The
Lincoln
League

*To Kathy and Ric.
Thanks for putting up
with that pesky baby
brother of yours.*

THE LINCOLN LEAGUE

Inspired by a True Story

by
Doug Peterson

Cover Illustration by DogEared Design
Interior Design by Bookmasters

Published by Kingstone Cinema
An Imprint of Kingstone Media Group
P.O. Box 491600
Leesburg, FL 34749-1600
www.KingstoneCinema.com

Printed in the United States of America by
Kingstone Cinema

Library of Congress Cataloguing-in-Publication information is on file.
ISBN 978-1-61328-129-1

Doug Peterson's
History by the Slice Novels

Pre-Civil War

The Vanishing Woman
Based on the true story of Ellen Craft (1848)

The Disappearing Man
Based on the true story of Henry "Box" Brown (1849)

Civil War

The Lincoln League
Inspired by the true story of John Scobell (1861)

European History

The Puzzle People
A Berlin Mystery

Inspired by the true story of
John Scobell

Also, based on the true stories of fellow Civil War spies
Timothy Webster
Hattie Lawton
Elizabeth Van Lew
Mary Bowser

"We were a family. How did it break up and come apart so that now we're turned against each other, each standing in the other's light? How did we lose the good that was given us—let it slip away . . .? What's keeping us from reaching out, touching the glory?"

—The Thin Red Line,
screenplay by Terrence Malick

"The chief source of information to the enemy is through our Negroes."

—*General Robert E. Lee, 1863*

Acknowledgments

I don't know what I would do without the faithful early readers who provide so much wonderful advice at reasonable rates (a lunch treat). So let me begin with my wife, Nancy, who is my first line of review and provides so much valuable input on character development. Thanks for being willing to read certain chapters over and over and over during revisions.

Also, thanks to Tom Hanlon, Dave Evensen, Heath Morber, Carol Browne, Ric Peterson, and Kathy Gullang for your extensive notes and faithful assistance. I am so fortunate to have such bright, talented people keeping a close eye on these words.

Thanks to Art and Kelly Ayris for supporting my vision to bring forgotten stories from the antebellum and Civil War periods to life, particularly little-known heroes such as John Scobell, Henry Brown, and Ellen Craft. And thanks to my agent, Jonathan Clements of Wheelhouse Literary Group, for helping me to bring this vision into focus.

There are so many reasons to be thankful and so many people to thank, but here are a few more:

—Jenny Goran, for your passion in bringing to life on stage characters such as Ellen Craft and Elizabeth Van Lew.

—Jim Kestner, for your guidance on the educational front.

—My prayer partner, Scott Irwin (no relation to the Scotty Irwin who shows up inside a Confederate submarine).

—Michael and Molly, Jason and Kristen, for your encouraging presence.

—Kirk DouPonce and DogEared Design for an incredible cover.

—Bookmasters, for your excellence in editing, proofing, and text design.

—Pat East and Irenka Carney, for making my website manageable for a non-techie like me.

—The University of Illinois library, for making the research so much easier.

1

Richmond, Virginia
June 23, 1861

"Don't go," said Peg.

"I gotta," said her husband, John.

"It's a white man's war."

"It's our war, too."

"Don't believe it."

Peg and John Scobell stood at arm's-length from each other, just outside the servants' door of the Atwater house. They boarded in an attic room of the three-story home, which was tall and narrow with a V-shaped roof that shot to the sky like a church steeple. Peg wiped away a bead of perspiration from under her right eye. It was early morning but already hot as blazes without even the hint of a breeze.

"I'm goin' North to fight. I can't just sit idle durin' this war," said John.

"Stay with me. For the first time, we're free."

"And I'm free to fight."

Master McQueen had just set them free, and now John wanted to leave her for a war. It wasn't fair, she thought.

"You actually think the Yanks are gonna put a gun in your hands?" she asked.

"They will if I'm gonna fight for 'em."

"They'll put you in the front line to block the cannonballs. And what's gonna stop the Rebels from snagging you before you even get North?"

"I'll make it through the lines."

"Choose me instead of the war."

"It's not a choice between you and this fight."

"It is."

John had a backpack stuffed with food and a hunting knife hidden beneath his shirt. But his most unique weapon was a pencil and paper hidden in a pocket that Peg had sewn inside the cuff of his pants. John said that if he couldn't fight in the war, he was planning to gather information for the North. But spying sounded just as dangerous as shooting a gun to Peg, maybe more so.

"What do I tell people?" she asked.

"Tell 'em I'm goin' to Fredericksburg for work and that I'm bringin' you there when I got enough money."

Peg wondered if people would believe such a story. She buried her face in his chest. "I ain't lettin' you go."

John stood a head taller than her, and he put his lips to her hair. "I *gotta* go."

"You ain't leavin'."

Those were the very words her mama had used when her papa bought his own freedom and left the family high and dry. She was ten years old at the time, but she had a stark memory of being in their small cabin with her mama screaming that he couldn't leave them, and she kept pounding on his chest, like some crazed person pounding on a locked door. Her father shoved her small mother aside, like he was pushing aside a wild child, and he charged out the door without so much as a backward glance at Peg or her younger brother Shadrack. "You ain't leavin'!" Peg's mother screamed at the door, but she didn't even try to chase him down. Peg never saw her papa again.

And now this.

"You ain't goin'," she repeated to John.

"It's a matter of honor."

"Then honor me."

John leaned in and gave her a long kiss. Then, pulling away, he stared at her hard, as if he was printing her image in his mind like one of those daguerreotype photographs. With daguerreotypes, you had to hold a pose for what seemed like forever while the camera's eye memorized every living part of your body. Peg held her pose, staring back at him without a smile.

John said he wanted to say good-bye right there by the house, but she wouldn't let him. She hiked alongside him all the way through town, still trying to convince him to stay, although she knew by now it was a losing battle.

"Now in those times many shall rise up against the king of the South," John declared, as they moved toward the edge of the city. He recited this passage from the Book of Daniel to her almost daily. It was as if he was trying to convince her that he was being sent on a Biblical mission, like Moses or Joshua, and she shouldn't stand in his way.

"So the king of the North shall come and build a siege mound, and take a fortified city; and the forces of the South shall not withstand him," he continued. "Even his choice troops shall have no strength to resist. But he who comes against him shall do according to his own will, and no one shall stand against him. He shall stand in the Glorious Land with destruction in his power."

John's eyes lit up whenever he spoke those words.

"Let me go with you, laddie," she said when they finally reached the very edge of Richmond. "Laddie" and "lassie" were terms of affection that they often used—words picked up from their Scottish master, Dugall McQueen.

"Too dangerous, lassie," he said.

"If it's too dangerous for me, then it's too dangerous for you."

He didn't respond. They had reached a path leading north into the woods, for John told her he was planning to take a less-traveled route, skirting any Confederates along the way.

"I'll come back soon, when this is over, Peg. It's gonna be a short war."

Peg was suddenly so angry that she was tempted to punish him with cold silence. But she didn't. She held on to his arm, twisting the fabric of his sleeve in her hands. She didn't want to cry, but she couldn't help herself.

"Please. Choose me, John." She had also vowed she wouldn't beg, but so much for vows. "Choose me, please."

Silence was his answer.

So she gathered herself and tried to command his loyalty. "I expect you back here in no time."

"Very soon, my lassie," he said.

He gave her one more kiss—good and long, so the daguerreotype had plenty of time to process.

2

Manassas Junction, Virginia
Saturday, July 20, 1861

FOUR WEEKS LATER, JOHN SCOBELL HAD BEEN CAPTURED AND pressed into service for the Confederate States of America.

On his way north, Confederate scouts had caught him sleeping in a barn near Fredericksburg and put him to work for the South cooking, digging latrines, and building rail breastworks. He toiled alongside a number of other slaves and free blacks, forced to labor for the Rebel war effort. And on this particular Saturday, he helped to set up camp for the Eighth Georgia, a prelude to battle.

It had been a hot, humid day, and his clothes hung on him like a wet blanket. But it had begun to cool in the early evening, and the air rustling through the woods felt refreshing on his damp shirt. He sat on a log, a stone's throw from the soldiers, and he nearly broke his teeth trying to bite down on hardtack. Most of the Georgia soldiers were gathered in small clusters, trying to talk the fear out of their gut and drinking coffee so thick you could float a piece of iron in it. Some had gotten their hands on 150-proof liquor, strong enough to pop the top of their skulls, but John had neither liquor nor water.

"How y'all doin', John?" came a voice from behind. It was Augustus Young, or "Gusty," a soldier who looked to be in his mid-twenties.

"Thirsty, sir." John stood to his feet and stared straight ahead, very soldierlike.

Gusty came to a stop and stared at him. Gusty had long brown hair, a thick moustache, and the tuft of a beard on the tip of his chin. He was the son of a horse-capper, a dealer in worthless horses, and his mother had died from the fever when he was six. John had picked up heaps of information such as this by just hanging on the fringes. He listened. He watched.

Gusty looked around, as if to make sure no one was looking. Then he lifted the strap of his canteen over his head, used his body to block any view of what he was doing, and slipped the leather canteen to John. John stared at it, disbelieving. The last time a white man had offered him a canteen of water, he discovered the man had urinated in it.

"Go on now. Drink."

Was this some kind of trick? Gusty was a friendly sort and didn't seem to be the kind of person to pull something like that on him.

"Thank you, sir." John reached out and took the canteen; then he yanked out the stopper and drew the canteen to his mouth slowly, to give his nose a chance to take a whiff of the contents. Just in case.

He took two healthy swigs. His throat was as dry as a riverbed in drought, and the gush of water felt good going down. Glory be, it was pure water.

"God bless you, sir." He wiped his mouth with the sleeve of his shirt and slipped the canteen back to Gusty, who nodded and headed for the gathering of soldiers. John sat back down on the log, where he listened and observed. Later, when he was out of sight, he would take notes, using the scrap of paper and stub of a pencil tucked away in the hidden pocket inside the cuff of his pants. If anyone found out what he was writing, they would have taken him into the woods without hesitation and sent a lead Minié ball through his brain.

"Let's hear a song, John-boy!" called out a young recruit named Peter.

John groaned inwardly, for the boy was always asking him to sing—probably to calm his rattled nerves and yank his mind away from the impending battle. But John would oblige, for he really had no choice. So he launched into a soft ballad, and the men went quiet.

As I roved out one morning in June,
To view the sweet fields and the meadows in bloom,
I spied a fair damsel, she appeared like a queen,
With her costly fine robes and her mantle of green.

The men found it especially amusing to hear a black man singing a Scottish ballad about "fair damsels," but John was filled to the brim with such songs, thanks to his former master. John even learned from Master McQueen how to imitate certain accents, and he gave the song a Scottish brogue, which astounded these Southern boys. A black man sounding Scottish? They looked at him like some curiosity from P.T. Barnum, and he continued to sing.

I stood in amazement, I was struck with surprise,
I thought her an angel that fell from the skies;
Her teeth shone like ivory, her cheeks like the rose,
She was one of the fairest that nature composed.

One of the men guffawed—probably a fellow who hadn't heard him do his Scottish accent before—but another soldier shushed the man. John had the soldiers mesmerized, he could tell. He was a snake charmer. The song told of a Scottish lass who lost her beau in the battle of Waterloo, and when John had finished the song, an air of melancholy hung in the silence. He had sent their thoughts back to the girls they left behind, just as John's thoughts went back to his own wife. He felt guilty leaving Peg so soon after they had been freed, but he had a duty to do. It was a matter of honor, and his father had taught him that a man's honor was the flag of his soul, and it was made evident through loyalty, courage, respect, and sacrifice. Peg had to learn to make sacrifices as well.

After the melancholy of the moment had dissipated, the soldiers moved on to other things—mostly storytelling and joking. They let

John alone, which suited him just fine. Playing the role of a "happy darky" could be exhausting—and depressing.

The encampment was on the southern side of Bull Run, the stream that snaked its way through the rolling land of northern Virginia. There was still plenty of light left on this evening before a fight, and the men battled demons, a warm-up for their upcoming battle with the Yankees. One man tossed his playing cards into the fire, his burnt offering to God. Off to the right, John heard a man in the dark reciting the Lord's Prayer over and over and over.

"But deliver us from evil . . ."

The pop of gunfire was sporadic. Probably skirmishers shooting at Yankee pickets or wild pigs. Then a man dressed in civilian clothes but carrying a gun entered the camp and immediately became the focus of attention; he had stories to tell, and the men were still looking for distractions. The civilian, a thin whip of a man named Hancock, was obviously known by many of the soldiers, and he was introduced to the others as a loyal copperhead—a Northerner who worked for the Southern cause. That explained his lack of a Southern accent—and the copper penny he wore around his neck.

"You were there?" Peter asked.

"I was," said Hancock. "I was in the headquarters of General Bonham when there was this tremendous bustling about outside and whistling and men calling out like tomcats. And then this beautiful young woman came sweeping into the headquarters, wrapped up in a cloud of the sweetest perfume I ever did smell."

John rolled his eyes. The man obviously loved to spin tales, but John became more attentive, wondering if there might be some truth hidden away in the midst of the perfume and beautiful damsels.

"I heard of lady spies comin' to and fro between Washington and our lines, Mister Hancock," said Peter, jamming a large wad of tobacco into the corner of his mouth. His cheek bulged, and his teeth were black with tobacco when he grinned.

"Well, this woman was the most beautiful spy I ever seen," said Hancock, seated on a tree stump. "As I stood there, basking in her beauty, she plucked the tucking comb from her hair, and her long locks came cascading down to her shoulders."

John was continually amazed how the soldiers and even the officers would talk so freely around him and other Negroes, for they thought he couldn't possibly do anything with their information. They were probably more concerned about talking in front of a boulder than a black man.

Hancock continued, leaning forward, and John got a good look at his face. It was long and narrow, and he had a thick black beard, deep-set eyes, a long nose, and a single crease running down his left cheek like a rill.

"The lady spy pulled out a small, rolled-up note, wrapped in black silk and hidden away in her long hair," Hancock said. "The note carried vital information gleaned from the inner circles of Washington."

"Such as . . . ?"

"Don't rightly know. The general dismissed me, and I hung around outside the headquarters, waiting for the lady to exit. I hadn't seen a woman like that in nearly a month, and I wanted another peek."

"I heard of a lady spy dressed like a milkmaid and carryin' a milk bucket that brought intelligence to our camps," chimed in another.

Hancock laughed and motioned with his hands as he spoke, obviously in his element. "This beauty wasn't no milkmaid, believe me. She came out of the headquarters about fifteen minutes later, and she encountered an enraptured audience of men soaking up her radiance. Word had spread, and I think half the regiment had come to gawk. I strode up to her and thanked her personally for her brave deeds, and she told me her name was Miss Bettie, and she gave me a kiss on the cheek before riding off."

John nearly laughed out loud at this ludicrous fabrication. He caught himself in time, but a muffled snort leaked out.

Hancock snapped his head around, and he stared at John in surprise, as if he hadn't seen him sitting there in the shadows of the trees. "What's that, boy?"

All eyes moved in John's direction. He just grinned back, trying to conceal the sudden jolt of fear behind his smile.

"Aw, it's just John Scobell," said Peter. "Don't fret 'bout him. He's harmless."

Hancock stood up, stretching to his full height of almost six feet. "Come over here, boy."

John silently rebuked himself for being a fool to let out any sound at all. He rose from the log and made his way closer to the men, keeping a smile on his face. Hancock scratched at his beard, as if rooting around for insects in the thick hair. He looked John up and down, sizing him up for a fight. John was about five feet, ten inches—not quite as tall as Hancock, but being twenty-seven, John looked to be younger by more than ten years. John had close-trimmed hair, a thick neck, and an off-kilter nose that had already been broken by knuckles a couple of times before. It showed he wasn't afraid to fight.

"What're you doing lurking behind us like that?" Hancock asked.

John stared back at him, which was not what a subservient black man was expected to do. But he couldn't help himself; he suddenly felt a deep hatred for this copperhead fool.

"I am not doing anything, sir. Just sitting here wishing I could whip some Federals," he said, suddenly moving into a Scottish accent. A couple of the soldiers laughed, but Hancock was not amused.

"That so, John Scobell. And whatya going to use to whip them with? The branch of a tree? I assume you ain't carrying a gun."

John patted himself down, as if he wasn't quite sure if he had a gun hidden somewhere in his clothes. "I do not appear to have a weapon, sir."

This time he used a British accent. Another snort of laughter from one of the men.

"You think you're funny, Scobell?"

"C'mon, just leave him be," said Gusty, putting a hand on the civilian's shoulders.

Hancock shook Gusty's hand loose. "I wanna know, boy. What are you gonna do to help fight off this invasion of Virginia?" The man took a step closer, and John could smell the spirits on his breath. He gave John a shove in the chest. Not too hard, but John stumbled back two steps. "You good with your fists, boy?"

Gusty tried to insert himself between Scobell and Hancock, but the civilian nudged him aside. Then Hancock gave John another shove, this one harder. John wanted so much to haul off and break this man's jaw, as he knew he could. But if he did, he would have half of these soldiers pouncing on him. The last time that he had hit a white man, it took five men to beat him down, breaking his nose and two ribs. In a one-on-one fight he was a wildcat, but this time he would have about a dozen beating on him, and that was too much, even for John.

"You loyal to the South, boy?" Hancock said.

Time to bring out his finest acting skills. "Yes, sir! I'd love nothin' more than to fight and shoot alongside the Eighth Georgia, sir!"

John could see amusement emerge on Hancock's face.

"Are you a good shot?"

"Yes, sir! A very good shot!"

John spoke the truth. Back in Richmond, his former master trusted him enough to put a gun in his hands and hunt game. Master McQueen was an old Scottish soldier, and he taught him how to load with an uncanny speed and take down a rabbit from a fair distance.

"You really think you're good at it, eh?" said Hancock.

"Yes, sir!"

Hancock smiled and turned to the other soldiers gathered around him. "You believe this darky? He says he can shoot better than any of you!"

John's smile vanished. "Ain't what I said, sir."

"I think you oughta prove it. Let's see who's the better shot. John Scobell or one of these men."

"Hold on," Gusty said. "We don't want no distractions the night before a battle."

"Distractions is just what we need," chimed in Peter. "I wanna see if Scobell can draw a bead better than Watkins."

Another man, a short squat fellow with a square-shaped head, stepped forward: Watkins. "He ain't better, and I'll prove it."

"But we don't want to be usin' up cartridges and caps that we'll be needin' tomorrow," Gusty said.

Hancock grinned, reached into his jacket pocket, and pulled out a handful of cartridges. "Then let me contribute these. Four for each man. It'll be worth it to see this."

He handed four cartridges and four percussion caps each to John and Watkins, and the contest was quickly arranged. They set up a makeshift shooting range in a field not far from the encampment. Hancock set out two targets—two pairs of dirty long johns—and he hung them side-by-side from a low branch on a tree about one hundred yards yonder. From a distance, it looked like the legs of two men dangling from the branches. The sun was getting low, but there was still plenty of light to shoot.

"The first one to blast three holes in the drawers wins, which means you only have one bullet to spare out of the four," announced Hancock.

Watkins fetched his gun, while Gusty let John borrow his rifled musket. "I sure hope you know what you're doin', John-boy," Gusty said under his breath.

"Oh, I do, sir." John smiled, acting more confident than he felt.

"Did you have much to eat today?" Hancock asked, slapping an arm around John's shoulder. It draped across his shoulders like a python.

"No sir. Just some dried peas and hardtack—and weevils."

The men laughed, for hardtack was a stiff kind of cracker that dulled your teeth and harbored so many insects that the men called them "worm castles." It was best to eat hardtack at night so you couldn't see what you were swallowing.

"Well, John Scobell, I hope you're hungry. If you lose, I'm gonna watch you eat a plateful of good Virginia soil."

John felt the perspiration building on his forehead. He was fast at loading, and dead-on in shooting, but he hadn't practiced in months, and these men had been drilling regularly. A good soldier could load and fire three times in a minute.

"If you're really here to protect Virginia soil from the Northern invasion, then you should have no problem eating a pan load of good Virginia dirt."

John turned away. "It will go down smoothly with a cup of tea, sir." He used his British accent once again, but he spoke too softly for anybody to really hear what he said.

John and Watkins took their positions facing their long-john targets, which flapped in the breeze like gray flags. The moving air, which had felt so good after a hot day, was going to make their target shooting all that much harder. John smiled and tried to look as good-natured as possible.

"On my signal," Hancock said.

About two dozen men had gathered around for the entertainment. They had been joking and snorting, but now the only sound was the constant hum of insects. A fly hovered in front of John's face and brushed against his nose, and he swatted it away with his left hand.

"Begin!"

Hands flying, John pulled from his pocket his first paper cartridge—about the size of a cigar. He bit the end with his teeth and tasted the acidic flavor of gunpowder. A set of teeth, uppers and lowers, were the most important physical requirement in the military, and John had a strong set of choppers.

The cartridge contained both the gunpowder and Minié ball, and he poured the stream of powder into the barrel first. Then he squeezed the Minié ball out of the cartridge and slipped the bullet inside the muzzle with the flat end first; this was the trickiest part, for slippery fingers could easily drop the lead ball. But not this time. John picked up the ramrod, twirling it in his fingers with a skill that came back to him in a rush, and he used the cup-shaped end of the rammer to pack everything down in the breech of the weapon. He pushed the ramrod with only one finger, knowing that if the gun accidentally went off, he'd lose only one digit rather than most of his hand.

Next he pulled the hammer to half-cock and grabbed a percussion. This posed another tense moment, for a cap was as small as a tooth and could easily be dropped as well. He slipped the cap onto a narrow firing cone, fully cocked the gun, brought it up to his shoulder, and took aim.

John put a bullet hole cleanly through one of the legs of the flapping long johns. One of the soldiers, field glasses trained on the target, confirmed his first strike.

Another man whistled and said something about how "that darky can sure shoot."

The only problem was that Watkins' rifle had gone off seconds before his, and his direct hit had also been confirmed. Watkins was a step ahead of him, already loading for a second shot. The man was fast. Blazing fast.

John held the musket firmly in front of him, and he raced through the steps again, yanking out another cartridge. Rip. Pour. Squeeze. Ram. Retrieve a cap. Ready. Aim. Fire. With his natural ability flooding back into his muscles, he loaded the gun even faster than the first time, and his bullet made the long johns twitch as it went through, like a hanged man dancing at the end of a rope.

Meanwhile, Watkins was complaining. "My target got blown by the wind! Not fair! It moved!"

Obviously, he had missed.

"The Yankees ain't gonna stand still neither when we fight tomorrow," said Gusty.

This meant John could be patient on his third shot. He needed only one more direct hit, and Watkins needed two. He had time. He tore open the third cartridge with his teeth and poured in the powder. Then came the Minié ball. He squeezed it out of the wrapper, but he fumbled the bullet and tried to snag it in midair. Missing, it hit the ground, but he followed its descent and knew exactly where it landed. He snatched it back up, but he had lost precious time—and composure. No wonder he missed on his third shot.

Watkins hit on his next shot, which meant they had both hit their targets twice. They were neck and neck once again.

John pulled out his last cartridge, conscious from his peripheral vision that Watkins was a step ahead of him. John's hands were flying, and he loaded his gun faster than he had ever done before. But not fast enough. As he was putting the percussion cap in place, Watkins was already taking aim and firing.

Cursing quickly followed. Watkins' gun had jammed.

John took careful aim. He had time. He had time. A gust of wind whipped at the long johns, and they danced from side to side like there was an animal trapped inside of them. He fired. A direct hit!

The men roared with laughter, while Watkins cursed and Hancock steamed. Gusty clapped John on the back, and the others needled Watkins for getting whipped by a black man.

John was mightily relieved that the Rebels were too busy teasing Watkins to pay much attention to him. He had been afraid he would feel their wrath for showing up a white soldier, but even Watkins seemed more miffed at his jammed gun than at John.

He had only Hancock to worry about.

When he turned to check out the expression on the civilian's face, he found himself facing the muzzle of a loaded rifle. Hancock aimed the gun directly at John's face, only about three feet away. This time, John was not acting when his jaw dropped and his eyes went wide.

3

Richmond, Virginia
Saturday, July 20, 1861

PEG SCOBELL DANCED ALONE. STANDING IN DANCE POSITION, AS if she were face-to-face with John, she spun clockwise with her imaginary partner while traveling counterclockwise around the ballroom. She had taken a break from polishing the ballroom floor in Captain Atwater's home—preparations for the evening's festivities. The room was empty, but she tried to imagine it filled to capacity with women in colorful hoop skirts and men in black dress coats.

Feeling a little dizzy, she paused to catch her breath, and she wondered for a moment if it was really true, as some said, that the spinning motion of the waltz could injure your brain and spinal marrow. She decided that if high-society ladies could waltz without doing observable damage, then so could she. So she curtsied to her invisible partner and continued dancing, even though she knew she should probably get back on her knees and return to working the beeswax into the oak floor. She wished it were possible to strap a brush to one foot and a slipper on the other, so she could polish the floor while dancing.

"Peg Scobell, what on earth do you think you are doing?"

Peg nearly jumped out of her skin. She turned to the open doorway, where Missus Henrietta Hicks stood glaring at her. Missus

Hicks was a petite old woman, close to seventy years old, but she was anything but frail. She was a friend of the Atwater family and had lived in the captain's house for the past five years. Even at a little more than five feet tall, she could be scarier than a six-foot mountain man.

Peg diverted her eyes. "Sorry, ma'am. Just testin' out the floor."

"Just *scuffing* the floor is more like it. Get back to work because you have a full day of chores in preparation for tonight's party. I want that floor shining so brightly that you can see your face in it."

"Yes, ma'am."

Peg got back to her knees and returned to polishing, ever conscious that Missus Hicks hadn't left the room. She felt the old lady's eyes boring down on her.

"I don't like it," Missus Hicks announced.

Peg looked up, confused. "I'll make the floor shine, ma'am."

"I'm not talking about the floor, you silly girl. I'm talking about your hair."

Peg instinctively shot a hand to her head and ran her fingers across her rows of braids, which she had worked into a circular design like the swirls on a conch shell. Now that she was a free woman working for Captain Atwater, she had more time to tend to her hair, and she had meticulously crafted the braids—something special for the night's festivities. She figured even the help should look done up.

"Makes you look like a savage."

"But Missus Hicks—"

"Don't sass back. You cover that wooly hair like a proper woman should. I expect you to don a head wrap, the same as all the other colored girls."

Ah! There was the real reason: Missus Hicks didn't want any of her servants to stand out. She preferred them to blend in with the furniture.

"But don't you think—?"

"I will hear nothing more on the matter, and I trust you will not spoil the day with any more bellyaching."

At that moment Peg's employer, Captain Matthias Atwater, popped his head into the room, completely oblivious to the tension.

He focused his smiling face on Peg. "Excellent job, Peg. And when you are done, do not forget that I promised Miss Doris that you would help her prepare her hair for tonight."

"I haven't forgotten, sir."

"Good girl."

Miss Doris was a spinster who lived next door, and Captain Atwater, a widower, showed a keen interest in her. It was obvious to anyone who had eyes.

Peg was happy that the captain seemed enthralled by Miss Doris, for that reduced the risk that he would let his eyes wander toward her. Captain Atwater struck Peg as an honorable man, not the type to take advantage of a black servant. But you never knew. Peg, twenty-five years old, had been well-endowed by the Lord, and she had a dimpled cheek that drove men crazy when she flashed a smile. Her smile had worked on John when they were courting, but she tried not to smile at white men, which was difficult because she was a good-natured woman, easily drawn to laughter.

"Very good, Peg!" Captain Atwater repeated, rubbing his hands together. He was trim for a man in his fifties, with a face that could almost be described as gaunt. His most striking features were his facial flourishes—a thick, completely white moustache and a monocle perched on his right eye. "I will leave you to it, then!"

The captain disappeared, heading in the direction of his drawing room, leaving Peg alone once again with Missus Hicks. The old lady didn't say anything; she just gave her another good hard stare and vanished.

Peg returned to her work, and as she pressed the cloth into the floor in a circular motion she imagined that she was wiping the self-satisfied expression off of Missus Hicks' face.

*****

A ballroom was a woman's battlefield. That's what Peg's old master, Dugall McQueen, liked to say, quoting one of his favorite Scottish writers. Peg thought the words were fitting. During the afternoon, she helped Miss Doris don her war paint—red rouge made from vegetables, which Peg helped to apply with a ball of muslin. Miss Doris' war helmet was her full head of hair, spruced up with a wreath and a sprig of false hair on the back of her head, spilling down her neck in curls. Peg even helped Miss Doris don her armor—lacing her corset so tightly that it was a wonder the woman could even speak. Perhaps that was why she was so quiet most of the time.

Miss Doris was in her early forties, making her fifteen years younger than Captain Atwater, and she too seemed smitten.

Come evening, everything was set and the guests began arriving, with a line of carriages depositing them at the front door of the Atwater house on Franklin Street. Peg was on the constant move, helping the cook, Matilda, in the kitchen, and setting up refreshments. Captain Atwater had hired reinforcements for the evening, including Peg's good friend, Mary Bowser.

"I love to watch the women use their fans to flirt," Mary said as they maneuvered through the crowded ballroom carrying two pitchers of fresh tea. After setting down the pitchers, Mary motioned with her head toward a young belle. "She's carrying her fan in her left hand, and that means she desires an acquaintance of the man she is gazing at."

Peg wasn't sure if Mary was pulling her leg. She seemed serious, but she could be a bit of an actress.

"How do you know all that?"

"Miss Lizzie taught me the language of fans and handkerchiefs."

Miss Lizzie was Miss Elizabeth Van Lew, an eccentric Richmond lady who freed all of her slaves years back, including Mary Bowser. Mary continued to work as a housemaid for Miss Lizzie.

"And look over there," Mary said. "Miss Gamble is letting her fan rest on her right cheek. That means 'Yes.' If you draw the fan across your cheek, that says 'I love you.' If you twirl it in the left hand, that means 'I love another,' and if you draw the fan through your hand, that means 'I hate you.'"

"Seems awfully complicated," said Peg. "Wouldn't it be easier to just use words?"

"Easier, but less fun."

Mary laughed. She was a petite, pretty girl in her twenties, wearing a full-length dress with a wide black belt that accentuated her narrow waist and a collar that buttoned tightly around her neck. Her eyes lit up with mischief, and her skin was dark and smooth—darker than Peg's. She led the way back to the kitchen, where they would receive their next orders from Matilda.

Throughout the evening, Peg occasionally found opportunities to stand and gaze at the dancers. The Atwater ballroom was not so large that they could invite a great number of guests—especially since ladies' dresses had become so enormously wide that you couldn't fit more than a dozen on the dance floor at one time. It's a wonder some of these women could even fit through doorways in their hoop skirts. But they were still a wonder to behold—double skirts of so many colors, spinning like whirligigs. Music was provided by a pianist, violinist, and harpist, hidden behind a screen of vines.

"Did you notice the nice new flag?" she overheard Missus Hicks telling a couple of older women, standing off in a corner with the other matrons.

"Oh yes. I am glad to see the flag—*at last*," said Missus Cavendish, with the words "at last" a not-so-subtle dig at Captain Atwater's tardiness in raising the flag of the Confederate States of America.

"It takes time to have such a beautiful flag made," said Missus Hicks, a scowl showing through her forced smile.

Missus Cavendish said nothing, but Peg noticed that the woman drew her fan through her fingers.

Peg had followed the changing flagscape within Richmond over the past year. Back in February, the United States flag, with its 33 stars, still flew from the Virginia capitol, as well as from public buildings and many homes. After Fort Sumter in April, secessionists ran a Confederate flag above the capitol, only to see it yanked down during the night. But when President Lincoln called for troops to put down the rebellion, the Commonwealth of Virginia finally pulled out of the Union, and everything changed. The flag of the secession, with its circle of stars and three wide bars, two red and one white, conquered the front porches and public buildings throughout Richmond. Although a few good friends and family knew that Captain Atwater harbored sympathy for a unified country, he immediately pulled down his U.S. flag in April because it was safer to keep his opinions secret. Many Unionists had fled Richmond in fear of their lives, and the captain's house remained without a flag until today.

The remainder of the evening went smoothly, with nothing of consequence, until close to the end when several men, including Captain Atwater, slipped away to the drawing room. When Peg entered the room carrying a tray of sandwiches, four men were gathered in a circle by the mantle, and they continued with their conversation as if she was invisible.

"Do you believe the war will end quickly with a great Southern victory?" one man asked her employer, Captain Atwater.

"Yes, I do. The next month should decide the outcome."

Peg noticed that Captain Atwater avoided any prediction of a Northern or Southern victory—just a quick victory. Although he still harbored Unionist sympathies, he also had a son in the Southern Army and he held a position on the board of the Tredegar Iron Works, supplier of cannons and other weaponry for the Confederates. Peg wondered which loyalty carried more weight.

"So you agree with Senator Chestnut, who predicted he would be capable of drinking down all of the blood that is going to be spilled in this short-lived war?"

"Well, I am not so sure I would put it in those terms."

"Will the torpedo boats hurry along the outcome?" asked another man. "And how is work coming on these boats?"

"Excellent, excellent."

"A torpedo boat just doesn't seem honorable to me," said a gentleman by the name of Malone.

"I admit that I too have had reservations about such a weapon. I still do," Captain Atwater said. "But the men making these boats are doing what's best to end this war speedily—and to break the blockade."

"But to attack using a boat that travels underwater?" said Mister Malone. "A ship above water would not have a fighting chance against one of these infernal machines. Troops and ships should face each other in the light of day in full view of each other. That is the honorable way. None of this skulking around."

"With the weaponry we have today, fighting in the wide open is the way of sure death," added another man.

"Are you saying that a machine that hunts ships from beneath the surface of the water is *not* the way of death?" asked Mister Malone.

The captain shrugged. "You needn't worry. I am not sure such a machine will actually work."

"Let us pray not," said Mister Malone. "Ships that travel underwater would be as terrifying as a ghost ship, striking unseen with no warning."

Peg had no idea what they were talking about. Torpedo boats? Ghost ships that sail beneath the surface of the water?

"Ghosts are not honorable combatants," added Mister Malone.

Those were the last words that Peg heard before she exited the room with her tray loaded with empty cups. As she slipped through the door, she very nearly ran into Missus Hicks, who hovered near the open doorway, as if eavesdropping on the men. The old lady had strong opinions, and she never liked it when the men separated themselves to discuss major matters, such as the war.

"Pardon me, ma'am," Peg said, stepping to the side to go around Missus Hicks.

Missus Hicks struck her closed fan on her left palm, and Peg wondered what kind of unspoken message the old lady had just sent her way.

4

OHN'S EYES FLASHED TO HANCOCK'S TRIGGER FINGER, AND HE said nothing. He didn't dare breathe.

"Mister Hancock, stand down!" The voice was that of Gusty, who stepped beside John and faced Hancock squarely, one arm extended.

The other soldiers gathered around in a half circle to see if the civilian would actually do it. Would he fire a bullet through the head of a black man who had the audacity to win a sharpshooting contest? Several men were grinning and one was egging Hancock on. John's mouth had gone dry again, and his heart was pumping pure panic through his veins.

"I said stand down!" Gusty, bold as a bull, reached out and touched the barrel of the gun. John closed his eyes and braced for impact, but there was no burst of gunpowder, no bullet ripping into him from point-blank range. When he opened his eyes, John saw that the gun was now aimed at the ground.

"Are you a fool? You're gonna kill someone," Gusty said.

"That's the point," Hancock said.

"The bullet mighta gone clean through Scobell and killed one of us to boot. Besides, I have uses for this here John Scobell, and I don't want you blowin' out his brains."

He has uses for me? This was news to John.

Gusty turned to face John and smiled. "I'm takin' him with me in tomorrow's scrap with the Yanks. I could use a servant to carry and load my musket. Seein' how fast he is at loadin', I'm gonna take advantage of that."

John was thunderstruck. Evidently, so was Hancock.

"You're gonna what?" Hancock said.

"If gentlemen soldiers can bring their servants with them, then I'm gonna have John here carry and load my weapon."

It was true that some masters forced their body servants to carry their rifles and other equipment, and John had always felt compassion for the poor souls lugging those heavy loads. Now, all of a sudden, he was in their sorry shoes.

"If you let him load your weapon, this fool will probably put a bullet through your head and skedaddle off to join the Yankees," Hancock said.

"He ain't gonna do any such thing," said Gusty. "If he did, he knows he'd be shot down in seconds."

"I don't know if it's proper for me to be carryin' a gun," John suggested nervously, looking for any way out.

Gusty scoffed. "Nonsense, John!"

Watkins, the sharpshooter whom he had just bested in the contest, grinned and slapped John on the back. "You said you wanted to shoot some Yankees, so this is your chance to help the cause!" John wondered if Watkins might just put a bullet through his head on the battlefield while he wasn't looking—an easy way to get his revenge for being made to look the fool in their contest.

John studied the faces of the other men. Some scowled, but others had the same sly smirk as Watkins. He was afraid there were a half dozen men anxious to fire a bullet in his back during the chaos of battle.

"From this moment on, I'm declarin' ya'll to be my servant, John! Whatya think of that?" Gusty said.

John didn't know what to say.

"Suit yourself!" Hancock told Gusty before turning on his heels and marching off, flinging out one last warning. "But I think you'll live to regret it—or die to regret it!"

As Hancock disappeared into the darkness, Gusty smiled at John. "If you'll be my servant for the next day, ya'll will get the chance of a lifetime. How many men get to see a battle from front row seats?"

It made John sick just thinking about it. "Yes, sir," he said. This time, no phony accents. Just a nervous catch in his voice.

*****

It was a short night, but a cool one, with a full moon and clear black sky unfurling above their heads. John curled up under a blanket that Gusty had provided and caught a few winks. When John's eyes blinked back open, men were moving about in the dark, and the realization that he would be marching into battle came down on him like the weight of a falling horse. He knew he would never get back to sleep, nor did he care. If this was going to be his final night on earth, he would rather not dream it away. So he sat up, leaned his back against a tree, hugged his knees to his chest, and prayed the Book of Daniel.

And the king of the South shall be moved with rage, and go out and fight with him, with the king of the North, who shall muster a great multitude. . . . So the king of the North shall come and build a siege mound, and take a fortified city; and the forces of the South shall not withstand him.

An image came to his mind of him standing in a wide-open field, and two bulls were charging at each other from either side. Two great powers were colliding, and he was caught in the middle, but just before the bulls struck, goring him on their horns, he took off running. Maybe that's what he needed to do on the battlefield—run for his life. He wasn't one to flee from any fight, and he had the broken nose to prove it. But he was fighting on the wrong side!

From out of the dark, John heard an eerie sound, like the whinny of a ghostly horse coming from the trees. He was well versed in birdcalls and songs, and he knew it was a screech-owl—a short, stubby bird with almost no neck and ear tufts that stuck up like a devil's horns. Any time he heard a bird, he couldn't help but think of Peg, who shared his love for birds and wildlife; in fact, it was one of his earliest memories of her, six years back.

*****

"Sounds like an Orchard Oriole," Peg said as they passed the border of a forest just across the field from their church, First African Baptist. They walked side by side, so close together that their shoulders sometimes brushed against each other.

"No, it's a Baltimore Oriole," John countered. "Listen. It sounds more like a flute."

They paused, and the rich warbling streamed down from the trees like liquid sound.

"No, it's definitely an Orchard Oriole," Peg said.

"Would you like to wager?"

"I ain't got money to spare."

"Then wager a kiss. If I'm right, I get to kiss you."

"And if I'm right?"

"Then you get to kiss me."

John grinned, but Peg looked a little shocked by his wager, and he hoped he didn't insult her with his boldness. He kicked himself for acting a fool. They had known each other for only three weeks, ever since he caught sight of her coming out of church with the most unusual head wrap he had ever seen. It was a colorful wrap, and she had taken the long twisted tail and brought it down under her chin and then back up, where it was tucked into the turban. They had talked several weeks in a row, and today he took the risk of asking her to go for a walk with him for the first time. And now he might have gone and spoiled everything.

He locked eyes with her, looking for any sign that she had been amused by his wager.

Finally, Peg's smile blossomed. "All right. Deal."

They approached the edge of the forest, but they didn't go any farther because they did not want to raise a scandal among the congregation members, some of whom had their eyes on them from back at the church. They began to scour the branches for the bird—Baltimore Oriole, Orchard Oriole, whatever it was. The bird continued to sing, so it was still in the branches somewhere close.

"There!"

Peg followed John's pointed finger, which he had aimed at a flash of orange amidst the green leaves. It was a Baltimore Oriole, for its bright orange chest was a dead giveaway. An Orchard Oriole would be chestnut-colored if it was male, yellow if it was female.

They listened to the bird serenade them for another minute before it finally lifted off and disappeared into the summer sky. Then they walked on in silence, with John beaming a self-satisfied smile. He was prepared to initiate the kiss, but something held him back. He had recently learned things about Peg—about her master, Cager Johnson, and the way the man took advantage of her. He didn't want her to feel like he was just another man taking liberties with her. He wanted to do the honorable thing.

"I don't have to collect on my bet if you don't feel right about it," John finally said. "With people watching and all."

They stopped and faced each other. Peg smiled. "John Scobell, are you losin' your nerve?"

"No, no, I just want to do the right thing, seeing as . . . I mean I don't want to take advantage, especially considerin' the things . . ."

John didn't finish his sentence, and Peg's smile vanished.

"Whatya mean, 'the things'?"

"Nothing. I just don't wanna take advantage—the way some masters do."

Peg stared into space, her smile completely gone, the moment completely ruined. Why in the world did he have to open his big mouth?

"I'm sorry," said John. "I didn't mean to spoil our time."

"I'm sorry, too."

John looked down at his feet and said nothing. They heard the song of another bird, but neither ventured a guess of what kind.

"Shall we head back to the church?" she finally said.

"Yes. That would be best."

They walked back to First African Baptist, side-by-side, with a little more distance between them.

*****

John felt like such a fool that afternoon, but their first walk did lead to one of the favorite traditions of their marriage. Whenever they heard the sound of a bird, they guessed the type; if John was right, he would kiss her, and if Peg was right, she would kiss him. They kissed quite frequently.

By this time, most of the men were awake and moving about in the dark, and John was put to work helping to prepare breakfast, a Last Breakfast for many. He made coosh, frying up bacon and then adding grits to the sizzling grease. The result was a flavorful mash that stuck to your ribs. Most food in the camp wasn't fit for cockroaches and would give you the Tennessee Trots, but not John's food.

In the distance he heard the muffled rumbling of cannons, like a growling stomach on a grand scale. The Eighth Georgia, from what John picked up, was positioned well behind a place called Blackburn's Ford, where General Longstreet's Rebel forces had amassed. They were in the rear, and John wondered if perhaps they might be spared any action on this day.

He received his answer not long after the men had finished breakfast.

General Bartow rode into their camp and announced, in dramatic fashion, "Get ready, men! A battle is already raging near the stone bridge across Bull Run, so you're going to see yourselves some action this day!"

They had to wait as they brought in one of their companies, which had been out on picket duty, and then the chaplain said a prayer. John heard one man heaving up his bacon and mash in the brush. The cool of night was gone, and the muggy morning air was already soaking their shirts like an invisible rain by the time the Eighth Georgia began moving, at least a full hour after General Bartow had given the command.

Gusty had John carry his haversack, cartridge box, and gun—a rifled musket, which could shoot much farther than a smoothbore—and they marched in a row four abreast. Marching with Rebs: It was the strangest feeling that John ever experienced. He had told Peg he was heading north to help the Federal cause and rid the land of slavery, but now he was about to help a man shoot down Yankees. She would be so angry if she knew what he had left her for.

They marched double-quick, and John's right foot felt a knife stab at every step; he had picked up a sharp rock through a hole in the bottom of his shoe, but he couldn't stop to take it out. As they got closer to the battlefield, the sounds became louder—the cannons, the guns, the shouting—and a wave of dizzying panic swept over him. But he kept moving forward, the gear of the men clanking and rattling on all sides.

Next, they saw men coming toward them, but they weren't moving fast and they weren't Yankees. These were Southerners, wounded men being removed from the battlefield, bloodied and battered. Some men hobbled along on their own power, covered in blood. John tried not to stare, but he couldn't help himself. He saw one man with a big chunk of his left shoulder missing. Another man's face was covered entirely in red, as if he was wearing a mask. Two men dragged another soldier along—a man with a mangled leg. It looked like the limb had been flattened by an elephant or some other powerful force, and the man moaned something awful.

Lieutenant Colonel William Montgomery Gardner led the five hundred men of the Eighth Georgia past a plain two-story white house at the crest of a hill. He ordered them into a cornfield, a patch of green growth that gave them welcome cover. The only thing rising from the corn was a solitary apple tree, like the Tree of the Knowledge of Good and Evil standing in the very center of the Garden of Eden.

Eden was a long way away.

Colonel Gardner ordered them to get down, and John was happy to oblige. Staying closer to the earth would be safer, he figured. It also gave him a chance to pull off his shoe and rid himself of the sharp stone. Gusty was only a few feet away, and John loaded his gun and handed it over. The regiment had been ordered to load, and that could mean only one thing. The fight was upon them.

A few men made a break for the apple tree, unable to resist the temptation to eat from the tree. It was hard for soldiers to walk by apples or berries without snacking, but climbing a tree so close to the Yanks was insane. The lower branch was too high off the ground to grab hold of, so the men took turns shimmying up the trunk.

"Stay down!" one soldier shouted at them.

"Fools!" another said, speaking the obvious.

But Colonel Gardner didn't say a word. He had his eyes on the Yanks.

Suddenly: A tearing of the air. A cannon blast. There was a monster roar, and John heard something fly overhead like a demon spirit of the air. The cannonball didn't hit a thing, but the three men in the tree were back down to the ground so quickly that you'd think they had been shot from the branches. One fell on his head.

Colonel Gardner seemed unfazed. "Poor shots, those Yankees. That had to be over our heads by a mile!"

But the cannon shot was close enough for John. He clawed at the soil and wished he could dig a hole with his bare fingers and bury himself eight feet down. The battle had begun, but he was fighting for the wrong side and he had never been more terrified in his life.

5

"**A**RE YOU SURE YOU HEARD CORRECTLY?" ASKED PEG'S FRIEND, Mary Bowser.

"I'm sure," said Peg. "The men were talkin' about a ship that traveled beneath the water. Never heard such a thing in my life."

Mary nodded and said nothing. They were moving up Richmond's 14th Street on this warm Sunday morning, heading in the direction of their respective churches. A haze of airborne dust hung in the air as the morning wind stirred up the dirt roads.

Peg Scobell was a member of the all-black church, First African Baptist, which the vast majority of slaves and free blacks in Richmond attended, while Mary was on her way to St. John's Episcopal Church—the very church where Patrick Henry once said, "Give me liberty or give me death." Not many blacks attended the Episcopal Church, let alone been baptized there as Mary had. But Mary always was a bit different; she was as curious as the family that had freed her. The wealthy Van Lew family had sent Mary to Philadelphia for an education—something that Peg could not fathom. Mary had even spent some of her years as a missionary in Liberia, so she was also well traveled. Freed slaves were required to leave Virginia within a year, unless they successfully petitioned the legislature, but the Van Lew ladies flouted the law and let Mary continue to work for them anyway.

"Ships that travel under the water sound to me like important information," Mary said after they had gone a half block in silence.

"Captain Atwater said he wasn't sure the machine would even work."

"But if it did . . . That could make all the difference in the world. It's important."

Mary motioned for Peg to step off of the street, which was busy with foot traffic to the various churches. The city was packed, for soldiers had poured into Richmond after states started peeling away from the Union. Mary led Peg into an alley and glanced up and down the passageway, making sure no one was lurking nearby. Was there a reason to be so suspicious or was this simply her melodrama? Even for Mary, it was unusual behavior.

"Promise you will not say a word to anybody," she said.

"What's with all the shiftiness, Mary? You know I wouldn't tell anyone something you told me in confidence."

"I know, but I need you to promise regardless."

Peg sighed, exasperated by her friend's uncharacteristic lack of trust.

"Promise?" she insisted.

"Promise," said Peg.

Mary leaned in so close that Peg got a strong whiff of the flowers on her Sunday hat. "I know of people who would very dearly love to see the kind of information you have access to."

Peg was staggered. Was Mary talking about spying? Mary knew that Peg had sewn a secret pocket into the cuff of her husband's pants just before he headed north—and that John had said that if he wouldn't be allowed to use a gun, he would use his wits to collect information. Was Mary asking her to do the same?

"You want information about infernal machines?" Peg asked.

"The what?"

"Infernal machines. That's what Mister Malone called the underwater boats. Who's lookin' for this information?"

Mary smiled. "Infernal machines? I like that. Vivid. Very vivid."

Her friend had gone off track, so Peg repeated her question. "Who is lookin' for such information?"

Mary leaned in even closer, just inches from Peg's ear. "She wouldn't want me saying just yet. I'm only asking you to keep your ears and eyes wide open."

She? Mary was collecting information for a woman?

Peg pulled back and sized up her friend. Mary could be a jokester, but even Mary wouldn't jest about something like this. Spying in this environment was a dangerous game, for people were suspicious of just about everybody, except for black servants. But that could change.

"I'd really like to meet this woman who's askin' for information," Peg said.

Mary frowned. "Who said it's a woman?"

"You just did."

Mary's eyebrows shot up, as it evidently dawned on her that she had let slip that her contact was female.

"Oh."

"So could I meet her?"

"Perhaps later."

Mary took hold of Peg's hands and laughed. This all seemed to be a game to her. She could be fearless, sometimes bordering on recklessness. Mary was once arrested for not carrying a pass on the streets, and she had spent some time in jail before the Van Lews got her out. After that experience, Mary always liked to say, "Once you've been in a Richmond prison, not much makes you afraid."

"We're going to make history," she said.

Peg squeezed her friend's hands. "Don't do anything foolish, Mary. They'll string people up for gatherin' information."

Mary didn't seem to hear the warning. "When will you be working at the Atwater house next?"

"This afternoon. I'm servin' at dinner."

"Then keep your ears open. That's all I'm asking. They don't string people up for just listening to people talk. You'll do it then?"

"I'll listen. But I ain't writin' anything down." Putting information on paper: Now that was dangerous.

"That's fine then. You have a powerful memory."

"And don't be tellin' anyone that I'm listenin' for y'all."

"Of course I would never do such a thing."

"Don't even tell your lady contact about me. Not until I can meet her myself."

"There's no need for her to know your name. Does this mean you agree?"

Peg sighed. Every little bit of intelligence helped. How could she reject doing something that might help her husband's cause—and maybe end this war quickly, before he became cannon fodder?

"I hate secrets," Peg said.

Peg had been forced to keep secrets most of her life growing up in the Shockoe Bottom neighborhood down by the river, where many slaves and free blacks packed into tenements. Whenever she saw her papa drunk, he told her she better not tell Mama or he'd wallop her, and whenever she found her mama with another man (which was often), Mama said to keep it a secret or she'd be sorry. Peg reluctantly kept their secrets, but Mama and Papa knew what was going on.

"If you hate secrets, then all I'm asking is for you to find out Confederate secrets and pass them on. Then they won't be secrets any longer."

Peg took a deep breath. "I'm not sure John would approve."

"You told me John is collecting information himself. Why would he object?"

"He's protective of me."

"As he should be. But there isn't a risk here. Trust me."

Trust Mary Bowser? The last time Mary convinced her to take a risk, they went out after the curfew for blacks in Richmond and nearly got nabbed by the night patrollers.

"I'll do what I can."

Mary beamed. She linked arms with Peg and drew her back toward 14th Street. "We're making history, Peg," she repeated, whispering in her ear.

That's what Peg was afraid of.

6

THE BULLETS WERE BEGINNING TO BUZZ PAST. THE EIGHTH Georgia was back to its feet, rushing through a patch of oak trees and across a field, heading for a thicket of pine trees. Cannonballs were also whipping overhead, for the Yankees were still shooting high. If they could only reach the trees before the Northerners got their aim corrected . . .

This wasn't as bad as John expected it to be. He thought that men would begin dropping on all sides, but as the Rebel force jogged across the field, with bullets clattering all around like grasshoppers in the cornstalks, he didn't see anyone collapsing. The Yankees were still shooting from a good distance away, so he tried not to get overconfident about his chances of surviving.

The next moment, they were in the trees, and the organized lines of the regiment were broken by the obstacles in their paths—tree limbs, brambles, and blackberry bushes. They were in the shade, and that felt good, but John nearly got knocked off his feet from behind when he stopped to climb over a rotted fence running right through the woods. When the soldiers reached the other side of the thicket of trees they came to a stop, as if some invisible barrier was holding them back, and they began firing from the protection of the forest. Just beyond the trees was an open field where a lonely icehouse stood; a little further beyond was a farmhouse—and Yankees. Thousands of them, John guessed.

John loaded the rifle and handed it off to Gusty, who fired and handed it back to John, who loaded it again, and on and on it went.

With guns going off all around, he was just as terrified of the weapons being fired by the Confederates at his back as the ones being fired by the Yankees in front. He glanced over his shoulder, afraid he'd see Watkins taking aim at the back of his head. But all he saw were soldiers who looked just as afraid as him.

Then the fighting got hot. The Yankees fired coordinated volleys that sent swarms of lead into the trees, and men began falling. The Yankee cannons had been adjusted, and the black balls ripped into the pine forest. A tree, only twelve feet away, exploded under the crushing impact of a black ball, and it toppled over. Pieces of wood flew in all directions, some of them piercing soldiers. Now that the bullets were finding targets, John heard screams and groans. Everything in his body was telling him to hightail it and run, but he knew that if he fled, one of the Rebels would definitely kill him on the spot for deserting. He had a better chance facing the Yankees, who were still a good distance away.

When John reached out to grab the rifle again and reload, he saw Gusty leaning over and picking up another gun from the ground where a fellow soldier had fallen. Gusty now had two rifles, and he shoved one of them into John's hands.

"We need all the firepower we can get. Go on and take it," Gusty said, proceeding to reload his own.

Just like that, John found himself armed. He stared at the rifle in his hands—thankful he was no longer defenseless on a battlefield, but torn by the prospect of firing on Yankees.

"Go on, John, use your gift!" called out Gusty.

John grabbed some cartridges and percussion caps from the fallen soldier, and he stared across the field, which was clouded with the thick fog of gunfire. He knew Gusty was expecting him to fire, so he shot high. No one was going to be evaluating the accuracy of his aim in this chaos because the men had better things to do—like stay alive. He loaded, fired, loaded, fired, each time aiming above the enemy's heads. The most common mistake, even when you were trying to aim straight, was to shoot high. So by intentionally aiming high, he was probably posing a bigger threat to the birds flying by.

Gusty cheered him on. "That's it, John. I think y'all hit one!"

Hit one? That was not possible, unless these soldiers had discovered a way to hover in the air. But if Gusty wanted to believe that he had dropped a Yankee, then that was fine with him.

John thought he heard the command to charge, but he remained in the trees—as did all of the men. The idea of sprinting out into the hailstorm was sure suicide. He would have a better chance dodging raindrops in a gully washer. His clothes were drenched through with sweat, and his mouth felt like it was packed with cotton. And the noise. It had become deafening. Guns going off on all sides, trees cracking, men shouting. The cacophony had a disorienting effect, and John suddenly felt sick to his stomach. He didn't want to die pretending to fight for the South.

The Yanks started firing canister shot—cans packed with lead balls and sawdust. As the canisters soared above their heads, they disintegrated and rained balls on the heads of the soldiers, creating a torrent of pain. A cannonball shrieked past, and he glanced to his left and saw a headless soldier collapse backward. Another man was sprawled out on a fallen tree, his arm draped over a branch, his mouth gaping, and his eyes glazed and sightless. He saw the standard bearer hold the Confederate flag high, and it made John sick thinking he had gathered beneath an enemy banner. He scoured the terrain ahead for any sign of a Yankee charge, but the smoke of so many guns pouring out bullets from both sides made it almost impossible to see a thing across the field. He couldn't hear, couldn't see, couldn't think. He loaded and fired and loaded and fired, like some mechanical contraption gone awry.

John took off his slouch hat and wiped his forehead with his forearm, and something went zipping by, inches from his nose. A bullet had gone cleanly through the hat in his hand. He was going to die. He felt it in his bones.

And then came the most terrifying sight of all. Breaking through the fog of smoke were Federal soldiers, thousands of them it seemed, running toward them, charging, screaming, bayonets in full view.

"I hope y'all are as good fighting hand to hand as shootin'!" Gusty shouted.

John looked for an opportunity to run. Maybe he could escape to Federal lines during the chaos. It might work. Soldiers on all sides were wearing uniforms of all types and colors, and John's raggedy clothes were mud brown; there was no telling what side he was on. But did the Yankees even have black folks mixed in with their ranks?

He remembered the image of two charging bulls coming at each other, preparing to gore each other to death, with John trapped in the middle. This was it—the image come to life. The bayonets were the horns of the bulls, as two enormous beasts prepared to converge.

John had his bayonet fixed, and he wondered what it would feel like to drive it through a man's chest; he usually fought with his fists and had been in only one knife fight, and he had knocked the man cold before either of them could even use a blade. One thing was certain: You cannot fake hand-to-hand fighting, so he would have to kill or be killed. He got into a crouch, looking for an opportunity to run. The Yankees were close, and there were so many of them. If he could simply turn around, maybe the Yankees would assume he was on their side. That's all it would take. A simple pivot. A turning of the body. One moment he was fighting for the South, the next moment he was a Yank. As simple as that.

Then a hand snagged his sleeve, and John was sure that Gusty had read his thoughts and was trying to stop him from running. His friend had locked onto his arm, as if he knew! His grip was strong.

Turning, John expected to see anger and disapproval in Gusty's face, but he saw fear, not judgment.

And blood.

Gusty had been hit in the side of the head, and his right ear was a mangled mess; John looked away from the blackened wound, for it made him sick to his stomach. Suddenly, Gusty fell backward, although he didn't let loose of John's arm. He was still alive, his eyes were fixed on John, and he was saying something. In the noise, John couldn't hear a thing. The two forces were about to collide, and John knew this was his best chance to slip into the Federal lines. He wanted so badly to run, but Gusty was still clutching his sleeve, twisting the cloth in his hand, and his eyes brimmed with fear. John knew he couldn't desert Gusty; it wasn't in his blood to leave a man who had been uncommonly kind to him. So John pulled out his handkerchief and pressed it to the side of Gusty's head, which was raw and red with blood. He was ashamed to find himself wishing that Gusty would just die and close his eyes, so he couldn't see him run off to the Northern side. But Gusty's eyes were wide and they wouldn't leave John's face. Gusty's lips moved, but he had no idea what the man was saying.

John leaned in closer and said, "I got ya, sir, I got ya."

With his rifle slung over his shoulder, John squatted down, put both arms beneath Gusty's body, and rose up from the ground, lifting the wounded man.

"I ain't lettin' go of you."

Then John began to jog, but not toward the Yankee side, where he wanted to be, but back to Rebel lines. Men were dying all around him, and John moved through the carnage with Gusty in his arms. He wondered why he remained unscathed, and then it dawned on him. The Yankees were not bothering to target a black man carrying a dying soldier in his arms and leaving the battlefield. Even in this patch of hell, some soldiers followed rules of honor. The Federals focused their wrath on the Rebels who were trying to kill them.

Strange. It was as if Gusty had become his guardian angel, providing a circle of protection and safety. It may have looked like John was the one rescuing Gusty, but in reality it was the other way around.

"Y'all gonna be fine, sir, y'all gotta know that."

John felt tears coming down his cheeks, cutting a tributary through the dust on his face. Gusty was trying to say something. From the shape of the words on his lips, it seemed as if the man was telling him, "Thank you." But it was John who should be thanking Gusty. This dying man was his protection.

John heard an awful crack and wondered if it was a breaking tree or breaking bones. But still, he went untouched. He nearly tripped on a branch as he moved back through the forest of pine, back to safety, back to life. The smoke was choking them both, and Gusty began to cough. But at least it meant he was still alive—until John realized that his friend was coughing blood.

"Stay with the livin', sir!"

Finally, they came out of the back end of the trees and into the light. Then something stung his right thigh, and John nearly collapsed. He caught his balance and kept trudging, trying to catch a look at his leg to see if he was all right. He didn't see blood and was able to keep walking, so if a bullet had struck him, it must have come from a long distance and had lost all of its power.

Gusty's head suddenly flopped to the side, and John shook him as he walked, trying to shake the life back into him. His friend's eyes were still open, but there was no light in them. Gusty's spirit had left the body, and John could sense that he was carrying nothing more than flesh and bones. Strangely enough, the body seemed heavier. Remove the spirit and a body got heavier, not lighter, it seemed.

He kept walking with the body in his arms because Gusty deserved a proper burial, even if it meant that John had missed his chance to go over to the Federal lines. He owed the man that much. Gusty had saved his life, first with Hancock and now on the battlefield. So he kept walking, even though the body felt heavier and heavier. It was like trudging in a dream, where your legs feel so heavy that you can barely lift them. He moved across a patch of open ground, conscious of movement on all sides, other injured soldiers hobbling away from the battle. The Rebels seemed to be retreating from Matthew's Hill, and he wondered if a wave of Yankees was about to break through the forest at his back.

The smoke had thinned, but the fog inside John's head had become thicker. He was confused and disoriented, and he thought men were talking to him, but he could not hear what they were saying. Something about him being a loyal slave lugging his master's body. Then two men lifted Gusty's body from his arms and placed him on a stretcher—and John felt so vulnerable again. Without Gusty in his arms, he was an individual black man again, and he had lost the protection of his white friend. He turned and surveyed the scene. The

Rebels were pulling back, and soldiers were falling on all sides. The battle was coming after him, the bull was still charging.

So John did what anyone would do if a bull was coming right for him. He ran for his life. But he didn't retreat with the Rebels, and he didn't run toward the Yankees. He ran for the woods.

7

I T WAS SO STIFLING THAT PEG FELT AS IF *SHE* WAS THE ONE BEING cooked for dinner, not the roast pig. No air moved through the kitchen in Captain Atwater's house, and the heat gathered in a concentrated mass. The oven had ratcheted the temperatures up, and Peg dripped with sweat.

Peg was helping out Matilda, an older Negro servant who could cook the carpet and still make it tasty. Peg was the only one she would allow to help her in the Atwater kitchen. Today, Matilda even let her score the skin on the 7-pound pig leg before they started roasting it. Matilda knew just how to roast the thicker, upper part of the leg so it was cooked through and through without burning the thinner parts to a crisp.

Matilda, a pint-sized cook, barely five feet tall, also had rhubarb tarts and hominy muffins in the making, and Peg couldn't resist nibbling on the crumbs. Matilda didn't allow the help to sample the food, except for the occasional taste test, but Peg figured there was no harm in scooping a handful of morsels off the counter and surreptitiously licking them from her palm.

This afternoon, Peg was going to try spying; the way she looked at it, she was simply gathering morsels of information, like scooping the crumbs of hominy muffin off the counter. So there was really no danger to this kind of spying. Was there? She wasn't writing anything down. How could they suspect a thing?

"You go clean up now and let me finish this," Matilda ordered. She would have made a fine Napoleon on the battlefield. "I don't want you serving the family smellin' like a cooked pig."

Peg savored the smell of food in her clothes, but she was quick to obey. "Yes, ma'am."

She changed into her serving clothes in the quarters upstairs, but not until she had washed away the cooking smell from her hands. She covered her hair with a head wrap, as Missus Hicks ordered, but she had decided to wear the yellow one, dyed with hickory bark and bay leaves. Peg loved the splash of sunlight on her head, and she adjusted the yellow head wrap before hurrying back downstairs.

Captain Atwater had invited Mister Clifton Ballard and his wife Abigail to dinner, which was promising. Mister Ballard was an older gentleman, a banker, and he had been on the board of the Tredegar Iron Works forever. She hoped they might spill some tidbits about what was going on in the iron works, and Peg would be there to sweep up the scraps of information. The irascible Missus Hicks was also dining at the table, as was Miss Doris from next door. As Peg went about her duties, she felt Missus Hicks' gaze fixed on her. And when she cast a sideways glance, it was obvious where the old woman was looking—at her head.

The folks spent considerable time talking about some widowed woman named Missus Baker who was coming to visit from Chicago of all places. It seemed as if Peg's first attempt at gathering intelligence was going to be a complete waste of effort, when the conversation suddenly made a turn for the dramatic. They began to discuss two men squabbling over a belle and the possibility of a duel.

"Will it actually come to that?" asked Missus Ballard. "Surely not."

"It very well might," said Captain Atwater. "Mister Thompson was very disconcerted with Mister Crawford for the words he dared to write in the newspaper."

From what Peg could gather, Mister Thompson and Mister Crawford had been vying for the attentions of the same Southern belle.

And when Mister Crawford was spurned at a recent ball, he printed a poem that brazenly insulted the lady.

"Did he really say that her lips speak falsely?" asked Miss Doris.

"He did," injected Missus Hicks. "And if you ask me, he was right on the mark. Her lips *are* false."

Captain Atwater shot a look at Missus Hicks, but she ignored him.

"I believe it is noble that Mister Thompson is standing up for her honor," said Mister Ballard. "Mister Crawford had no cause to walk up to him on the street and pull his nose."

Peg looked around at the table at the bobbing heads, for most agreed that pulling another man's nose was an ultimate insult, directed at the most prominent feature of a man's face and therefore deserving of a duel. She thought it all seemed so silly. After all, what's a tweak of the nose in comparison to a whipping with the lash?

"But surely they could settle their differences another way than to duel. Isn't someone going to stop it from happening, my dear?" said Missus Ballard.

"Fighting like gentlemen is far superior to brawling like wild dogs in the streets," he said, as Peg began to clear the dishes. "Two men in an open field, staring each other in the eyes. . . . Much more honorable."

No one had an immediate response to that statement, but Peg could see the light of mischief in Missus Hicks' eyes.

"If fighting a duel in the open is honorable, then what would you call sneaking up in a submarine boat and attaching an explosive torpedo to the bottom of a ship?" Missus Hicks suddenly said. As Peg suspected, the old lady had probably overheard the men's conversation in the drawing room during the dance the night before.

Her words went off like a bomb. Everyone went deathly quiet, just as Peg was leaving the room with several plates in her hands. She wished she could linger a little longer in the dining room, but that would raise suspicion. She cast a quick look over her shoulder and saw old lady Hicks dabbing at her mouth, pretending to be oblivious to the shocked looks on the faces of their dinner guests.

Peg moved around the corner, into the short hallway leading toward the kitchen, and she stopped. She listened.

"Missus Hicks, you make a very good point," she heard Mister Ballard say. "I have raised the very issue myself on the Tredegar board."

"I would hope so, Mister Ballard," said Missus Hicks. "I am pleased to hear it."

"Speaking of the Tredegar Iron Works, I think it is time for myself and Mister Ballard to retire to the drawing room, for we have some business to discuss," said Captain Atwater, obviously looking for an opening to whisk Mister Ballard from the presence of Missus Hicks. "If you will pardon us, ladies."

Missus Hicks couldn't resist a final jab. "You are retreating from the field of battle already? I would like to hear more of what Mister Ballard has to say."

"Perhaps another day."

Peg was still taking in these words when she felt a pair of eyes burning into her back. She spun around, the plates still in her hands, and saw Gilbert Mann, a butler and sometimes coachman for Captain Atwater. He smiled at her, moved in uncomfortably close, and whispered, "Pick up any fascinatin' gossip?"

Gilbert put his hand on her shoulder, and Peg cringed. Ever since her husband went north, she had caught Gilbert staring at her, and now this. She shook loose, turned away from Gilbert, and headed for the kitchen.

"You don't have to go, Peggy. I like gossip too. Let's listen together."

"You can call me Missus Scobell."

Gilbert let out a laugh, which drew the attention of the cook, who popped her head out of the kitchen door and shot a look at Peg. Wiping her hands with a towel, Matilda's eyes moved to Gilbert.

"No dawdlin' now, the two of you."

"Sorry, ma'am," said Peg, lowering her eyes and scurrying into the kitchen.

When Peg had deposited the dirty plates in the sink, Matilda presented her with a silver tray, topped with a pitcher of blackberry tea and two glasses, for Mister Ballard was active in the temperance movement and could not abide even the sight of liquor bottles.

Earlier in the afternoon, Peg had removed all alcohol from the drawing room. Peg hated the sight of drink herself, after growing up with a papa who painted his tonsils with alcohol every morning and night. Her brother had become a stinking drunk as well.

"Try not to snoop when y'all are deliverin' refreshments," Matilda said, glaring.

"Yes, ma'am," Peg said. But when she reached the door leading into the drawing room, she paused before going in—to listen.

"With the Baltimore copper depleted, do we have a source for copper?" she heard Captain Atwater asking Mister Ballard.

"We're aimin' to get it from the Ducktown mines in Polk County, Tennessee."

"Is that our only Southern source of copper?"

"Our only. I always said we were too dependent on Northern sources."

Peg tried to memorize the key ideas. Shortage of copper. Ducktown mines. But what county in Tennessee did they say? She had vowed she wouldn't put anything on paper, but now she wondered if she needed to write this down when she got back to her room.

"It's not only a problem for copper," said Captain Atwater. "We're looking for steel for our rifling machines and lead for rifle projectile sabots."

"Any possibility of finding sheet zinc for the ammunition boxes?"

"We're hunting for sources."

"At least we have no problem with lumber for the gun carriages."

Peg could not linger any longer without raising suspicions, so she entered the drawing room, where the two men lounged in chairs. Captain Atwater puffed on a cigar, while Mister Ballard poked around at his teeth with a toothpick. As she poured their drinks, they continued to spill information, not seeming to care a whit about her presence. She was a Negro servant, and a woman to boot. They didn't think their words meant anything to her.

"What about the ironclad ship?" Mister Ballard asked. "Thank you kindly, Peg."

Smiling, Peg nodded and poured Captain Atwater's tea.

"It's looking like they will be contracting with us to produce the iron sheathing for the ship."

"Excellent. But where are we going to obtain the iron for this vessel?"

"Good question. The railroads?" said Captain Atwater.

"Discarded rails?"

"It's probably our best source of iron."

Peg left the room, her head spinning. So much to remember. Iron sheathing for a ship? An ironclad ship? Did they really mean that a ship was going to be made out of iron? Wouldn't the thing sink to the bottom like a heavy stone? She wondered if the two men had been making it all up, just to tease her ears. Iron, copper, sheet zinc. The information was a clutter in her head.

She lingered at the door a little longer, until she felt a cold presence at her back.

"And what do you think you are doing?"

Spinning around, she found old lady Hicks giving her a stern stare. Had Missus Hicks already caught her spying?

Missus Hicks reached out and put a finger on Peg's head wrap and played with the bow. She sighed heavily. "I don't like it."

"Pardon me, ma'am?"

"I said I don't like your head wrap, Peg. Do you have ears to hear?"

"But ma'am, you asked me to wear a head wrap."

"I assumed you would be wearing a *white* wrap, not a yellow one. I don't like it."

"I'm sorry, ma'am, but—"

"*Change it.*"

"But, ma'am, I—"

Missus Hicks marched on, and Peg watched her go, determined to hold back the tears that were coming. She didn't entirely succeed, and Matilda the cook noticed the sheen of tears pooling in her eyes when she appeared in the kitchen.

"What's wrong, baby child?"

"Missus Hicks."

"Oh yes. *That woman.*"

This simple exchange said it all. Matilda wrapped her arms around Peg and patted her back, but her comfort made it all the more difficult to hold back the tears. Peg had to deal with Missus Hicks day after day, but sometimes the frustration overwhelmed her.

Matilda soothed her like she would a young child with hurt feelings. "Let it out, baby child, let it out."

The older woman pulled out a handkerchief and handed it to Peg. Peg noticed that the handkerchief had been dyed red, and she couldn't help but laugh; she smiled through her tears as she dabbed away the moisture from her eyes. Matilda guessed correctly why Peg had suddenly smiled.

"I got the good sense to keep my splash of color hidden away in my pocket," she said. "You're wearing your color on your head like a proud flag."

Peg's smile broadened. "I should've known better."

"That's it, honey. Bring that smile back."

"Missus Hicks wouldn't let me wear no braids, so I thought I could . . . I could wear some color."

"There's only two colors in Missus Hicks' world. Black clothes and white skin. Anything else is a sin before God."

That was true. Missus Hicks wore only black clothing, and with three husbands gone and buried, she was probably planning to wear mourning clothes for the rest of her life, even if she lived to one hundred. Matilda gave Peg a peck on the cheek and sent her off, like she was her own daughter.

By the time Peg returned to her room in the hothouse attic of the Atwater home, her mind was jumbled. She tried to remember all of the information she had heard from Captain Atwater and Mister Ballard, but Missus Hicks had upset her so badly that it was hard to keep the information fixed in her mind. She ran the details through her head and realized that it was becoming more confused by the moment. She sat on the edge of her bed, fanning her face and trying to retrieve what she had heard. Iron. Zinc. Copper. Ironclads. The idea of an invincible ship seemed terribly important. But she couldn't write this information down. Could she? It was just too dangerous.

Then she thought about her husband John and how he might be fighting for the Yanks, if they allowed him. She thought about how he had hidden that pencil and paper in the cuffs of his pants and was taking down notes in a far more dangerous place than a comfortable house. She felt like such a coward.

Peg went to the nightstand, where her Bible sat. She flipped it open and hunted for words that might guide her decision of what to do. She searched through the Psalms because they were chock full of fears and confusion and pain. The Psalms didn't provide an answer about what she should do . . . until her eyes landed on a verse number . . . then flitted to a chapter number.

Numbers.

The numbers made her realize: She could take notes, but she could do it in a code of her own making.

Quickly, before she lost her nerve, Peg dug two scraps of paper and a pencil out of a drawer and wrote down everything she remembered about the ironclad, infernal machine, zinc, copper, Tennessee, and so on. Then she transposed each letter of her note into a specific Scripture verse that began with the same letter. Second Kings 6:30 began with, "And it came to pass . . ." So that verse would stand for the letter "A."

When she was done, she had several slips of paper that appeared to be nothing more than a list of her favorite Bible passages. She burned the paper with the information written out in clear English, but she still had to find a place to stash her coded message.

Her eyes scoured the room. It was a bare room, as most servant quarters were. Under the mattress? Too obvious. Under the floorboard? If anyone found it, they would know it was a coded message. There was only one logical place to hide the note.

Peg opened her Bible to the Book of Daniel, the eleventh chapter.

So the king of the North shall come and build a siege mound, and take a fortified city; and the forces of the South shall not withstand him . . . He shall stand in the Glorious Land with destruction in his power.

Peg closed the Bible on her coded message and placed the Good Book back on her nightstand.

8

WHEN JOHN PLUNGED INTO THE WOODS, HE HEARD SHOUTS from behind, and he shot a look over his shoulder to catch sight of two Rebel soldiers hot on his tail. He leaped over a log, his rifle still slung over his shoulder and slapping against his thigh. A gun went off from behind, but no bullet burrowed into his back; he was still on his feet, dodging between trees, leaping over brambles, his legs pumping and burning, and branches smacking him in the shoulder. One sharp branch put a cat-scratch across his face, and he heard more warnings to stop as he picked up speed.

The battle was soon far behind him, but he could still hear the crashing footsteps of the pursuing Rebels. Panic had powered his initial sprint, but now the heat had become oppressive, and he felt as if his shirt, drenched with sweat, weighed him down. He considered spinning around and fighting the men hand to hand, but one of the soldiers had not yet fired his gun. If he tried to fight, he would get a bullet in the face before he even had a chance of taking them down.

"Hold on, boy!" shouted one of the Rebel soldiers, clearly out of breath as he strained to get out the words. "If y'all halt, we'll take you back to camp unharmed."

John didn't believe it for a moment. These two white boys obviously couldn't stand the idea of even a single black man slipping away in the midst of a battle. Why else would they be so persistent? If he was caught, they would make an example of him. His death would be slow—and very public.

John scrambled down a steep ravine, his feet slipping and sliding on the leaves. He maintained his footing until the toe of his right shoe caught on a rock, and he went flopping down on his hands. His knee struck stone and sent a hot flame of pain into the joint; his gun went flying about five feet to his right. He heard the clanking of his pursuer's equipment, and he scrambled to pick up his weapon. But as he pushed himself back to his feet, gun in hand, he saw that one of the Rebels was only about twenty feet away, his gun leveled directly at John's face. This was his moment to decide. Should he give himself up and hope and pray for mercy? Or should he turn and keep running, providing an easy target for this Southern boy, who probably spent his days shooting small squirrels out of trees?

He never had a chance to choose. The soldier's gun went off and John heard a grunt, and for a moment he wondered if he was hearing himself groan with pain. But the cry came from behind, and he spun around to see a Yankee soldier crumpling to the ground, his gun dropping from his hand. The Rebel had gone for the greater threat—a Yankee soldier who had suddenly appeared in the woods, probably separated from his regiment.

The Rebel began to reload and John took off, the pursuit renewed. John had witnessed the marksmanship of this Confederate, and the man had put the bullet squarely in the forehead of the Yankee soldier. Fear added momentum to his legs, and he ran with even greater speed. For a moment he thought he had lost his pursuers. He came to a halt, ducked behind a tree, and caught his breath. The blistering heat was unbearable and perspiration flooded his face, turning his clothes into a sopping sponge.

Then a sound came from his left, and he wheeled around to see the second Rebel coming at him with his saber raised. This soldier had circled around to catch him unawares, and the man let out a scream like a high-pitched Indian war cry—*"Wa-woo-woohoo, wa-woo woohoohe!"* Dropping to the forest floor, John heard the swoosh of steel slicing inches above his head. The sword sank into a tree, cutting through a branch like butter. The Rebel was knocked off balance when his blade hit bark, and John picked up the branch that had just been lopped off and jammed it into the Confederate's gut. The man buckled over, and John followed with a crack to the back of the man's head, and the Rebel fell face down.

As John took off running again, he knew there would be no such thing as mercy in the minds of these two men. Not now. His body reached deep for strength, and he gained speed, never looking back. When he finally came to a stop and slipped behind a tree, about ten minutes later, he no longer heard the sound of his pursuers. In the distance, he could hear the thunder-rumble of cannons and men shouting and the popping of guns. From far away, the battle sounded so muffled and harmless. His breathing steadily came under control, and he fought the urge to cough. Peeking around the tree, he saw no sign of either Rebel or Federal soldiers, so he stepped out and tried to get his bearing. He supposed that off to his left was the Warrenton Turnpike, the road that stretched off in the direction of Centreville and Washington. He began moving through the woods once again, praying that he was heading northeast. Sunlight broke through the trees in spots, lighting up the forest floor like a cathedral.

About fifteen feet away, off to his right, his eyes landed on a wolf den dug into the base of a slope and partially concealed by vegetation. Wolves usually build their dens near sources of water, so he went off rummaging nearby. But he hadn't gone far before he heard voices moving in his direction. Rebels? Yankees? Either blue or gray could be trouble, so he hurried back toward the wolf den—a nice hiding spot.

Wolves used dens for giving birth to pups, and that happened in the spring, so he stood a good chance of finding the home unoccupied at the height of summer. He dropped to the ground, and his rifle clanked on the dirt as he slid inside the den, feet first, twisting onto his belly and pushing himself backward, like a crab retreating into its hole. The hole was about fifteen feet deep with the birthing chamber at the very back. He savored the shade of the den and the cool feel of the ground on his arms and belly.

Only one problem: Another critter was borrowing this space, and something began moving inside the den. John resisted the urge to shout in surprise, as something moved across his leg—slithered actually. A snake slowly slid over one leg, then another. Surely it was not a rattlesnake, because it would have sent out its telltale warning long ago. The snake continued to cross his body like an unending train, but if it was typical of snakes in these parts it probably wasn't more than three feet long. John knew his wildlife, and the primary ones he had to fear, not counting the timber rattler, was the copperhead and the cottonmouth. He remained perfectly still as the snake crossed his body and curled up in a coil, only a few inches from his gut.

He heard more voices in the distance, muffled voices, and he wondered if it was the two Rebel soldiers, still scouring the forest for him. Between a rock and a hard place, he remained still for about a half an hour, although it was hard to judge time when you have a snake dozing inches from your belly. He had his gun aimed at the den opening, in case one of the Rebel soldiers peeked in his head. But all was quiet in the woods, except for the constant chatter of wildlife. He occasionally heard the rustle of leaves and prayed it was just the sound of squirrels and other small mammals.

The snake was going nowhere and he hadn't heard voices or human movement for a spell, so he considered making a dash for it. Carefully, he adjusted his position, moving slowly onto his right side, and the snake didn't react. He raised his head from the ground and looked off toward the circle of light—the den exit only about six feet away. He could crawl for safety and pray the snake wasn't a copperhead.

His right leg had gone to sleep, even though the rest of him was very alert, and he tried to shake it to life without rousing the snake. He was so thirsty and his throat ached every time he swallowed. Frustrated, he shook his leg a little harder, trying to wake it up.

He roused the snake instead.

In the dark, only inches from his belly, he heard the snake hissing. He looked back and could barely make out the snake's black body, but he could see the head rising from the ground and its face expanding to the sides like the hood of an angry cobra. The next moment, the snake struck. The black body shot straight for his face like a cannonball in the dark. It happened in the space of a single breath. The snake's thick head thumped him directly in the forehead, and he felt the full force of the black bullet hitting him hard. John kicked at the snake, pushed up to his hands and knees, and scrambled out of the hole as fast as possible. Behind him, the snake was still hissing.

Staggering out of the den, he felt his forehead for any sign that he had been bitten, but he could find no telltale marks through the skin. He scanned the area and saw no sign of soldiers, either Yankee or Southern. So he calmed himself down and decided to check out his reptilian enemy to find out if he had been attacked by something poisonous. He returned to the den, crouched down, and peered inside. He could make out the muscular snake just inside the den, but now it was stretched out, as if dead to the world. Carefully, he used his bayonet to reach in and lift the four-foot-long serpent. The snake was no longer hissing. It had gone limp.

John laughed lightly. This was no copperhead. This was a hognosed snake, which was more bluff than bite. They were good actors and could puff out their faces like an intimidating cobra. But when they struck, they usually didn't bite—and they weren't poisonous if they did. They typically butted you in the head like a battering ram, and John felt the spot where he had been slammed by the snake. Hognosed snakes were also good actors when it came to playing dead, and the snake was putting on a show.

Gently, he placed the hog-nosed snake back inside the den, and then he saluted the creature before continuing on his way.

As suspected, John found a creek a short distance from the den; it was barely a trickle, but there was enough water to hold his thirst at bay and wet his face. He soaked his slouch hat with water and then jammed it on his head. But as he made a move to go, he noticed the most curious object, propped up against a tree like a living thing. It was a doll, about a foot tall. The doll had a pure white face, red bonnet, salmon-colored dress, and blue apron, and it seemed so strange, so out of place, sitting all alone in the middle of a forest, only a mile from a battlefield. He picked it up and stared into the black eyes on the papier-mâché head. Peg had never owned a doll growing up—not a single toy. Her father satisfied his own desires by spending his money on drink, and her mother was more interested in satisfying the desires of every man in the slave neighborhood of Shockoe Bottom than in satisfying Peg's need for a mother. The doll would be a gift for Peg, so he slipped it into his backpack and continued on his way.

It was early evening, judging by the sun and the lengthening shadows, and he thought about how he had encountered the Tree of the Knowledge of Good and Evil on the battlefield, complete with apples, and now he had met the serpent. What's next? Flaming swords and angels? He wondered if these were signs from God, but for the life of him he had no idea what it all meant.

John began to hear commotion in the distance, coming from the direction of the Warrenton Turnpike. He veered a little to his right to stray farther from human contact. But avoiding soldiers on the move was becoming more difficult. Three times he had to hide behind vegetation as Federal soldiers came crashing through the forest. The traffic increased, men fleeing, many tossing aside unnecessary equipment that weighed them down. Haversacks. Tin cups. Sewing kits. John had a sinking feeling, and he feared that the Confederates had won the war in one fell swoop. He felt so tired, and his legs began to ache, and he wondered if he was feeling the first touch of sunstroke, even as the darkness slowly settled down.

A little deeper into the woods, and he nearly walked right into the side of a hut. The squat little shack was so well hidden that he didn't see it until he was a few feet away. The shack was about seven feet high and barely big enough to hold more than four or five people. The sides and roof were completely covered with vegetation, but behind a curtain of branches he could see a wooden door. The Lord had led him directly into the path of a shelter for the night.

He set aside his rifle, peeled away the branches, and put his ear to the door. Not hearing a sound coming from inside, he reached for the door handle. But as he did, he heard the cock of a gun from behind. Someone had snuck up on him, as quiet as a feather. He turned and found himself staring into the face of a black man. The man pointed a gun directly in his face, only a few feet away.

The man's expression softened, but he didn't lower his gun. "Friends of Uncle Abe?" the man asked.

John had no idea what the man was asking. He licked his parched lips and stared back blankly.

"Friends of Uncle Abe?" the man repeated, in a tone that demanded an answer.

John could only suppose what he meant. "Abe Lincoln? I'm fightin' on Abe's side, if that's what y'all mean."

The man blinked away a drop of sweat, and John noticed his finger ease away from the trigger. He must have answered correctly.

"You mean you ain't heard of the League, you bein' a black man and all?"

"I ain't heard of any League. I'm just doin' my part for Uncle Abe." He held up a hand and said, "Let me show y'all."

Slowly, John moved into a crouch. "I'm just gonna reach for the cuff of my pants."

The man became suddenly defensive again and firmed his aim. "You keep your hands away from your leg. Don't want you pullin' no hidden gun on me."

"I ain't got no hidden gun. But I got a piece of paper and pencil hidden away."

The man furrowed his brow. "Piece a paper? You write?"

"I do. Please. Let me show you."

"Do it slowly. So I can see."

John obliged. Carefully, he turned the cuff of his pants inside out, revealing the pocket that Peg had sewn into it.

"Well, I'll be . . ."

"Here. My paper." John reached in and plucked out about a dozen small slices of paper—and the stub of a pencil.

"Well, I'll be . . ." the man repeated. He lowered his rifle, and John took a deep breath. The man stared in wonderment as John held out the paper, with its scribbled notes. "What's it say?"

"Troop movements. Troop numbers."

The man's eyes moved from the paper to John's face. He looked puzzled. "You been spyin' and you're tellin' me you ain't hearda the League?"

"No, sir."

The man set his rifle against a tree and shot out his right hand. "Then let me be the first to welcome you, brother. The name is Cleon Fisk, and welcome to the Lincoln Legal Loyal League."

The man shook John's hand as vigorously as a well pump.

9

CHABOD PAGE SAT IN THE BACK OF THE BOAT AS BILLY O'MALLEY rowed them farther out on the James River, with a dangerous object on board—a small keg filled with rifle powder. It was night and the sky was filled with as many stars as there were drops of water in the river. Most of the sky was clear, and the moon cast its image on the river, but Ichabod could see shreds of clouds scudding across the sky. Rain was coming.

Among the stars was a single moving light—the Great Comet, which had appeared earlier this year to the astonishment of everyone on both sides of the country's divide. Comets always mean the death of a king, and he believed that this comet meant doom for the Yankees and their new king, Abraham Lincoln.

"Lookee how the tail of the comet nearly touches the North Star," Ichabod told Billy, who strained at the oars.

"What's it mean?" asked Billy. The young man, barely twenty, had no education to speak of, so Ichabod made it his mission to teach him things.

"It's as plain as day. The comet's tail is about to smack the North Star across the sky, a clear sign the North is gonna fall from their lofty perch, and the South will triumph gloriously."

Ichabod stared at the keg of gunpowder, which sat near the bow of the boat, looking as innocent as can be. "We are the comet come to earth, Billy boy, and we're gonna send the Northern ships up in a blaze of fire. We're an earthbound companion to that comet in the sky!"

"Yes, sir," said Billy, but Ichabod could tell that the boy had no idea what he was talking about. The boy had no sense of wonder, no feeling for the poetry of war. Billy just looked plain afraid, and most people wouldn't blame him, seeing as he was sitting with a keg of explosives at his back.

Ichabod and Billy were not the only occupants of the boat, for Ichabod had brought along his dog, Ahab—a fierce creature, a Cuban bloodhound. Bloodhounds were so named for their ability to smell and track scents, including blood, but one look at these animals and you can see why people thought their name also meant they could *spill* plenty of blood. Ahab, with his light brown coat, had an enormous head and powerful jaws, and a sturdy body of solid-steel muscle. This animal could tear out a person's heart in a heartbeat, but Ichabod had used a cudgel to mold the dog, shape him to his will, and make him obedient to him alone.

"Why does he have to look at me that way?" Billy asked, pulling on the oars and trying not to connect eyes with the dog. Ahab sat at Ichabod's feet in the back of the boat, just staring at Billy and panting with his tongue hanging out.

"Don't worry, he's just hungry," Ichabod said with a chuckle.

Ahab was Ichabod's only companion in the world, and all he really needed in life. He had lost pretty much everybody else, because ever since he was a lad he had been dancing with death. When he was only six years old, he would hold his hand as close to the fire as possible before it began to bite and sting. He also remembered venturing up to his papa's bull when he was nine; he touched the unsuspecting bull from behind and barely cleared the fence before the bull could ventilate his behind with its horns.

Ichabod believed he had a strange and almost mystical invincibility. He was only twenty-nine, but he had seen enough death already for two lifetimes, and yet he was always spared. His parents had died before he was twelve—both victims of the speckled monster, smallpox. His wife had died in childbirth, his newborn son didn't survive the week, and his best friend drowned a year ago, caught in the weeds when they were swimming together.

Ichabod felt like a human comet, cutting a flaming blaze through life, while people died in his wake, breaking off and burning up like sparks.

Only Ahab remained in his life, for the dog was also a survivor. Keeping such a dangerous dog, bred for tracking down slaves, made Ichabod feel as if he had made a pet out of Death itself. As his dog's master, he was a Master over Death.

"Don't worry, Billy. Long as I'm with you, y'all gonna be fine," Ichabod said. "I can touch Death, but Death don't touch me."

Billy nodded and cast another glance back at the torpedo. Ichabod wasn't sure what scared the boy more—the keg of gunpowder or the dog staring at him.

Ichabod and Billy were testing new torpedoes after their failure just a few weeks ago. Ichabod had been part of the team that took several kegs of gunpowder, equipped with percussion triggers, and floated them into the heart of the Union fleet in Hampton Roads. They had done everything correctly, and the tide carried the two torpedoes along the sides of two ships. Each torpedo was connected with thirty fathoms of lanyard—a cord that would trigger the bombs when it pulled taut.

Only the torpedoes never went off.

The boss, Mister Maury, eventually figured out what went wrong: Water must have gotten into the casks, wetting the powder. So here they were, testing out the new construction; but if they made any mistakes, he and Billy would go up in a whoosh of water and flame.

"Did you really touch Death?" Billy asked.

"Many a time. When we drifted into Hampton Roads, Mister Maury and me, we got right up beside one of the Union vessels, and I touched the hull with my own hand."

Ichabod held up his hand as if the oil from the side of the Union ship was still visible on his palm.

Billy nodded and sniffed. Then he scratched his head for a moment before changing the subject. "You really gonna go down into the torpedo boat?"

"'Course I am. I told you I ain't afraid of Death, and Death knows it."

"But a ship that goes beneath the waters . . . How they gonna keep the water from comin' in?"

"The iron is watertight."

"Then how you gonna get yourself air to breathe?"

"The air is pumped in through a hose that connects to a flotation device on the surface of the water."

"And you think it'll work?"

"'Course I do. What better way to break the Union blockade? Sneak up on them as silent as a snake, then blow them to bits. That's why we're doin' these tests. Gotta make sure the explosives work."

The explosives they planned to use with the submarine boat were slightly different than the floating torpedo they were testing this evening. But floating torpedoes and submarine boats were all part of the same big plan to break the Yankee blockade.

Billy turned around, his eyes landing on the keg of gunpowder, and Ichabod could tell he was probably picturing himself getting blown to bits, his body flying a hundred different directions.

"This is the spot," said Ichabod. He climbed past his dog Ahab and set the trigger on the keg of gunpowder. Then the two men carefully lowered the torpedo into the water; it had been weighted to float about two feet below the surface, and the trigger was connected to a thirty-foot rope lanyard.

With the torpedo set and floating away with the current, Billy began rowing in the opposite direction with greater urgency. Still standing in the boat, Ichabod faced the torpedo while the lanyard continued to spool out, as if a big fish was on the other end of the line and running away from the boat.

"Soon, Billy, soon."

Billy rowed like a man possessed.

"Take it in, boy, and use every sense—sight, hearing, smell, touch."

Ichabod held out his right hand, like he was giving a benediction to the dark. The lanyard suddenly went taut, and a big grin appeared on his face. He looked straight into the darkness. Then a brilliant flash erupted, as if the Great Comet itself had come flaming down from the sky and had landed in the James River. Ichabod felt the energy from the explosion and the heat and the reverberating sound, but he didn't flinch. He kept his hand extended as if the explosion had been triggered by the electricity of his skin.

Their test was a success. Ichabod had touched Death once again and lived to tell about it. Pleased with himself, he sat down in the boat and ran his hands across the back of his dog. Ahab softly growled beneath his touch.

*****

Peg sat down on her bed, and two moths fluttered into the glow of the light, disturbed from their dinner of devouring her blankets. The straw-filled mattress crunched beneath her as she set the candle on the nightstand, next to the Bible, next to her coded messages tucked inside the Book of Daniel. She would have to find a way to get in touch with Mary Bowser and pass on the information as soon as possible. She wanted this information out of her hands, because she felt as if she was storing something as dangerous as gunpowder right next to her bed.

Peg had been living in the Atwater house for four years now, because even when she was a slave, Master McQueen had hired her out to Captain Atwater as a maid. The master had also hired out John at a hotel in town for several years, but John lost his job when he was freed; that was why she hoped people would believe their story that he had gone to Fredericksburg for fresh work. She had no idea where he really was right now, and she wondered if she'd ever share a bed with her husband again.

Rising, Peg hurried over to the room's sole window and opened it even wider. An open window meant plenty of bugs would be joining her, but it also meant a cool breeze; being tucked away on the third floor, the room was stuffy and boiling on days like this. Leaning out the window, she looked down on the dark city and caught the fresh whiff of approaching rain. The black sky was clouded, so she saw no sign of the Great Comet. Many black folks said the comet was a sign that they would soon be freed—like the fire at night that the Israelites saw when they fled Egypt.

Alone with the silence, Peg found herself drawn to thoughts of John and how he had left her. She tried to fight away such thoughts, but it was like trying to keep a wasp from entering the wide-open window. She thought back on how Master McQueen had brought her and John to his study and said he had always known it was wrong to keep slaves. He said he had been trying to outrun his conscience for far too long, so he freed them on the spot. Four months later, John left her for war. It made her spitting mad.

Peg felt a different sort of bondage knowing that she could be a widow at this very moment and not know it. What if John was killed and his body was left on the battlefield for the wild dogs and vultures to erase from the world? She couldn't imagine that the gravediggers who scour a field after a battle would bother burying a black man. His body would simply vanish, and she'd never know for sure what became of him. John was all about honor, but what kind of honor was that?

Of course, it was honor that drew her to him in the first place, six years ago. All of her life, the men around her had been as dishonorable as could be. Her father and brother? Both were drunks who beat on her and her mama. Before Master McQueen came along, two of her previous masters had taken advantage of her. There were those words again—"taken advantage"—the same words that John had used when he ruined their first walk together. The words sounded so plain and polite, but they covered terrible sins. Peg's mother had been sold to a brothel in the Deep South, and Peg might have been destined to follow if not for John.

*****

"Let her go," John told Peg's brother Shadrack. This was on a street in Richmond, in the Shockoe Bottom neighborhood down by the James River, where she boarded out with her brother and Mama.

Shadrack had a tight grip on her wrist, and he was twisting it, sending shafts of pain up her arm.

"I said let go," John repeated.

"She's my sister, and this ain't any business of yours," said Shadrack.

"You're hurtin' my arm, Shadrack!" Peg squirmed in his grip, and his thick fingers clamped down like a vise on her right bicep. A small crowd gathered, mostly men drawn by the potential for violence.

"Master Johnson said to fetch you, so I'm fetchin' you," said Shadrack. Her brother made a living fetching things for Master Cager Johnson—tracking down escaped slaves, hauling his sister back to him—all for the payment of whiskey.

"You let go of her," said John, taking a step closer. She thought that John better be careful because her brother stood well over six feet tall and was as burly as a bear. She didn't know what John was capable of at the time. They had only just met in church two months earlier.

"Peg, you come with me peacefully, you hear," Shadrack said. "The master is needin' y'all, so stop your squirmin' or you're gonna get the back of my hand."

Peg spit in her brother's face, hoping to startle him into letting her loose. It worked, and she slipped away, but for only a moment. Shadrack was quick for a big man, and he latched onto her left wrist. With his other hand, he slapped her across the face.

That's when John launched himself at Shadrack. He lowered his head and hit her brother in the mid-section like a battering ram. Shocked, Shadrack went down onto his back with a groan and a roar, and John leaped on top of him, pounding on his face. Then John climbed off, and he moved into a boxer's position. Her brother scrambled back to his feet with a maniacal look in his eyes, but John simply danced around the big man, popping him in the face and telling him to back off. But the embarrassment and the bloody lip just riled Shadrack even more. As John danced around him, Peg noticed him moving closer to the edge of the dock, drawing her brother toward the water. Shadrack let out a grizzly bear roar and took a sweeping right hook, but missed. As John ducked to the side, he grabbed her brother's arm and used his bodily momentum to pull him forward and toss him into the river. Shadrack came up sputtering and spitting water.

The spectators applauded, and John took Peg's hand and led her away, and they disappeared into the crowd. John never let go of her.

*****

Fighting for her honor brought them together, but it was his stubborn sense of honor that had also driven him into another fight. John knew how to take care of himself, but this war was a different beast, and she was afraid. Peg blew out the candle and slept on top of the covers, as she usually did on hot summer nights. Then she felt the brush of a breeze on her face, as the rain began to fall.

10

THE RAIN BEAT DOWN ON THE ROOF OF THE SHELTER IN THE woods. John Scobell sat on the dirt floor and felt trickles of water seeping in at the walls. After such a hot day, he didn't mind. He had already refilled his canteen with rainwater and splashed his face. His stomach throbbed with mild nausea as he sat in the cabin alongside a black man named Cleon Fisk. A single candle was their only feeble light.

Cleon was telling him about the Lincoln Legal Loyal League, a loose network of Negro spies that stretched all across Virginia and into other Southern states. Cleon looked to be in his twenties, with hair in braids, ears that stuck out slightly, and light brown skin.

"Next time you hear one of us say, 'friends of Uncle Abe's,' you respond with 'light and liberty,'" Cleon instructed. "You hear me? That's our sign."

John nodded. His eyes had adjusted to the dark.

"You a free man?" John asked.

"We're all free men," snapped Cleon.

"Not in the eyes of Virginia."

"Then Virginia needs spectacles."

"What I mean is do you have free papers?" John asked.

"I don't need no free papers when I got the Holy Spirit burning in my chest. The Spirit makes me free, not some papers."

"Well, I find they come in handy, Spirit or no Spirit," said John, patting his pocket, where his own freedom papers were tucked away. "My master, he freed me and my wife—"

Cleon erupted. "Don't you *ever* use the word 'master' around me unless you're talkin' about the Lord God Almighty. Ain't no master on this earth except God Himself."

John went quiet, suddenly afraid to talk, for fear of using the wrong words. The rain picked up in intensity, pounding away at the roof.

"How many are there in the League?" John was beginning to fear that the Lincoln League was a figment of this man's wild imagination. Maybe there was only one member, and he was looking at him.

"I don't have a count. Gotta be hundreds, though. Just in this here parts, there are dozens."

"Are they both slave and free?" John asked before he realized he had blundered again.

"*They're all free I told you*! Ain't no slaves in the eyes of the Almighty! Paul the apostle told us not to be slaves of men 'cause we were all bought with a price."

John wasn't going to argue with that, so he steered the conversation down another trail. "Do you know what happened in today's battle? When I left the field, the Federals were routing the Rebels on Matthew's Hill."

"It's a dark day, John. The Rebs became a wall of stone, and the Federals broke apart on that wall. They retreated. They're runnin'."

John suspected as much, but hearing it confirmed was like a bayonet to the belly. "You think the war is over?"

"No, sir. The war is just beginnin', and by the time it's over the rivers are gonna run red. Bull Run is already red, but this rain is washin' it all away, and those white boys will be back to scrap again."

Cleon glanced down at John's backpack, which was propped up against the wall, and he furrowed his brow. "Don't look now, John boy, but there's a little person in your pack."

John followed Cleon's gaze and noticed that the top of his backpack had popped open, and the head of the doll he had found peeped out. He smiled. "Oh. That. Just a gift for my wife back in Richmond."

"You always got a habit of snatchin' up dolls in the middle of a battlefield bloodbath?"

Shrugging, John said, "I found it lying about. Struck me as strange, too. But I figured my wife would like it."

"Your wife still play with dolls?"

"She never played with dolls. Didn't have those kinda parents."

"I see. Kind of looks like a little demon, the way it's peeking out of your backpack, like it's alive." Cleon shook his head. "The thing's gonna give me nightmares. Let's talk 'bout something else."

That was fine with John. He noticed the rain begin to let up, just a bit, and then he picked up a distinct and familiar sound through the drumbeat of drops. Something was moving through the woods, and it sounded like more than a solitary man. He heard the snort of a horse, and Cleon blew out the candle and whispered ominously, "Black Horse Cavalry."

John had no idea what the Black Horse Cavalry was, but he didn't like the sound of it. Cleon certainly had a flair for the dramatic, slapping a Biblical meaning on everything, so John couldn't be sure just how serious the danger might be. They sat there silently as the horse approached. They could also hear the tramping of feet, and there seemed to be several approaching men, judging by the sound. He saw flashes of light through the cracks in the shelter, because one of the approaching men carried a lantern of some sort. Even in the dark, he could tell that Cleon had pulled out a revolver, so he picked up his rifle. The horse was perhaps only a dozen feet away by the sound of it. Men were talking softly, but it was impossible to discern words in the thrumming rain. Could it be the same two Rebels, still tracking him down? Surely they couldn't be that persistent.

Cleon aimed his gun at the cabin's narrow door, and John did the same. If the horsemen investigated and opened the door, they would get a face full of lead. John felt himself coil up inside, like a bull snake.

The Rebs moved even closer, and John heard every step of the horse. Then movement ceased, and all he could hear was the constant rain. But he sensed that the men hadn't moved on. Were they standing a few feet away, inspecting the shelter? John heard another snort of the horse, only a few feet from their door.

Then, at last, a voice. "Friends of Uncle Abe?" someone said.

John looked over at Cleon and saw a big smile blossom on his face. "Go on, John," he said. "Answer the man."

"Friends of Uncle Abe?" repeated the gruff voice outside the door. Cleon nudged him.

"Light and liberty," said John.

"I'm opening the door," called out Cleon. "Don't be shootin' the nose off my face now."

John and Cleon scrambled out of the cabin, and they found three black men and a chestnut-colored horse caught in the feeble glow of a single lantern. The rain was still coming down steadily, but it felt good.

"Who's this?" asked an older man, with gray eyebrows and salt and pepper hair. Despite his obvious age, the man looked as solid as a fortress with enormous hands. He extended one of them to shake John's hand.

"The name's Scobell. John Scobell."

"Pleased to make your acquaintance, John Scobell." The man's handshake was powerful, almost painful. "They call me Gallus Turner. And this here is Abram Fox and Hackey Pickens."

John shook hands with the other two men. Abram Fox was tall and lean, probably pushing forty, with enormous side-whiskers, while Hackey Pickens was a young man, with hair parted directly in the middle. Hackey wore an ornate Zouave uniform—a blue, collarless jacket with red trim, a red sash, billowing red pants, the kind you might see in Arabia, and a brilliant red kepi hat with a flat, round top and blue visor.

Gallus shot a look at Cleon. "What's the story?" he asked, flashing a glance at John.

"John Scobell here, he's been observin' and countin' troop movements. He's loyal to Uncle Abe."

Gallus sized up John from head to toe; he didn't look happy with Cleon for bringing a new member into their fold, someone they knew nothing about, and John couldn't blame him for his suspicions. Cleon had a reckless spontaneity about him.

"John Scobell here knows how to write and read," Cleon said, slapping John on the shoulder.

That brought Gallus and the other two men to attention. "This true?"

"It is," said John. "My wife and I, we both been taught. I can show you if you like."

John started to go for his pants cuff when Gallus held up a hand. "Not now. Let's get outta the rain."

"Good idea," said Cleon.

The five of them crouched low and climbed, one by one, inside the small shelter. They somehow managed to squeeze inside the shack, sitting shoulder to shoulder, with their body heat turning the interior into a steam room. But John paid it no heed. He was excited, for he was about to begin his first meeting as a member of the Lincoln League. He was no longer a solitary spy. He was part of something larger.

11

Richmond
November 1861: Three and a Half Months Later

PEG SNUCK INTO THE SECOND-FLOOR GUESTROOM WHEN ALL was clear because she needed a mirror for what she was planning. Then she went to work with her white head wrap. She angled it across her head, covering all of the hair in the back, and then she twisted the end of the scarf into a tight tail and wrapped it into a compact bun over her right ear.

Hearing a noise, she hopped up and stepped behind the door for a moment, until she realized it was just the creaking of the house. Her hands were shaking.

Back in front of the mirror, she took a second head wrap and angled it across the other side of her head, creating a tightly wound bun just above her left ear. The first attempt to create the second bun failed, and the whole fabric nearly unraveled; she began to panic that Missus Hicks was going to catch her using the guestroom mirror and give her a tongue lashing. But on the second attempt, she had it—two overlapping head wraps combined to create a beautiful covering.

After one final check in the mirror, she hurried downstairs. Her head wraps were both white, as Missus Hicks demanded, but she knew she was playing with fire by adding her own personal touch. Missus Hicks wanted submissive uniformity from all of her servants, and that meant white head wraps with a single bow in back. However, if Peg was ever going to get away with this, it would be now because Old Lady Hicks had more important matters on her mind—namely, a woman by the name of Missus E. H. Baker.

Missus Baker, a widow from Chicago, had come swooping into the Atwater home a week ago, and she turned everything upside down, especially the world of poor Miss Doris next door. Missus Baker was a handsome woman—short, trim, and energetic with chestnut hair, a woman who preferred a bracing hike to indoor, social activities. She also had an insatiable curiosity that made her a striking contrast to the shy, staid Miss Doris.

Miss Doris was clearly panicked by the presence of a woman like Missus Baker staying under the same roof as Captain Atwater. Evidently, Missus Baker's family had once lived in Richmond and been close to the Atwaters, and the captain had known her growing up. Childhood sweethearts, perhaps? It sure looked that way in Peg's eyes. She made it her job to hover as close as possible, in case Captain Atwater leaked Southern secrets. She was becoming good at this spy business.

On this particular evening, Miss Doris and Missus Baker sat on opposite sides of Captain Atwater at the dinner table, and it was a sight to behold, each woman vying for the man's attention. Also in attendance were Mister and Missus Cavander, Richmond society folk—and Missus Hicks, of course. The meal was lavish, but it was also an ordeal because Old Lady Hicks insisted that the household conform to the new, more monotonous dining fashions. Instead of putting out all of the food at once, it was *service à la russe* for the Atwaters. Course after course came out, one at a time, and everyone had to wait for the slowest eater to finish before moving on to the next course.

As Peg served the meal, she caught Missus Hicks studying her with the eye of a hawk, following her as she moved around the table. The lady would not say anything in front of guests, but Peg wondered if her head wrap design was going to pass muster. She didn't make eye contact with Missus Hicks, and concentrated on listening to their table talk. At first, the conversation was nothing a spy would care about: the weather, the tobacco industry, the Richmond social scene. Leave it to Missus Hicks to suddenly make it interesting.

"I cannot believe that authorities would let the Van Lews continue to provide comfort to our enemies in Libby Prison," declared Missus Hicks, loud enough to bring every other conversation to an abrupt halt.

Even Peg paused in what she was doing—removing the plates of the second course. Over the past few months, as she gathered intelligence and reported it to her friend Mary Bowser, she had discovered that the woman to whom Mary was passing on their information was the eccentric Elizabeth Van Lew.

Miss Van Lew, along with her mother, stirred up scandals on a regular basis in Richmond because they insisted on bringing food and comfort to Union prisoners in Libby Prison. So Peg perked up when she heard the name "Van Lew" spoken.

"We are told to love our enemies," said Captain Atwater. "The Van Lews are simply following the admonition of our Lord to comfort the prisoners."

Leave it to Missus Hicks to argue with the Almighty.

"Sometimes the most loving thing we can do is let those prisoners suffer the consequences of their actions—not be pampered in prison."

"I doubt very much if anyone is being pampered at Libby Prison," said the captain.

"Mister Calvin Huson was certainly being pampered in the Van Lew estate."

Miss Van Lew and her mother had been given permission to bring Mister Calvin Huson, a dying Yankee officer, into their home. They buried him last month.

"Mister Huson is no more. A dying man deserves care and concern, no matter the uniform he wears."

Peg vanished into the kitchen, arms loaded down with plates, so she lost the trail of conversation. But when she returned with the third course, the Van Lews were still the topic of conversation. Even Miss Doris had joined in.

"I agree wholeheartedly, captain, that our Lord tells us to love those who do us ill," she said. "What I had the most contention with was Miss Van Lew's unwillingness to make shirts for the South Carolina troops."

Peg was shocked that the normally mild Miss Doris would put forth such a bold opinion, but perhaps she was trying to compete with Missus Baker, whose Northern bluntness seemed to appeal to Captain Atwater.

"Yes, that behavior was perplexing," the captain agreed.

"But I heard that the Van Lews brought books and flowers to the South Carolina boys," chimed in Missus Baker. "So they have provided comfort to both sides."

"True. Very true," said Captain Atwater, diplomatically agreeing with the women on both sides of him. He was caught between Northern and Southern ladies, much the way that his allegiances were trapped somewhere in the muddy middle ground.

"Traitors and spies should be hung in the public square," announced Missus Hicks out of the blue, bringing the conversation to a shocked standstill. An uncomfortable silence descended like an eclipse, and Peg hurried from the room, feeling as if the words were meant for her, even though the Van Lews were the subject of the conversation.

"No one is accusing anyone of being a traitor or a spy," she heard the captain say as she hurried down the hallway to the kitchen.

Peg placed the serving dish on the kitchen table and looked over at Matilda, who was putting away food. "I don't know why the captain puts up with that woman," she said.

"You know as well as I do why he puts up with her," Matilda said. "The captain is a man of honor."

Peg felt like saying "the captain is an honorable fool," but she bit her tongue. Six years ago, the captain had foolishly told a friend, Thaddeus Hicks, that if anything happened to him, he would take care of his mother. Then one year later, Thaddeus Hicks dropped dead from a heart attack, and Missus Hicks moved into the Atwater home within the month. The captain was a man of his word.

"I like your wrap," Matilda said, motioning toward Peg's head. "Never seen two of them put together that way."

Matilda wore her plain white head covering the most common way—with a knot tied at the back.

"Thank you."

"Missus Hicks say anything 'bout it?"

Peg shook her head. "And I'm prayin' she don't."

"If the Good Lord can handle Pharaoh, He can handle Missus Hicks."

When Miss Doris and the Cavanders had left for the evening and darkness descended, Captain Atwater, Missus Baker, and Old Lady Hicks capped off the evening relaxing on the front porch. Peg worked beyond sundown on many days, and she was tidying up the ladies' parlor when she heard voices drifting in from the porch. The windows were wide open to let in the breeze, for it was an unusually warm night for November, and their words floated lazily into the house.

When she peeked out the window, she was shocked to see that Missus Hicks had retired for the night, leaving the captain and Widow Baker alone on the porch. She was surprised, but not just because the captain and Missus Baker had been left to their own devices; she was shocked that the old lady had retired for the night without making a comment about her unconventionally tied head covering.

Peg slipped behind the curtains, into the shadows, and stood there listening to the captain and the Northern woman. They talked in hushed tones, but they were sitting right by the open window, so Peg could absorb every word.

"You are at heart a Union man," she heard Missus Baker say. "Am I correct in my assumption?"

Silence. Was the captain angry that the woman had spoken such dangerous words?

"Yes. I do believe that our Southern cause is . . . misguided."

Captain Atwater must be smitten by this woman to speak so openly about his Unionist sympathies.

"Our people have been led into the war by designing politicians," he added.

"Do you believe in slaveholding?" Missus Baker asked bluntly.

"I believe we should have given up our slaves, rather than leave the Union."

"It can be dangerous to hold such beliefs. I hope you do not share this with others as freely as you share them with me."

"I do not. You are . . ."

Peg could not make out the rest of the sentence. Was the man professing his devotion to this Northern lady?

"I will not breathe a word of this to anyone," Missus Baker said. "But tell me honestly, do you think the war will end soon?"

"I once thought it would be short, but ever since Manassas . . . I don't know. I only know with certainty that the South will fight to the last man. It will be bloody."

"I am sorry to hear that." Another silence followed, and then Missus Baker ventured down another course. "I have always desired to see the Tredegar Iron Works before I leave Richmond."

"If you will not leave Richmond until you see the Iron Works, then I may *never* want to show the operations to you."

Missus Baker laughed coquettishly.

"Being a gentleman, however, I would be happy to show you the iron works. I will be visiting the site tomorrow. Would you care to join me?"

"I couldn't think of a more delightful day, spending it with you and seeing the mightiest iron works in the South."

Peg rolled her eyes, for the captain seemed willing to do anything this woman wanted.

"Oh, but I forgot," the captain suddenly said. "I am afraid I cannot take you to the iron works tomorrow because I have to witness the test of a submarine battery."

"Submarine battery?"

"A new type of ship."

"Then perhaps I can accompany you there. The James River is beautiful, and I admire ships of any type. What kind of ship is it?"

The captain laughed, a light chuckle. "I will let you be surprised. We could do a very quick tour of the Tredegar Iron Works, and then continue on to the demonstration. Many of the officers will be bringing their wives along, making a picnic of it."

"Capital!" Missus Baker exclaimed. "I look forward to our day together."

Our day together. Missus Baker knew what those words would mean to an infatuated man like Captain Atwater.

No words followed from the captain, and Peg wondered if the two of them were embracing. She didn't mind scooping up morsels of military information, but she suddenly felt guilty to be listening in on more intimate matters. Hearing the two of them suddenly rise from their chairs, Peg scurried across the ladies' parlor in the dark, and then she disappeared up the stairs.

As she neared the top of the stairs, she paused and looked up and discovered Gilbert Mann, the butler, just standing there, staring down on her. Smiling.

"Evenin' Gilbert," she said, reaching the top of the landing and making a move to go around him.

He stepped in front of her.

"I seen y'all peekin' on those two lovers," he said, smiling. "You gettin' lonely for a man?"

"Ain't none of your business, Gilbert."

Gilbert, a young man in his mid-twenties, held up his hands and smiled. "You're right, you're right, I'm talkin' disrespectful. I just can't figure out that John Scobell of yours."

"What's there to figure out?"

"I can't figure out why he went and left y'all."

"You know why. Lookin' for work in Fredericksburg."

Gilbert scratched his head and cocked it. "Why not look for work 'round here, so he can stay close to you? That's what I woulda done, Peggy."

"Wasn't no work in town." Peg made another move to slip around him.

Gilbert scoffed. "Must not-a looked all that hard. Makes me wonder if he's gone off to fight."

Peg turned slowly to face him squarely. "He ain't gone to fight, and don't you be spreadin' lies, Gilbert."

Gilbert must have caught the fire in her eyes because he backed off quickly. "I'm sorry, Peggy, I was just speculatin'. I'm just sayin' I think he'd be a fool to leave you for a white man's war."

Peg bit her lips. He had used her very words in saying it was a "white man's war." However, hearing it from Gilbert raised her hackles, and she found herself suddenly defending John's opinions.

"We should be doin' anything we can to help take down slavery, Mister Mann. Slavery's the common enemy between us and the Northerners."

"Fiddlesticks. The North ain't fightin' to abolish slavery. You really think the Federals are goin' to sacrifice thousands of their young men's lives for us black folk? That ain't what this war is about."

"But John said it's a big part of the war and that's why he—"

Peg caught herself before she let spill the fact that John was off fighting.

"John said there wouldn't be no war if the states weren't squabblin' about our freedom in places like Kansas and Missouri," she said.

Gilbert smiled and shook his head. "A war still ain't a good enough reason for him to be leavin' a woman like you."

Peg had to agree there, but she didn't say so. "It's work he's lookin' for, not war, and he'll be back to fetch me," she simply said, turning away.

"Well if he don't come back, then let me be the first to know."

Peg hurried up the next flight of stairs, and she prayed that Gilbert would have the good sense not to follow.

12

Washington
November 1861

"I WANT TO FIGHT," JOHN FLATLY TOLD ALLAN PINKERTON, THE head of the Union Intelligence Service.

John had spent the past three months collecting information for the Lincoln League in northern Virginia, but he wanted more. He wanted to fight with honor as a soldier, not a spy. So he and Cleon had told the Lincoln Leaguers that they were heading to Washington, with forged passes in hand, to show up at the first recruiting office they found. John had heard that recruiting offices were closed to Negroes, but he thought he might be allowed to serve in the Home Guard. He had to at least try.

However, the moment they crossed the Potomac, Yankee soldiers brought them into Washington to appear before Pinkerton, who had made his name with his famed Chicago detective agency before becoming head of the Union Intelligence Service. Pinkerton sat behind a large oak desk. He had a rounded face, close-set eyes, and a receding hairline that was compensated for by his thick, finely trimmed beard.

The intelligence director gave John a sympathetic smile. "You want to fight? That is good. That is precisely why I make it my policy to interview Negro contrabands that come through the Federal lines—to find out who might be of service."

"But we ain't contrabands," Cleon said emphatically.

Pinkerton's eyebrows shot up and his smile faded; John sure wished Cleon knew when to bite his tongue.

"We are free men," Cleon added.

"Ah." Pinkerton smiled. "I see."

Technically, it was true that John and Cleon were not contrabands—escaped slaves claimed by the Yankees as spoils of war. Cleon had told John he hated the term "contraband" because it lumped escaped slaves alongside inanimate property confiscated in battle. But John could care less what the Yankees called escaped slaves if it meant they would no longer return them to their Southern masters; before the North declared escaped slaves to be contraband, that is exactly what was happening.

"I would like to fight in the Army," John said, speaking with much more tact than Cleon.

"But you do know that the Army is not accepting Negro soldiers," Pinkerton said. "There have been volunteer colored units sprouting up all over—Boston, Cleveland, Philadelphia. But the Secretary of War is adamant: no colored soldiers."

"It don't make no sense," Cleon said. "The North can't be such fools to put themselves at a disadvantage to the South. The South has black labor doin' all the work on the farms growin' food while the white men are away fightin'. The North ain't got that, so it needs to use every man they got, white or black."

John cringed. Cleon had used the word "fools"—not the best choice of words. But Pinkerton didn't seem angered by it. On the contrary, he smiled.

"You will not get any argument from me," he said. "But the fact remains. No colored soldiers. Can either of you men read and write?"

John hesitated because he had learned over many years that reading and writing was something you kept secret from white people, seeing as it's illegal for slaves to be taught in many states.

Cleon answered for him. "John here can write. Real good at it too. Show him your writin', John."

Still feeling hesitant and suspicious of Pinkerton's motives for asking the question, John paused before reaching down to his pants cuff, turning it inside out, and extracting some papers from the hidden pocket. When he raised his head back up, Pinkerton had a curious smile. John slid the papers across the desk to him.

As the intelligence chief read the papers, which contained some of the information he collected in Virginia, Pinkerton kept glancing up at John. "How'd you learn to read and write?"

Again, John was hesitant to answer. Would he get Master McQueen into trouble for teaching him? He kept his answer vague.

"Some white folks taught me," he said.

Pinkerton didn't seem upset by this revelation; in fact, he seemed pleased. "I could use a Negro man who can read and write. I would like to bring you on board to run errands for me."

"Errands?" John asked.

"Delivering messages in Washington. Things of that sort. We'd also like to see more of what you can do—reading and writing."

John studied his hands. He didn't know what to say.

"He'll do it," Cleon suddenly said—to John's complete shock.

Mister Pinkerton's smile grew wider. "Do you agree with your friend here, John? Will you help us out—on a trial basis?"

"Yes, he agrees." Cleon jumped in when John delayed in responding.

"Are you sure?" Pinkerton kept his gaze on John.

Finally, John spoke up—anything to keep Cleon quiet. "Yes, I agree. I'd be honored, sir."

When they eventually left Pinkerton's office on I Street, John was beginning to feel more comfortable about Pinkerton's proposal. But Cleon seemed even more pleased about the new appointment than he did. He was beaming.

"It may be a trial period like he said, but I think it could really lead somewheres," Cleon pointed out, walking backward in front of John, so he could look him straight in the eyes.

John shrugged. "I'd still rather be soldiering than spying."

"Maybe God's got other plans. Why else would the Good Lord put those words in my mouth?"

John smiled, wondering if the Good Lord would really want to be credited with any of the words coming out of Cleon's mouth. As they turned the corner, they came upon a bustle of activity, for they had reached the local recruiting office. Washington, like cities throughout the North, was ablaze with enlistment fever. The Battle of Bull Run, so disastrous for the Union Army, had roused the North, and recruiting offices in every state were overrun with men, young and old, who wanted to get their licks in at the Confederates. Boys, barely big enough to lug a rifle, tried to pass themselves off as men. Old men, with more gray on their face than a Rebel has on his uniform, deluded themselves into thinking they could still fight.

John spotted one such old man, the buttons of his old uniform popping on his belly; he argued with his wife in the street.

"They need every able-bodied man they can find," the man told his wife, as he marched—hobbled really—down the muddy road toward the recruitment office.

His wife dogged his heels, waving a white handkerchief at him every step of the way. "Look at yourself, Joshua. Your body hasn't been 'able' for twenty years now!"

The only thing missing from the scene in front of them were black faces. All of the recruits were white, even though black men all over the North had asked for a chance to prove their honor and patriotism. It made John's blood boil to think how they had been turned back. His strides became longer, and he made a beeline for the enlistment office.

"Whatcha doin', John?"

"Enlistin'!"

"But what about Pinkerton? You told him you'd work for him."

"I have to at least try to become a soldier."

John and Cleon slipped to the end of the line, which snaked around the side of the building. But as they took their places in line, John couldn't miss the hostile glares and curses. The man at the very end of the line was a sturdy fellow who looked to be in his thirties, with a heavy cape over his shoulders, a trimmed moustache, and a gallant feathered hat.

"They ain't takin' coloreds, you know." He spoke in a helpful tone. It wasn't a threat.

"White's a color, ain't it, and they're takin' *you*," said Cleon. "So it seems to me they *are* takin' colored people."

Not helpful, Cleon, John thought. The stranger hardened his look.

"Get out of line," the man commanded.

"We're free men," Cleon said.

John began to regret stepping into this line with Cleon at his side. He should have done it alone, for this was risky. There were still slave laborers everywhere, and John knew there was always the risk that someone might tear up their freedom papers and claim they were slave material.

"I think y'all are better suited to that there kind of job than fightin'." The stranger motioned toward a slave who passed by pushing a cart loaded with human dung. The waste was dumped in a field only ten blocks from the White House and could probably be smelled by President Lincoln himself when the breeze was right.

"Would you like to see how well we can fight?" Cleon said, slipping his arms out of his jacket.

"Yes, I would," said the stranger, removing his cloak and handing it to another man.

Things were spiraling wildly out of control. John knew how fights wound up when the odds were ridiculously lopsided. He could easily take on this white man alone, but there were thirty others standing right there in line. He wished Cleon had the same sense.

"My friend here wasn't talkin' about showin' you how he fights in the street," John explained. "He was referrin' to fighting in the army."

The stranger was already rolling up his sleeves—and so was Cleon.

"No I wasn't and you know it, John. I was referrin' to the kind of fightin' you do with clenched fists," Cleon said.

"You don't wanna do this," John told him.

"What's wrong? It's not like you to run from a fight."

"I ain't runnin' from a fight. I'm here tryin' to sign up to fight for my country!"

"Then show these fools you can fight!" Cleon said. "Show them right here and now!"

The white man gave John a stiff-armed shove in the shoulder. "Listen to your friend. If you won't fight here, how are you going to fight a thousand white men on a battlefield?"

That did it. John took off his coat and slapped it against Cleon's chest. Fighting like this was pure suicide, but he could not let the challenge go unanswered. John spun around to face the white man, fists raised.

"That's enough!"

Two Yankee soldiers suddenly broke through the cluster of on-lookers, and John couldn't help but feel a sense of relief.

"There will be no fighting here!" one of the soldiers said, using his gun to shove John away from the crowd. "And there's no recruiting of coloreds here neither, so clear off!" the soldier added, driving John back several more steps. The soldier was huge; it was like being shoved by a ship. John put up his hands to show that he carried no weapon, and he backed away slowly. Thankfully, Cleon did the same, although he was still snapping at the stranger, saying something about John being one of the finest shots he had ever seen and the Army could sure use him. But at least Cleon was obeying the soldiers' orders.

John continued to backpedal from the recruiting office, and he didn't dare turn his back until he was a safe distance away. He knew what happened when a black man turned his back to a white man, and he wasn't going to make that mistake.

13

PEG RODE IN THE BACK OF THE WAGON, AS THE CAPTAIN STEERED them down the road leading to the Tredegar Iron Works alongside the James River. Beside him was Missus Baker, dressed in a practical, but striking, blue dress, with a light coat wrapped around her shoulders.

Peg's dress wasn't such quality, of course, but her head wrap had become bolder. She wrapped the cloth around her head like a turban, leaving the braids on the back of her head exposed. Missus Hicks wasn't around to complain, and the captain was too smitten by Missus Baker to even notice or care that the back of her head was uncovered.

As promised, Captain Atwater impressed the Northern woman with a brief tour of the mighty factory—the iron heart of the South. Peg had to wait outside with the wagon while the captain took Missus Baker into the complex. Mary Bowser told Peg to keep her eyes open and try to memorize every detail, but there wasn't much to be seen from the outside. Perched by the James River, the Tredegar Iron Works churned out every type of rifle and cannon they could conjure. Peg made a note that the boiler shops, blacksmith shops, and brass foundry hugged the river, while the gun foundry, rolling mill, and slave quarters sat back a ways from the water.

Captain Atwater's tour of the iron works was brief, and they were soon on the narrow road alongside the river, heading for the demonstration of this new ship.

"I cannot believe that the young boy I once knew as a child, the boy who used to run around our neighborhood turning sticks into guns, is now turning steel into cannons," Missus Baker said.

Captain Atwater beamed. "There is still some of that little boy inside of me."

Peg, jostled by the movement of the wagon, shook her head. This Northern lady couldn't be more obvious in her flirtations.

"The iron plates you are rolling . . . Did you say they are for a ship to be made of iron?" Missus Baker said.

"Oh yes. Our rolling mills are almost entirely devoted to creating iron for this new ship. Our ships will be like knights of old, wearing armor that cannot be pierced."

"How thick is the armor?"

Peg wished she could be writing all of this down. She concentrated her mind.

"We are combining two layers of two-inch iron because three layers of one-inch iron was not enough to resist the penetration of solid shot. Four inches should do it."

The captain seemed determined to impress Missus Baker with his knowledge and position on the iron works board. Peg's head was crowded with details by the time they reached the demonstration site, about ten miles down the road from the Tredegar Iron Works. The afternoon continued the recent string of warm days, but Peg had packed an extra shawl for Missus Baker in case they returned late when the temperatures dropped. The trees were almost stripped bare of leaves, and the cloud cover was a thin white sheet.

When they arrived at their destination, Peg's nervousness heightened. Gathered along the banks were at least a dozen Confederate military men in uniform, along with their wives. It was a picnic atmosphere, but it terrified her to be gathering information right under the noses of so many officers. She told herself they would pay her no heed, for she was just a servant—and not the only one on the site. Each of the wives was tended to by at least one black servant, who handled the food.

As Peg spread out their blanket, she kept listening to Missus Baker, for she was one inquisitive lady.

"What is the purpose of a ship that swims beneath the water?"

"We hope to use it to break the blockade at the mouth of the James River. The North's blockade is causing pain, and if we do not do something soon, the suffering will become intolerable."

Missus Baker continued to pelt him with questions, but the couple wandered closer to the river, so Peg could no longer pick up their conversation. Like the other servants, she remained in the background and didn't dare move any closer to the demonstration. One of the military men explained to the observers what they were about to see, but Peg could only catch snatches.

Then the crowd parted just enough for Peg to notice an odd vessel. Most of the ship was submerged in water, but a portion of it stuck out above the surface, and it appeared to be long, almost cigar-shaped. On the very top of the ship was a round portal, and two men climbed in through the opening. Then, right before her eyes, she saw the ship sink beneath the water and vanish. She blinked in disbelief.

*****

Ichabod Page had never been so excited. He felt like he had climbed into a floating casket and was taunting Death by stepping into this submarine boat. His mind raced with anticipation.

"Don't breathe so deeply," said Samuel Thomas, one of Ichabod's two companions in the submarine boat. The third man, Scotty Irwin, was inside a compartment at the bow of the ship, separated from Ichabod and Samuel.

Ichabod laughed at Samuel's caution. He leaned back and breathed in deeply and audibly. He was not afraid, for plenty of air was being pumped in through an India-rubber air hose that stretched from the submarine to a flotation device on the surface of the water.

"There's plenty of air to go around, Sammy," said Ichabod.

Samuel scowled. Ichabod knew that Samuel disliked him, but he loved to get under the skin of cautious people like him. Samuel had written up a long list of precautions, for several people had already died testing submarine boats. He was determined to control every variable, take every precaution, but Ichabod believed in Fate, and no amount of planning could change their destiny. What happened, happened.

The interior of the submarine boat was long, narrow, and starkly furnished, with two wooden chairs being the only nod to comfort. At the back end of the boat was the rudder, as well as a hand crank to spin the enormous propeller that measured almost four feet from top to bottom. They let the water into the ballast tanks, weighing them down, and the submarine slowly dipped beneath the water, into the gloom of the dark, cold river. An aneroid barometer measured air pressure and estimated the depth of the sub, and their only light was a single candle, so it truly felt as if they were in the darkest of caves. If the candle went out, they would know that oxygen was a problem.

"I'll crank," Ichabod said.

Samuel tracked their position with a compass and adjusted the rudder, and Ichabod went to work, cranking away like a human extension of the machine. Within minutes, Ichabod's face was drenched with sweat, for the compartment was as stuffy as a two-man tomb.

Ichabod could tell that Samuel was worried that his gulping breaths were consuming too much oxygen. "Need a break? I'll take a turn," Samuel suggested.

Ichabod ignored him and kept cranking. A cramp formed in his leg, for he had to crouch low in the tight quarters, and this put a strain on his bent legs. The movement of the boat was barely discernable, although the velocimeter showed a speed of about one mile per hour.

"I'm taking over," Samuel said a few minutes later, and the man crowded against Ichabod, trying to nudge him away from the crank.

Ichabod erupted with a curse, and he pushed back with his body. "You take care of the compass. I'll take care of the crank."

"Don't work so fast. You're consuming too much oxygen."

"Don't worry, you're lettin' out enough hot air to more than make up for it."

This time, Samuel put his hands on Ichabod's shoulders and tried to push him away from the crank handle, but Ichabod shot out a stiff arm and knocked his crewmate back two steps. Ichabod knew Samuel would not press the issue because he would probably worry that two men fighting would consume even more oxygen and the candle would flicker off, and then he would really begin to panic. Ichabod was right; the man backed off and returned to his seat and his compass. The candle flickered, but kept on burning.

When the submarine was finally in position, it was Scotty Irwin's turn to move into action. He was sealed off in a separate compartment, and his job was to exit the submarine and swim underwater to an old tub of a boat, which had been towed to the middle of the river. He would attach the magazine loaded with gunpowder and connect the fuse. Then, when he was back in the submarine and they were a safe distance away, they would trigger the explosive and blow the boat out of the water.

Ichabod had to smile, for poor Samuel was taking the shallowest of breaths to conserve oxygen. Just for sport, Ichabod opened his mouth as wide as possible and inhaled deeply, as if trying to consume all of the oxygen in one big gulp like chugging a glass of beer. Samuel didn't say a word, but Ichabod could see that he was getting to him.

Done cranking for now, Ichabod sat down and examined his hands. He was dripping with sweat and grinning. These hands had touched the torpedo, loaded with gunpowder, and he was sure he wouldn't die today.

*****

Peg drifted closer to the riverbank, straining to get a look at what was happening on the river. No one rebuked her, no one told her to stay away, because all eyes were on the water, which looked serene. Out in the middle of the river floated a dilapidated hulk of a boat. The man in charge said something about, "Pretty soon, now," but "pretty soon" stretched on for a long time. Eventually, the crowd lost their attention and began to chatter among themselves, casting occasional glances toward the river.

"Where is the camouflaged flotation?" she heard Missus Baker ask, getting up on tiptoes and peering closely at the river.

Captain Atwater pointed, gently placing one gloved hand on Missus Baker's shoulder. Their heads were only a few inches apart. When they turned to speak to one another, their mouths were the closest to each other that Peg had yet observed. The captain handed his field glasses to Missus Baker and helped her direct the instrument toward the flat flotation moving away from the boat. Captain Atwater had his arms around her as he helped her adjust the field glasses. Peg was so captivated by their romantic maneuvering that she almost forgot what she was there for.

The sudden explosion reminded her.

Peg's entire body, inside and out, leaped at the roar, and she jerked her head to the right just in time to see the boat also jump. There was a blaze of fire, and the old boat was thrown upward as it split in half, as if a whale had hit it from beneath. But this was the work of something even more dangerous and potent than a whale.

Several women screamed at the explosion, but after recovering from the shock of the blast, the crowd clapped, as if they were at the opera and a singer had just hit a high note. In a way, it was the South's high note, for they now had in their hands a weapon that could rip apart the Federal fleet, and the Yankees would never know what hit them.

14

OR SEVERAL DAYS, JOHN RAN ERRANDS FOR ALLAN PINKERTON—
mostly delivering messages. To his surprise, he was also given
some basic training on how to read ciphered messages. But when
Mister Pinkerton asked for another meeting, he didn't think anything of it.

Cleon did.

"He may have a spy mission for y'all, and wouldn't that be something," he said. "A mission from Mister Allan Pinkerton himself is
like Moses sendin' them spies into Canaan, sayin' to them, 'Go up
this way into the South, go up to the mountains'!'"

John smiled, for Cleon always looked for ways to insert Scripture
into every conversation, whether he was talking about coffee or the
Confederacy. Cleon had once been a revival preacher, so his thoughts
were crammed with the Bible.

John and Cleon ambled down the muddy streets of Washington, and John doubted very much that Mister Pinkerton was actually
going to send him on a mission for the Union Intelligence Service.
If the Yankees didn't want black men in the ranks of their army, he
couldn't believe the head of the intelligence service would want to use
a black man on a mission.

"Pinkerton's impressed by your ability to read and write," said
Cleon.

John shrugged and said nothing as they turned a corner and
had to sidestep a wandering hog. The hog sized them up, its snout
dripping with mud. Soldiers stood on every corner, for Washington

was under martial law as people braced for a Confederate invasion. The streets were drab and dirty, and a sour smell followed John and Cleon everywhere; there were so many people packed into the city that soldiers had turned every nook and cranny into a latrine.

Cleon waited outside of Pinkerton's headquarters while John was ushered into the intelligence director's office. The secret service man was seated once again behind his oak desk, studying papers and not looking up to recognize John's entry. John stood, hat in hand, and Pinkerton continued to ignore him until another white man entered the room. Finally, Pinkerton looked up, grinned broadly, and motioned to two chairs.

"Mister Timothy Webster, let me introduce you to John Scobell," said Pinkerton, and John immediately wondered about the rules of Northern etiquette. As a free black man, should he extend a hand to a white man like Webster? Webster answered the unspoken question by shooting out his hand, and he and John shook.

"If you're trying to place Mister Webster's accent, don't try," Pinkerton said. "He's from Wales, but he can sound Northern or Southern—whatever the occasion calls for."

John nodded and smiled awkwardly. Webster sported a beard, and he had a high forehead and swept-back hair that curled down to the top of his ears. His eyes were sleepy-looking, and he was tall and lanky—a stark contrast to the more compact, tightly wound Pinkerton. Where Pinkerton was intense, Webster seemed relaxed, almost shy, and he folded one long leg over another and leaned back in his chair.

"John Scobell has performed well these past few days, and I have found him to be a remarkably gifted man for one of his race," Pinkerton said, talking as if John wasn't sitting right there in front of him. "He can read and write, he is full of music, and he can put on an act—like you, Mister Webster."

Mister Webster nodded and cast a sidelong glance in John's direction.

"I feel sure that John need only assume the character of a light-hearted darky and no one would suspect that he is a cool-headed detective," the director continued.

John bristled at the description but remained quiet. He could sense Webster's eyes studying him, as if gauging how he reacted to Pinkerton's characterization.

At that moment, there was another rap on the door and Pinkerton announced, "Enter."

Both Pinkerton and Webster stood to their feet, and John scrambled to rise the moment he saw who was entering the room. It was a woman in her twenties, with long, golden hair, blue eyes, and the kind of looks that would set a man running off a cliff if she asked. John averted his eyes, while Webster helped her into a chair.

Mister Pinkerton didn't bother introducing her to him, and John remained standing as the intelligence service boss related their plans.

"Miss Hattie and Mister Webster, I would like the two of you to travel south to Richmond, posing as man and wife," he continued. "You've had plenty of practice at that by now."

Mister Webster patted Miss Hattie's hand, and she blushed like a bride.

"This time, however, I would like you to take John with you, posing as your servant."

Miss Hattie offered a smile in John's direction, and he looked away. He was stunned. Was Cleon right? Was Pinkerton actually sending him on a mission?

"We have reason to believe that Confederate chemists are devising explosives to destroy our blockade of Southern ports and wreak havoc—explosives the likes of we've never seen before."

"Such as . . .?" Webster probed.

"Explosives that can be hidden anywhere—floating in canisters in a river, hidden beneath the ground, even placed in homes and triggered by cleverly hidden tripwires. They're called torpedoes."

"Is such a thing allowed in the rules of war?" asked Miss Hattie.

Pinkerton leaned back in his chair and thought that question through. "In this war, there are no rules."

"What specifically do you want us to do?" Webster asked.

"Start by heading to Leonardtown. We have reason to believe that Confederate couriers are passing through the town with information on various types of torpedoes. After that, I want you—Mister Webster and Miss Hattie—to head on to Richmond to find out what you can on how Confederates are smuggling gunpowder into the South. The South is suffering from a shortage of saltpeter for the creation of gunpowder. They're so desperate for the substance that they have taken to extracting it from, shall we say, *material* taken from outhouses, latrines, and chamber pots in Richmond."

They didn't have to ask what he meant by "material." Human and animal waste was a prime source for niter, another name for saltpeter.

"I beg your pardon for my frank use of words," Pinkerton said to Miss Hattie.

"No offense taken. I know what a chamber pot is used for."

Pinkerton told Mister Webster and Miss Hattie that they were to head for Richmond after they did their work in Leonardtown, but he made no mention of John.

"Where am I to go after Leonardtown, sir?" John asked.

"I want you to head for Dumfries, Manassas, and Centreville, where the Rebels have their winter camp. Find out what you can on troop strength and movements."

"Yes, sir."

John was disappointed not to be heading for Richmond, where he could have been reunited with Peg, but the mention of Manassas meant he would be back among familiar faces in the Lincoln League—people he had been working alongside for the past three months.

This time, however, his return to northern Virginia would be entirely different. He would return as the first black man on an official mission for the Union Intelligence Service.

*****

Timothy Webster, Hattie Lawton, and John Scobell did not draw any attention to themselves as they departed Washington on a brisk November morning. How could they? They were caught up in a flood of people, all heading across the Potomac River on Long

Bridge—thousands upon thousands moving by horseback, carriage, and foot. The crowd was so great that it took several hours just to wait their turn to cross the bridge.

Everyone was heading for Bailey's Crossroads on the Virginia side of the river, where the Yankee General McClellan was putting on his Grand Review—a display of military pageantry never before seen on the American continent.

"Can't believe y'all still carryin' that thing," said Cleon, patting John's backpack, which sat between them on top of a carriage. The doll, which Cleon had taken to calling Lucy Ann, peeked out from the top of the pack.

"And I'll keep on carryin' it till I see Peg and can give it to her as a gift."

"Just seems a bit amusin': a man on a mission, a man workin' for the Union Intelligence Service, carryin' around a doll. She still spooks me with her black painted eyes."

Cleon was not any part of the official mission for Pinkerton, but Webster told him he could tag along for a spell, since he was heading in the same direction—toward the Lincoln League camp in northern Virginia. Heading into northern Virginia wasn't the most efficient way to reach Leonardtown, Maryland, but Webster said he needed to connect with a fellow Pinkerton man at the Grand Review, and then they would cross into Maryland farther south.

The string of mild winter days had ended, and the weather had turned decidedly nippy, with patches of snow on the ground. John and Cleon were perched on top of the carriage, buffeted by the November wind, while Webster and Miss Hattie rode inside in comfort. On such a day, carriage space was at a premium, so you had to be white if you hoped to find a seat; even then, you had to be of the right sort of white—well-to-do or well-connected.

"How many troops you suppose there gonna be in this Grand Review?" asked Cleon. He wasn't one to let a silence last very long.

"I heard up to a hundred thousand," John said.

"That'll make the Johnny Rebs shake in their boots."

"Parades don't win wars."

John drew his overcoat around him tighter. He pulled his slouch hat down tighter, but it didn't cover more than just the tops of his ears, which were stinging cold.

"You scared?" Cleon asked.

"Of what?"

"Of dyin', of course. You're headin' off on your first mission, so it's gotta occur to you that you might wind up shakin' hands with St. Peter sometime soon."

"I try not to think of it."

"Mmmmm. I think on it all the time. It's gonna be pretty remarkable."

John shook his head. "Sounds like y'all lookin' forward to dyin'. Isn't that unusual for a man who gets spooked by a doll?"

"Dyin' will be like wakin' up from a long sleep. You take your last breath, and the next moment you're touchin' the glory and strollin' down the gold-paved streets of the Kingdom."

"All I know is that Peg'll be awful mad if I wind up dyin' before I get a chance to see her again."

Cleon laughed. "What's she gonna do? Track you down in the afterlife and give y'all a tongue lashing?"

"Wouldn't put it past her."

It was only a seven-mile trek from Washington to Bailey's Crossroads, but by the time they reached it, the Grand Review had already begun. The carriage pulled off the road, and they found a good vantage point overlooking the vast plain. From atop the carriage, John and Cleon had an eagle's-eye view of the most magnificent array of soldiers they had ever seen. Blue uniforms must have stretched a mile. John saw polished gold cannons, flags fluttering everywhere, bands playing martial music, and rows and rows of soldiers, all streaming past a reviewing stand. There was no mistaking the tall man who stood at the center of it all. Even from a distance, John could see Abraham Lincoln's towering black hat.

John kept his hands warm beneath his armpits, happy that Mister Pinkerton had supplied him with a heftier coat. The cold weather hadn't kept the ladies away from the Grand Review, for there were many in attendance, bundled up with coats over their wide crinoline dresses. As the parade unfolded in front of them like a panoramic painting, Timothy Webster and Miss Hattie finally left the warmth of the carriage arm in arm, pretending to be man and wife. Webster was a congenial sort, and he talked with a few observers before he and Miss Hattie approached someone in the crowd. The face was familiar. Where had he seen the man before?

"I can't believe it." John gawked.

"You know that man?" Cleon asked, motioning toward the tall man shaking hands with Webster.

John slowly nodded. But surely he was seeing things. Mister Hancock, the man who had shoved a musket in his face back at the Battle of Bull Run, was talking with Webster as if they were long-lost brothers.

"Who's the man?" asked Cleon.

John didn't answer. He just stared.

"You gonna tell me or not?"

"Hancock's his name."

"Ah. Hancock." Cleon cupped his hands around his mouth and blew warm air on them, then rubbed them together like two sticks to start a fire. It took about ten seconds for the name to register. "*Hancock*?" he exclaimed.

Cleon said the name so loudly that Webster, Miss Hattie, and Hancock turned and stared right at them. When Hancock caught sight of John, he looked just as surprised as John figured his own face appeared.

"You mean he's the Reb who nearly shot you in the face?" Cleon said under his breath.

"That's the one."

"What's a Reb spy doin' talkin' with Mister Webster and Miss Hattie? You don't think . . .?"

"I don't know what to think." John didn't take his eyes off of Hancock.

Hancock, Miss Hattie, and Webster continued to chat, and they occasionally threw glances in John's direction. Then Webster broke out in a smile and approached the carriage with Miss Hattie still on his arm and Hancock one step behind.

"Come on down, John!" called Webster, still looking amused by the whole thing.

John didn't budge.

"Deliver us out of great waters, from the hand of strange children," said Cleon, softly.

Hancock spread his arms and smiled up at them. "Don't worry, John. I'm on your side."

"If he's on your side, I'd hate to encounter an enemy," Cleon whispered.

John was determined to show no fear. He had hesitated long enough, so he climbed down from the carriage and marched up to Hancock.

"I would introduce you to Ethan Hancock, but it appears you two have already met," said Webster.

"I must apologize for my show back at Manassas," said Hancock, "but I had to be convincing. I did a pretty good acting job, don't you think?"

Acting job?

John didn't answer. Was the man saying that nearly shooting his face off was all a performance?

"He's one of us," said Webster. "He's one of Pinkerton's men behind Rebel lines, one of the best double agents. He's the man I needed to meet here."

"It is true," confirmed Miss Hattie.

If Hancock stuck out his hand, John would not shake it, he decided. Fortunately, Hancock did not even try.

"I am as surprised as you are, seeing you here with Mister Webster and Miss Hattie," said Hancock.

John would not give him the satisfaction of a smile or even a word of conciliation.

"Trust me, I would not have shot you, John. I wouldn't have gone that far with my theatrics."

John didn't believe it. An awkward silence.

Finally, Webster laughed and slapped Hancock on the shoulder. "Believe me, John, when I say that Mister Hancock here is a Union spy. You have nothing to fear."

"I ain't afraid," John said, finally cracking his silence.

"And I believe you, for you were fearless when we last met, even with my gun in your face," said Hancock. "But also believe me when I say I was just putting on a show. You should know a thing or two about acting. You had me going with those British and Scottish accents of yours."

Webster cocked his head. "Scottish accent? I had not heard of that ability."

Suddenly, laughter erupted from the top of the carriage. "Show Mister Webster your accent, John! Come on now!" Cleon shouted enthusiastically. He was always asking him to perform his accents.

As they stood there in silence, the band in the distance struck up a tune. Finally, John let break a sly smile. "This day would be jolly good if the band would play 'God Save the Queen.'"

His British accent was spot on.

Webster, Hancock, Miss Hattie, and Cleon all laughed, Cleon loudest of all, and several people nearby gave them disapproving stares for breaking the solemnity of the occasion.

"Mister Pinkerton made a good choice with this one," Hancock said to Webster. "Believe me, he'll make a fine spy."

John wouldn't argue with that.

15

EG HAD TO LIGHT THE KITCHEN FIRE, SHAKE OUT RUGS, LAY
the hearth, make the beds, wash the breakfast dishes, clean the
pantry, prepare tea for Missus Hicks, wash the privies, scour
the tables, wash the windowsills, and pick and gut two ducks.
As she worked on one of the ducks, she felt like a battlefield surgeon,
wielding a knife sharp enough to slice through bone, running an
incision from the bird's breastbone to its rear end. Then she reached
into the duck and hauled out all of its organs in one scoop, being
careful to preserve them all. As Matilda liked to say, "We eat everything but the quack."

Peg was good with a knife.

By late afternoon, she was dead on her feet, but she continued on,
sweeping the second-floor guestroom, where Missus Baker stayed.
The house had gone quiet, so she took a moment to sit down, remove
her shoes, and massage her feet. Her arches ached, as they always
did, and she let out a yawn; then she rolled her head to work out the
kinks in her neck.

Peg stood and trudged over to the room's closet. Not many bedrooms had closets, and this one could be accessed from two different
rooms. You could enter the closet from the guestroom, as Peg was
doing, or you could enter from Missus Hicks' room on the other side.
This closet was a no-man's land, caught between Missus Hicks and
Missus Baker.

Peg hesitated before entering because confined spaces set her
nerves on edge. Before she even stepped into the small space she

noticed that her heart was beginning to race. She wiped her sweaty hands on her waist, picked up her broom, and entered. Last week, Missus Hicks had been angry with her because she ignored cleaning the closet, so she couldn't very well skip the chore again this week. Closets brought her nothing but fear.

*****

Peg hid herself away in the closet on the third floor of Cager Johnson's sprawling house. The room was small and dark, and it had a musty smell. She heard the sound of her brother Shadrack moving around on the third floor, opening and closing doors. Looking for her. Stalking her.

Shadrack had a reputation as a tracker, which was why Master Johnson had nicknamed him "Blood," as in bloodhound. Shadrack was often called upon to help hunt down escaped slaves—a job that earned him extra rations of food and, even more importantly, liquor. In fact, Shadrack was almost as good at tracking down escaped slaves as a Cuban bloodhound.

Peg placed a hand on one of her bruised ribs, where Shadrack had punched her hard. Then he had left her alone for about an hour, retreating to his room and his bottle. But now his fury had returned, and Peg was afraid he was primed for more violence.

Thou art my hiding place, Peg said to herself. Thou shalt preserve me from trouble. Thou shalt compass me about with songs of deliverance.

Peg heard Shadrack's footsteps moving along the third-floor hallway, and she heard him cursing under his breath. She wished the master, Cager Johnson, were in the house right now to put a restraint on her brother. Master Johnson could be brutal as well—even more so than her brother Shadrack—but she didn't think he would allow her to be bruised or broken. Not today, at least. Cager Johnson had just agreed to sell her to Master McQueen, and he knew that if she arrived at the McQueens damaged in any way, her sale price would go down dramatically. Master Johnson needed every penny from the sale.

But Cager Johnson was gone for the afternoon, and Shadrack wanted his revenge.

"Ollie ollie oxen free!" Shadrack called out in a taunting tone. She heard him banging around in another room, possibly the one directly across the hall. It was difficult to tell. As children, they had played many games of hide and seek; even then, Shadrack scared her with the amount of force he put behind his fist when he "tagged" her.

"Ollie ollie oxen free!"

Shadrack had moved into the room with the closet. Peg shuffled backward into the dark corner, squeezing into a narrow space between the wall and a chest of drawers. As she did, she knocked a coat from one of the hooks against the wall. The coat fell over her head like a shroud, and she let out a stifled shriek.

The room went completely quiet. Carefully, she peeled the coat off of her head and held her breath. He must have heard. He had to have heard.

All of a sudden, the closet door was thrown open, and daylight poured in, and Peg screamed as Shadrack reached in, all shadow and strength, and his hand clamped down on her forearm, and he yanked her into the room.

"Shadrack, let go!"

He hurled her across the room, and she struck the corner of a low dresser, the edge catching her in the hipbone. She tried to bolt for the door, but he shoved her as she went running past, and she went flying against the wall shoulder first, before slumping to the floor. A picture on the wall was nearly knocked from its nail; it tilted sideways and swung above her head like a pendulum.

"Who you think you are, leavin' me like this?"

"I ain't leavin' you, Shadrack. I won't be far away, I promise."

"You'll be under the same roof as that man, and I can't have that."

"That man" was John Scobell.

John's master, Master McQueen, had agreed to purchase Peg, and Cager Johnson had just sealed the deal this morning. Peg would be sent to Master McQueen's house come morning—if she lived that long.

"It ain't my fault Master McQueen is purchasin' me," Peg said, looking up at her brother. She remained sprawled out on the floor, leaning

against the wall. Her brother, all two hundred and fifty pounds of him, stood over her, and it almost looked like he was about to cry. There was a deep sadness mixed in with the anger. Peg had taken care of her brother most of his life, for their mama and papa were never there to do the raising. And now it was obvious by just looking into his eyes: He was terrified of being separated from her for the first time in his life.

She spoke soothingly. "Shadrack, Master McQueen's house ain't far, so I'll be near. Don't you fret. I'll be sure to help y'all when I can."

Shadrack rubbed his right eye, obviously embarrassed that he was showing any emotion beyond anger. He breathed heavily. "It was you who asked John Scobell to talk to Master McQueen, didn't you? You got Master McQueen to buy you and take you from this house."

"I wouldn't a done that. I wouldn't desert you, Shadrack."

It was true that she hadn't asked John to convince Master McQueen to buy her; it was all John's idea. John was well aware that Cager John-son was in dire financial straits and might jump at the opportunity to make some quick cash, as he did when he sold Peg's mama away to a house of prostitution in New Orleans.

Peg stood up and took two slow steps toward her brother. He seemed to be calming. She spoke kindly. "I'll be close, brother. I won't ever desert you." She reached out, laid a hand on his shoulder.

Shadrack stared at the floor and sucked in two big mouthfuls of air. He bit his lip.

"Don't you worry none, brother."

He raised his head and looked her in the eyes. She saw a softness in his expression.

"I'll always be close. I will take care of you."

Suddenly, his gaze hardened and he slapped her hand away. "Liar!"

One second later, his right hand shot out, and he took hold of her by the hair, and he yanked, hurling her across the room. She seriously wondered if she would live long enough to join John at Master Mc-Queen's house.

*****

Peg never told John about what Shadrack did to her that day. Shadrack made sure that any bruises he left were not visible—nothing on the face. So Cager Johnson never found out, and neither did John or Master McQueen. If John had found out, she was certain he would have killed her brother.

Peg and John married in June of 1857—four years before they were given their freedom, if you could call this freedom. She still had to tiptoe around explosive people, like Missus Hicks, and she still hated to enter the narrow confines of a closet. She decided to work quickly. She swept the floor and began to dust the shelves inside the closet, cleaning with extra elbow power. After clearing out a patch of cobwebs, the throbbing of her feet intensified, so she took another moment to sit and massage her arches.

"She is not to be trusted."

A muffled voice came from Missus Hicks' room. Peg felt immediate panic, for she suddenly realized that she had neglected to open the closet door leading into Missus Hicks' adjoining bedroom. She had been under strict orders to always open the doors leading into *both* rooms whenever she was cleaning the closet—just to alert people she was there. Too late now. Missus Hicks was talking, completely unaware of her presence just a few feet away, behind the closet door.

Even more to the point, was Missus Hicks talking about *her* when she said, "She is not to be trusted"?

"For all we know, she could be a Northern spy," Missus Hicks said, plunging Peg into deeper panic. Had she been uncovered?

Peg thought she heard someone else say a few words, but it was even more muffled. It was a female voice.

"We should search her room," Missus Hicks announced.

Search my room? Peg's latest coded message, written just last night, was still tucked inside her Bible. She suddenly wondered if the code was too obvious, too amateurish. If they searched her room, with suspicions already in their minds, they would see through it in a moment.

Peg had to get back to her room and hide the evidence before they got there. So she rushed toward the closet door, but her foot caught on the broom, which she had leaned against the wall, and it clattered to the floor. She let it lie, in too much of a hurry. Then she snatched up her bucket of water and three rags, and she hurried for the door, hoping to slip silently up the servant's staircase and burn her coded message. But before she could even cross the threshold, a figure stepped in front of her, and they very nearly collided.

It was Missus Hicks, and she did not look pleased.

When Peg came to an abrupt stop, she could not keep the water from sloshing out of her bucket. The sudsy water came just short of landing on Missus Hicks' shoes, and the old woman glared at Peg as if she had just discharged a firearm a foot in front of her face.

Missus Hicks put her hands on her hips. "Is there a fire?"

"No, ma'am."

Peg crouched down and began to wipe up the small puddle with her rag, and she noticed Miss Doris standing just a few feet behind Missus Hicks. She must have been the other female voice that Peg had overheard. Miss Doris seemed nervous, fiddling with her necklace and biting her lower lip.

At that moment, Missus Baker appeared at the top of the staircase, looking clearly baffled. She stared at the strange gathering just outside her room.

"I am sorry, Missus Baker, but Peg here has been dawdling, and she still has much more cleaning to do before your room is ready," said Missus Hicks.

"That is all right," said Missus Baker. "I don't mind a little dust."

"But I do." Missus Hicks strode into the guestroom, swiped a finger along a dresser, and displayed the smudge of dust to Peg. "Does this look like you have finished cleaning this room?"

"No, ma'am. My apologies, ma'am."

"Then I suggest you finish the job before you go bolting out of a room as if you are being chased by a ghost."

"I will, ma'am. But I need fresh water."

"Don't you worry about getting fresh water. Just get in there and clean."

"Yes, ma'am."

Missus Hicks proceeded to explain to Missus Baker that the room would be occupied for at least another hour, and the Northern lady shrugged and retreated down the stairs. Missus Hicks and Miss Doris headed upstairs, while Peg went to work and began dusting the bookshelf. She paused and leaned against the fireplace mantle. Her right hand was shaking, and her mouth had gone bone dry. Spying was a hanging offense, even for a white person. Imagine what they would do to a black maid if they discovered she had coded messages tucked in her Bible upstairs. Should she run? That would only make her look guiltier. Besides, where in the world would she run?

She moved around the room, her mind barely connecting with her work, as she wiped down bookshelves aimlessly, expecting the thump of footsteps any moment, expecting Missus Hicks to appear in the doorway, waving the latest coded message in her hands.

Peg lifted books, three at a time, to dust beneath. Then she hurried to the window, raised it, leaned out, and snapped the dust cloth in the crisp November air. She paused to stare out on Richmond and suck in the air, wishing she could be far away, with John. Why did she ever let Mary Bowser convince her to take on such an assignment? Who did she think she was? John would be furious if he knew the chances she was taking. Of course, if he truly cared for her safety, he would not have run off to join the Northerners in the first place, would he? Sometimes, Peg's blood boiled just thinking on it.

Peg continued to dust, moving books, dusting some more, and then rushing to the window to snap the rag. Crazy thoughts came to her, like the temptation to shimmy down the tree, just feet away from the window, and run for her life. *Stay calm, don't do nothing rash.*

Back to the bookshelf. She lifted three books. Dusted. Moved on. Lifted three books. Dusted. Lifted two books.

Paused.

Pieces of paper peeked from the inside of one of the books—a commentary on the Book of Romans. Captain Atwater was very particular about the treatment and display of his books, and Peg was well aware that he did not approve of anything being jammed inside one of his volumes. Ever. His books were perfectly aligned, standing in a row, like a perfectly disciplined line of soldiers. But if he would never insert loose paper into a book, then who did?

Pulling out the papers, Peg could not believe what she was seeing. There were drawings—sketches of the submarine boat! And there were notes. Three pages of handwritten notes in print so small that she had to squint to read it. It was all there—how the submarine operated, how it was propelled, how it received oxygen, and how it could detonate an explosive from beneath the water.

Missus Baker? This was her room, the guestroom. She was a Northerner, and she had the captain wrapped around her little finger.

Could Missus Baker be a Union spy?

Peg had no other explanation for these notes. The writing looked to be the work of a feminine hand—clearly not that of Captain Atwater. Besides, he would never have jammed them inside the pages of a book, and Missus Baker was the only other person in the house who witnessed the demonstration of the submarine along the James River.

Missus Hicks had said: "The woman cannot be trusted." And Miss Doris had been by her side, probably agreeing wholeheartedly. Peg realized that perhaps they were not speaking about her after all. Perhaps they were talking about Missus Baker! Miss Doris had good reason to suspect something sinister about Missus Baker—anything to pry her loose from Captain Atwater.

Footsteps approached. Quickly, Peg jammed the papers into the deep pocket of her apron. She didn't have time to return them to the book on the shelf, but she didn't think it would be wise to put them back anyway. If Captain Atwater strolled into this room, he would be sure to spot pages sticking out of one of his books, even if they were well concealed. He inspected the books in all of the rooms as regularly as a captain inspects his troops.

Missus Hicks was back in the doorway, looming.

"Peg, what in the world is taking you so long?"

Peg noticed, once again, that Miss Doris stood a few steps behind the old lady, still playing with her necklace.

"Sorry, ma'am. Just finishin' up, ma'am."

"Then skedaddle! There's plenty of cleaning still to be done in the parlor downstairs."

"Yes, ma'am."

It was obvious that Missus Hicks and Miss Doris wanted access to this room while Missus Baker was gone. That's probably why they had insisted that Peg keep cleaning—anything to drive Missus Baker away. If that's true, then perhaps it was Missus Baker's room, all along, that they wanted to investigate—not hers. Peg slipped out of the room, careful not to spill any more water. Before hurrying down the nearby staircase, she looked back at Missus Hicks, but the woman had already disappeared into the guestroom. Miss Doris glanced at Peg, gave her an awkward smile, and then followed Missus Hicks into the room.

Peg smiled back and moved down the stairs, terrified but still strangely satisfied that she had saved Missus Baker from certain discovery. She hoped the woman would thank her for the risks she was taking.

*****

Ichabod Page marched through the dark Richmond streets, lantern in one hand, gun at his waist, and his Cuban bloodhound, Ahab, trotting by his side. Because of his duties with the torpedo boats, Ichabod had not been brought into the regular Army; but while he waited for the boat to be readied for action, he wanted to do more for the cause, so he patrolled at night and hauled Negroes off the streets. He also acted as a courier, delivering important messages for Confederate spies.

"You sure you wanna go down into the water?" asked his fellow slave patroller, Erasmus Klew.

"Why would I be afraid of a torpedo boat? I've faced worse and lived."

"You'll need a heap of luck on your side to survive."

"Luck has nothing to do with it. It's Fate."

Ichabod told Erasmus how his mama once explained to him about the Fates—three women who controlled your destiny. One spun the thread of your life, the second measured out the thread, and the third cut it off when you died.

"My thread is strong 'cause I have something that needs to be done before this war is over. I'm gonna be on the first torpedo boat to sink a ship. Mark my words, I'll be remembered throughout history."

Erasmus whistled, obviously impressed to be walking the beat with such a man. They patrolled the Church Hill area, where many wealthy lived, just a little north of the river, factories, and makeshift prisons.

Erasmus was an old man with a hobbled right leg that left him limping. With so many men going off to fight, the nightly slave patrol in Richmond had to fill its ranks with old men and the lame—and Erasmus was both. The officer in charge of the night patrol told Ichabod he could not release his dog on any slaves caught on the streets at night because masters would be upset to have their property damaged by the jaws of such an animal. Reluctantly, Ichabod had no choice but to agree to these terms because otherwise Ahab would not be able to accompany him at all. Just having his Cuban bloodhound at his side was enough to stir fear on the street.

"They say Miss Van Lew was out and about today, bringing aid to them Yankee prisoners again," Erasmus said.

Ichabod grunted. He hated Elizabeth Van Lew with a passion. He didn't understand why the authorities hadn't already tossed her carcass into prison for treason. Just because she was a woman—and a wealthy one at that—shouldn't make her immune to justice. They had already arrested one woman—a Yankee lady named Missus Curtis, who was suspected of spying—so ladies weren't off limits. The South had many enemies in petticoats.

"I curse Miss Van Lew," Ichabod said, and he meant it. His curse was not just an expression. It carried real power, he thought. "Our Army underestimates the wiles of women—and coloreds."

"Coloreds? You really think an African could collect intelligence? Don't seem to me like they'd be capable."

"They're more capable of fouling the works than you'd think," Ichabod said. "They got African voodoo."

"Oh."

Erasmus stared into the dark, as if he thought voodoo spirits lurked in the shadows on all sides.

"There's even coloreds out in the woods 'round Manassas and Fredericksburg," Ichabod said. "The Lincoln Legal Loyal League, they call themselves. The 4 L's."

"Where'd you hear such things?" Erasmus sounded skeptical.

"I have my sources. Good sources, and I believe those devils are out there."

"You think there's colored spies here in Richmond?"

"'Course I do."

Ichabod and Erasmus reached Franklin and 17th, where the notorious "Cage" was located—an octagonal cage where prisoners were put on display. A lone Negro man sat in the Cage, probably caught without a pass and gobbled up by night watchmen. He was either asleep or dead.

Ichabod and Erasmus made a left turn onto 17th Street and headed for the river, where Ichabod hoped to find a few more curfew breakers that he could toss into the Cage.

"I've a mind to round up some fellows and hunt down those Lincoln Leaguers myself," he said.

"You need any help?"

Ichabod cast a glance at Erasmus' bum leg. "It's a long ride between here and Fredericksburg and even longer to Manassas. Pretty hard for an old man."

"I can ride, and I can shoot straighter than any man I know."

"I will ponder on it, old man."

That seemed enough to satisfy Erasmus, even though Ichabod had no intention of making this old codger part of any posse he put together. They went silent as they continued to walk along the James River, which was as dark as oil. Ichabod thought back to how he and his pappy used to clear out rattlesnake dens by firing away at them from a safe distance, and he figured that destroying a nest of spies would be pretty much the same thing—only more entertaining.

He'd be sure to bring Ahab along for the hunt.

16

Leonardtown, Maryland

OHN HAD STRUCK A WHITE MAN ONE OTHER TIME IN HIS LIFE, when the fellow had tried to hit him with a whip. John had snagged the whip in mid-air with his left hand, and he planted his fist on the man's nose with his right. He was immediately pounced upon by five men and nearly beaten to death, and his nose had been broken for the second time. But now, incredibly, he was being *ordered* to strike a white man. The *United States government* was telling him to thump a white man in the back of the head! Never in a million years would he have guessed this would happen.

It was late afternoon in Leonardtown, and John crouched in a cluster of trees, where he had a good view of the hotel where Webster and Miss Hattie were staying. Webster had come across a man named Doctor Gurley in the hotel—a Union deserter whom he discovered to be one of the Confederate couriers that Pinkerton told them to watch out for. Doctor Gurley was carrying important papers, and Webster's idea was for John to ambush the man and retrieve them.

Webster had given him a description of Doctor Gurley—about forty years old; five feet, ten inches tall; wire glasses; trim black beard; smartly dressed. Webster had also told him that Doctor Gurley was staying the night with a family in a cabin, requiring him to cut through the woods. John's plan was to waylay him on the way and lift the papers from his person. Even trickier, John had to accomplish his mission without being seen, so he would have to strike Gurley from behind.

As the afternoon dragged on, the wind picked up and John could smell rain in the air. It wasn't cold enough for snow or sleet, but the rain would be chilly. Finally, two men emerged from the hotel, followed by Mister Webster, who was giving them his farewell. Webster said he would walk their target to the door so that John could identify him, but John wasn't expecting *two* men. The men were about the same height, and they both wore the same nondescript black coat and top hat, but one had a beard and the other did not. He figured that the dark-whiskered man was his target, Doctor Gurley.

They approached the woods, and John kept waiting for the beardless man to break away and go off on his own, but he didn't. John cursed his poor fortune. He couldn't attack *two* men without being seen, so he slipped back a little deeper into the woods and stayed low. The two men were visible through the bare trees, moving along the narrow trail. Even though the leaves had fallen from the beech, hickory, and maple trees all around him, the forest was still thick enough to provide ample cover.

John blew on his left hand, which was becoming stiff with the cold. The fingers of his right hand tightened around the club that he had brought along for the job. The trick would be to hit the man hard enough to knock him out, but not so hard that he killed the man. If he killed the fellow, a manhunt was sure to follow, and he might wind up swinging on the end of a rope.

Keeping at a safe distance, John followed the men, staying parallel with the path and treading lightly. He kept one eye on his feet, making sure he didn't crack a twig, and the other eye on the two men. But there was one big problem with splitting his vision: He soon forgot which man had the beard and which man didn't. From behind, at a distance, the men looked pretty much identical walking side by side. Same coats. Same hats. Similar height.

He couldn't afford to attack the wrong man.

The forest became thicker, and the vegetation cut off much of the late afternoon light, so identifying the right man was going to be even more difficult in the gloom. He had to walk slowly, deliberately, and the men kept gaining, moving farther out of view.

When John had been a slave, Master McQueen would send him out hunting regularly, so he had learned how to track game while making the least noise. Most of the tips came from an Indian scout he knew. John slung his shoes over his shoulder, so he could walk in his bare feet. He looked for clear patches of soil and placed his feet on these little islands of dirt, making sure he placed the heel of his foot down first, then slowly rolled it forward. He also moved in bursts, pausing every so often to assess the terrain just ahead.

When the path turned sharply right, the men disappeared completely from view. But at least this gave John the opportunity to move onto the trail where they wouldn't be able to see him. He hurried up the path, still running as light-footed as possible. Then a light rain began to fall, and the pattering on vegetation worked to his advantage. His steps blended with the noise of the rain, so he slipped his brogans on his feet and continued on.

When he came around another twist in the path, the men were gone. The trail branched off in two directions, but he had no idea which one they had taken. If the two men hadn't been together, he could have waylaid the doctor a long time ago. He was furious, but he tried to stay under control. Control meant silence. Frustration led to noise.

Arbitrarily, John chose the trail on the left, guessing that it was more likely to lead to the cabin in the woods. He hurried along, his footsteps still covered by the patter of rainfall. The path curved to the left, and he spotted a figure just ahead. The man was alone, so the two of them must have split off on opposite trails. But which man was he following? Doctor Gurley or the beardless man? From behind, it was impossible to tell.

Picking up a rock, John slipped behind a tree on the left side of the trail. Then he hurled the rock past the man and into the woods on the right side of the path. It worked. Hearing the crash and thump of the rock in the underbrush, the man stopped. He turned.

John saw his profile. No beard. *It was the wrong man!*

The man spun around, looking for any sign of life in the woods, but John pulled back behind the tree in time. When he dared to venture another peek, the man was gone. He had continued up the path.

Swiftly, John backtracked down the trail, returning to the spot where the two paths diverged. This time, he hurried up the right path, hoping he hadn't failed his first assignment. When he finally spotted Doctor Gurley, the man was approaching a clearing, where a lone cabin was visible in the growing gloom. He had to get to him before he reached the cabin.

Slipping off of the path and into the midst of the forest, John crouched behind a tree and called out—in a British accent—"Doctor Gurley, sir, Doctor Gurley, please come here!"

No response at first. John heard no sound, except for the low-pitched warbling of a bluebird coming from the upper branches of the trees. Then: "Who's there?"

"It's me, Doctor Gurley! Down the path! I'm hurt!"

"Who is that? Do I know you?"

"I need help! I turned my ankle!"

John pressed himself against the tree, hoping that the fringes of his body were not exposed. Then he heard movement. Doctor Gurley was approaching, moving down the path.

"Where are you?" Doctor Gurley asked. He was close. John didn't dare respond, or the man would be able to pinpoint the voice.

"Answer me! Where are you?"

The bluebird answered with a harsh chattering, almost a chipmunk sound.

Carefully, John ventured a look. He spotted Doctor Gurley, still on the path, facing another direction, searching the woods for any sign of the British bloke who had called his name. John tightened his grip on the piece of wood in his right hand.

"Hello?"

Doctor Gurley's voice seemed even closer. John braced himself against the tree with his left hand, staring at the bark only inches from his face; the smell of the forest was strong. The rain came down a little harder now, but that only worked to his advantage.

Movement again. Had Doctor Gurley given up? Was he getting suspicious about the voice?

John took a quick peek around the tree. The doctor was walking away, so John had to act quickly—and silently. He slipped noiselessly around the tree and onto the path. Doctor Gurley was about fifteen feet away now, moving fast. John had to act before the man spun around. If Gurley saw his face, he might as well tie the noose himself.

He rushed forward, his arm raised, and—for the first time—his footsteps gave him away. Doctor Gurley heard the rustle of clothing, the soft compression of leaves, and the man began to turn, but John struck before he could pivot around. His club connected with the back of the doctor's skull, and wood hit bone with a thick clunk. The doctor grunted—nothing more than that—and his knees buckled, and he dropped. His knees hit the ground first, and then he fell forward, his face striking the wet leaves. His arms had gone limp and didn't brace his fall.

Oh God, I hope he's alive.

John was on him a moment later, holding the man's head down, just in case he was still conscious. He didn't want the doctor twisting around and seeing his black face. If he did, Gurley would put together a posse and raid the black side of town, and someone would pay for this attack.

A soft groan. Doctor Gurley was still alive, thank God, but he was regaining consciousness. John moved his left hand off of his head and gave him a second strike. A whoosh of air came out of Doctor Gurley, like a deflating goatskin canteen.

Quickly, quickly, John rummaged through the doctor's coat pockets and came up empty-handed. The same with the pants' pockets. Nothing. Surely, John hadn't attacked a white man and risked his neck for no good reason. Webster said the man was carrying papers, but where? He went through the pockets again and began to panic, and then he looked inside the hat for any sort of hiding place. Still nothing. Crouching over the body in the rain, his eyes scanned the body from head to toe. *The shoes.* He noticed that the heel of Doctor

Gurley's right shoe was askew, so he slipped off the shoe and found that the heel unscrewed completely, revealing a secret compartment. Tucked into the sole were some neatly folded papers, and he found the same treasure trove in the left shoe. Fingers trembling, he quickly scanned the documents. On top was a letter addressed to Judah Benjamin, Confederate Secretary of War.

John lifted Doctor Gurley's limp wrist and felt for a pulse. It throbbed faintly.

Before fleeing, John looked around to make sure he didn't drop anything that would link him to this attack. The doctor's wound was bleeding, but not as badly as most head wounds. A moist circle of red had appeared in his hair, like the red glow of a coal fire.

John took off, the papers tucked in his coat, and when he turned the corner of the path, he slowed down. He had to be careful not to be seen by any white person on this trail, or he would be connected to the crime, and he wouldn't live another day. Slipping off of the trail and into the woods, he picked his way back toward Leonardtown, increasingly frightened.

When he reached the Negro side of town, he found a secluded spot near the edge of the forest, plopped down on a fallen tree, and tried to calm himself. His heart was still galloping. The rain had let up, so John reached into his pocket and pulled out the papers, for he had decided to read the documents thoroughly before passing them on to Webster. He was a slow, deliberate reader, and he took in every word, trying to fix them in his mind. The first paper was mostly about Union troop movements, but it also mentioned Rebel work on explosives being done by George and Gabriel Rains—something about a sub-terra explosive shell, whatever that might be. The most shocking part, however, came at the end of the missive, where it listed the names of three suspected Union spies in Richmond. None of the names were familiar, but one of the spies gave John pause. The name was that of Missus Elizabeth Baker, a Yankee lady suspected of gathering information while visiting the home of Captain Atwater.

Atwater.

With Peg working as a housemaid for the Atwaters, he wondered if he should head for Richmond as soon as possible—to warn this Baker woman, and to warn Peg not to get involved with her. Surely, Peg would not be so foolish as to get mixed up with a Northern woman spying right under Confederate noses. She had more sense than that.

17

ISSUS BAKER WAS UNCHARACTERISTICALLY QUIET THROUGH-
out breakfast. Peg noticed that she was fidgety and distracted.
But the Northern lady had good reason to be nervous. She
must have discovered by now that the papers in her room
had disappeared, and she probably expected Confederate officials to
come crashing through the Atwater door at any moment, ready to
lock her up in Libby Prison.

Peg needed to let her know, as soon as she could, that the information on the submarine boat was safe with her. Unfortunately, finding a chance to talk to Missus Baker was going to be difficult because
old lady Hicks wanted her to work on making buttons this morning.
There were no button-making machines in the South, so people had
to make their own. Peg cut them from gourds, wood, and even peach
pits, and then covered them with fabric.

After a little time had passed, Missus Hicks came by to check on
her progress, and the old lady frowned and folded her arms. "Can't
you work a little faster? I need a couple of buttons finished sometime
before the war ends, if you don't mind."

"Yes, ma'am."

Missus Hicks just stood there staring at her, and Peg could tell
that her eyes were on her head wrap, which had been tied with a
good-sized bow in the front.

"Now that just looks plain ridiculous," Missus Hicks said. She
reached out, grabbed the end of the bow and tugged, unraveling it.
"Tie it again, and this time do it properly."

Then Missus Hicks strode off, leaving Peg to rework her head wrap with a more modest bow in the back, rather than in front. Matilda strolled by not long after, and she told Peg she should be working a little slower.

"Take your time!" Matilda scolded, as she passed through the kitchen where Peg had set up her worktable. "You're movin' so fast, your buttons are lookin' like you cut them blindfolded with a potato sack over your head and the lights out."

"Yes, ma'am."

As Matilda exited, it dawned on Peg that the cook had varied her head wrap, and had placed her tie on the side, rather than behind her head. It was the first time she had ever seen Matilda with a variation in her head wrap.

Finally, after Peg had several buttons complete, she picked up a corn broom as an excuse for leaving her post. She peeked around the corner of the kitchen. The path to the staircase was clear, so she hurried over, grabbed the railing with her right hand, and swung around and up the stairs. But before she could reach the turn on the first landing, she heard the scolding voice of Missus Hicks. It sounded like the woman was prowling the second-floor hallway, complaining about something.

Peg shrank down the stairs, pausing at the bottom.

When Missus Hicks' rant dissipated, Peg continued back up the stairs, carefully. She heard sounds again—muttering, and it seemed to be coming from the guestroom. She reached the second-floor hall and found that she was right. The noise was coming from Missus Baker's room. But Peg also heard Missus Hicks rustling about in her room at the opposite end of the hallway, and she panicked because she knew the old lady would be furious to see that she had left her button-making post. So she slipped inside the guestroom without stopping to knock—not a single rap on the door.

Missus Baker stared at her in horror. A black maid had just entered her room without so much as a warning.

"And what do you think you're doing?"

Peg's eyes fell on the bookshelf, where it was obvious that the woman had been rummaging for the papers. Peg put a finger to her mouth.

"Don't shush me," Missus Baker said, volume rising. "And get out of my room."

Peg had to act quickly, before Missus Hicks came to investigate the ruckus. So she reached into her deep pocket and plucked out the Northern woman's papers. Missus Baker stared in disbelief, as if she had just pulled out a rattlesnake.

Missus Baker struck quickly. Her hand shot out in a blur and smacked her across the cheek with a stinging crack.

"What business is it of yours, stealing my papers?" Missus Baker hissed.

"But, ma'am, I was only trying to—"

"Where did you get these?"

"I found them cleaning, ma'am, but that's the thing. I was afraid—"

"You have no business taking my papers."

Peg was on the verge of tears. Missus Baker's anger and judgment stung as much as the slap. The last thing this lady should be doing was making a fuss and drawing the attention of Missus Hicks down the hall. If she would only pause in her fury for just a moment, Peg could explain that she was keeping the papers from falling into the hands of Captain Atwater, who surely would have found them when inspecting his bookshelves.

"Get out of my sight."

"But—"

"You heard me. Get out of this room."

"But Missus Baker, I was just tryin' to—"

Two raps on the door. "Is there a problem in here, Missus Baker?" It was Missus Hicks' voice from the other side of the door.

Missus Baker's eyes went wide and her mouth parted, as if she finally realized the mistake of drawing the old lady's curiosity. She glared at Peg and said, with a soft snarl, "Not a word of this to anyone, or I will have you horsewhipped."

Peg could only nod. Missus Baker slipped the papers beneath some clothes in her trunk just as the door opened. Missus Hicks stepped across the threshold and put her hands on her hips.

"What seems to be the problem, Missus Baker?"

Peg wondered if the old lady noticed the flare on her cheek, where she had been slapped.

"It's nothing, Missus Hicks. Just your maid startling me when she came in here to sweep," Missus Baker said in a lilting, carefree tone. She put on a fine acting display, changing on the spot from fury to forgiveness.

"Peg, what do you think you are doing in Missus Baker's room?"

"I'm so sorry, ma'am, but I thought I would take a break to do a little sweeping upstairs."

"And who told you that you could take a break from making buttons?"

Peg kept her eyes on the floor. "My mistake, ma'am. It will not happen again."

"It is all right, Missus Hicks." Missus Baker was a little late in trying to be conciliatory. If she had been reasonable from the start, then Missus Hicks would not have been alerted in the first place—and perhaps Peg could have explained why she had the papers.

"Back downstairs. I will deal with you later," said Missus Hicks.

"Yes, ma'am."

Broom in hand, Peg slunk downstairs to her buttons. As punishment, Missus Hicks would probably give her some extra chore to do—without pay.

*****

The day was off to a dramatic start, but it became even more intense when Missus Baker suddenly announced at lunch that she was leaving Richmond this very afternoon. The news came as no surprise to Peg, who figured the woman would clear out of town the first chance she had now that she had her documents back. But Captain Atwater couldn't have appeared more shocked if the news had been scribbled on a piece of paper, wrapped around a cannonball, and shot into his front parlor.

While Gilbert served the chicken soup, Peg refilled the captain's cup of coffee, and her eyes flitted from Captain Atwater to Missus Hicks to Missus Baker. Missus Hicks didn't even try to hide her obvious pleasure at Missus Baker's announcement, while the captain couldn't conceal his pain. It was as if that cannonball had hit him squarely in the gut.

"But Elizabeth, why so sudden?" asked the captain.

Missus Hicks groaned. She clearly hated it when the captain called Missus Baker by her Christian name.

"I have an aunt in Fredericksburg who is near death," Missus Baker explained. "I just received the telegram this morning."

"Odd. I don't recall a telegram being delivered this morning," said Missus Hicks.

"How could you? You were still asleep when it arrived."

Missus Hicks scowled, but it was true that she had a hard time pulling herself out of bed lately. When Peg first started working for the Atwaters, the old lady would bound out of bed at daybreak, eager to create havoc.

Peg made a move to refill Missus Hicks' coffee cup, but when the lady redirected her scowl at her, she backed off.

Captain Atwater looked like a mournful old hound dog as he stared at his lady friend. "But will you return to Richmond as soon as you can?"

"Perhaps, but I am not sure when. The land north of Richmond is the most dangerous turf in the war. It might be difficult convincing my uncle to let me go—at least until the war ends."

Peg had never seen the captain look so helpless. His hand was shaking so hard that he nearly tipped over his cup of coffee.

"Then I will escort you north."

"You will do nothing of the kind," commanded Missus Hicks. "You cannot leave your household undefended. Those Yankees might come swooping into Richmond, pillaging like barbarians."

"She is right," said Missus Baker, which was perhaps the first time she and Missus Hicks had agreed on anything. "Have hope. I will return to Richmond just as soon as I am able."

As Peg exited the room, she couldn't help but think that no Yankee would dare tangle with Missus Hicks. But she knew that the old lady's argument hit Captain Atwater where he was most vulnerable—his sense of duty and honor. Peg listened from just around the corner, and she remained in this position, even as Gilbert passed by with a knowing grin.

"Why, Miss Peggy . . ."

Peg put a finger to her lips, and Gilbert obediently went quiet. He was terribly amused by her persistent eavesdropping. Words dribbled from the dining room to the hallway, and Peg listened for another minute before continuing to the kitchen.

By mid-afternoon, Missus Baker had left town on the stage, and Peg had finished with making buttons. While she washed smoke grime from the ceiling of the second-floor hallway, she noticed Captain Atwater sadly moving from room to room, doing his regular inspection of the bookshelves. She passed by the open door of the guestroom, where the books stood at attention; the captain adjusted a few and made sure they were dusted properly and in alphabetical order, by author.

The captain had been moping all afternoon since Missus Baker had left, but it was the best of news for Miss Doris. When she came by for dinner and heard about Missus Baker's abrupt departure, she was positively dancing on air. It was clear that in Doris' mind, Missus Baker, the Northern woman, was in full retreat, and the South had won another decisive battle.

18

Centreville, Virginia
December 1861: One Month Later

JOHN MISSED PEG SOMETHING FIERCE. TRUDGING ALL OVER northern Virginia with the Lincoln League made him desperate for just a glimpse of her. John had traveled up the Rappahannock River on a steamboat, and now he was in Centreville, where he linked back up with Cleon, Gallus Turner, Hackey Pickens, Abram Fox, and other members of the Lincoln League. John had already told Cleon what had happened with Doctor Gurley, but now the others were asking questions.

"Did the doctor suspect it was a black man who clubbed him?" asked Gallus, as he stepped over a narrow fallen tree. They moved through the forest, five abreast.

"That's the good part!" said Cleon, answering for John. "John used his British accent in calling out to the doctor, so Gurley thought he'd been thumped on the head by a Brit!"

Cleon asked John to demonstrate his British accent for the others, and John reluctantly obliged.

"But that don't make sense. What good did it do to lift the papers off of him?" asked Abram. "Didn't the doctor have the information memorized?"

"No, he—"

"No, the fool!" exclaimed Cleon, cutting off John and hopping in front the group. He walked backward, facing the others as he talked. "The doctor didn't think he was allowed to read papers addressed to the Reb's Secretary of War, so that addlehead never even laid eyes on the words, and the information was never delivered!"

"We sent the letter north to Pinkerton with one of the Lincoln League men based near Leonardtown," John added, finally squeezing in a few words of his own.

"That's right! John introduced Mister Webster to a whole cabin-load of Lincoln Leaguers," said Cleon. "I bet Webster was feelin' a might uneasy bein' the only white face amidst almost two dozen black men. But I gotta give it to the man, he was willin' to put the letter in the hands of one of our Lincoln League agents to deliver to Pinkerton. That's sayin' somethin'!"

"There's gotta be a double agent workin' for the Rebs in Washington then," said Abram. "How else would the doctor get his hands on the names of spies in Richmond? Someone is leakin' information south."

"Oh, I don't doubt it. There's probably double agents everywhere," said Cleon. "If the Yanks have double agents, like Hancock and Webster, then the Rebs do too. Someone is stealing information from right under Pinkerton's nose."

On this morning, John, Cleon, Abram, Hackey, and Gallus were carrying sacks of bread to the Rebel winter camp at Centreville. They had been posing as vendors of delicacies because the best way to stay in good graces with the Rebs was through their stomachs. It seemed as if Cleon talked pretty much every step of the way, but John heard only some of what he had to say. Most of the time he was thinking about Peg.

*****

John stumbled but kept his balance as he came down the steep street leading into Shockoe Bottom. Richmond streets were laid out like a parable. The rich folks lived up on top of the city's seven hills, and everything drained down to the lower reaches of the city, where the poor lived—like the Shockoe Bottom slave neighborhood down by the river. That's where John and Peg boarded out in a two-room tenement, sandwiched between two shacks, one of which had a tin roof that was always flying off in pieces in a big wind. John was afraid that one of these days a piece of tin was going to whizz past and lop off his head.

Turning off of Cary Street, John went two blocks past a row of shanties, where someone was always porch-sitting on a Sunday afternoon like this, when church was over. As he approached their tenement, he heard a man's voice coming from inside. It wasn't an angry voice, but John didn't like the idea of a strange man inside their house without him around. He pounded up the stairs, threw open the door, and there, sitting in his favorite rocker, was Peg's brother Shadrack. Peg stood off to Shadrack's right, and John wondered what kind of devilment her brother was up to now.

"What do you think you're doin' here?" John demanded. Now that he and Peg were married and both working under Master McQueen's roof, he had hoped Peg wouldn't have any more contact with her brother.

Shadrack slowly stood, hat in hand, but it wasn't an intimidating move. In fact, the man looked scared. He was still as big as ever, but somehow less threatening.

"Afternoon, John."

His tone was conciliatory, almost meek. This caught John by surprise, and he didn't know what to say at first. But he gathered his wits and spoke harshly.

"I asked y'all. What're you doin' here?"

Peg answered for him. "Shadrack come here for a favor."

"That don't surprise me."

"Hear him out, John."

John didn't understand Peg's sympathy for her brother after all he had done to her. Shadrack never stood up for her when Peg's pappy roughed her up as a child, and when her pappy ran off, leaving Shadrack in charge the house, it was his turn to man-handle Peg whenever the fury came over him.

"Cager Johnson is fixin' to sell me South, down to where he sent Mama. I can't let him be doin' that to me," Shadrack said.

"Then run."

"You know I can't do that. There's dogs."

John laughed. It was amusing to hear Shadrack speak about the dangers of running. Cager had kept him around all these years because Shadrack was a good tracker, and he had helped track down many runaway slaves, with whiskey being his primary reward for successful captures. And now he speaks of being afraid of the bloodhounds! God's judgment fits the crime like a glove.

"Then what do y'all expect us to do?" John said. "If we had money to buy someone's freedom, it's gonna be Peg's freedom, not yours."

Shadrack dipped his head. "I know, I know. But I was thinkin' you might ask Master McQueen to buy me from Cager Johnson—the way he done with Peg. I can't be sent Deep South, John. Y'all have to help me."

"I don't gotta do anything."

"That's not what I meant. I mean I'm beggin' y'all to help me."

If the man got down on his knees, John would blow his top.

"I thought you were Cager's favorite," John said. "Whatja do to get him wantin' you shipped down South?"

Shadrack shrugged, looked away, and said nothing, so Peg stepped in and explained for him. "He tried some conjuration on Cager Johnson."

John had to contain his laughter. "You tried conjuration! What kind of conjurin'?"

Shadrack still didn't answer—probably too ashamed.

"A voodoo lady told him to get some fresh cow manure, mix it with red pepper and white people's hair, and cook it in a pot over the fire," Peg explained. "Once he had it all ground to a snuff, he was to sprinkle it all over the master's bedroom, and in his hat and boots."

For Peg's sake, John did not laugh out loud, but a smile still leaked through. "And what did you think all that would accomplish?"

"The lady told me the master would not flog me if I sprinkled the dust around his bedroom," said Shadrack.

John stifled another laugh. "And what happened?"

"The master and his wife started sneezing and wheezing when they climbed into bed, and they discovered that the source was my conjurin' powder," said Shadrack, not making eye contact with John.

"I assume he walloped you a good one," John said. "Some conjurin' that was." He could contain his laughter no longer.

Peg stared at him with fire in her eyes, as if daring him to laugh any more. So John reined in his sputtering laughter, for her sake. Truth be told, he almost felt sorry for Shadrack, standing there so helpless and hopeless. But the key word was "almost." John tried to stifle any feelings of sympathy, fixing his mind on the things that Shadrack had done to Peg throughout her life.

Shadrack raised his head and stared John in the eyes. "I'm askin' with all my power, John. Would y'all help me? Would you talk to Master McQueen about purchasin' me?"

John stared back and sized up the man. If Shadrack had come here before he was being threatened with being sold down the river, he might have been more sympathetic. If Shadrack had truly repented and given up his slave-hunting ways, then maybe. But not now, not today, no way.

"No. I will not help. Now leave our house."

*****

It took a long time for Peg to forgive John for what had happened that day. Her brother was sold South, and they had no idea what became of him. Sometimes, John felt guilty—especially on days when Peg would start crying about her lost family. But he had to do what was best for her. He had to protect her.

John's mind snapped back to attention when the words of Cleon broke through to him. He was talking about heaven again.

"So that's why I ain't got no fears of Rebel bullets," Cleon told the others, although they had heard it all before. "I already been to heaven a coupla times in my visions and touched the glory, and if I could go back there today, so be it. But God'll keep me here on this piece of dirt long enough to do the work He got for me. And then I'll be whisked away, and I don't rightly care if it's a bullet or something else that sends me back home."

John nodded slowly, and Cleon turned to face him.

"So don't have no fear 'bout yourself or 'bout your wife Peg."

John was startled. "What do you mean, my wife Peg?"

"I know that the letter you found on Doctor Gurley got to you—it bein' filled with the names of Richmond spies, includin' a spy in the very house where your wife works. I can put two and two together. I know it's eatin' at you."

John shrugged and stared at the palms of his hands. "I asked Webster and Miss Hattie if I could go with them to Richmond, to see Peg, but they said my mission was in the direction of Centreville."

"The Lord'll protect your missus. Besides, your Peg wouldn't get caught up with spying business in the heart of the Confederacy, would she?"

"Not Peg. But the Law has a way of snaggin' black men and women and fixin' the blame on them, even if they are as innocent as Abel. I'm afraid for her."

"Fear no man," Cleon said.

Easier said than done.

John, Cleon, and the others continued their trudge through the woods, sticking with the job at hand—keeping track of Confederate numbers, which John recorded and then sent north with black couriers known as the Black Dispatches. It was a clear day, and the clouds were narrow strips, all in a line, as if a large cloud had been cut into thin, white bandages. It was a welcome relief after days and days of sleet and snow. It was only December, and already it had been a rough winter. As they worked their way up a steep slope, Cleon asked him to sing, and John struck up a Scottish ballad.

What makes that blood on the point of your knife?
My son, now tell to me.

It is the blood of my old grey mare
Who plowed the fields for me, me, me.

It is too red for your old grey mare
My son, now tell to me.

It is the blood of my old coon dog
Who chased the fox for me, me, me.

It is too red for your old coon dog
My son, now tell to me.

It is the blood of my brother John
Who hoed the corn for me, me, me.

What did you fall out about?
My son, now tell to me.

Because he cut yon holly bush,
Which might have been a tree, tree, tree.

What will you say when your mother comes back,
When she comes home from town?

I'll set my foot in yonder boat
And sail the ocean round, round, round.

When will you come back, my own dear son?
My son, now tell to me.

When the sun it sets in yonder sycamore tree
And that will never be, be, be,
And that will never . . .

John stopped singing. He came to an abrupt halt, shocked by what suddenly appeared before them as they came to a rise in the ground that leveled off in the midst of the forest. A black man was sitting on the cold ground, propped up against a tree, with his hat tipped down over his eyes, as if he was snoozing. But something told John that the man had gone deeper than sleep. His left hand was wrapped around the pole of a Union flag, which hung down like a limp rag.

John set down his satchel of bread and approached the man cautiously, with the others trailing just behind. He nudged the man on the shoulder. The man was stiff and solid, like he was made out of wood, and his long coat was powdered with frost. John took a breath before working up the courage to tip the hat up and get a good look at the man's face. He worried that it might be a familiar face.

Carefully, he raised the hat and found the man's eyes wide open, as if in shock. A bullet hole, crusted black with dried blood, was nearly perfectly centered on his forehead. And yes, the face was familiar. He was one of the Lincoln League couriers, a man by the name of Reuben Moon. John didn't know him very well, but Reuben had recently carried one of his reports to a safe house outside of Washington. John paused to look around, wondering if Reuben's killer might still be lurking nearby. But considering how cold the body was, that was doubtful. He had probably been killed a day ago. John noticed that Hackey, being the youngest of them and maybe not as accustomed to violent death, looked especially shaken.

Abram stretched out the flag clutched by the corpse, and John was shocked to see that it was attached to the pole upside down. Flying the flag upside down was sometimes a sign of disrespect, sometimes a way of signaling for help. Perhaps this flag meant both; perhaps the murderer had slipped the upside-down flag into the dead man's hand as some bizarre joke. But strangest of all was that someone had scrawled words across the flag.

"What's it say?" asked Gallus.

"It says, THIS IS THE FIRST."

"The first? What's it mean, 'this is the first'?" asked Hackey.

"It means there will be more."

Cleon stared at John for a few moments, taking it all in. Then he looked back at the face of Reuben Moon, which was frozen in an expression of shock and disbelief.

"You mean more deaths?" Hackey said.

"Yes. More death."

*****

Allan Pinkerton's friend from New England put it best: The public buildings in Washington were like "diamonds in a dunghill."

The White House was a beautiful architectural gem, surrounded by muddy streets after a cold December rain, and its grand pillars ironically made it look a bit like a Southern plantation house. The Capitol building, meanwhile, resembled a layered wedding cake, but the new dome was still only partially constructed, so it looked as if wedding guests had already nibbled away much of the cake. Pinkerton couldn't help but see the unfinished Capitol building as a fitting symbol of the country, which had been nibbled away by secessionists.

Pinkerton stopped to wipe the muck from the bottom of his shoes on the edge of a tree stump. If he didn't stop every so often to clean the bottom of his shoes, by the time he reached the White House his feet would be caked with enough soil to create a small island. Besides, he was off to meet with the President himself, and it would not do to show up with so much muck, even though Abraham Lincoln, being a backwoods bumpkin, was no stranger to mud.

The Union intelligence director entered the White House from the north side and was escorted down a long vestibule to the President's reception room on the right. The motto of Pinkerton's detective agency back in Chicago was "We never sleep" and the symbol was a single open eye—alert and watchful. But on this day Pinkerton was exhausted from the never-ending work, and he nearly drifted asleep while waiting to be ushered into the President's office. Fortunately, he was called before he could completely embarrass himself by dozing in the chair.

When Pinkerton was finally ushered into Mister Lincoln's office, the President was sitting behind a large walnut table, on which were piled books and maps. In fact, there were maps everywhere—rolled-up maps leaning against the wall, maps strewn across a horsehair sofa, and even a couple of maps peeking out from behind the sofa. President Lincoln stood up to shake hands, rising to his gangly height of six feet, four inches. He smiled slightly, and Pinkerton noticed that his cheeks seemed even more sunken than the last time they had met together; his cheeks were like two gray valleys, and he had one lazy eye where he had been kicked by a horse and nearly killed as a boy.

Right away, President Lincoln started in on one of his stories, as the secret service man knew he would. "When I was a boy, I remember a farmer who had a bull that would take off after anyone who dared to cross the field. He was an ornery beast, and one day a neighbor climbed the fence, thinking he could dash across the field before the bull could catch him."

The President scratched behind his right ear—an oversized ear in proportion to his rail-thin body—and he smiled.

"The man was fast enough to reach a tree, but he knew there wouldn't be time to climb it, so he began running around and around and around that tree, and the bull chased him, getting angrier by the moment. Finally, the man circled around the tree and caught that bull by the tail and held on for dear life. The bull was in a froth because it couldn't shake the man from his tail, and he bellowed so loudly that we could hear him from a mile away."

President Lincoln paused for effect, and Pinkerton leaned in closer.

"Finally, the bull broke into a dead run, with the poor man still holding onto the tail and hanging on with all he had. 'Darn you!' the man shouted at the bull, as the two of them tore across the field. 'Who commenced this fuss in the first place?'"

Pinkerton laughed along with the President, not sure what the story had to do with their business at hand. President Lincoln rubbed his hands together; they too were oversized, like two paddles.

"In this conflict, we have got the bull by the tail, Mister Pinkerton, and no matter who started this fuss, we have to hold on for dear life if we intend to come out the other side unscathed."

"Well said, Mister President."

President Lincoln leaned back again and stroked his beard, and Pinkerton—a no-nonsense Scotsman—marveled at how different they were. The once clean-shaven President had grown his beard on the advice of an eleven-year-old girl, of all things. The girl had suggested the President grow a beard since his face was so cadaverously thin, and Pinkerton had to admit that she had a point. Still, he couldn't imagine ever being possessed to grow whiskers because a young girl wrote to him.

It was time to get down to business, although Pinkerton had no intention of informing the President that he suspected a double agent in his service; he had no idea who was leaking information about their agents, but he wondered if it could be someone working for Miss Rose Greenhow, the Washington socialite he had under house arrest for espionage. He decided to concentrate his report on submarine warfare.

"Mister President, I wish to tell you that we have received fresh intelligence about Southern efforts to build a torpedo boat," Pinkerton began, hoping to finally get down to business.

"Torpedo boat? You mean those submarine boats?"

"That's right. We received intelligence from one of my female agents in Richmond, who witnessed a demonstration of a torpedo boat on the James River, not far from the Tredegar Iron Works."

"And . . . ?"

"It appears to work, sir. Blew a skiff right out of the water."

"And this torpedo boat was not visible at all? It was completely submerged?"

"They connect the air hoses to a flat platform that blends in with the color of the water, and that's all you can see—but only if you look at the water very carefully."

President Lincoln's demeanor changed instantly, from the homespun storyteller to a serious, saddened man. His eyes could sometimes be the saddest that Pinkerton ever saw.

"Have you sent word to Hampton Roads?" the President asked. "We must maintain this blockade at all costs and sustain our superiority on the water, since our abilities on land have been . . ." He paused, obviously searching for the most tactful words. "Our abilities on land have been sorely lacking, even in the face of inferior numbers on the Confederate side."

President Lincoln had slipped in a veiled criticism. He was not happy with General McClellan, who had been convinced that the Confederates threatened Washington with 150,000 men. The numbers turned out to be vastly overblown. Even more embarrassing, Federal soldiers had discovered that many of the Confederate cannons they feared were only logs painted to look like cannons. "Quaker cannons" they were being called. The Federal Army had become a laughingstock.

Pinkerton quickly switched the subject back to boats. "Commander Smith is planning a defense of some sort." Pinkerton immediately regretted adding the words "of some sort," because it sounded unsure and vague. "I have confidence that the torpedo boat will be stopped."

"Good. What about our efforts in creating a torpedo boat of our own?"

"There have been delays with the Frenchman de Villeroi's submarine boat. But we hope to see it completed in forty days."

"Forty days? Can it be done?"

"It can."

"Excellent." President Lincoln's gaze drifted off into space, in the direction of the maps pinned against a far wall. Then he snapped back to reality and looked Pinkerton in the eyes. "Tell me, though, do you believe that torpedo boats are an immoral form of warfare?"

"Civilized war does not allow for killing for its own sake, Mister President. But if it achieves a military advantage, it is acceptable. Torpedo boats are no different than an ambush on land or concealing cannons."

The President didn't respond. He stared into space again and ran his hand down the side of his face. Then he cracked a smile, and Pinkerton knew what was coming: another one of his homespun stories, this one about two parsons arguing about how to cross a river. When he was done, Pinkerton gave him a charitable chuckle and stood to his feet.

"Why, Mister President, I do believe you'd still be telling jokes even if you were only a mile from hell," he said.

President Lincoln gave this some thought and then took his parting shot. "Yes, sir, that's about the distance to the Capitol."

19

Thomas Cannon leaned over the ship's rail and stared down on the water. The evening sun had not yet set, so there was still light, but he didn't know how they could be expected to see something lurking beneath the dark waters of Hampton Roads—the waters where the James and Elizabeth Rivers converged just before spilling into Chesapeake Bay and the Atlantic Ocean beyond.

Thomas Cannon and Spencer Fish kept watch by the starboard cathead—the wooden beam used to keep the anchor a safe distance away from the hull. They were usually teamed together on the watch because the captain thought it was amusing to pair a "Cannon" with a "Fish"—two fitting names for seamen on a ship like the USS *Congress*.

"Soon it'll be too dark to see," said Thomas.

"Don't fret, the net'll snag 'em."

"Nets don't catch everything."

Commander Smith had ordered them to connect a thirty-foot-long netting to the jib boom, and then they lowered it into the water, fourteen feet deep. Weights on the bottom of the netting kept it vertical to snag any torpedo boat, like a massive underwater spider's web.

"If the net don't get 'em, the dragrope will," said Spencer.

Other men were pulling a dragrope through the water, hoping that the hook on the end would catch on the torpedo boat's air hoses and yank the air supply apart.

"Think of this torpedo boat as just an oversized gator with a skin of steel," Spencer added. "My pap and I would wade through the marsh, probing for gator holes with a hooked pole. When we hooked us a gator, we'd thump it on the head with an axe. Simple as that."

"But gators can't blow you up with a torpedo."

Thomas and Spencer remained silent for the next ten minutes, their eyes riveted to the water. They were told to look for a flat flotation device that blended in with the surface, and after staring at the black, rippling water for more than twenty minutes, Thomas' mind started playing tricks; he thought he saw the flotation device three or four times, but it turned out to be an illusion. They each carried rifles, but Thomas wondered what good bullets would do against a steel beast. It was one thing to face an enemy ship on open water, but it spooked him to know that a ship might be lurking beneath the water, attaching a torpedo to their hull—right beneath his feet.

Thomas' stomach rumbled, for his dinner didn't set well, and he leaned on the rail, wondering if his meal of cheese and biscuit might decide to come back up for an encore. The cheese had been moldy, but that was nothing new, so he didn't think it was the reason for the nausea slowly growing in his gut. They had removed the maggots from the sack of biscuits the usual way—placing a dead fish on top, drawing maggots out of the biscuits and into the fish. But maybe they hadn't gotten all of the buggers. Maybe he had eaten more maggot than biscuit.

Thomas stared directly down on the water, wondering if he was going to be sick. And when he slowly raised his head, he saw it. He blinked his eyes a couple of times, expecting the illusion to evaporate and the surface of the water to return to normal, but the vision didn't disappear into ripples. A flat piece of wood, floating on the water, approached their boat quickly, and he suddenly realized that they could be blown to bits at any moment.

His shout carried across the ship. "There! I see it!"

*****

Ichabod Page was going to make history. He was intent on being aboard the first torpedo boat in the history of the world to sink a ship. And they were close. Below the surface, in the darkest of waters, they were operating blind. Samuel Thomas, his companion in this cramped vessel, estimated they were close enough for the third man, Scotty Irwin, to leave his chamber and affix a torpedo to the hull of the nearby ship. So Ichabod stopped cranking, the propeller stopped turning, and the submarine boat came to a stop, suspended like a big steel fish in the murky waters of Hampton Roads. The waters swarmed with Yankee boats, preventing Southern goods from going out or coming in. The blockade was strangling the Confederacy, but with torpedo boats and soon-to-be-finished ironclads, Southern ingenuity was going to blow this blockade to kingdom come.

"Any idea what ship we're close to?" Ichabod asked.

"The USS *Congress*, by my estimations."

Samuel stared at the candle, their only illumination, as if fearing that low oxygen levels were going to snuff it at any second—and snuff *them*, as well. Samuel's obsessive fears made him a liability, Ichabod thought. He had unsuccessfully campaigned to get Samuel tossed from this mission, for the man was too cautious, too fearful for his own good. The boss said no other person knew as much about the operation of these torpedo boats as Samuel did, other than the ship's inventors. But Ichabod thought that head knowledge was useless if your gut was yellow.

Samuel had caught wind of Ichabod's attempts to drop him from the mission, and their strained relations got even worse. Not that Ichabod cared.

"What's taking Irwin so long?" Samuel fussed.

"Just stop your frettin' for once."

Samuel muttered a curse under his breath—an insult meant for Ichabod.

"What's that you say?" Ichabod asked, walking two steps in Samuel's direction.

"Nothing you would understand."

Samuel, sitting in a chair with the candle in his hands, looked up—his face eerily lit by the small light. Ichabod was tempted to smack the man with the back of his hand, but he didn't want Samuel to drop the candle and plunge them into complete darkness.

Darkness came anyway.

The candle suddenly snuffed, just like that.

"Whatya do?" Ichabod demanded. "Did you blow it out, you fool?"

"I didn't!"

"Then light it!"

Ichabod heard fumbling in the dark. A match ignited, sending up a miniature flare—and then it too went out just as quickly.

"Light it right!"

"I am!"

Another match flared, another match went out.

Ichabod could hear Samuel breathing rapidly. "We've lost air!" Samuel shouted.

"You're just panicking! Breathe easy."

"I can't! We've lost air, I tell you!"

Ichabod cussed him out, but he was beginning to notice that he too was short of breath. He sucked in air, but it didn't satisfy. He began to breathe rapidly.

"We need to surface!" Samuel shouted. He was nearly screaming.

Ichabod heard him scrambling in the dark, probably trying to locate the pump to eject water in the forward ballast so they would rise.

"Don't panic, man!"

In the dark, Samuel stumbled into Ichabod and then lashed out at him, throwing out an elbow that caught him in the mouth. Ichabod tasted blood, and he went dizzy. Was it from the elbow to the face, or the lack of air? He fought the temptation to panic. He had never lost his composure in the face of Death before, but he felt a tightening in his chest, a mild paralysis of the lungs.

He suddenly began to fear that Samuel was right. Their air supply was gone.

Sucking on his swelling lip, Ichabod wondered if the Yankees had torn away their air hose using a dragline. So he moved to the opposite end of the torpedo boat and began pumping out the ballast tank. His breathing sped up, his heart was racing. *Don't panic, don't panic.* He sensed that he was reaching out and putting his hand on Death itself.

Then Samuel rushed for the ladder leading up to the hatch, and Ichabod knew what he was aiming to do; he was going to open the hatch before they had surfaced. He was going to bring the freezing Hampton Roads water pouring into the vessel, the surest way to turn this ship into a coffin.

Grabbing him by the legs, Ichabod tried to pull the man down from the ladder, but Samuel kicked loose, fueled by the flame of pure panic. If the man would just give it time, they would reach the surface before their air ran out. Ichabod latched onto the man's legs again, but Samuel's shoe caught him square in the eye, and he saw sparks in the dark as his eye erupted with pain. Ichabod stumbled backward and fell onto the floor of the submarine.

This gave Samuel just the time he needed to release the hatch, which opened inward. Dark water poured through the open hatch, knocking Samuel from the rungs of the ladder. Ichabod latched onto a bottom rung as he was hit by a gush from above—freezing cold water that nearly stopped his lungs instantly. He felt Samuel trying to scramble over him and back up the ladder, but Ichabod had had enough of him. With the submarine filling fast and beginning to sink, he pulled a hunting knife from the sheath at his waist, grabbed Samuel from behind, and thrust the knife into the man's side and turned the blade. Furious, he peeled the man from the ladder and pushed him aside; then he held onto the rungs as the water continued to pour down on him, like standing underneath a waterfall in winter. The water had knocked off his hat and struck his bare head, and it felt like he was being scalped by an icy knife. He gasped for breath as the small submarine quickly filled, the frigid water rising up to his chest, then neck. He moved to the very top of the ladder, finding a small air pocket at the top, where he could still gulp oxygen.

Moments later, he was completely submerged in cold water and had to get out immediately. If the submarine sank any deeper, he would freeze before he reached the surface. The air pocket was gone, the submarine was filled, and he made his move—until a hand from below latched onto his ankle. Samuel was still alive, submerged in water, and he had grabbed Ichabod's ankle. Holding his breath, Ichabod crouched, and he stabbed at the hand, one, two, three times, until it finally let go, minus a finger. Then Ichabod pulled himself up and out of the hatch and into the water, rising, rising, his lungs bursting, the cold squeezing his head like iron clamps.

He burst through the surface, gasping and opening his mouth as wide as possible to take in every drop of air. The submarine boat was gone, drifting down to the bottom, taking Samuel with it. Ichabod treaded water and tried to calm himself, gauging the distance to the Southern shore. He could swim the distance, as long he didn't freeze first. To the east loomed the hulking ship like a mountain in the gloom, and he heard men shouting, muskets firing. Were they firing at him? Had he been spotted?

He began swimming, and the muscles in his arms ached with icy pain. He had to keep moving, keep swimming, or he was a dead man. He thought of his best friend, who had drowned when he became tangled up in weeds at the bottom of the river, and Ichabod remembered his bloated body and face when they hauled him out of the water. Ichabod was not about to end up that way. He swam hard with long, strong strokes, hoping that the rhythm would calm his nerves. Then his head struck something hard, and at first he thought he had swum straight into the side of the submarine. But that couldn't be possible because the torpedo boat had sunk. Treading water, he reached out and touched a wooden platform. He had swum directly into the flotation device that had once held their air hose.

The wooden platform was his savior, and Ichabod felt that Blind Fate once again had saved him by directing him toward this flotation platform. Gripping the slippery surface, Ichabod hauled his body onto the wooden frame—his raft, his savior. For a moment, he laid spread-eagle on the raft, and he let exhaustion overwhelm his senses. It was tempting to just close his eyes and drift away like smoke, but Ichabod realized that the cold was putting him to sleep, and some people never woke up from such a hibernation. He owed it to Fate to stay alert and alive. Then he heard the pops of gunfire, and something pelted the wooden frame only six inches from his face.

He was being shot at from the ship.

That woke him up, and it was all the incentive he needed to rise up into a crouch and start paddling for land.

20

Peg Scobell couldn't decide which was more foolish—continuing to gather information in the Atwater house, where suspicions were growing, or riding out into the Virginia countryside with Mary Bowser.

"I'm wonderin' if I should find employment in another house," Peg said to Mary. They sat side by side in a wagon, heading south out of Richmond along the Osborne Turnpike. Mary did the steering while Peg cradled a basket of fresh eggs in her lap.

"But they're blamin' Missus Baker, not you," said Mary.

News had reached the Atwater house that the Yankees had been waiting for the Confederate torpedo boat with nets and draglines. The submarine had been successfully sunk, and Missus Baker could be blamed. There were stories circulating that she had supplied the Yankees with a wealth of information about the South's torpedo boats, but Captain Atwater couldn't believe that his childhood friend, the woman he was head over heels for, would betray him that way. Missus Hicks had no trouble believing it.

"The news about Missus Baker has them suspicious of *everyone*," Peg said to Mary.

"Then lay low for the next month and wait for it to blow over."

"Mmmmm." Peg stared at the eggs in her lap. Three of them were hollow, and they contained coded messages from Elizabeth Van Lew for Federal eyes. "I wouldn't call this layin' low."

"Captain Atwater doesn't have to know how you spend the Lord's Day," Mary said, shooting a quick look at Peg. "You aren't his slave. You didn't tell him you're with me today, did you?"

Peg shook her head. "No, but he knows we're friends. I never worried about Captain Atwater because he's been sympathetic with what Miss Van Lew is doin' for Yankee prisoners. But after what happened with Missus Baker, that could all change."

Mary shook the reins. "I wouldn't fret about it, Peg."

That was Mary's solution for everything. *Don't fret about it.* She may have nerves of steel, but not Peg. Mary regularly conveyed messages from Elizabeth Van Lew to a farm that the lady owned on the southern outskirts of Richmond. The farm was run by William Brisby, a free black employed by the Van Lews—another part of the ever-growing Van Lew spy network. It was a frigid day, with a slate gray sky and a scattering of snowflakes swirling across the ground when the wind kicked up. Peg sneezed and coughed, and she wondered why on earth she had gone out in this weather with a soreness scratching at her throat.

"Rebel pickets ahead," Mary said.

Three armed Rebel soldiers, one standing and two crouching, guarded the turnpike. Peg had made this delivery several times with Mary before, so she knew what was coming. But that didn't make it any easier. Peg placed the basket of eggs in the back of the wagon, along with bread, blankets, a coil of rope, and other supplies for the farm. She didn't try to hide the basket, however, because that would raise suspicions. Their coded messages were hidden in plain sight.

The three soldiers stepped into the road, and one signaled for them to halt. Mary brought the wagon to a slow rolling stop and offered them her brightest smile. Peg didn't know how Mary maintained such composure.

"Good afternoon, sirs," Mary called out before lowering her eyes.

One of the soldiers actually tipped his hat—a friendly gesture that calmed Peg just a bit. A second soldier looked bored by the routine, but the third man was clearly not in a friendly mood for two Negro women.

"Passes," he demanded.

Mary obliged, handing over the passes that Miss Van Lew had written out.

"We's headin' out to the farm to pick up vittles for Confederate men who be convalescing back in Richmond," said Mary, shedding her educated tone and talking like the men expected. Peg said nothing. She shivered.

The irritable man stared at the pass, which carried the name of Elizabeth Van Lew. The soldiers had probably heard of the infamous Richmond lady, but if they knew their duty, they would also know they could not harm the servants of a wealthy Southern family, no matter what her reputation might be.

"What you got back here?" asked the friendlier man, craning his neck to peer into the back of their wagon.

The bored soldier reached in and fondled one of the blankets. "Could use one of these to warm my nights," he said sullenly.

"Ain't our property to take," said the friendly one.

The irritable soldier finally finished reading the pass, shoved it in Mary's hand, wandered around back, and rummaged through the supplies. "What's the eggs for?" he asked. "Thought y'all were pickin' up food at the farm. Why you *bringin'* food then?"

"The hired hand on the farm, he like the eggs we gots from the birds back at Miss Van Lew's house," Mary said.

"The eggs sure look tasty." The bored soldier reached out to grab the basket.

Peg's heart was in her throat. Three of the eggs contained secret messages, but Lordy, she forgot which was which.

Mary moved quickly, without looking panicked, and she lifted out the basket before the man's fingers could latch onto an egg. "Let me pick out a dandy one for y'all, sir. I know which ones are finest."

Peg stared in wonderment while Mary looked over each egg carefully, as if assessing the quality. "Here y'all be."

She handed over a single egg to each man, and the sudden spark of generosity softened the expression of the irritable-looking man. Food had a way of doing that.

"Tell Miss Van Lew that we thank her kindly." The friendly soldier tipped his hat once again. The grumpy soldier was already using his knife to poke a hole in his egg and drink it down. His fingers looked red and raw and stiff with cold.

Finished with the egg, he tossed aside the empty shell. "That went down smooth. I'll take another."

Peg let out a soft gasp. There were nine remaining eggs, and three of them contained coded messages. Peg prayed that Mary knew exactly which three they were.

"We need some eggs remainin' or our farmer friend'll be sore at us," Mary said, handing another egg to each man.

The grumpy soldier told her where her farmer friend could go before he sucked another egg dry. Then he reached out his hand and motioned with his fingers.

"Another."

"But sir . . ."

"Another!"

The friendly soldier said that he had had enough thank you, so Mary handed out eggs to the other two men. That left four eggs in the basket—only one of them real. If they asked for more . . .

Yellow yoke dripped in the grouchy man's beard, and he ran his tongue around his mouth after finishing off his third egg. The bored man burped and tossed aside his shell.

Then the grumpy man held out a hand and motioned with his fingers.

"Another."

This was it, Peg thought. They were going to be discovered, hauled into town, and hanged. This was her last day on earth.

Mary stared, not handing over a single egg. She had only one to spare, and two of the soldiers wanted one.

"Another!"

"But sir . . ."

"Another!"

Mary didn't budge. Then Peg leaned over and lifted the basket out of Mary's hands. She had no idea which of the four eggs was real, but she heard herself saying, "Mary, dear, these soldiers sure are hungry. We should just give them the rest of the eggs."

Mary's eyes widened. She must have been wondering if Peg had gone mad.

Then Peg sneezed. It was a walloping big sneeze, and it showered a fine saliva mist over all of the eggs in the basket.

"God bless you," Mary said, her eyes brightening.

"Thank you."

Then Peg sneezed a second time for good measure, making sure that her spit was as clear as rain. The eggs glistened with spittle.

The soldiers said nothing. The grumpy man, his right hand still extended, stared—his mouth gaping like a guppy.

Peg wiped her nose with her right hand, ignoring the lace handkerchief up her sleeve. She snorted and coughed and picked up one of the eggs with her right hand.

The soldiers continued to stare, and Peg prayed that they believed, like many people, that she had just ejected her life force—a *Negro's* life force—all over the eggs. Other people believed you were emitting an evil spirit when you sneezed, and not too many people would want to down an egg covered in an evil spirit, especially one that had just shot out of the mouth of a black woman.

"Another?" Peg asked, holding out her basket.

The grumpy man withdrew his hand, while the bored one burped again. "Don't know 'bout you, but I'm filled to the brim," the bored soldier said.

Peg coughed again, for emphasis.

"Move on," the irritable one said, but not until he reached into the back of the wagon and ripped off half of the loaf of bread. That was fine with Peg. No messages were buried there.

"Thank y'all," said Mary, shaking the reins, and the wagon lurched forward. They didn't look back until they were long past the three Confederate pickets.

"Thank you," Mary said to Peg. "I knew there was a reason I bring y'all along on these missions."

21

THE HALF-FROZEN GROUND CRUNCHED UNDER JOHN'S FEET AS he and four members of the Lincoln League trudged in the direction of the Rebel winter camp in Centreville. Alongside him were Cleon, Gallus Turner, Abram Fox, and Hackey Pickens. Hackey, the youngest of them, barely twenty years old, was still wearing his Zouave uniform with the red cap. John didn't know how Hackey kept the uniform so snapping bright in these rough conditions.

Once again, John, Cleon, Gallus, and Hackey all carried sacks of rolls, for if they were spotted by Rebel pickets, they could simply say they were delivering food to the troops. Abram Fox carried a bottle instead of a sack of rolls, and he held out his whiskey for any to grab.

"Care for a swig?"

None of them dared, for they knew better than to go near any concoction of Abram's.

"I would just as soon put my arm in a bobcat's mouth than drink that down," said John.

"Wouldn't surprise me if that bottle was a mixture of bark juice, tar-water, turpentine, brown sugar, lamp oil, and alcohol," added Gallus.

"Puts fire in the blood." Abram downed a mouthful, his Adam's apple bobbing up and down.

As they crossed a narrow, trickling stream using long strides, Cleon started talking about the Four Horsemen of the Apocalypse, and a light snow began to fall. He went into excruciating detail about the symbolism of the Red Horse of War, the Black Horse of Famine, the White Horse of Conquest, and the Pale Horse of Death, but all that John could think was that his toes ached in this weather.

They tramped about another half mile through the woods until Abram let out a curse, came to a sudden standstill, and pointed to the sky. "Tell me if I ain't seein' the End of Times right before my very eyes. Or is the drink puttin' strange pictures in my head?"

All eyes followed his pointed finger, and John could barely believe what they saw in the sky, partially blocked by the treetops, but clear as day. It was a hot air balloon, drifting across the land like some strange beast. John had heard about the use of balloons by Union spies over the past year, but he had never seen one in real life.

"Your eyes ain't deceivin' you, Abram," said John. "That's a spy balloon."

"You can come out from behind the tree," said Gallus to young Hackey, who had obviously never seen a hot air balloon before. "It ain't a livin' thing."

The five Lincoln League men were fascinated by the sight so they followed the balloon, no longer paying close attention to the direction they were heading. When they reached a clearing, they got a good view of the balloon, and that's when they heard the first boom of artillery. Confederate soldiers were firing on the aircraft.

"They ain't gonna be able to angle their artillery to shoot that thing out of the sky," said Gallus. "Mark my words."

No sooner did Gallus voice his opinion than something from the sky came crashing into the woods like a meteor. A cannonball smashed through the trees, snapping limbs not too far from where they were standing.

"They might not be able to shoot it out of the sky, but they might just shoot us right off this mortal world!" shouted Hackey, and he hightailed back in the direction they had come. Realizing they had wandered into the path of cannon fire, the other four followed on his heels. Hackey led the charge as another boom sounded, and another cannonball crash-landed in the woods behind them.

Safely out of range, they stopped to catch their breaths, exhaling steam into the air. John leaned over, hands on his knees, trying to catch his breath. When he straightened up, his eyes scanned the sky for any sign of the balloon, but it seemed to have drifted out of view. The cannon fire had ceased as well, so perhaps the balloon had retreated back in the direction of Washington. His eyes lingered on the trees as he scanned the sky, for he had noticed something peculiar, something very strange among the branches.

When John finally realized what he was staring at, he bolted forward.

"What you think you're doin'?" called out Cleon. "You're headin' back for where we just ran!"

John stopped at the base of a thick tree and stared up. By this time, the others had seen what he had spotted, and they all came running over. They stared up at the branch, from which a body dangled. John's heart sank, for the body was that of another black man. This one was wrapped up in a U.S. flag, like a cocoon hanging from a tree.

"Cut him down," John told Hackey. The young man was up the tree in no time; as he shimmied along the branch, the stiff body swung back and forth slightly, wood creaking.

"Y'all ready?" asked Hackey, drawing out his knife.

"We'll catch him," said John.

Belly-down on the branch, Hackey carved away at the rope. No one said a word as the body dropped into their arms, about six feet below the branch. Like the other victim they had found, the dead body had stiffened, and it was like catching a massive marble statue. John was almost afraid the body would shatter like stone if it struck the ground full force. They braced the body's fall and drew it carefully to the ground.

The men pulled off their hats in respect, for the face of the dead man was painfully familiar, at least to John. The man was Charley Jones, who had been a member of the Lincoln League for about six months now. A married man with six children. There was writing across the flag again, and John unrolled the banner to read the words.

"What's it say?" asked Gallus.

John scratched the side of his face. "It says, THIS IS THE SECOND."

No one said a word. They looked at each other, stone-faced all of them, except for Abram. He looked away, tears building in his eyes.

Gallus finally had the courage to say what everyone was thinking. "I do believe that someone is huntin' us down one by one."

22

EG AND MARY MADE SEVERAL MORE RUNS OUT TO THE FARM for Elizabeth Van Lew, carrying additional messages. But after the close call with the eggs, Miss Van Lew had Mary sew a leather pocket into the bottom of her shoes, where they concealed the coded messages.

On this Saturday, a day as cold as ice, they had brought back a treat from the farm—several pigs ready for butchering. Peg helped out when her chores were done at the Atwaters. Working alongside Mary Bowser and some of the free black men employed at the Van Lew house—Oliver Lewis and James and Peter Roane—she toiled into the night, hand salting the pork before packing it into tubs of salt, which drew the moisture out of the meat, readying it for the smokehouse. She was exhausted, but she knew that Miss Van Lew would reward her with a sizable hunk of pork, maybe even give her the pancreas to fry up for sweetbreads. It would be well worth it.

The next day was Sunday, a day of welcome rest, so Mary and Peg decided to stay the night at the Van Lew house, rather than venture across town in the dark. After working late, they retreated to the room on the top floor because they weren't about to risk being on the streets after the curfew fell for black folk in Richmond. They sure didn't want to wind up in the Cage.

The Van Lew house was a large mansion on Grace Street, between 23rd and 24th Streets. It stood three and a half stories tall, with an enormous two-story Doric piazza on the back facing the sprawling gardens, which had retreated into a bleak dormancy this time of year.

Peg shared the cramped bed with Mary, who was almost as active while sleeping as she was by day. Peg tired of Mary's jabs in the ribs and kicks to the shins, so she eventually curled up on the floor to sleep. Mary had taken the entire blanket and clutched it around herself tenaciously, even in slumber, but Peg managed to scrounge up a thin blanket for herself and find a spot on the cold wood floor.

By first morning light, a bird outside the window started singing, and Peg could sense that she was too wound up to go back to sleep. Besides, the sun was already beginning to appear on the horizon, so they would be rising soon anyway. She raised herself from the floor, listening carefully to the birdcall—a habit that always reminded her of John. It sounded like the bird was singing "Cheer-up, cheer-up, cheer-up." Definitely a robin. She went to the room's lone window and pulled aside the curtain, but not too much because she didn't want a torrent of light to wake up Mary. Then she followed the sound and scoured the bare trees, her eyes finally landing on an orange-breasted early bird, perched on a branch. If John had been here, she would have been rewarded with a kiss for guessing correctly. She missed him so much that it was painful.

Peg let the heavy drapes fall back in place, plunging the room into darkness. But before she could make an attempt to go back to sleep, she heard a soft rapping on their door. Then the voice of the butler, William Sewell: "Miss Mary, Miss Mary, you're needed downstairs."

"I will wake her, Mister Sewell," Peg called out, and the butler said, "Thank you, Miss Peg," before thumping down the stairs.

Waking Mary was easier said than done. But after about five minutes of tugging, Mary roused and they dressed rapidly.

"I was out like a log," Mary said. "I hope you slept as well as I did."

Peg didn't answer, and when they got downstairs, they found Miss Van Lew in a state of agitation. Miss Elizabeth Van Lew, better known as Miss Lizzie, was a small, energetic woman with bright blue eyes, ringlets spilling down her head, and a sharp pointed nose that added to her bird-like qualities. When she was agitated, she fluttered with hummingbird energy.

"Mary, we need to make a custard and some hot bread for the prisoners," she said. "We are needed at the hospital."

By "we," she obviously meant that Mary was the one who needed to make the custard and hot bread—with Peg's assistance.

"The hospital, ma'am?" said Mary.

"Yesterday, Secretary Memminger finally agreed to let us visit Federal soldiers in Harwood's prison hospital. With all of the work going on in the house, I was going to wait until Monday to visit. But I woke up inspired and thought we'd jump at the opportunity today."

Peg wished she felt equally inspired. But she had to admit that this was big news. Miss Lizzie had been taking food, blankets, and reading materials to Yankee prisoners of war since the Battle of Manassas in July, but no amount of flattery had convinced authorities to let her into the prisons to see the men in person. Now, that had suddenly changed. She was going to see Yankee prisoners in the hospital.

So they set about baking. Peg had planned on this being a morning of well-needed rest, with church at First African Baptist, but Miss Lizzie had other ideas. Not being employed by Miss Van Lew, Peg didn't have to help out, but she worried that the mistress might forget about her reward of pork if she didn't.

So, while Mary prepared the crust, Peg beat twelve eggs, mixed them with a quart and a half of new milk, and strained it all through a fine sieve. Then she added sugar and a pinch of salt. They cooked three custard pies and several loaves of bread, and the kitchen filled with delectable smells that made Peg's stomach rumble with hunger.

When all was ready, Miss Lizzie motioned for the custard pans. Carefully, Mary lifted up the custard pie, and Peg was shocked to see that the pan had a false bottom. Beneath the false bottom was a secret space, where Miss Lizzie placed money and messages. Then Mary put the custard pie back in place and did the same with the second and third pies. Peg figured they were bringing food to the prisoners, but she hadn't bargained on smuggling messages. Was there no end to Miss Lizzie's subterfuges? Did she not even rest her spying on the Lord's Day?

On the way to the hospital, Mary was in high spirits, considering the early hour they had been roused and the fact that they were carrying dishes that could get them thrown into jail. Whenever they approached someone on the streets of Richmond, Miss Lizzie would cock her head like an inquisitive bird and mutter to herself. It was all part of her act as she cultivated the role of an eccentric woman. In fact, some people had taken to calling her Crazy Bet, and Peg had heard the name bandied about in the Atwater house. Captain Atwater was too much of a gentleman to use it himself, but Missus Hicks thought it was quite amusing.

Harwood's Hospital stood on the southwest corner of 26th and Main Streets. It was a rectangular block of a building, three stories high—a former tobacco factory owned by George D. Harwood. Hospitals had sprouted up all across Richmond since the war began, but most of them tended to Confederate casualties. The Confederate hospitals attracted an army of volunteers—loyal Southern women who showered the injured soldiers with care. Miss Lizzie, Mary, and Peg were about to become the first Richmond folks to provide similar volunteer nursing attention to injured Federal soldiers.

As they approached the building, which was a combination prison and hospital, they found it heavily guarded by Rebel sentinels. No surprise there. Peg looked up and saw the silent faces of Yankee prisoners staring down from the barred windows on the second floor. One of the prisoners grinned and gazed straight at her, so Peg immediately averted her eyes and looked straight ahead. Miss Lizzie stopped at a white line, painted on the brick surface, and two guards approached swiftly.

"Good morning, young men," said Miss Lizzie. "We are here under the authority of the Secretary of Treasury Memminger to provide ministrations to the injured soldiers inside. On the Lord's Day, we all need solace."

"No one enters without a permit," said the first guard, a young man, clean-shaven. The second guard lifted up the cloth covering the pies in Peg's hands and took a whiff of the sweet custard smell.

"I understand," said Miss Lizzie. "I carry a permit that allows me and my two servants to enter."

Peg felt a bit odd being described as one of Miss Lizzie's servants. She wasn't a servant in any official capacity, but had she become so closely linked to this infamous woman that she had become an unofficial servant of sorts?

While one guard studied the permit, the second one pulled out a knife, and for a moment Peg wondered if he meant them harm. Instead, he inserted the knife into the custard.

"Young man, what do you think you are doing?" asked Miss Lizzie.

"Gotta be sure you ain't baked a weapon inside this custard."

"Then I hope y'all are using a clean knife."

"A little rust ain't never harmed no one." The guard continued to probe, slipping the knife through the custard in at least a dozen different spots.

"We worked hard on these pies, sir, so I would thank you not to destroy them in your investigation."

"They don't need to be pretty. All custard looks the same once it's snaked through a person's gut," said the guard with a grin.

Miss Lizzie displayed her disgust, but at last they were approved, and the guards escorted them toward the front door.

"Don't know why y'all want to help the enemy," said the second guard as they approached the door. "These men should be shot, not given delicacies."

"If we wish our Southern cause to succeed," Miss Lizzie said, "we must begin with charity to the thankless. It is the Christian thing to do."

In two simple sentences, she had connected on two counts—devotion to the Southern cause and devotion to Jesus. She may be Crazy Bet to some, but she knew what she was doing.

The guard grunted his response.

"Love is the fulfilling of the law," Miss Lizzie added, a phrase that Peg had heard her use many times before.

The first thing Peg noticed as they entered the dimly lit, former tobacco factory was the odor. The fetid smell of bloody bandages hung in the air, combined with the stink of bedpans, and Peg almost gagged. She brought the custard closer to her nose, hoping it would mask the odor. Rows of narrow beds flanked each wall. Every bed was taken—close to one hundred, Peg figured. As they ran this gauntlet, some men moaned, most were asleep, and a few offered their thanks. Peg tried to keep her eyes on the back of Miss Lizzie, who turned and smiled to the men on either side. Miss Lizzie didn't look the least bit flustered by the suffering and the smell.

While Miss Lizzie tended to the men, Peg and Mary cut thin slices of custard pie, trying to feed as many as possible. But three pies were not going to go nearly far enough, unless they could perform some Sabbath Day miracle of the loaves and the fishes and the custard. They cut the pies on a wooden table positioned right beside another table where the surgeon had laid out an assortment of knives and saws used for lopping off limbs. Peg hoped that the knife she used hadn't doubled as a surgeon's knife. And as the custard wobbled beneath her knife, she pictured for a moment that she was cutting into human flesh, and once again she came close to getting sick. The last thing these men needed was her vomiting all over their food.

Peg was relieved when they finally exited the hospital over an hour later, although it had felt like an eternity. Miss Lizzie sure better be giving her plenty of pork as a reward for this mission, and she hoped she would never have to make such a visit again.

"The bread and custard pies did not go far enough," announced Miss Lizzie as they headed back to her mansion on Church Hill. "We will have to do this again. Soon."

Peg groaned inside. As she walked with an empty custard pan in her hands, she couldn't contain her curiosity, so she lifted up the false bottom and noticed that it was now empty. Somehow, some way, during all of her ministrations, Elizabeth Van Lew had slipped the money and messages to some of the wounded men. The woman was a magician.

Miss Lizzie marched into the Church Hill neighborhood with Peg and Mary following in her wake. As she passed a husband and wife of high standing, she muttered to herself and cocked her head. Peg noticed the elderly couple stare over their shoulders, and the old man shook his head in judgment.

Crazy Bet paid them no heed. She never did.

23

ABRAM FOX STARED AT JOHN WITHOUT THE TRACE OF A SMILE.
He tossed a rock in his hands and glowered.

"You go on now. Just run back to the white men who is pullin' your strings," he snapped at John.

"Now Abram, you know that ain't fair," said Cleon.

Abram hurled the rock into the woods, and it clunked off the side of a tree. "What's not fair is Mister High and Mighty Scobell leavin' for Washington City right at the time when someone is huntin' us down, one by one, puttin' a bullet through our heads. Very convenient, I'd say."

"I was ordered back by Mister Pinkerton," John said, tossing another log on the fire that they were using to toast their shins. "He has another mission for me."

"I understand," said Gallus, in a much more reasonable tone of voice than Abram. "But do you really have to jump when they call?"

John's right fist curled into a clench. He was not Mister Pinkerton's boy. This morning, the Pinkerton double agent, Ethan Hancock, had tracked down John and told him he was wanted back in Washington to meet up with Mister Webster and Miss Hattie. Hancock said he would escort John as far as Fairfax, and then a different white agent would accompany him the rest of the way to Washington, ensuring that he wasn't snatched by Rebels along the way. At the moment, Hancock was off making contact with another agent, but just as soon as he returned, he and John were leaving. Cleon insisted he was going to Washington too, and that didn't sit well with Abram and Gallus.

"Don't you think you can ever say no to them?" Gallus asked.

"I have a duty to our country," John said.

"Washington white folks ain't part of *my* country," said Abram. "This here is my country, this square mile right here in Virginia." He waved his hand at their concealed cabin in the woods.

"This country you see 'round here is *slave* country, you fool. And if we want to make it free country, we gotta help the Yankees, like John is doin'," said Cleon. "You're just jealous 'cause you ain't been given a mission by the intelligence service."

Abram scoffed. Gallus stared at John like a skeptical judge, while Hackey tried to stay out of the argument. He hated seeing people get riled up.

"*Jealous?*" Abram said, as if the word had a foul taste. "I ain't jealous. Why would I want to go off and serve a white man, while people here is gettin' killed, one right after another?"

"I'll speak to Mister Pinkerton about what's happenin' down here," said John. "Maybe he can help."

That set Abram to laughing. "You think he's gonna help out a pack of colored spies?"

Even Gallus didn't seem convinced there was any chance of that ever happening. "Be realistic, John."

"I don't like leavin' neither, not with what's been happenin'," said John, trying to appease Abram. He spoke the truth, for he did feel guilty about leaving. He felt guilty leaving Peg, and now he felt like a deserter by leaving his friends in the Lincoln League. But he had a duty to perform.

Abram dug another rock from the cold soil, sat down on a fallen tree, and jiggled it in his hands. "You know, all of this dyin' started happenin' when you made your acquaintance with that Webster man."

"What're you sayin'?" John narrowed his eyes.

Abram smiled back sardonically. "I'm sayin' it's mighty suspicious that Lincoln Leaguers started dyin' not long after you told him 'bout us and even had him come to one of our meetings near Leonardtown."

Cleon shot to his feet. "You sayin' Mister Webster is betrayin' us?"

Abram leaped to his feet in turn, and the two men moved toward each other, squaring off about three feet apart.

"I'm sayin' you can't trust a white man!"

John stepped between, pushing Cleon and Abram apart, but Abram slapped his hand away, and John struck back. He shoved Abram backward, and the man tumbled over the fallen tree and came back up spitting mad. Cleon didn't even try to contain his laughter, while John put up his fists, ready for action. His blood was boiling. Abram may be ten years older than him, but even old men needed to be taught a lesson.

"Stop it!"

Hackey had been getting increasingly agitated as tempers flared on all sides. But now he was on his feet, squeezing his eyes shut and yelling at the top of his lungs. It was like he was having a fit. Hackey was usually so quiet that it was sometimes easy to forget he was there—and that he hated conflict among his friends. Tensions sometimes pushed him to a breaking point.

"*Stop it Stop it Stop it Stop it Stop it Stop it!*"

John backed away from Abram, hands up, while Gallus worked to calm down Hackey.

"We're stoppin'," said Abram, who seemed genuinely alarmed by the young man's frenzy. "Calm down, Hackey, we ain't fightin'." He put his hands in the air, like a man surrendering.

Hackey continued to stare at his feet, and his body seemed to convulse, as if it was being shot through with electricity. Gallus put a hand on both of his shoulders and said, "It's all right, it's all right."

"Hackey, look, we're shakin' hands," said John, extending his hand to Abram.

Abram stared at the hand for a few moments, not moving, as if John had offered him something poisonous. Finally, he reluctantly took one step forward and gave John's hand a cursory shake. Abram wouldn't make eye contact.

It took a good five minutes to calm Hackey down, and when they finally did, the group went stone cold silent. Even Cleon was quiet for a change—until Ethan Hancock showed up back in their camp, all smiles.

"You about ready to go?" Hancock asked John.

"We were ready yesterday," said Cleon.

Hancock looked around at the others. "You boys keep up the good work. Y'all are servin' your country with courage."

"Thank you, sir," said Gallus with a monotone voice. Abram didn't answer; he just stared at John. Hackey was the only one who gave Hancock a smile; it was an awkward smile, but at least it was something.

"I'm really sorry to be takin' John away from y'all, but Mister Pinkerton has some important work for him."

John flinched inside. Hancock probably didn't mean it, but his words made it sound like staying here with the Lincoln League would *not* be important work. No one responded.

"Cleon, you still plannin' on comin' with us?" Hancock asked.

"Lord, yes."

"If anyone stops us along the way, you tell him you're my free-born indentured servants," Hancock said to Cleon and John.

As John nodded, he noticed Cleon grimacing and sensed him bristling at the words "indentured servant," which weren't much better than the word "slave." But for once, Cleon kept quiet. He probably didn't want to say anything that would give Hancock an excuse to leave him behind.

John shot a look at Abram, as if daring him to say something about them pretending to be indentured servants. But Abram's mouth remained firmly closed. He folded his arms across his chest.

For a moment, John was tempted to tell Hancock that he had decided to stay, to prove he wasn't afraid of any madmen in this forest. He felt embarrassed to be heading off, trailing a white man, while the others had to grapple with whatever was out there.

John spoke up. "Mister Hancock, sir . . ."

"Yes, John?"

John kept his eyes on Abram and didn't speak for several seconds. "I'm as ready as ready."

And so they marched off in the direction of Washington, and neither John nor Cleon ever looked back.

*****

"You're going back to Richmond," said Allan Pinkerton.

John was thrilled to hear those words from the intelligence service director. It was a new year—1862—and he was back in Washington sitting in Pinkerton's office along with Timothy Webster and Hattie Lawton, who looked striking in a snug-fitting green vest and a gold hairpin adorning her hair.

John hadn't seen his wife Peg since he had left Richmond six months ago. He tried to keep his eyes from wandering to Hattie, but being in the woods for so long, he had almost forgotten how nice a woman could look and smell. He was happy to be in fresh clothes, for one of the first things he did upon arriving in Washington was find a tub of steaming water and a bar of soap.

"Your work has been invaluable," Pinkerton said, looking from Webster to John. "I have passed on the details to General McClellan, and he was very interested to know that General Johnston was operating with 104 regiments and General Magruder had 29 regiments."

Pinkerton said he still needed more information on Confederate defenses in Richmond, so Webster and Miss Hattie would go there posing as husband and wife, while John would be their servant.

"You're a hero throughout Virginia and Maryland," Pinkerton said to Webster. "People see you and Hancock as two of the Confederacy's finest spies."

Webster smiled at Pinkerton's confidence in him, and he was about to say something when he was overcome by a brief coughing fit.

"I hope you didn't catch anything during your Potomac crossing, my husband," said Miss Hattie. "I sure wouldn't want to catch anything from you."

"I doubt you would let me near enough," said Webster, smiling again until he was convulsed by another paroxysm of coughing.

Webster had told them about the miserable river crossing in December, when he was being ferried across the Potomac in a cold, driving rain with the wives and children of two Confederate officers. In a safe house across the river, Webster noticed that one of the women had dropped a bundle of papers wrapped in oilcloth and tied with red tape. Inside the bundle were maps of the terrain around Washington and quite accurate counts of Federal troops.

Webster coughed again, from deep in his chest, and he buried his face in his handkerchief.

"Are you certain you are up for this?" asked Miss Hattie, and John's heart dropped. If Webster didn't go to Richmond, then neither would he.

"I would never pass up an opportunity to pose as your husband, ma'am."

"Then you leave for Richmond immediately," said Pinkerton—music to John's ears.

It was obvious that Timothy Webster would have to be on his deathbed to consider giving up the chance to pretend he was Miss Hattie's beloved. But their love was all a show, while John had something much more substantial. He had a real wife waiting for him in Richmond, and it was about time they had their arms around each other again.

24

OHN PAUSED TO STAMP THE JANUARY COLD OUT OF HIS TOES, and then he resumed his trudge down Franklin Street in Richmond under a slate-gray afternoon sky, heading in the direction of the Atwater house. He pulled the coat around himself tighter, and the snow came down in fine flakes, covering the frozen mud in a white veneer. He still had his pack on his back because he was finally going to be able to give Peg the doll he had been carrying all over tarnation.

Before heading to the Atwaters, John had helped to settle Webster and Miss Hattie into Richmond's finest establishment, the sparkling new Spotswood Hotel on the corner of 8th and Main. The task took longer than he had hoped, given the rapidly deteriorating condition of Timothy Webster. Upon entering the luxurious hotel lobby, Webster put on a fine performance as his many Richmond friends greeted him. But the moment he reached their room, he collapsed on the bed. John wet some rags for Miss Hattie to put on Webster's forehead, which she said felt like touching a hot stove. Then she finally told John "to go on and see his missus," and she would tend to Mister Webster, whose cough had become buried deep in his chest.

Now that John was on his way to see Peg for the first time in six months, he was as nervous as the first time he met her at church six and a half years ago. He knocked on the servant's door in back, and Gilbert Mann answered. They had never been friends, and John didn't trust the man within a mile of his wife.

Gilbert looked shocked to see him, and then his face shifted to obvious disappointment. Gilbert forced a smile, and it looked as if he was about to snap a facial muscle just trying to crack the faintest glimmer of a grin.

"John! Welcome home, brother." There wasn't a trace of sincerity in the man's tone.

"Good to be back, Brother Gilbert."

Gilbert stepped aside and let John enter. John stamped the snow off his shoes, wiped them on the mat, and shook the moisture from his hat.

"Find any work in Fredericksburg, John boy?"

John stared back coldly. "I'm serving a gentleman and a lady, a Mister and Missus Webster. They're settled in at the Spotswood."

Gilbert whistled. "The Spotswood! Must have pockets lined with gold."

John wasn't in the mood for idle chatter. "Where's Peg?"

"Your wife? Wasn't sure if you'd remember her name after all these months."

If that was a joke, John didn't smile at it.

"What's that supposed to mean?"

"I'm just sayin' you been gone so long, it's easy for a man to forget he's married—and sometimes even a woman forgets."

John didn't want to spoil his reunion with Peg; that was the only thing preventing him from knocking Gilbert to the floor. He moved within a foot of the man.

Gilbert backpedaled quickly and put up his hands. "Let me fetch her for you. Seein' as you don't live here no more, I don't think Mister Atwater would care to see a strange black man tramping through his house, drippin' snow everywhere."

John remained at the back door, creating a puddle around his brogans and trying to calm down. He took a deep breath and tried to focus his thoughts on Peg. He finally decided his shoes were dry enough to step from the mat, and he wandered through Matilda's orderly kitchen, which seemed exactly the same as when he left it—not one utensil out of place.

"*John?*"

He spun around and saw Peg standing on the kitchen threshold, framed in the doorway like a beautiful portrait. Seeing her that way, he wondered if he had been a fool to ever leave her. Hard housework hadn't aged her in the four and a half years they had been married, but he knew that his six months in the wilds had changed his appearance. His face had become much thinner, and everything about him had become harder and sharper, more feral. Living on the ragged edges of an army will do that.

Gilbert stood two steps behind Peg. John waited for him to leave, but the man didn't budge.

"You can go now, Gilbert," John said, using the tone of a master dismissing a servant.

Gilbert glowered and didn't move.

"Please, we need to be alone," Peg said, using a much softer touch. Gilbert turned on his heels and left.

John took one step forward, and that movement acted as a trigger, sending Peg rushing across the kitchen. She threw herself in his arms, and he absorbed her warmth and smelled her hair, and he wondered once again if he was mad to have given her up, even for six months. They remained in this embrace for a long time, no words spoken. He moved his hands across her back, feeling the smooth fabric of her dress. Abram Fox had told him many times that he was a fool not to go tomcatting with him, but if Abram could meet Peg, the man would know why he chose the path of honor. Only a true fool would tomcat behind the back of such a woman.

"Why didn't you send word?" Peg asked.

John was disappointed that she had broken the spell by speaking.

"No opportunity. I didn't know until this week that I was even returning to Richmond."

"Are you back to stay?"

"I wish I could say I am."

"I wasn't sure . . . I didn't know if you were even alive," Peg said.

"You didn't need to worry none."

"Yes, I did."

Peg pulled out of the embrace. "I'm glad they didn't use y'all in the army. I seen the Federal soldiers taken half dead into the city as prisoners. I'm right, ain't I, that they didn't put you in the army? They ain't usin' black folk to fight."

"They didn't even use me to block cannonballs." John put his arms back around Peg. "But they did use us. They still are." He put his mouth close to Peg's ear. "I'm gatherin' information."

"Peg Scobell, who told you that you can take a break?"

Peg pushed away from John and whirled around. Missus Hicks loomed in the doorway, hands on her hips, just as John always remembered her.

"I'm sorry, Missus Hicks, but John has come home."

Missus Hicks stared at John. No smile. Nothing.

"I see him standing there. You think I'm blind?"

"No, ma'am." said Peg.

"Good afternoon, ma'am," said John, maintaining an even stare. He was a free man and wasn't about to give this woman the "down look" of a slave. Missus Hicks stared back, fiercely.

"You have work to do, Peg, so get to it!"

"May I please say good-bye to my husband, ma'am? I haven't seen him in some six months."

"I don't care if you haven't seen him in some six *years*. Back to work, or you can walk out that door alongside him and not return!"

"I'd better go," John said softly, giving Peg a peck on the cheek.

"Henrietta, I make all employment decisions around here," came another voice, and John was shocked to see Captain Atwater appear behind the old lady. From what John could remember, Captain Atwater was not one to challenge Old Lady Hicks. He wondered what had transpired in the past half year to give him a little more backbone.

Missus Hicks gave Captain Atwater her most terrible glare before charging off. Then the master of the house directed his gaze at John and smiled. "Good afternoon, John. Where are you staying?"

"At the Spotswood with my employers, sir."

"Ah, very nice. Peg, you may give your husband a proper good-bye, and then it would be best for you to finish your chores."

"Yes, sir, thank you, sir."

Hooking arms, Peg and John stepped out the back door and into the elements, with a fine curtain of snow still falling. John opened his great coat and wrapped it around her and they embraced again.

"Wish I could take you with me," John said.

"How long are your employers in Richmond for?"

"Don't rightly know. My boss-man is down with a bad sickness, so it could be longer than he bargained for."

"Y'all take care of yourself then. I don't want you catchin' the fever."

"And I don't want you catchin' the shivers," John said, giving his wife an extended kiss, to make up for lost time. Then he held her closely, not wanting to give her back to Missus Hicks and Captain Atwater.

"I almost forgot," John said, drawing back and swinging his pack off of his back. "I brought a present for you."

"A present? John Scobell, you're the only man I know who could go off to battle and return home with a gift."

"I know you're a little old for this, but maybe when we have a little girl someday . . ." John pulled the doll out of the pack.

He handed it to Peg, and she took it in her arms as gently as if it was a living thing. She and John had not been able to have children for the past four and a half years, and she worried whether she would ever have a child.

"I never had a doll growin' up, except the ones I made out of sticks and string."

"I know. That's why . . ."

Peg embraced John again with her left arm, the doll cradled in her right, and she sobbed into his coat, and John wondered if she was mourning the child she didn't think she would ever have. She had told him that she wondered if her barrenness was because of the treatment she received under Cager Johnson. Damaged beyond repair.

"Thank you, John. It's a treasure."

"Cleon is spooked by the doll, but I think she's quite handsome."

"Cleon?"

"A friend I made out there. He named the doll Lucy Ann."

Peg cocked her head, bird-like. "You have a friend who named a doll?"

"He's a rather unique person. But you better get back in before you catch your death, or Missus Hicks will come out here lookin' for you. I will be back to see you, soon as I can."

"When will that be?"

"Perhaps tomorrow."

"Good-bye, laddie." Peg got on tiptoes and gave him another taste of her lips, and she turned and hurried back inside the warmth of the Atwater house. John stared at the closed door for a minute before heading back for the Spotswood Hotel.

*****

Ichabod lifted his hat and scratched his head using only four fingers on his right hand. He had lost his pinky finger and a toe to frostbite after his frozen plunge in the waters of Hampton Roads, but it could have been much worse. He could have wound up in a submerged grave. But it still felt odd doing even simple things, such as scratching, minus one finger.

The afternoon was cold, and he pulled his coat tighter. Before the near-drowning, this cold would have been easily endurable. But it seemed as if his body had become more sensitive to temperatures after nearly freezing to death. His body's normal fire just wasn't enough to keep him warm. Sitting beside him, as faithful as ever, was his Cuban bloodhound, Ahab.

Ichabod and Ahab had been keeping an eye on the Atwater house ever since he heard that the spy who had given away the secret of their torpedo boat was a Northern lady staying with Captain Atwater. The fool. What kind of malt-horse drudge would bring a Northern woman into the Tredegar Iron Works and then show her a demonstration of their greatest weapon? The captain had been sorely rebuked, but Ichabod would have preferred to see him locked in the Cage for a few days to set an example.

From across the street, Ichabod had seen a colored man come to the house as bold as could be. The man went around back, and

Ichabod followed, and he watched him disappear inside the Atwater home. Ichabod had become familiar with the Atwaters' colored help, but he had never seen this fellow before. He had become especially suspicious of the pretty colored lady by the name of Peg, for he tracked her one Sunday as she strolled on over to the Van Lew residence. Any link between the Atwater house and Van Lew house was enough proof for him that something was going on.

Work had begun in earnest on a second torpedo boat, an improvement over the one that sank. Ichabod's ability to survive the sinking impressed his superiors, so he had a spot reserved on the next torpedo boat once it was finished. Some people questioned his sanity and eagerness to try again after such a close call, but his life was nothing more than a string of close calls.

In addition to the torpedo boats, he had heard that inventors, some of them crackpots, had been flooding the Confederate War Department with ideas. One man suggested dropping torpedoes from hot air balloons, which actually struck Ichabod as a pretty good idea. Another fellow had an idea for unmanned twin boats, propelled by rockets, which could slam into ships. But the War Department concentrated most of its energy on floating torpedoes, deadly kegs of gunpowder that were set off when a ship ran into a trigger cord in the water. There were even ideas to bury land-based torpedoes in the soil to blow up unsuspecting soldiers, but some said this went far beyond the proper rules of war. In Ichabod's way of thinking, anything was fair in war.

Ichabod perked up when he saw the colored boy and the maid, Peg, slip out of the back and embrace in the alleyway. Such open displays disgusted him, even among white couples, but he could do nothing but observe. Then the black man pulled the pack off of his back and reached in and pulled something out for Peg Scobell.

"My, my, what do we have here?" Ichabod said softly to Ahab.

The man was handing her a doll! That sealed it. Peg and this man had to be caught up in something because he knew what those dolls were being used for. After all, he had used one of them himself. He supposed it could be possible that the man was handing her an ordinary doll, but he doubted it.

With Ahab at his side, he followed the black man as he split off from Peg and made his way to the luxurious Spotswood Hotel, which had become the center of Richmond's wartime world—a bustling hub where politicians, military officials, and every sneak and spy gathered to exchange boasts, banter, and secrets. Ichabod tied up his dog outside because he knew that he would attract a lot of attention if he strolled inside with a Cuban bloodhound. Then he followed the colored fellow into the crowded lobby, with its gaudy chandeliers and ornate statues. The black man disappeared up a staircase, and Ichabod followed, mixed in with the crowd. The staircase was a stream of people, moving up and down like ants.

The colored man reached the very top of the hotel, the fifth floor, where the crowd thinned to a trickle. Ichabod pretended to be fishing for his door key in his pocket, keeping an eye on Peg's man. He made a note of the room that the fellow disappeared into, and when the hallway was clear of activity, Ichabod strolled on down and paused before the door. Room 510.

Making a mental note of the room number, he went downstairs to the hotel desk and inquired about the occupants of Room 510. A Mister and Missus Webster. But who was their black servant and what did he have to do with the maid at the Atwater house? It was worth investigating. He took out his pad of paper and jotted down the name "Webster." He wondered if the man in 510 could be Timothy Webster, the famed Confederate courier, but he doubted it. Once again, it felt strange performing routine tasks, such as writing, minus a finger.

As Ichabod exited the hotel, someone from the crowded lobby called out his name, but he kept walking until he was back outside in the elements, away from the noise and the nonsense. He was in no mood for socializing. He never was.

25

EG STARED AT THE CEILING AND PULLED THE QUILT UP TO HER neck. Morning was breaking across Richmond, and John was still deep in sleep next to her, his breathing heavy. Propped up on the dresser was Lucy Ann, the doll in the salmon-colored dress. The doll was white, of course, so that made it slightly disturbing to have her standing there and watching them sleep—like some slave-owner's daughter keeping an eagle eye on them.

John had been in the city for four days now, and for the past two days she had been looking for the right time to tell him about the spying she was doing for Mary. She considered not telling him at all, to keep it her secret, but Mary Bowser wanted John to know of their operation because she hoped to enlist his services.

"Have you told him yet?" Mary had asked yesterday—for what seemed like the tenth time.

When Peg said she was still looking for the right moment, Mary threatened to tell John about the spying herself. But Peg didn't think she would go so far as to tell John behind her back. Mary might lose her services—and their friendship—if she tried such a stunt. Mary could be exhausting to be around.

John shifted and grunted in the narrow bed, pulling the covers tight over his shoulder. It was soothing to have his warm body back beside her. Peg had vowed that today would be the day she told him, but she didn't want to spoil a good thing, now that she finally had him back, and especially since Captain Atwater had allowed him to stay with her. Mister and Missus Webster paid the captain to board John in the Atwater house, so the captain was being well compensated for the extra body in the house. Even Missus Hicks approved of John boarding out with them, because the old lady welcomed a little extra money—especially money from the hands of Timothy Webster and his "wife." When Missus Hicks heard that John was serving Timothy Webster, she started treating John with a little less vitriol. Missus Hicks had heard of Webster and how he had helped secessionists in Baltimore, so he was a true Southern hero in her eyes, a Son of Liberty who carried information from the Confederate Secretary of War himself.

"Good mornin', lassie," said John, using the Scottish term of endearment as they always did.

Peg turned her gaze from the ceiling to her husband and found his eyes wide open, taking her in.

"Mornin', laddie."

With the sun rising, Peg had very little time before she would be expected downstairs. If she was going to tell him today, it had to be soon.

"When you gotta be at the Spotswood?" she asked.

"Don't rightly care," said John, leaning in for a kiss. His breath preceded him, and she shoved him away.

"No kissin' till you use some tooth powder."

Captain Atwater was a stickler for servants with fresh breath, so he insisted that all of them use a tooth powder of his own making, which included bicarbonate of soda, brick dust, and a few other special ingredients she didn't dare ask about. Peg made tooth powder a habit, and she expected John to use the horsehair toothbrush that the captain had kindly given to her. John complained, especially after six months of letting his breath go wild. But Peg knew he would be willing to do whatever was necessary to get some love.

While John tended to his breath, Peg quickly dressed. "How is Mister Webster feeling?"

John responded, but Peg had no idea what he said with all of the tooth powder in his mouth. She heard him spit into the empty bucket they had set next to the bucket of clean water. "His fever is finally comin' down. He's talkin' about headin' outta Richmond for a few days."

His words woke her up like a splash of cold water. "Mister Webster's leavin' Richmond? Does that mean you're goin' with him?"

"No, thankfully. He's off for Nashville with a man named William Campbell."

"Thank the Lord. I didn't want to lose you again so soon."

John walked back into the room, wiping his mouth with a hand towel. He leaned against the doorjamb. "Well . . . I do have a short mission with Miss Hattie, but I won't be gone long."

"Miss Hattie?" Peg didn't like John being around such a beautiful white woman.

"She has to deliver some important papers to a person along the Chickahominy River. But then we're comin' right back."

"But it seems like y'all just got here."

"I won't be gone long."

"When you comin' back?"

"A few days."

John sat down on the edge of the bed next to Peg and put an arm around her. "I've still gotta job to do. This war needs to end with a Federal victory, and we all gotta do what it takes to make that happen."

If ever there was going to be an ideal time for Peg to reveal what she had been doing for Mary Bowser and Miss Van Lew, this was it. "We all gotta do what it takes," he had said, and "we all" certainly included her.

"I understand," Peg said.

She could see his furrowed brow immediately relax, and he drew her in closer and kissed the side of her head.

"My breath suit y'all fine?"

Peg ignored the nibbles on her ear. "You're right. We gotta do what it takes." She paused a beat. "That's why I'm doin' my part too."

Peg was afraid to look him in the eyes when she said this, but she felt the intensity of his stare. "What y'all mean by that?"

"It means I agree with you. It means I gotta contribute. I gotta . . ." She was afraid to finish her sentence. "It means I been collectin' information too."

John shot to his feet. "What're you tryin' to say?"

Putting a finger to her mouth, Peg shushed him. "Don't you be causin' no fuss now, John. Y'all will bring Missus Hicks into this room if you don't calm."

John put his hands on his hips and said, in a soft but stern tone, "You mean you been spyin'?"

"Mary Bowser asked me if I would—"

"*Mary Bowser.* Why ain't I surprised at that?" John stared at the ceiling and groaned.

Peg pierced him with her eyes and spoke just above a whisper. "John Scobell, you tone down that voice, or y'all gonna get us hung."

Sitting back down on the edge of the bed, John leaned in closer. "Have y'all been spyin' in this very house?"

"I'm just collectin' information. I put it in code and hide it in my Bible before passin' it on to Mary and Miss Van Lew."

John buried his face in his hands and rubbed his eyes with his fingertips. Then he glared. "I ain't gonna have a wife of mine playin' the part of a sneakin' spy."

"Sneakin' spy. What do y'all call yourself?"

"I'm a man, and that's different. I ain't gonna have my wife doin' this kind of work."

"Women are good at it, because most people don't suspect a lady to be spyin'."

"'Course they don't suspect women, because it ain't normal for a lady to be doin' that. It ain't natural."

"Miss Hattie is spyin'."

"She ain't normal. And she ain't my wife."

"Yeah, but you probably dream she was."

"We ain't changin' the subject here, Peg. This is about you spyin'. I won't allow it."

Peg felt like slapping John because she knew he wouldn't hit back. She was sorely tempted to take advantage of his chivalry, but she didn't. She bit her lip before snapping at him. "If it ain't been for me, that Missus Baker woulda been caught."

John stood up and walked to the door and back. "You mean the lady who watched the torpedo boat testin' on the James River?"

"I prevented Captain Atwater from findin' her papers. If it wasn't for me, she woulda been caught and maybe the torpedo boat woulda sunk some Yankee ships."

John paused in his pacing and pondered this. She wondered if she had convinced him, but John could be stubborn. "I ain't got a problem with y'all *protectin'* a spy. But I don't want you spyin' yourself. It ain't proper for a man's wife. It ain't natural for a wife to put her children in peril of losin' their mother."

Peg laughed. "If you haven't noticed, John, we ain't got any children."

"And we ain't gonna have any children if y'all get yourself killed. So yes, you're puttin' our *future* children in peril."

"When we have children, I won't spy no more."

"If y'all live long enough to have a child."

This conversation had to end, Peg thought. They were talking softly, but Missus Hicks was as crafty as a spy, snooping and then swooping in on you when you never expected it.

"Ain't y'all got a mission of your own to be goin' to?"

John didn't answer. He just glared back at her.

"Ain't the fair-skinned Miss Hattie waitin' for you?" she added.

John slammed the door on the way out. Peg sat on the edge of the bed, trying to fight back the tears. She didn't want to say goodbye this way, not when he was about to head off on a mission and this could be their last conversation. Suddenly filled with dread, Peg leaped to her feet and ran out of the room, hoping to catch him.

She ran into Missus Hicks instead.

"Peg Scobell, why aren't you downstairs in the kitchen by now, helping Matilda with breakfast? And put on your apron. I'm not having a servant of mine half-dressed."

"Yes, ma'am."

Peg hurried back into the room, and it took a minute to figure out where her apron had wound up. By the time she was down the stairs and to the kitchen, John was gone.

"Your man didn't look none too happy on the way out the door," Matilda said. She already had the skillet sizzling with butter. "But don't you worry none, baby child. Every marriage needs some sparks to keep the fires goin."

Peg stared out the window, contemplating whether she should run after him. But if she did, she might get fired for deserting her stove. She looked at Matilda, who could probably see that she was on the verge of crying. Then she set to work and helped her cook up some flapjacks and bacon. Smoke rose and grease hissed in the pan.

*****

Hackey Pickens jumped over a narrow creek, which wound its way through the forest. His foot hit a patch of half-frozen mud, and he nearly slid back into the water. The last thing he needed in this weather was a wet foot. He had already lost a toe to frostbite a few years back.

Hackey and Abram had spent the day serving up food to the Rebels encamped at Centreville. Ever since the conflict with John Scobell, Abram had been as ornery as a bear and still spouting suspicions about Timothy Webster. They were supposed to be scouting out troop numbers and movements, but Hackey had a hard time keeping numbers straight in his head when Abram was so busy filling it with suspicions and poison. Hackey never could tolerate squabbling, so he decided he had to get away from Abram for a spell, and he volunteered to collect firewood for the soldiers. So the sergeant wrote him a pass, and he plunged into the forest to clear his mind.

Before they parted ways, Abram told him to at least take off his red cap because it was so bright that it could be spotted from the Moon. If there was a murderer roaming the forest, the hat would give the man a blood-red target. But Hackey was not about to be separated from any part of his uniform.

He slipped his hand into his coat pocket, just to make sure his freedom papers were still there. The papers had once belonged to a friend named Pleasant Jones, a man he had known while living in the Great Dismal Swamp. Pleasant just curled up one night from what he called a broken stomach, and he died before the morning sun had risen. Hackey figured that Pleasant Jones, being dead and all, wouldn't mind it if he borrowed his freedom papers. Hackey liked the man's name, and he called himself Pleasant Jones whenever he showed up to work at the Confederate camp during a spy mission.

Dead folks had been good to Hackey. He got his fine uniform off of a dead Union soldier killed in some skirmishing just before the Battle of Manassas. It was a dandy Zouave uniform, much flashier than the drab gray or butternut brown of so many Confederate soldiers, or even the Yankee blue. A few Rebels threatened to strip him naked when they saw him wearing such a fancy uniform, but most of the Rebs were just amused; they said he should keep the uniform because it made them laugh seeing him so gussied up for war.

And then there were the ladies . . . they loved a uniform like this. The clothes had already drawn the eye of several pretty hens he had encountered in camps and small towns scattered about.

He continued to move silently for another ten minutes, his arms filling with wood. He spotted a couple of wild pigs, and he wished he had a weapon of some sort to take them down. But, alas, he was defenseless against their tusks. As he stepped over a log, he heard something crack and wondered if he had snapped a twig. At the same moment, he felt something smack him in his lower back, as if a master had just whacked him with a stick. He spun around and saw no one, and as he did, he used one hand to reach behind and touch his back. It felt moist, and when he drew his hand back, he noticed that it came away with blood on his fingers. Suddenly, the stinging set in, like his back had been lit on fire. He stumbled and staggered, and it dawned on him that he might have been hit by a bullet. But from where? He spun around, looking for any sign of life, and that just added to the growing dizziness. He fell onto his side, wood spilling out of his arms; his head began to spin and his vision narrowed, as if he was looking down a long tunnel through the forest. The pain in his back mounted, and it felt as if someone had jammed a burning torch into a hole in his skin. For a moment, he wondered if his skin was on fire, but he did not smell burning flesh, and whenever he reached back and touched the pain, he came back with more blood.

Somehow, Hackey pushed himself up, rose back to his feet, and began to run—hobble, more like it. And then he felt another sting, this one centered in his back, and he tumbled forward. He rose to his knees and noticed that the bullet had passed through his body, for there was a small exit hole in his chest, turning as red as his pantaloons. When he saw the hole, full panic set in. An intense pain spread all across his back, like spilled liquid soaking into his muscles and taking his breath away.

Delirious, strange thoughts and memories flowed over Hackey. He saw a black woman walking toward him in the forest, the most beautiful woman he had ever seen, and he wondered if this was the woman he would have married if he wasn't about to die. She floated past and evaporated, and then he saw himself as a young boy in the Great Dismal Swamp with Pappy, and a snake had wrapped itself around Pappy's leg. Memories continued to flow over him, submerging him in the past, and then he had the strangest thought of all. He suddenly wondered if the bullets and the blood had ruined his beautiful uniform. As he sank deeper, like slipping into quicksand, he also wondered if someone would come by, find him dead, and strip him of his Zouave uniform—just as he had done to that poor Union soldier. Strangest of all, he found himself smiling at the thought of one soldier after another using the same uniform over and over. As each soldier died, another one would strip the body and put on the uniform, until he too was shot down.

The uniform would live on forever, but the men would not.

26

J OHN WISHED HE HADN'T STORMED OUT ON PEG, BECAUSE HE HAD
no chance to patch things before riding out of town. As soon as
he returned to the Spotswood Hotel, Miss Hattie was ready to
leave with him in tow, so he rode out of Richmond with a cloud
hanging over them and no guarantee that he and Peg would see each
other again.

Miss Hattie said they had important papers to take north to
General McClellan—information on some new electric torpedoes
being built in Richmond, as well as another submarine boat being
constructed. So now their horses were carrying them southeast out
of Richmond, with cottonwood trees rising up on both sides and
the wind freezing his face until it felt like he was wearing a mask
of ice. They rode hard in the direction of the Chickahominy River,
taking them toward the village of Glendale. When they spotted a
church steeple peeking above the trees, they reined their smoking
steeds to a leisurely walk and stopped at an inn on the outskirts
of town.

John brought in Miss Hattie's bag, while a matronly woman
greeted her on the porch of the inn. He then led the horses to the
stables, left them in the hands of a stable boy, and hefted his pack
onto his back. John decided to scout the village to make sure they
hadn't been followed out of Richmond. The village consisted of about
two dozen houses, ranging from a small cabin to the two-story brick
home in the center of town. There were more animals than people
wandering the streets, a few dogs and cats, as well as some chickens

and one pig. John clenched his fist to work the stiffness out of his cold fingers.

As he turned the corner of the central street, his eyes landed on a curious fellow—a red-haired man with enormous side-whiskers. The man was loaded down with a heavy pack on his back, from which dangled utensils and tools of all sorts, everything from hammers and frying pans to mallets and axes. A peddler.

"Good mornin' to you," said the man, surprising John with his Irish brogue. "Which way to the tavern, boy?"

John stopped and stared at the peddler. There was something a little strange about the man. Was it the accent that didn't seem quite right? John knew his Irish and Scottish accents, and this man's accent was close but not on the money. But what really jumped out at him were the peddler's brown eyelashes—a poor match to the man's reddish hair.

"There's a barroom in the inn on the edge of town, sir," said John, pointing the way back toward where they had entered the village of Glendale.

"Thank you kindly, boy." The peddler tipped his hat and strode off, his gear clanking. John decided to keep an eye on this one, so he waited until the man was well down the road before he followed. When he reached the inn, John found the peddler already in the barroom ordering something to drink, with his hefty pack settled into the chair across from him, propped up as if it was his drinking companion.

"The charming young lady, Missus Webster, offered me your services," the landlady said, suddenly slipping up beside John and startling him. She was dressed in widow's weeds—black mourning clothes—but her face was bright and smiling. "So go on now and help set the table, John boy."

"Yes, ma'am."

After stashing his own pack in the kitchen, John carried out the plates, silverware, and cups and placed them on a long wooden table in a dining room with a ceiling so low that his head nearly scraped the dark-brown beams. The landlady, Missus Hawkins, handled the food preparations herself, and he found her to be unusually opinionated when it came to matters of food.

"Never, I mean *never*, use the same utensil for different foods," she said, shaking a finger at him. "I do not allow for promiscuity among my serving spoons and forks. Just as the good Lord meant for us to have one lifelong partner in marriage, each dish in my dining room has only one lifelong serving spoon. Stray from this rule, and you have disease. So keep the serving spoon happily married to the proper serving dish."

She went on to explain that the Science of Cookery and the Science of Health are closely connected, but John didn't understand half of what she said. Her talk of "happily married" serving spoons made him think once again of Peg and the way they had left matters back in Richmond. By the time he snapped to attention, Missus Hawkins was going on about how the secret to all good cookery is making fine meat jellies, and her rule was that no one ingredient should dominate, and then she said something in French, and John was lost again.

In the midst of the table preparations, however, John managed to slip a word to Miss Hattie.

"Keep an eye out for the peddler with the red hair," he whispered.

Miss Hattie knew better than to cast a glance at the peddler while John was talking to her. She kept her eyes fixed on John and took a sip of water. "What do you know of the man?"

"He's been watching you."

Miss Hattie didn't respond. She probably knew that most men kept their eyes on her, but she was too modest to say so.

"He's staring more than normal," John explained, "and I think he's wearing a wig. His accent ain't quite right."

"I will remember that. Thank you, John."

Missus Hawkins announced dinner, and fifteen people gathered at the long oak table. The dinner was in courses, and the clatter of knives and forks on plates made John's mouth water—but he knew he would have to wait for leftovers. The conversation touched lightly upon the war, with much of the focus being on the 1860 census, which showed the North growing much faster than the South.

"The census was rigged by Yankees, no doubt," observed one older gentleman, "so it's good to be done with the North and not have to watch states like Illinois and Michigan steal our seats in Congress."

"I say we spread our kingdom farther south," said another. "Let's spread our heritage into the Caribbean and Latin America. More land means more strength, and we will be invincible to Northern aggression."

Miss Hattie smiled and agreed. She had told everyone that she was from Corinth, Mississippi, and was traveling for her health. As John helped to serve, he noticed that the peddler remained quiet while the conversation bubbled all around him. But whenever Miss Hattie looked the other direction, the peddler's eyes fixed on her.

*****

After the meal, John helped settle Miss Hattie in her room, and she agreed that the peddler was most likely a spy.

"I'll need y'all to keep an eye on him," she said. "Can you do that, John?"

"Gladly." He was eager to please Miss Hattie, and he wondered if he would be as dedicated if Miss Hattie wasn't the most striking woman in a one hundred-mile radius. Once again, his mind went back to Peg and her comments about Miss Hattie. Everything seemed to draw his mind back to Peg.

After John returned downstairs, he collected his backpack and found the peddler settling his score with the landlady. "Business is dull, so I'll have to walk back to Richmond," said the peddler before exiting through the front door, his massive pack clanking with every step. John followed at a safe distance.

Outside, John watched the peddler light a short-stemmed clay pipe and head for the road leading back to Richmond. John rushed to the stable, where he recalled seeing a fishing pole leaning up against a wall, and he snatched it up; if he should be spotted following the peddler, he could say he was out to catch his next meal. But as he headed out of the barn, he realized he didn't have his gun, because Miss Hattie didn't want her servant caught carrying a firearm. There was no time to retrieve it now, so his hunting knife would have to do.

John knew of a shortcut to the river, where the peddler was heading, so he left the road and plunged into the trees, until he came abreast of the man. He couldn't see the peddler, but the clanging of the red-haired man's pack was like the bell on a cow's neck, telling him where he was moving. Three miles out of town, he heard the peddler turn left and leave the road and make for the river. The peddler, still hidden from view, passed directly in front of John, judging by the sound. And when he had passed, John carefully followed him down to a bluff overlooking the river. From behind a tree, John finally caught sight of the man, standing at the top of the steep bank and looking around, as if to make sure he wasn't followed.

After tightening the straps on his pack, the peddler took one final glance around and then scrambled down the bluff, clanking every step of the way. John moved from behind the tree, got on his belly on the cold ground, and peered over the edge of the bluff. The drop-off was extremely steep. Thick underbrush and young timber concealed the red-headed peddler from view, and he heard the continual clanking become fainter and fainter. John wondered what the peddler had in mind by heading for the river below. He couldn't swim the river in this cold and with such a weight on his back.

John didn't think he could get down the steep bank without creating a ruckus of his own, so he walked along the bluff for about a hundred yards before coming across a narrow, overgrown path leading safely down to the river. At the bottom of the cliff, he paused and listened for telltale sounds of the peddler's pack. He was sure he had lost the man.

Moving along the river in the direction where he had last seen the peddler, his sharp eyes spotted footprints in the unfrozen ground. Fresh prints. He tracked them along a narrow path by the river, which took a sharp right and then reached an open, level stretch. He followed the tracks until he reached another bend in the river, where he spotted a small cabin, half-submerged in vegetation.

John crouched in a thicket, which provided an obstructed view of the cabin, and he waited, blowing on his hands for warmth. He had the patience of a hunter, but he only had to wait a short spell before the cabin door opened and out stepped the peddler and a second man.

From this distance, the second man appeared to have closely cropped black hair and a swarthy complexion.

The two men went around to the back of the cabin, where John could see the corner of a stable and hear the whinny of horses. Moments later, the men emerged on horses, with the red-haired peddler atop a dark iron-gray horse, and they took off in the direction of the river road.

John waited a few minutes before rising into a crouch and approaching the house carefully. It appeared deserted, so he hurried forward with the fishing pole still in hand, pausing behind trees as he moved in closer. Finally reaching the front door, he put his ear to the wood. No sound.

Turning the handle slowly, he cracked open the door just enough to enter the dim, earthy-smelling cabin. As he guessed: deserted. Lying on the floor in one corner was the peddler's pack, and he caught a whiff of the pipe tobacco the man had been smoking. The main room spilled into two adjoining back rooms—probably bedrooms. A round table with uneven legs sat in the middle of the main room, and on it was a small stack of papers, weighted down with a rock. But then his eyes landed on something completely unexpected. Propped up on one of the chairs was a girl's doll. It wasn't what you would expect in the clutches of spies, and it immediately made him think about the doll he had found in the woods near Manassas. This doll wore a plain white dress and no bonnet; it was roughly the same size as Lucy Ann, but her head was a bit larger.

The doll couldn't just be a coincidence, so he approached the table to take a closer look. But as he did, he caught a glimpse of something in his peripheral vision. In one of the back rooms, something was stretched out on the floor. Something large. A dog with its eyes closed. But it wasn't just any dog. It was a Cuban bloodhound, the kind imported specifically to hunt down slaves. John had seen slave hunters using these dogs before, the brute animals straining at their leashes and sniffing the ground. John debated with himself. Should he make a quick retreat through the front door or should he snatch the doll and the papers on the table?

He chose the papers and the doll. He would soon regret it.

John took three silent steps forward, set aside his fishing pole, and stuffed the doll and papers into his backpack. He made hardly a sound, but as he slung the pack on his back and picked up his fishing pole, the dog must have sensed his presence. From the corner of his eye, he spotted the dog rise to its feet. Lordy, the dog was tall. The animal let out a rumbling growl, showing its teeth, with its head, shoulders, and body aligned like an arrow—a deadly posture. John didn't think he could dash to the front door in time. Too far away.

He had dealt with dogs before, so he turned to the side, hoping the dog would see that he was not in an aggressive position. John stood straight and still, no sudden moves, even though everything inside him was telling him to run. He kept his hands at his sides, the fishing pole in his right, because dogs go for extensions from the body. In his peripheral vision, he could see the dog still moving toward him. He had invaded the bloodhound's territory. He was prey.

John tried to push down any feelings of fear, for the dog would pick up on it. Taking authority, he shouted, "No! Back!" But the dog kept coming, slowly, patiently, emitting a throbbing growl. The dog showed its teeth again and the red of its gums. The teeth were larger than any he had ever seen before in a dog. The bloodhound didn't attempt to circle John and get at him from behind, as many dogs will do. This was not a nervous dog. It was a trained killer, but he should not be surprised, considering the breed. John would have to stand and fight, so he took several slow steps to the side, not making eye contact. He hoped to work his way around the table and then back up slowly to the door. But the dog kept advancing, and he knew it would attack at any moment.

The slightest movement of his arm could trigger the attack, but he had to get at his knife, hidden beneath his shirt at his waist. Slowly, he reached for his waist with his free hand, but that was all it took to ignite the attack. The Cuban bloodhound bounded across the room. He knew the dog would go for the arm if he raised it, but as the dog hurled its enormous weight at him, jaws open, John decided to try something desperate. He shoved the fishing pole into the dog's throat, deep into the animal's gullet. The dog gagged and let out a whelp, and it pulled away, temporarily stunned, claws clicking on the wooden floor. The pole snapped in half, and John tossed aside the stub of wood.

But the dog wasn't giving up. This animal was single-minded.

John took one step back and pulled out his knife with his right hand. He hoped the dog would take enough time to recover from the shock of a pole down the gullet to give him a chance to get out the door. But the animal was already back for blood, and it clamped onto John's right arm. Fortunately, the jaws gripped more jacket than flesh, but the dog had enough of his arm, and it felt like his limb was being crushed beneath the weight of a locomotive.

The shock and power of the bite nearly immobilized John, but he stayed on his feet—initially. The Cuban bloodhound gave him a powerful shake, like his arm was a rag doll, and John stumbled. He maintained his balance, but the knife dropped from his right hand. He jabbed his left thumb in the dog's eyes, which normally caused a dog to release, but this was no ordinary beast. The dog drove him backward, trying to force him to the ground. If he fell, the animal would go for his throat, and it would be over—unless he could get to his knife.

Backing up in a circle, John worked his way closer to the knife. Then the dog pushed at him with all of its weight, driving with its head, and John felt himself tumbling onto his back. As he hit the floor with a sickening slap, he threw out his left hand and groped, but his dancing fingers could not locate his weapon. The dog was on top of him now, his throat exposed and his arm clamped in its jaws.

His hand touched the edge of the knife. He couldn't see it, being on his back, but he felt the handle. He tried to get his fingers around the handle, but it was hard to do with over a hundred pounds of moving muscle on his chest. At last his fingers wrapped around the handle, and he brought it up in a sweeping arc and felt the blade plunge through flesh. The animal let out a squeal, which seemed odd coming from a big bruiser. Immediately the dog released his arm, and John pulled the knife loose and scrambled back to his feet, panting and sweating.

John had only moments before the dog was back in action, angrier and lusting for blood. He made a run for the front door, and he could hear the dog recovering and coming at him. He slipped through the door, spinning around and slamming it shut, and he saw the animal lunge, blood staining its shoulder red, teeth showing, killer eyes, ears back. John put all of his weight behind the door as it shut, and he felt the power of the animal slamming against the wood. The door cracked, but it held, and John took off running with blood staining his jacket and another doll in his backpack.

*****

Ichabod didn't know why Tobias insisted on wearing that ludicrous disguise. The red wig didn't even match his brown eyebrows. He regretted recruiting him to hunt spies.

Tobias and Rupert, another of his recruits, had tracked down Ichabod by the river, where he had spent a pleasant morning fishing. The only thing missing was his dog, Ahab, which he had left to guard the cabin. It was a good thing that Rupert was comfortable around Ahab, because Tobias was terrified of the animal.

As the three of them made their way back to the cabin by horse, Tobias told him he had tracked Hattie Webster and her black servant to the Glendale Inn. Ichabod had learned that the servant's name was John Scobell, Peg's husband, and he was convinced that the Scobells were a husband-and-wife team of spies. He asked Tobias for a description of John Scobell to make sure he had identified the right person at the Glendale Inn; but as they approached their cabin near the river, Ichabod heard a pitiful whimpering. His heart dropped, and he spurred his horse forward.

"What is that?" Tobias asked.

"It's Ahab, you fool!"

Ichabod had never heard such a mournful sound from his dog before, and he wondered if he had been shot. Ichabod had lost two parents, a newborn son, a friend, and a wife, but losing Ahab would be more than he could bear. Ahab was the closest thing he would ever have to a child—granted, a 140-pound killer, but still a child to him.

Leaping from the saddle, he barged through the back door and found Ahab curled by the front door, licking a gaping wound in his shoulder. He crouched down and gently put his hand on the dog's shoulder. The animal shuddered beneath his touch and squealed when he touched too close to the wound. Someone had plunged a knife into Ahab's shoulder, and he wondered who in the world would be able to get that close to his dog and live to escape this cabin. Ichabod looked around the room, half expecting to see the mangled body of Ahab's victim sprawled on the floor somewhere. He found splatters of blood in various parts of the room, and he wondered if human blood might be mingled with Ahab's blood.

"What happened?" asked Tobias, when he and Rupert finally caught up with him and entered the cabin.

"He's been stabbed! Now fetch me some clean water!"

"There, there," said Ichabod, giving Ahab a kiss on the top of his head and running his hand down the dog's neck. "You'll be all right, boy. Y'all will be fine."

Whoever had done this must have been going for the main artery in Ahab's neck, but he had not succeeded. The wound was deep, but it appeared to have missed anything vital.

"Were you followed here?" Ichabod asked Tobias, after Rupert had brought him a bucket of water and a clean rag. Tobias stood on the far side of the room, terrified of Ahab even when the dog was whimpering like a puppy.

"I'm *sure* I wasn't followed," Tobias muttered.

Squeezing water from the rag, Ichabod cast a look in the corner, where Tobias had dumped his peddler's pack.

"It wouldn't a been too hard for someone to follow you here with that clanging jumble of yours," he snapped.

"I wasn't followed," Tobias insisted.

"Y'all give me some help here," Ichabod ordered the two men. Rupert strode over and crouched down, unafraid of the animal, but Tobias wouldn't budge. "I said I need some help here!"

Reluctantly, the man in the red wig sidled over, staying as far as possible from Ahab's head.

"I'm gonna need y'all to hold his head while I clean the wound."

"Hold his head? That's where the teeth are located." Tobias peddled back two steps.

"Don't worry, boss. I can handle it," said Rupert. "Tobias will just make it worse."

"You're probably right." Rupert had a nice way with animals and he stroked Ahab's head as Ichabod carefully began to dab the wound. Ahab flinched and squirmed, but Rupert was good at keeping him under control.

Ichabod spoke to Ahab like he would a baby. "Don't you worry, boy," he said, almost in a singsong style. "I'm gonna make it all right. I'm gonna find out who done this to you. And then I'm gonna cut out his heart."

27

CLEON WAS WALKING ALONE IN THE WOODS WHEN HE HEARD THE voice say: "You gotta die before you can live." Then he heard the sound of trees cracking and crashing, and he turned and saw an entire wall of trees come tumbling down, as if an invisible giant was striding through the forest, pushing down trees as he walked. As this unseen force approached, Cleon noticed birds falling from the sky and hitting the ground dead at his feet, and he began to sense death all around him, as if he was immersed in it like air, and he began to choke. When he looked down at his leg, he saw a narrow cord of darkness wrapping itself around his foot and move up his leg like a serpent, and he cried out, "Mercy! Mercy! Mercy!"

Panicking, Cleon took off running through the forest, sensing that something was chasing him, and he heard his own heartbeat pounding in his ears. Then behold, he turned around and saw that he was being pursued by a hellhound larger than a horse, just a few feet behind him, and he heard the dog's teeth snapping at him, coming together with a click.

The forest became thicker, and the path narrower, and the dog was always right behind him, growling and snarling, but never quite snagging him in its teeth. Then Cleon felt a hand reach underneath his right arm and lift him off of the ground, and he soared high above the forest treetops and the sin-sick land below. He looked to his right and saw that he was being whisked through the air by an angel with wings tipped with gold. They soared above a deep, lush valley where he could see sheep grazing, and a voice in his ear whispered, "This is holy ground, this is holy ground."

Then the angel brought Cleon down before a vast sea of glass, mingled with fire, and he told the seraphim, "I can't pass through, or I'll perish." But before his eyes, a path opened through the fire, across the sea of glass, and he passed between the flames, which towered on both sides. Then he heard a voice like thunder, and it told him, "You are my workmanship and the creation of my hand, and I will drive all fears away. You have a deed to your name, and you will never perish."

Then Cleon looked down and saw that he was dressed in golden robes, and an angel was looking at him and smiling and saying, "Everything just fits." And Cleon began to shout in praise.

When Cleon came to, he found himself lying on his back in the middle of the forest, and he was shouting and praising God. The mat of leaves beneath his back and head felt cold and damp and smelled of decay. He raised himself on two elbows and looked around. The forest was quiet, except for the birds and the crunch of leaves beneath the feet of squirrels. He wasn't at all scared, for he had had visions like this many a time. They were as ordinary as breakfast.

Cleon had recently reunited with the Lincoln League near Manassas, and Gallus had warned him not to walk in the forest alone, not with a killer on the loose, but he wasn't afraid of death, and he wanted his time alone to talk with the Lord. It was getting late in the afternoon, and he figured he should make his way back to the Lincoln League camp. So he got to his feet, brushed the leaves from his clothes, and began walking. The damp cold seeped into his clothes, and he increased his pace to try to create some heat on a chilly day.

He hadn't been hiking for more than five minutes when he had a sense he was being followed. He wondered, at first, whether he was still caught up in a vision. Was he imagining the sound of a pursuing hellhound once again? He turned and looked, but he saw nothing but trees, a community of giants shooting straight and tall.

Then a crack, like a snapping branch. A bullet gashed a tree only one foot away from him on his right. Someone had taken a shot at him! Deep down, Cleon knew he should start running without delay, but he took a second to look behind, to see who was shooting, to find out who had been killing his friends. At first he saw nothing, but then he spotted a figure off to his left, a good distance away. To his shock, it was a black man, and this man was pointing directly at him. The man wasn't pointing a gun, though, just a finger. And then Cleon heard another shot, and a bullet hummed by his left ear.

This time, he immediately took off running, and he weaved through the trees, trying to switch directions every few seconds, throwing off the aim of his pursuer. He was definitely being hunted, for he heard crashing in the brush from behind. Cleon leaned forward as he ran, trying to keep his head down and his target small. Another shot sounded, but he felt nothing hit him. As he dodged around another tree, he didn't notice the thick, low-hanging branch, and it cracked him in the head like the slap of a heavy hand, and he was thrown backward onto the ground. His head pounded with pain, and it took a few seconds for the danger to sink in. His pursuer was close. He looked around as he rose to his feet, but he saw no one. Nothing but forest.

Another crack. This time he felt the bullet enter, and he felt himself falling, falling, and he hit the cold, damp leaves and he touched the glory and shouted, "Mercy! Mercy! Mercy!"

*****

"We told you not to walk through the forest alone," said a voice that came to him muffled, like his ears were clogged with water. His vision snapped into focus, and he looked up at Gallus, who was on one knee, examining his shoulder. "Don't worry, the bullet just grazed you. You lost a bit of blood, but I think you'll live."

"You fool, it's a good thing we came along lookin' for you." Abram's scowling face appeared directly overhead, and Cleon smiled back at him.

"Good to see you too, Abram!"

Gallus helped Cleon into a sitting position. Pain shuddered through his right shoulder, and he cringed.

"Did y'all see who shot at me?" Cleon asked.

"Just a glimpse," said Gallus. "We arrived on the scene as you were goin' down."

"Scared 'em off with a few shots of our own," said Abram, grinning and waving his revolver in the air.

Cleon laughed. "Abram, you couldn't hit an overweight buffalo if it was standin' close enough to lick your face."

"Yeah, but people don't know that. I scared 'im good, and he went runnin.'"

"Was he a black man?" Cleon asked.

Gallus looked surprised. "You mean you saw him?"

"Just before I started runnin'. But the funny thing is, I didn't see him holdin' a gun. He was pointin' at me, aimin' his finger like a gun."

"I saw him too, but I didn't notice whether he had a gun or not," said Gallus. "He went runnin' back in the general direction of the Rebel winter camp. Now let's get y'all back to the cabin, so we can treat your wound."

"Not yet," said Cleon, climbing to his feet. "If he went toward the Rebel camp, then I'm gonna go look for him."

"Don't be a fool a second time," said Gallus.

"But this is our chance to find out who's been huntin' us. We gotta do it before the man's long gone. I think I'd remember him by sight."

Abram sighed. "Hate to say it, but he's makin' sense."

"My shoulder'll be fine. If we're gonna snag this devil, we gotta do it now—before dark sets in."

"I suppose y'all have a point," conceded Gallus.

So the three of them marched toward the Centreville winter camp, and Cleon muttered to himself, "I will drive all fears away, I will drive all fears away, I will drive all fears away. You have a deed to your name, and you will never perish."

Gallus and Abram exchanged looks, but made no comment.

28

OHN AND MISS HATTIE RODE THROUGH THE DARK, THEIR HORSES moving in a free and easy gallop. When John had returned to the Glendale Inn after his tangle with the dog, Miss Hattie decided they needed to leave immediately before the red-headed peddler put two and two together, figured John had been in their cabin, and descended on the inn with reinforcements. After she treated John's wound—his coat had kept the bite from doing any serious damage—they informed the unhappy landlady that they were leaving that very moment. Then they departed when the sun was just beginning to set, and now they were moving swiftly, heading for the landing at the Chickahominy River.

"It appears we will get through this all right," said Miss Hattie after they had put Glendale far behind them.

"Still plenty of time for trouble," said John. "But perhaps we better walk the horses for a spell."

"You're right, we should give them a rest."

"Just wish we were closer to the landin', ma'am. I still fear that that confounded peddler will show up before we're done with this."

Miss Hattie laughed—not a rude laugh, just a friendly chortle that indicated she thought he was worrying too much. "There's an old saying, John. Don't borrow trouble until it comes."

"Yes, ma'am."

They slowed their horses to a trot and passed through highly cultivated land, with crops on all sides that hadn't yet been touched by war. The moon cast light over the winter wheat crop and the river to their left, while occasional farmhouses and barns loomed in the silvery glow to the right.

"I judge we're only about five miles from the landing," Miss Hattie said, "so you can stop any worrying, John. At the landing, my husband will be there to take our information."

"Your husband, ma'am?"

"Why yes, John, you didn't know my husband is an officer in the Union army?"

"No, ma'am, didn't know that." Truth be told, he didn't even know she had a husband, let alone was married to an officer. He couldn't imagine any man allowing his wife to pretend to be the husband of another man, as Miss Hattie was doing with Timothy Webster. He didn't dare say any of this, but Miss Hattie must have read his thoughts.

"My husband approves—all for the cause," she said. "He trusts me when I tell him that Timothy Webster occupies the sofa in our many adventures, even though his legs are two feet too long for most sofas."

John gave a polite laugh, and he didn't let on how horrified he was about the way she had chosen to serve her country. They continued on in silence.

"I think our horses are sufficiently rested," Miss Hattie eventually said, and they spurred them forward. The road led directly through a patch of timber, where the light of the moon was blocked and the road plunged into darkness. It was the ideal place for an ambush, but he didn't say a word of these fears to Miss Hattie. She already considered him a worrier. Nevertheless, they passed through the woods unscathed, and John thought that perhaps Miss Hattie was right to be confident.

Not long after they left the confines of the woods, John heard the faint sound of horse hooves coming toward them, and he realized they might not make it to the river landing without incident after all. In the glow of the moon, they picked out four horsemen emerging from the gloom directly ahead.

"You have your gun handy, John?" Miss Hattie said. When they had left Glendale, she made sure he was carrying a weapon.

"Loaded and ready."

"You pick one out from the two on the left, and I'll pick one out from the two on the right. They won't expect us to fire on them."

John had heard from Mister Webster that Miss Hattie was a fine shot, but he didn't believe it at the time. He hoped Mister Webster knew what he was talking about.

The approaching riders split into two pairs, with one pair shifting to the right side of the road and the other staying to the left, as if they were politely allowing them to pass through the middle. But John sensed it was a trap, a way to clamp them in a deadly vise. They were now close enough that it appeared that two of the men wore Confederate gray and had heavy sabers at their sides. The moonlight hit the red hair of one of the men. It was the peddler—the man he had trailed earlier in the day. He must have gotten ahead of them on the road while he and Miss Hattie were checking out of the Glendale Inn.

John and Miss Hattie increased the speed of their horses, but not dramatically. John had his left hand on the reins, his right hand on his gun. They were now close enough that he could see that one of the men had his weapon drawn—and two more were reaching for their holsters.

"Halt! Throw up your hands!" one of the men shouted.

Miss Hattie answered by raising her gun and firing point-blank, and John did the same—probably not the kind of response these men were expecting from a woman and a Negro. Two of the men tumbled backward off of their horses, and the other two must have been taken completely off guard. Webster was right. Miss Hattie was a sure shot and had knocked a man right out of his saddle.

"At 'em!" John hissed, spurring his horse, and the animal took off like a bullet. The remaining two men were in the process of aiming their weapons as John and Miss Hattie raced between them; but the men must have realized that they risked hitting each other if they both shot to the middle, for they held their fire until John and Miss Hattie had passed between. John didn't look back, but he sensed them taking aim, and he veered his horse left and heard the crack of gun-fire. He felt as if his back made one broad target.

John stayed low in the saddle and then moved his horse back to the right, staying as close to the side of the road as possible. Miss Hattie had done the same, for she obviously knew how to maximize speed and minimize target size. Her bonnet had flung off and her hair streamed behind her. More shots were fired, many shots, and John figured that the two men had emptied their guns by now—the fools. But the men still had swords and could do serious damage if they caught them.

John's horse was on the bit, running well, running confidently, and the path ahead seemed clear of obstructions until they made a right turn, hugging the edge of the road, which was lined by fenc-ing. Up ahead, a tree had fallen across the trail. He didn't know the abilities of this horse, because Miss Hattie had loaned it to him, and he prayed it had enough schooling to jump this obstacle. If the horse refused and came to an abrupt stop, it might send John hurtling for-ward like an arrow off a taut bowstring.

He and Hattie pulled away from the men, and they rode side by side, neither of their horses dropping the pace. He wondered if it would be wiser to slow his horse and let it take an awkward cat jump over the log, just to play it safe. But he hated to give up any ground to their pursuers. He had never run a horse this fast in the dark. Good thing there was enough moonlight to stay true to the path.

As they neared the fallen tree, John leaned forward in the saddle and gave his horse release, moving his hands up the animal's neck. He kept his eyes focused ahead, because any sudden head move-ments of his own could throw off the horse's balance; then the horse jumped cleanly, clearing the tree easily, barely losing a stride, and they thundered on. His horse was a natural jumper. Miss Hattie's horse had taken the fallen tree cleanly as well, and they were back on track, pulling away. But as they rounded another bend, John spotted a large shadow dart out of the woods on the right side of the road. *A deer!* The animal, equally alarmed, froze for a moment, stopping directly in their path. John's horse, which had been so calm, completely lost its composure, and as the deer bounded off of the road his steed veered to the right, almost clipping the side of Miss Hattie's horse. Suddenly, his clear-footed horse had become a fiddle-footed tangle of nerves, unsure where to put its legs. The horse stumbled into the fence along the road and lost its footing, crashing through the wooden rails, and John found himself in the middle of an unscheduled dismount, flung out of the saddle, soaring through the air, and wondering if he was going to slam headfirst into a nearby tree. He missed the trees, but he hit hard against the ground, his right shoulder first; he didn't hear anything crack. The horse fought back to its feet, and John did the same, feeling a sharp pain in his right thigh, but he had to act fast before his horse bolted. He took the reins in his fist and calmed his horse until it finally ceased its stamping dance.

"You all right?" called Miss Hattie.

She had reined her horse to a stop when she should have kept going. He looked back down the path and could hear the thunder of the approaching pursuers.

"Go! Go! I'm fine!"

Miss Hattie paused to stare at him, so he added one more "Go" before she finally took off. John still had his gun, and he knew he didn't have time to mount his horse and follow her. His right leg throbbed, probably bruised blue, but he could put his full weight on it, and his horse appeared to be unharmed. Using his horse as protection, he placed his arm on the saddle for support as he aimed.

In the moonlit road, the two men appeared, and it was obvious they had spotted his horse along the side of the road. They bore down on him, one of them pulling out his sword and raising it in the air as he let out a whoop. John aimed for the man with the sword, the one on the black horse. He waited until they were close, a half dozen yards away, before he fired. The man with the sword threw both hands in the air, dropping his weapon, and his horse reared up on two legs and clawed the air. The horse hurled the man backward, while the other man, on a white horse, held on tightly as his charger went right, clawing up dirt and coming to an abrupt stop.

The black horse snorted and wheeled around and went running off with an empty saddle, back in the direction it had come. John aimed his gun at the remaining man, who surely must know by now that he was a marksman. Putting one hand on his hat, the man wheeled his horse around and tore off down the road, retreating into the night.

John kept his gun aimed at the dark path, listening to the hooves disappear into oblivion before finally lowering his weapon. He put away his pistol and ran his hand down his horse's mane, soothing it with, "Good girl, good girl." Now that the tension of the moment was receding, the pain in his right leg began increasing, and he breathed slowly and steadily, wiping the sweat from his brow with his sleeve. When he had calmed his horse, he mounted, and his leg screamed as he swung it over the saddle. Then he moved back onto the road and continued in the direction of Miss Hattie.

It wasn't long before he heard the tramp of horses coming toward him, and he hoped he wasn't about to encounter a second wave of attackers. He paused to reload his gun, but he doubted he would have enough ammunition to fend off so many men, from the sound of it. He decided his best bet was to head off of the road and hope they went by without seeing him.

Too late. An entire band of soldiers swept into sight, at least a dozen of them. Miss Hattie was riding in the middle of this cluster, and he observed they were wearing Union blue. She spurred ahead of the men and was the first to reach him.

"John, are you all right?"

"My leg's awful sore, but nothing broken."

"What happened to the pursuers?"

"One down, one fled."

"I am happy to see you in one piece," said the cavalry captain, a handsome man with a trim moustache.

"John, may I introduce you to my husband, Captain Lawton."

So this was the man who let his wife race around the countryside, getting shot at by Confederate spies and pretending to be another man's wife?

Smiling, John nodded. "Good evenin', captain."

"You are a brave fellow, Scobell," he said. "Thank you for protecting my wife. You were fortunate you didn't break your neck when your horse fell."

"I'm just glad it was my horse and not your missus' steed that went down."

John suddenly began to feel a little light-headed and sat on a nearby log, while Miss Hattie dismounted and came to his side.

"You set awhile, John."

She helped him remove his backpack, for his right shoulder was also tender, and he winced. One of the strings holding the pack shut had snapped, and the doll he had found in the cabin tumbled out.

Miss Hattie picked up the doll and burst out laughing. "Shucks, John, I didn't know you played with dolls!"

Several soldiers joined in the laughter, and John felt pretty darn foolish. He was about to explain the presence of a doll, but the captain spoke first. He sounded deadly serious.

"Where'd you get that thing, John?" he asked, dismounting and approaching.

"Found it in the cabin of one of the men I followed back at Glendale."

Miss Hattie, sitting next to him on the log, looked at the doll with more curiosity and less amusement. She turned it over in her hands. "You found it in the cabin? Why didn't you tell me about this?"

"Really no time 'cause we were in such a rush to leave Glendale."

"Here, let me take a look," said Captain Lawton, taking the doll from his wife's hands. He had a knife in his left hand. The captain flipped over the doll and jabbed it in the back with his knife. John heard a tearing sound as the captain drew the blade down its back. Then the captain reached inside the doll, like a bloody surgeon reaching into a body to pull out a bullet. Only instead of plucking out a Minié ball, the captain managed to extract papers.

"Well I'll be . . ." said Hattie.

The captain unfolded one of the papers and held it into the moonlight. "Good work! These are Confederate papers, and those men were spies, although you probably already gathered that, from their behavior at Glendale."

"Good work, John," said Hattie.

"This isn't the first time we have seen them using dolls for smuggling information and supplies. We stopped a blockade runner that carried dolls containing drugs and medicines for Rebel troops."

Lucy Ann. John's mind went immediately to the doll he had given to Peg, and he realized his gift to her was probably not some innocent child's toy, lost in the woods outside of Manassas. Most likely, that doll was also a spy's tool, and he had put it in his wife's possession. He suddenly felt sick to his stomach.

*****

Ichabod felt the fool, beaten back by a Negro and a woman.

He had survived the gunfight, as he knew he would, as he always did. But his partners hadn't fared as well. When he returned to the scene of the shooting, he found that both of the men shot from their saddles were dead, one with a bullet through the head and the other with a hole blown into his chest. Lucky shots. No woman could shoot that well, let alone a black man.

He found Tobias' gun about four feet from where the fool had landed in a tangled heap on the road, and he slipped it into his belt. Tobias' red wig had also been flung from his head. Why the man insisted on wearing it was baffling. Worst disguise he had ever seen. Ichabod found that Rupert's gun was still in the man's hands, and he had to pry the fingers off of the weapon. As he reloaded his gun, Ichabod made plans to bring the furies down on the black man who had nearly killed him just down the road. He didn't get a good look at him, but he was pretty sure it was John Scobell. And he was pretty certain by now that John was spying for the Yankees. Why else would he pass on a doll to his wife Peg and then steal the doll right out of their cabin? Scobell couldn't have gone far. But as Ichabod started back up the road, anxious for the hunt, he heard the sound of many horses. Well aware of the presence of Yankee soldiers in the vicinity, he decided not to take any chances and gave up any hope of immediate revenge. He reversed direction once again and headed back for Glendale, where his dog Ahab awaited him.

His vengeance could wait. After all, he knew exactly where John and Peg Scobell lived, and he planned on killing two birds with one stone.

29

T HE ATWATER HOUSE WAS EMPTY, EXCEPT FOR MATILDA DOWN in the kitchen, so Peg decided to snatch a little time in front of the mirror in the guestroom on the second floor. She didn't often get a stretch of time in which she could experiment with head wraps to her heart's delight—with no Missus Hicks around. So she set her mop and bucket in a corner of the room, scooted one of the chairs in front of the mirror above the dresser, and went to work, trying several styles of bows and knots and tails tucked into the wrap. She even tried on the forbidden yellow head wrap.

Peg only intended to experiment with head wraps for a short spell because she had plenty of work to do, but she lost track of time playing with the limitless variations. She especially liked the head wrap with its twisted tail hanging down on her left side, and she checked herself from all angles.

"What in heaven's name you think y'all are doing?"

Peg nearly fell out of the chair as Matilda charged into the room.

"You tryin' to get yourself fired, usin' this mirror like you owned the place?"

"Just takin' a break to try on some head wraps."

"Missus Hicks gonna rap your head with a stick if she catches you in here. That's the kind of head raps you're gonna get." Matilda put her hands on her hips and paused. She stared at Peg as if she had just noticed the colorful wonder on her head for the first time.

"Say, baby child, I like that. Never seen no one wear it that way."

"I can show you if you like."

"Oh Lordy, you tryin' to get us *both* fired?"

"The captain and Missus Hicks, ain't they gone all afternoon?"

Matilda bit her lip and walked around Peg to get a good look at her from all angles. "Mmm, that's nice. Quickly, show me how it's done."

Breaking into a smile, Peg leaped from the chair and Matilda took her place before the mirror. It was a beautiful oval mirror, French style because Missus Hicks loved anything French. The mirror's white frame was adorned with carved swags, acanthus leaves, and roses.

Peg set to work, draping Matilda's head with the wrap, covering her short hair completely.

"Then you twist the knot several times over, and I like to leave the end free and dangling like so."

"Very nice. Although if I lean over pots, I'm afraid the tail might dangle in the soup."

"Then you can knot it together completely and tuck the tail into the back of the wrap, this way."

Peg patted both sides of Matilda's head, firming it up after she had finished this variation.

"I like that."

"Or you can wrap the tail around the front this way."

Peg ran through all kinds of variations, such as wrapping the tail around the head at an angle so it looked as if Matilda had a tilted halo perched on her head. They became so caught up in what they were doing that they didn't hear the door open downstairs. And when Matilda started laughing in delight, they didn't hear the squeak of footsteps coming up the staircase.

It wasn't until the top stair creaked loudly that Matilda and Peg stopped in the middle of a knot, and Matilda's eyes went wider than a skillet. The cook jumped to her feet so quickly that her head caught Peg under the chin.

"No time to undo the head wrap," Matilda whispered. "Oh Lordy, and I'm still wearin' the yellow one. The missus is gonna have my head, wrap and all."

"No time to get out of the guestroom either," said Peg, for they could hear the footsteps moving down the hallway. Peg stood behind the door, which was slightly ajar, with Matilda right behind her, as if using her for cover.

"We're dead," Matilda whispered.

Peg put a finger to her lips to silently shush her.

They froze. Perhaps whoever it was would walk right on by the guestroom. The footsteps moved slowly, like someone being extra careful, and Peg wondered if it might be an intruder. Missus Hicks would not walk so deliberately, for she preferred to enter a room like a general leading an army.

Peg nearly let out a scream, for a man's face appeared, peeking through the slightly open door of the guestroom. It was a black man, and Matilda grabbed the mop—the nearest thing to a weapon she could put her hands on. She held it in front of her like a sword and said, "Who're you, and whatya think you're doin' in our house?"

Peg was stunned. It was like a ghost had walked right out of her past and through a door to the present.

"Shadrack! What do y'all think you're doin' here?"

Matilda shot a look at Peg. "You know this fool?"

"This here's my brother Shadrack," Peg said, pushing the door open wide.

Shadrack gave them an uncomfortable smile and removed his hat. "Beg your pardon, ma'am," he said to Matilda. "Didn't mean to startle y'all, but no one answered when I knocked on the servant's door downstairs."

"So you just wandered into a white man's home?" Peg said. "You could get yourself killed."

"I was careful. It was obvious no one was home—until I heard your voice coming from upstairs, Sister Peg."

"Well, all I can say is you should thank the Lord you ain't been shot comin' in here."

"Or mopped," said Matilda, shaking the mop head in his general direction. "I'll leave y'all alone to talk."

Matilda set aside the mop and exited the room—only to return a few moments later. She removed the yellow head wrap still on her head and grabbed her white one, draped on the edge of the bed. Then she gave Shadrack the stink eye as she walked past, heading back downstairs to the kitchen.

"We better talk out back because if the captain finds you in here, he won't be pleased," Peg said.

So the two of them trailed Matilda down the stairs and headed out behind the house, where they stood by a small white gazebo near the flower garden, frozen over with winter frost.

"Is John around?" Shadrack asked.

"Not right now, but he'll be by shortly." Peg wasn't about to let on that John was gone for who knows how long. She didn't trust what Shadrack might do if he thought John wasn't around.

Peg folded her arms in front of her chest. "So what in the world brings you here?" She hadn't seen Shadrack since the day Cager Johnson sold him down South—five years long gone. "Are you back in Richmond with a new master?"

Shadrack leaned against the gazebo railing. He had put on even more weight since he left, and Peg worried that he might break the railing just leaning on it.

"I ain't got no master no more," he said.

The words stunned Peg. "You mean you're a free man?"

Shadrack reached into his pocket, extracted a folded piece of paper, brushed the dirt from it, and methodically unfolded it. He held it up to her.

"That's what these papers say."

"How'd you get your freedom? Did you buy it?"

Shadrack dipped his head, as if afraid to look at her. She noticed a scar above his right eye that she didn't remember being there before.

"I came into some money," he said softly.

"Where'd you come upon that kinda money?" Peg didn't even try to keep the skepticism out of her voice.

"I have my ways."

"What ways?"

"Many different ways."

They stood beside the gazebo, neither saying a word for a few moments. A dog wandered by, sniffing at the ground, and then took off when it spotted a squirrel. Shadrack still wouldn't look her in the eyes.

"I'm sorry 'bout the things that happened," he finally said, staring at the sprinting contest between dog and squirrel.

"What kinda things?"

"Things I done to you as a brother."

If he had looked her in the eyes, he would have seen the shock on her face. Eyes wide, mouth open. She didn't think her brother had ever apologized to her for anything in his life. This was something new.

"I ain't been much of a brother," he added, now staring at the hat in his hands.

That was an understatement. She still had a scar on her left side where he had cut her with a knife. She had been twelve at the time, and he was ten, and he said he just wanted to see how well the knife worked.

"I ain't disageein' with y'all," she said.

Finally, he raised his head and looked her in the eyes. "But I can make it up to you, Peg."

Peg bit her lip and tried to fight back the memories of the times he beat on her. What was his excuse for that? Was he just trying to see if his fists worked?

"How y'all gonna make up for what you've done?"

"Maybe Mister Atwater is lookin' to hire on a new butler or somethin'."

"We already got one. Besides, how does that help me? Sounds like it's more for your benefit."

Shadrack scratched the back of his head. "If I'm near to you, I can do things for y'all to help you out."

"I got a husband for that."

Her brother nodded slowly. "In these war times, maybe you can use more menfolk to protect you."

Peg had to fight to keep from laughing. The idea of her brother acting as her protector seemed ludicrous. For all of her life, he was one of the people she needed protection from, and now he was proposing to shield her from the white world? She wanted to say no. She *wished* she could say no, but she didn't. She never did. Even growing up, when he was tormenting her, she felt a responsibility to look after her little brother and make sure he always had enough to eat. If John were here, he would send Shadrack packing. He might also do much more to her brother for inserting himself back into her life. Why couldn't John be here, rather than off with that white woman?

"I'll talk to Captain Atwater," she finally agreed. "Maybe he knows of somebody lookin' for help."

The last thing she wanted was her brother working under the same roof, but maybe Captain Atwater could find employment for him somewhere on the other side of town.

"Thank you, sister."

Without warning, he suddenly rushed forward and wrapped his big arms around her and squeezed. Peg had to stifle a scream, because she had always seen his hands as weapons, and any move in her direction was usually malicious. This was too much, and she felt panic in his embrace, like a steel trap had snapped on her leg. She pushed away, and when he tried to hug her again, she slapped his hand and shouted, "No!"

He backed away, like a scolded dog. "I'm sorry, Peg. I know I ain't got no right to ask you for help of any sort."

"That's right, you don't."

He toed the ground, kicking a rock loose. "So you'll help?"

She took care of Shadrack when their father got his freedom and left for Pennsylvania, and she took care of him whenever their mama spent nights in the tenements of various men in the Shockoe Bottom neighborhood, leaving the two of them alone in the dark. They had both come to see her as the real mother of the family.

"I said I would, didn't I?"

"Thank you, sister."

30

OHN FOUND PEG FINISHING SOME SEWING FOR MISSUS HICKS in their narrow, low-ceilinged room at the peak of the Atwater house. She nearly knocked over the single flicker of a candle, perched on the table next to her, when she saw him in the doorway and launched herself out of the chair, throwing her arms around his neck.

"Careful, you're gonna set a fire," John said, sitting down on the edge of the bed and drawing Peg into his lap. They kissed.

John had arrived at the house late at night, even though he and Miss Hattie had returned to Richmond in the afternoon—several days after the chase along the river. He helped Miss Hattie carry her things to the hotel room, and they were both shocked to find Timothy Webster lying in bed, his fever back and raging. So, for the rest of the afternoon, John helped Miss Hattie tend to Webster, and it was dark by the time he showed up at the servant's door of the Atwater house. Fortunately, Missus Hicks was sound asleep in her dragon's den, so Matilda let Captain Atwater know he was back, and the master of the house welcomed him cordially. Then John had bounded up the stairs.

"I have a surprise for you," he said to Peg, spotting the doll, Lucy Ann, in the same place where he had last seen her—propped up in a chair by the lone window.

"Then let's douse the candle. There's not much more than a stub left and Missus Hicks is sparing with her candles. We don't need light to be greetin' each other."

"But we need light for this surprise." He drew Peg aside and made for the doll in the chair.

"John Scobell, now is not the time to be playin' with dolls."

"Ah, but this ain't no normal doll." He drew out his knife and plunged it into the back of the doll, and Peg let out a gasp.

"John, you're scarin' the wits outta me. I've taken a likin' to that doll."

"We can sew Lucy Ann back up, once we've extracted this."

John realized that he was going to look quite foolish in the eyes of his wife if he found this doll to be empty. Squeezing two fingers into the opening in Lucy Ann's back, he didn't find papers, but he did touch something metal.

"This is all very strange," Peg said. "What do you think y'all are doin' rootin' around in that doll's back?"

John pulled out a 5-ounce tin with the words "Sulfate of Quinine" emblazoned on the front. He held it in the candlelight, and Peg stared in amazement, as if he had pulled the tin out of thin air, rather than from the doll's cavity. He dug around a little more and found a second 5-ounce tin.

"This must be one of the dolls that Captain Lawton was talkin' about—dolls used to smuggle medicine to Rebel troops."

"Captain Lawton?"

"Miss Hattie's husband."

"She has a husband? And he lets her pretend to be Mister Webster's wife?"

"I wondered the very same thing. But her husband told me that secessionists smuggle documents and medicine usin' dolls."

John told Peg how he had discovered a similar doll in a cabin in the woods, but he left out the rather important detail about the Cuban bloodhound that nearly ripped his throat open, as well as the night-time gunfight on horseback. Peg didn't need to know.

"Quinine? Can we hold on to it?" she asked.

Quinine was a wonder drug used to treat chills, aches, fever, and headache, often caused by bad air.

"Don't see why not, but it wouldn't be right to keep it all for ourselves. We should dispense it whenever we know someone who needs it."

Peg took one of the tins and flipped it over in her hands. "John Scobell, you sure are full a wonders."

"I know," he said, leaning over and blowing out the candle.

*****

The day was warm for January, with a light breeze that felt good on John's face. He sauntered down Main Street in the direction of the Monumental Hotel, which Mister Webster and Miss Hattie had checked into after finding no room at the Spotswood. John had helped Peg serve breakfast in the Atwater house and needed to find out how Mister Webster had fared during the night. The city pulsed with activity, with wagons rolling by, and several slaves pushing carts loaded with coal. He knew many of the black folks he passed, and it was a nice day for dawdling. It was even nicer to be back with Peg. They had patched things up, but neither had made any mention of her spying activities. He had decided to let the matter rest for a spell.

"Where y'all been?" called Dabney Smith. Dabney, a free man, had been running a cake shop after the previous owner hightailed it out of town because of suspicions that he had helped a slave escape to the North sealed up in a wooden box. "Ain't seen you at church in a coupla weeks."

John and Dabney attended the largest black congregation in town—First African Baptist. "Just been out of Richmond, doin' work for my employers."

Dabney whistled. "Ain't you the important one! Doin' out-of-town work." Dabney, a large, good-natured man, unfolded a cloth to reveal two miniature cakes, each small enough to fit in a person's palm. "A new recipe, and I cooked these in cups. Give her a go."

John took a nibble of the light cake—a cinnamon-flavored treat. "Mmmm. No wonder every white family in town has you making delectables for them."

John thanked Dabney for the cake and continued up the street. It certainly was a fine morning. No worries clouded his mind—until he was a block from the Monumental Hotel. He was shocked to see Cleon Fisk heading his way, looking deadly serious. What in the world was he doing in Richmond? Cleon always greeted him with a smile, especially when they hadn't seen each other in a long time. But there was no sign of a smile today. Something told John that his brief respite from worry was over.

Cleon didn't even start with "hello."

"Hackey is dead," he said bluntly.

That stopped John in his tracks. "That can't be."

"It *can* be. Hackey was shot down in the forest—just like the others."

John noticed that his hands had automatically balled into tight fists, clenched hard. His entire body had clenched.

"Was there a note left?"

"He was draped in the flag—a desecrated flag with words scrawled on it, just like the others. A fellow told us it said, THIS IS THE THIRD. But we guessed that already."

John laced his hands behind his head and groaned. "Is that why you're in Richmond? To ask me to help you track down this killer?"

"I don't need no help in trackin' the killer because I know exactly where he's at. He's here in Richmond. And I was just on my way to hunt you up at the Atwaters to tell you."

Cleon proceeded to relate the most remarkable tale—how he had almost become the fourth victim, escaping with a shot to the shoulder.

"And you ain't gonna believe it, John, but he was a black man. The Lincoln League is bein' hunted by a black man."

"And all this happened near Centreville?"

"Not far from where we found the body hanging in the tree."

"Then how do y'all know the killer came to Richmond?"

"When the killer run off, we tracked him all the way to the Rebel camp in Centreville. Watchin' from an overlook, we glimpsed him from a distance, and we saw him get in a wagon with a white man.

Abram and Gallus helped me track the two men and are in the city with me now.

"Could you see the white man's face?"

"No. Tall fellow, but that's 'bout all. His hat was down low, and like I said, we were at a distance." Cleon paused and looked at John directly. "Where was Mister Webster 'bout a week ago?"

"You suspect Mister Webster?" John had a hard time believing it. "He was off on a mission to Nashville, while I was doin' some work for Miss Hattie."

"Off on a mission. That so?"

"That is so. You really think he's the white man you seen leavin' in the wagon?"

"Could be. I hate to admit that Abram mighta been right about Webster. The timin' of his mission to Nashville seems awful suspicious to me, John. Where is he now?"

"Back in Richmond in the Monumental Hotel, taken ill again."

"Sick from bein' out in the woods huntin' black men?"

"We don't know that. Did the man you saw look anything like Timothy Webster?"

"He was tall, like I said, and Mister Webster's tall."

"How can you be sure the white man and black man came here to Richmond?"

"I can track a wagon in any season, and we followed the tracks to Richmond. Mark my words. These killers is in this city."

31

T WAS PROBABLY A GOOD THING THAT BARTHOLOMEW ("BAT") Cuthbert lived on the outskirts of Richmond, a good distance from any neighbors. His line of work was developing explosives, and not many neighbors would put up with occasional blasts, not to mention the risk of an entire row of houses being sent up in flame like kindling.

It took a while for Ichabod to locate the house, which was set far off the main road, down a winding path. The house was also hidden behind a wall of vegetation, and when it finally came into view, Ichabod was shocked by the condition of the premises. The yard surrounding the house was cluttered with the remnants of wooden barrels, a hundred twisted pieces of rusted metal, a couple of broken-down wagons, some tattered furniture, deserted rabbit hutches, and wheels everywhere. It was as if there had been some great explosion, casting all of these objects in every direction, but it was more likely that Bat Cuthbert simply wasn't the tidiest of persons.

Ichabod, with his dog by his side, approached the porch. Ahab was still recovering from the stab wound and showed the trace of a limp. But before Ichabod could reach the door, which hung loosely on its hinges, Bat stepped into view, framed by the doorway. Bat looked to be in his thirties and was covered in fine powder and dirt from his feet to his face. His light jacket was ripped in several spots, and he was missing his left arm, which ended in a stub at the elbow.

Ichabod considered Bat Cuthbert to be one of the best explosives men working for the Confederacy. He wasn't in the same league as

Mister Maury or the Bomb Brothers, Gabriel and George Rains, but he knew a thing or two about how to blow a person to atoms. He also happened to blow his left arm to atoms in a mishap one year earlier. Ichabod had gotten to know Bat Cuthbert while working with the torpedo boat and Mister Maury's floating barrel torpedoes.

"Ichabod! Haven't seen you since you almost drowned like a cat," Bat said, reaching out to shake with his only hand.

"Didn't quite go as planned. But I'm gonna try again."

"That's the spirit! Gotta get back on the horse." He nodded toward his missing arm. "I got back to work as soon as I could after this piece of me went flying into the trees, blown clean off. I figger I got plenty more parts to lose before I give up this line of work. Take a seat."

By "seat," Bat evidently meant a small, upside-down barrel on the front porch. Bat lit up a cigar—not the wisest of ideas on the porch of a house where gunpowder was stockpiled. But maybe he too liked to test the limits, brushing up as close to Death as possible. He waved his cigar in the direction of Ahab, who sat on his haunches, eyeing him. "I see y'all still have that killer by your side. One of these days he's gonna take your arm off while you sleep."

"Losin' *your* arm didn't stop you from surroundin' yourself with explosives."

"Very true. But your dog is eyeing me like tonight's dinner. Is he safe?"

"Safe as anyone can be."

"That's not very safe. So what brings you to my humble abode?"

"You can create just about any kind of explosive, can't you?"

Bat smiled. Ichabod knew he loved to be flattered. "I sure can . . . within reason. I been workin' on some subterranean torpedoes for the Rains brothers. You hide them under the ground, and when a soldier steps on 'em . . ." Bat made the sound of an explosion, waving his cigar in the air. "With subterra-torpedoes, pursuin' soldiers will be too afraid to chase our men, for fear of hidden bombs. Gabriel Rains says he thinks these subterranean torpedoes will do away with offensive warfare entirely, but he don't know human nature."

Bat went into detail, describing how he planned to make primers for the torpedoes that could be triggered by seven pounds of pressure when stepped upon. It was hard to stop him once he started talking, so Ichabod finally had to cut him off. "So you think you can make an explosive for me?"

"What did y'all have in mind?"

Ichabod reached into the haversack slung over his right shoulder and pulled out a doll about a foot and a half long, with short black hair and a white sleeping gown. He tossed it on a lopsided table set between them. It was a Negro doll—a rarity.

"Can you insert a bomb into somethin' like this?"

Bat spit off to the side and scowled. "I ain't in the business of blowin' up children, Ichabod, even colored children. What do y'all think you're doin'? Soldiers is one thing, children another."

"Don't worry, I ain't aimin' to kill any young ones. I'm aimin' for some full-grown Yankee spies."

"With a doll?"

"Yes, with a doll."

Ichabod told him all about the dolls being used to smuggle information and medicine for the South, and how two Negroes had discovered them. He wanted to wipe these Negro spies off the face of the earth.

"Black devils, you say?"

"That's right."

Bat lit up another cigar and blew out a puff of smoke. "Sure. I can do it. Be glad to."

32

FIRST AFRICAN BAPTIST SEEMED TO HAVE GROWN DURING THE
time John had been away from Richmond. The sanctuary had
hit capacity, and all 1,500 seats in the church were filled by
slaves and free blacks. A white preacher, Reverend Robert
Ryland, ran the service, as the law stipulated, but every other face
in the sanctuary was black. The galleries were so full that John was
afraid someone was going to get bumped over the balcony railing—
especially with all of the movement during worship, people sway-
ing and waving. The choir was strong this morning, and the Spirit
didn't just move. It galloped!

"I'm proud to be promenadin' with my man for the first time
in half a year," Peg whispered to John, hooking him by the arm, as
they strolled in front of the church after the service had ended. This
was a timeworn tradition, even in February as long as the weather
was nice. Folks dressed in their Sunday best clothes and strolled up
and down the avenue outside of the church at Broad and 14th. The
clothes worn by slaves and free blacks were plain during the week, but
all of that pent-up desire for looking sprucy exploded on Sundays;
the women wore extravagant brooches and colorful hats adorned
with ostrich feathers, and the men wore embroidered waistcoats and
patent-leather shoes. If you strolled on down the street to a white
church, you wouldn't find clothes as fancy.

John threw a glance over his shoulder, where Cleon trailed,
wearing a jacket with so many patches that it looked like he was
wrapped in a quilt. Cleon had the look of a man trying to work

out a complex puzzle. Throughout the sermon, he would regularly whisper to John about all of the spots where the preacher had gone wrong, which evidently was quite a number of places. It was a good thing Reverend Ryland didn't preach on the need for slaves to submit to masters, as he did a couple of times per year. This was Cleon's first visit to First African Baptist, and he would have thrown his shoe at the preacher if the man had started talking about slaves and masters.

"I ain't ever been in a church this large," Cleon said. "Made me feel like I was gettin' a little taste of heaven, except for that sermon. I don't think I'll hear any preachin' in heaven lackin' so much in spiritual exactitude."

John wasn't going to even ask what "spiritual exactitude" meant because Cleon was just showing off.

"You had a problem with parts of the sermon, Cleon?" asked Peg, and John sighed audibly. He should have warned Peg not to ask Cleon about the finer points of theology.

Five minutes later, Cleon was still talking about his opinions on the third chapter of Romans and justification by grace. He must have used "propitiation" a dozen times; he hurled the word like it was a verbal firecracker.

Peg finally extricated herself from Cleon's lecture by stopping to talk with her friend, Mary Bowser, who liked to promenade at First African Baptist after her much shorter service at St. John's had ended. They discussed hat styles, and John joined in, because even hat styles beat listening to Cleon go on. As he stood there, soaking in the boredom, he caught a sight out of the corner of his eye that nearly knocked him down. He turned his body forty-five degrees to get a good look and determine if he was seeing things. His eyes didn't deceive him: Peg's brother, Shadrack, was talking to one of the deacons. *Shadrack!* The last time that John had seen him was five years ago, just before Cager Johnson sold him South. What in the world was he doing back in Richmond?

John nudged Peg, who was still talking about hats with Mary. "Peg . . . Peg . . . *Peg.*"

Frowning, Peg turned from her friend and whispered, "John, y'all are bein' rude."

"Peg, did you know about this?"

"Know about what?"

John pointed across the way, where Shadrack was still deep in conversation with Deacon Lubble. Shadrack leaned over the smaller man, looking strange in his spruced-up clothing; John had never seen him wearing much else than overalls.

Peg's mouth opened, forming a near-perfect O.

"What's Shadrack doin' here?" she said.

"He never went to church when he used to live here, but maybe he has repented," said Mary Bowser. "When you saw him the other day, did he say anything about comin' to church?"

John gave Peg a scolding eye. "You saw your brother the other day?"

Obviously realizing she had said too much, Mary mouthed the word "sorry" to Peg and backed away—quickly.

"John, can I talk to you?" asked Cleon, tapping him on the shoulder.

John ignored him. "Peg, why didn't you tell me your brother was back in town?"

"I was afraid you might get angry at me."

"Why would I get angry at you? You ain't got control of your brother's movements."

"John . . ." Another tap from Cleon.

"Shadrack came by the Atwater house, askin' me to help him out. He's free now, and he needed a job."

"And you said no, I hope."

Peg didn't answer.

"John . . ." Cleon persisted, as annoying as a mosquito.

"Don't tell me y'all said you'd help him." John could not understand Peg when it came to her brother. If Shadrack had been part of his family, his father would have banished him years ago; in fact, his father did banish one of John's brothers for lesser crimes than

Shadrack's. "What did you do? I sure hope y'all didn't ask Mister Atwater to hire him on."

"No. I asked Mister Atwater if he knew of any jobs in a different house, far from us. John, you shoulda seen him. Shadrack apologized to me for what he'd done all his life, and he ain't never done that before."

"He couldn't apologize enough as far as I'm concerned."

"People change."

John grunted.

"I'm prayin' to God he's changed," Peg added.

"Well, you better pray harder," Cleon said, finally stepping between the two of them and forcing his way into their conversation.

"Cleon, what do y'all think you're doin'? We're tryin' to talk about somethin' important, and you keep tryin' to stick your nose in."

"What I got to say is more important." Cleon's eyes drifted toward Shadrack, who had finished talking with the deacon and was melting into the crowd near the church entrance. "I seen that man before. You say he's your brother, Peg?"

Peg nodded.

"Where'd you see him?" John asked.

"That man—your brother-in-law, John—he was the black man who tried to kill me in the forest."

33

Allan Pinkerton was worried about Timothy Webster. He hadn't heard from his best operative for close to a month, and he wanted to know why. No one had penetrated the South as deeply as Webster, and he couldn't afford to lose him.

"What do you think about going to Richmond?" Pinkerton said to Pryce Lewis, another of his prize agents.

Lewis, a Welshman like Webster, was blunt. "It would be folly for me to go to Richmond."

"And why is that?"

"Because I am known by certain people in the South."

Pinkerton bristled whenever people mistrusted his judgment. He had built the best detective agency in the country by operating on his instincts, and he was sure that Lewis would be safe going south on this job.

He liked Lewis, and found him to be a sharp operator, so he was surprised to receive resistance. Pinkerton considered himself to be a good judge of character, for he was a student of phrenology, which maintained that the skull contained twenty-seven different organs and that by measuring and feeling the skull, you could determine the mental strengths and weaknesses of a person. He required many of his agents, like Lewis, to undergo a phrenological test, as he had done. His own phrenological description, by Professor O. S. Fowler, reported that his characteristics were "enthusiasm, heartiness, whole-souledness, impetuosity, excitability, and earnestness."

Today, he was earnest about one thing—sending Lewis to Richmond to find out if Webster was in trouble.

"If you went to Richmond, who are you afraid would know you there?"

He hoped using the word "afraid" would work on Lewis' pride. But it didn't seem to have much effect, and Lewis started rattling off names. "Mrs. Phillips and Mrs. Levy for starters."

Pinkerton gave a wave of his hand. "They're in New Orleans, not anywhere near Richmond."

"The Morton family."

"The family went to Florida."

"Lieutenant Dr. Garradeiu."

"He's in Charleston."

Their conversation became a fencing duel. For every name that Lewis threw at him, Pinkerton blocked it with a reasoned answer.

"You haven't even asked why I am sending you to Richmond," Pinkerton finally said, leaning back in his chair.

An awkward silence fell between them.

"Well? Aren't you going to ask me?" Pinkerton said.

Scowling like a schoolchild being asked to recite, Lewis finally said, "All right then. What's in Richmond?"

"Timothy Webster is in Richmond. He went there with Miss Hattie Lawton, posing as husband and wife, and we haven't heard from him in a month. That's not like him. I need to send you there to find out what has happened to Webster and to pull him out of the fire if need be."

Pinkerton relaxed some. He could tell that the very name "Timothy Webster" had made an impact. Lewis stroked his enormous sidewhiskers, which grew bushy on his cheeks like tumbleweeds.

"You're to go to Richmond with Scully," Pinkerton said.

"What would my cover be?"

"You're a British businessman with sympathy for the South, and you're on your way to Chattanooga for a transaction on cotton."

Lewis frowned, and it looked to Pinkerton that the man was wavering again. So the intelligence director fortified his argument.

"General McClellan is beginning a major offensive, and the information that Webster is collecting in Richmond could determine the success or failure of that operation. You *must* find out what has happened to Webster. The Union depends on it."

At first, Pinkerton was afraid he had laid it on too thick, but Lewis softened and let out the hint of a smile.

"Let me think on this," he said, steepling his fingers and staring Pinkerton in the eyes.

"You have until next Sunday then," the intelligence director said, sensing that he had already hooked the man.

*****

Shadrack was clean gone.

When John had spotted him vanishing into the crowd outside of First African Baptist, he and Cleon ran after him but couldn't track him down. Shadrack must have seen Cleon outside the church and realized he had been identified by one of his would-be victims. So he fled. Peg told John where Shadrack had been staying for the past few days—in a dingy boardinghouse near the river. But when John investigated, the landlady said Shadrack had grabbed his things and left in a hurry, and she had no idea where he might be.

Another day passed, and John became frustrated because he had no opportunity to hunt for Peg's renegade brother. Mister Webster had become even sicker—a severe case of rheumatism the doctor called it—and John spent much of his day helping him and Miss Hattie in the Monumental Hotel. He couldn't tell Webster or Miss Hattie anything about Shadrack because Cleon had stirred up serious suspicions that Webster might also be involved, and he didn't know whom to trust.

It wasn't until another day had passed that John finally had a few hours free from his duties with Webster to dig through the back alleys of Shockoe Bottom for any sign of Peg's brother. He went to Barney Litman's grocery store, where he found several tobacco slave hands playing checkers; he also tried Letty's cookshop, a popular hangout, but no one there even knew who Shadrack was, let alone where he had gone.

John wandered up a narrow alley, cluttered with refuse and rutted so badly that a wagon could break a wheel maneuvering through the space. The last place he ever wanted to go near was Lumpkin's Jail, the most notorious slave trading operation in all of Richmond. But he forced himself to do it; the place was his last hope for locating Shadrack.

Lumpkin's Jail sat on a plot of land appropriately named "The Devil's Half Acre," and it was where slaves were temporarily held before they were put up for sale on the nearby auction blocks. Some described it as a purgatory, but that didn't quite fit. Purgatory was a stopover on the way to heaven, while Lumpkin's Jail was a stopover on the way to hell. In fact, it was hell. When Shadrack used to help track runaways, he would often operate out of Lumpkin's Jail. So if anyone knew where he might have gone, the monsters at Lumpkin's probably did.

John approached the compound, where there stood several brick buildings for the more cooperative slaves awaiting auction. The troublemakers wound up in the two-story jail where the most ungodly things happened. There was also a guesthouse for out-of-town slave traders, but John headed for the main house, where Mister and Missus Lumpkin lived.

He passed by three guard dogs, bringing to mind the stories his father used to tell about Cerberus, the three-headed dog that guarded the entrance into the Underworld. His father would talk of the twelve labors of Hercules, one of which was to capture Cerberus and bring him back to the land of the living. These three large dogs went berserk as John walked by, and he hoped the ropes holding them to their stakes were strong. They snarled and growled, low rumblings from one, a wild ripping sound from another. They crawled over each other to get nearer to John, and their ropes and bodies tangled, giving them even more of an impression of a three-headed dog.

"John Scobell, y'all got a nerve comin' onto the premises," came a voice off to his right.

It was one of the prison overseers, Lazarus Hope—an odd surname for a man who worked in such a place.

"Mornin', Laz," said John.

Laz was a skinny white man who seemed to have trouble growing a full beard. His face displayed a patchy stubble of growth, and he was missing an awful lot of teeth for a man barely over thirty. He carried a whip in his right hand.

"If y'all are fixin' to stay long, got a nice cozy cell for you," Laz said. "The best view in town."

"I can't afford your rates in this kinda hotel."

"Not many can afford to stay here. But I can guarantee you a memorable time."

"I'm lookin' for Shadrack Collier. You seen him here?"

"Good old Shadrack!" Laz pointed the end of his whip at John. "This ain't no lost and found, John, so you're wasting your time askin' about Shad."

John heard the sound of a door creak open behind him, and he turned to see a woman appear on the front porch of the Lumpkin log home. It was Mary Lumpkin, wife of the owner, Robert.

"You can go on now, Lazarus," she said, folding her arms across her chest. "I'll deal with this."

Lazarus gave Missus Lumpkin the evil eye, and he strode off without so much as a "Yes, ma'am." Missus Lumpkin was probably used to such impudent treatment by the white help. After all, she was a black woman.

People say that Robert Lumpkin, monster that he was, really loved Mary Lumpkin, as well as the five mulatto children they had together. But it was hard for John to reconcile the strange arrangement. Here was a white man who ran the most foul slave trading operation in Richmond—perhaps in all of the South—and John was supposed to believe he fell in love with a slave woman like Mary. They weren't husband and wife in the legal sense, but Lumpkin had freed Mary and called her his wife. He had even sent Mary and two of his children north to Pennsylvania for a spell to keep them safe—safe from slave traders like him.

"Mornin', John," said Missus Lumpkin wearily. She was a tall, generous-sized woman—much better fed than the slaves in the jail. But she had a haggard look in the eyes, probably from years of reconciling this life in her mind. Some said she had convinced herself that she could soften the treatment of slaves if she remained Lumpkin's woman, but people will always try to find their own justification in a world of compromises, John figured.

"Can I help you?" she asked.

"I'm looking for Shadrack. You seen him?"

Missus Lumpkin eyed him stonily. "What do y'all need him for?"

"He's a suspect."

Her expression cracked, and a smile appeared. "A suspect? Y'all act like you're the sheriff in town. What's he done?"

"Don't know for sure, but he mighta killed three black men."

The smile vanished. Her mouth parted, but only slightly. "Oh. I see. Were these friends of yours who done died?" John heard sympathy in her tone, but he wondered if it was all part of the act she had developed over the years.

"Yes, I was friends with them. He tried to kill a fourth friend, but failed, and the friend claims it was Shadrack he saw runnin' from the scene."

"Shadrack is a good tracker, but I never took him to be a murderer. He preferred to let the white men and the dogs do any killin'. How do you know the same man done all three killin's?"

"'Cause each victim was wrapped in a Yankee flag with messages scrawled on it. So you seen him?"

Mary looked behind her, toward the front door, as if to make sure her "husband" wasn't lurking anywhere near. Then she moved closer to John and said, softly, "Shadrack was here the other day, and he looked in an awful state. I wondered if he was on the run from his master."

"He told my wife Peg he didn't have no master. He had been made a free man."

"He sure didn't act like no free man. He was trapped, and I know trapped looks when I see it."

Of course she did: Her husband specialized in trapping human beings.

"I thank you kindly for the information, Missus Lumpkin, but do you have any idea where he's gone?"

"Ain't got no idea, but I don't think he planned on stayin' in Richmond. He was troubled, that for sure."

"You think he's already left town then?"

"I'm sure of it." She paused and sighed, and John recalled how people often described Lumpkin's Jail as "a place of sighs." Then she reached out and gave John's hand a squeeze. "I hope y'all find justice."

John nodded silently.

"This ain't gonna be the Devil's Half Acre forever, you know," she added.

"I hope y'all are right, Missus Lumpkin."

John gave his farewell and turned. As he passed the dogs, the three beasts went wild once again, and John thanked the Lord for good strong rope.

34

RYCE LEWIS HADN'T STOPPED WORRYING SINCE THE MOMENT
he and the Irishman Scully had arrived in Richmond on their
mission to find out what had happened to Timothy Webster.
They had arrived on a Wednesday, one day ago, and he couldn't
wait to be back on a train, heading away from the heart of the
Confederacy.

It didn't take much sleuthing to find out that Webster and Miss
Hattie were holed up in the Monumental Hotel, and that Webster was
sicker than a dog, suffering from a severe case of rheumatism. Just
like that, he and Scully had done their job, and they would be leaving
on the Friday morning train. He doubted whether he would be able
to shake his sense of doom until then.

A night at the theater on Wednesday didn't make matters any
better. If anything, the program by British comic Harry Macarthy at
the Metropolitan Hall made him feel even more isolated and vulnerable. Macarthy's raucous bits were all in support of the Rebels, and
the wild cheering nearly shattered his eardrums when the performer
started singing Confederate songs. Everyone in the audience leaped
to their feet and joined in, including Lewis and Scully, because, after
all, they were supposed to be Confederate sympathizers. But the lyrics tasted like poison.

Come, hucksters, from your markets,
Come, bandits, from your caves,
Come, venal spies; with brazen lies

Bewildering your deluded eyes,
That we may dig your graves;
Come, creatures of a sordid clown
And driveling traitor's breath,
A single blast shall blow you down
Upon the fields of Death.

He nearly choked on the words "venal spies."

The most nerve-wracking moment had come on this very after-noon when he and Scully checked in with General Winder's office, as everyone who crosses the Potomac must do upon entering Rich-mond. General Winder had a reputation for ferocity; he had been known to tie prisoners by the thumbs and suspend them from a crossbeam. But Winder was genial to them, and he declared that they would not need a pass to be in Richmond, since they were "stalwart friends of the Confederacy."

It was now early Thursday evening, and Lewis and Scully headed for the Monumental Hotel to check in one last time with Webster and Miss Hattie. It made Lewis sick thinking of the risks they had taken simply to find out that Pinkerton's favorite agent was convalescing. After running the gauntlet of prostitutes near Capitol Square, they entered the modest Monumental Hotel. Truth be told, he did not mind one final glimpse of Miss Hattie before leaving the city. As a single man, he wondered why he never landed an assignment from Pinkerton in which he could pose as the lovely lady's husband.

When they entered the room, they found a full house. It was a long, narrow room, and Webster was propped up in bed on the right side, with Miss Hattie seated at his side, holding his hand. Even in sickness, Webster had all the luck.

Standing behind Miss Hattie was a Negro servant, a fierce-looking sort, and P. B. Price, a garrulous white man, a member of the Young Men's Christian Association and an avid theatergoer. They had met Price the day before, and he was the one who had recommended the evening's entertainment.

"Mister Lewis, Mister Scully!" called out Price, rising from his chair and pumping their hands. "That was a grand show, wasn't it?"

Lewis grunted his agreement, and then Scully and Price began chatting about the best bits by the comic.

"There is another show tomorrow night," Price said, slapping Lewis on the back. "Mary Partingon is playing at Franklin Hall in *The Hunchback*. You should not miss it, fellows!"

"Afraid we're going to have to pass, but thank you all the same," said Lewis. "Tomorrow morning we hope to be on a train out of town."

"Are you sure we can't postpone leaving for a day?" suggested Scully. "*The Hunchback* sounds like a corker of an evening."

Lewis could not believe Scully's stupidity. He controlled his reaction, toning it down to a mild rebuke. "You know better than that. We cannot postpone our business in Chattanooga."

Scully looked like a child whose toy had been pilfered right out of his hands. "I suppose you're right."

The group chatted a little more about the theater, and then Mister Price departed, at last leaving Lewis and Scully alone with Webster, Miss Hattie, and the servant. Lewis cast a couple of looks at the Negro, wishing he would leave. Webster caught his eye movements.

"Don't worry, Pryce, you can trust John Scobell here."

So that was John Scobell. Lewis had heard about the colored spy, but he had no idea what the fellow looked like. Lewis nodded to him, and Scobell nodded back in silent salute.

"You seem to be feeling better," Lewis said to Webster.

"With these two saints waiting on me hand and foot, I hope to be back on my feet soon."

They spoke for about five minutes about the steady increase in food costs in Richmond, due to the Union blockade, and Lewis considered leaving right then and there. But he decided to linger a little longer, because he couldn't peel his eyes off of Miss Hattie. He didn't often get a chance to socialize with young women of such enticing features, and he loved it when she smiled in his direction. He would pay for this indulgence.

"Richmond sure is more crowded than I remember," Lewis said.

"That's true," said Miss Hattie. "We were lucky to get a room in this hotel. I hear some establishments have taken to renting out their billiard tables as beds."

They talked about the number of soldiers crowding into the city, and all the while Lewis kept shooting glances in the direction of Miss Hattie. Another ten minutes went by, and there was a sudden knock on the door.

"Probably just Price again," said Webster. Then he called out, "Come in."

The first man to enter the hotel room was a stranger, but a second man held back in the darkness of the hallway. When the second man finally crossed the threshold and moved into the glow of the gaslight, a pain stabbed Lewis in the chest. He recognized the second man immediately. It was nineteen-year-old Chase Morton.

In January, Pinkerton had ordered Lewis and Scully to lead a raid on the Morton home in Washington because the family was under suspicion for espionage. Chase's father, Jackson Morton, was a former senator and one of the largest slaveholders in Florida, and Pinkerton had questions about their loyalty to the Union. Lewis hated such an unsavory task—turning this distinguished family's house upside down—and he had spent some of the time smoking cigarettes in the parlor with Chase Morton, the very young man standing right before him now. They never found any evidence questioning the Mortons' loyalty, but Chase Morton had seen him, and he knew he was a Pinkerton man.

This was the worst possible turn of events.

"Hello, Mister Webster, I came to see if your condition has improved," said Morton.

So Webster knew Chase Morton. Of all the foul luck, Lewis thought.

"Mister Clackner and Mister Morton, may I introduce you to Mister Scully and Mister Lewis," said Miss Hattie.

They all shook hands, and Morton said nothing about having already met Lewis. But he gave him a good hard look when they shook. The air between them was electrically charged. Lewis did a good job maintaining his composure, but Scully—who only moments ago had suggested they stay another night—was showing signs of panic. Some of the electricity in the air must have been flowing through Scully, because he became jittery in his seat, and Lewis could see the sweat sheen on his forehead.

Finally, Scully got to his feet and mumbled something about "needing to be back at the Exchange Hotel," and he darted out of the room.

Strangely, Lewis almost felt a sense of relief. He had been on edge ever since they stepped foot in Richmond, but now that Morton had entered the room and knew who he was, Lewis actually felt the tension begin to drain away. Was this a symptom of shock or simple acceptance of fate? He felt so relaxed that he was almost tempted to ask Morton how his family was doing. He didn't.

"Care for a smoke?" Morton said, offering his gold cigarette case to Lewis. He smiled knowingly, and Lewis grinned back.

"Thank you, you read my mind," said Lewis, plucking out one of the cigarettes.

Morton lit up and then handed his box of matches to Lewis. "So what brings you to Richmond?" He leaned back in his chair and blew smoke from the corner of his mouth.

"I carried a message from our Rebel friends in Baltimore," Lewis explained. Pinkerton had supplied him with two forged letters from Rebel sympathizers, as part of his cover, but he thought it would be too obvious to produce them now as evidence of his Confederate loyalty. Perhaps he could hint to Morton that he was a double agent working for the Confederates and infiltrating the Pinkerton ranks.

"Mister Morton, I believe we have a mutual friend in Washington," said Lewis. "Miss Rose Greenhow."

Miss Greenhow was one of the most prominent Southern spies in Washington.

"I somehow cannot picture you as one of Miss Greenhow's confidantes," Morton said.

"People are not always who you think they are."

"And sometimes people are *exactly* who you think they are."

Throughout this exchange, Webster and Miss Hattie kept a hawk's eye on both of them. From their baffled looks, it was obvious they knew something was terribly wrong between the two of them.

"Miss Greenhow was put under house arrest in Washington, wasn't she?" said Morton, picking a piece of tobacco from his tongue.

"I believe she was. Such a shame to treat a lady like that—a pillar of Washington society."

"Who was it who put her under house arrest? A Mister Pinkerton, wasn't it? Do you know the fellow?"

"I think we all know that Mister Pinkerton is a scoundrel," said Lewis. "If I could destroy his organization from the inside, I would."

There. He couldn't make it plainer than that.

"I am truly glad to hear you say that," said Morton. "But I think it would take much more than one man, such as yourself, to take down the U.S. Intelligence Service. Perhaps Mister Scully will help you. Where did he run off to in such a hurry, by the way?"

"It's hard to know with Scully. An excitable man." Lewis pulled his gold watch from his vest pocket and popped the cover. "And I believe I must take my leave as well."

"So soon?" said Morton.

"Yes, I am sorry. It has been a long day."

"And perhaps an even longer day tomorrow," said Morton. "Don't forget your friend's coat."

"Oh, yes. Thank you." Scully had bolted in such a hurry that he had left his coat on a nearby hook. Lewis put his soft felt hat upon his head and made his farewells. He kissed Miss Hattie's outstretched hand and savored her perfume, and he wondered if getting to spend a little more time in her presence had been worth what was about to happen to him.

When he left the room, he found Scully waiting for him in the hallway, a frenzied mess. Scully paced back and forth.

"What're you still doin' here?" Lewis asked. "Thought you'd be runnin' down the street."

"I saw Samuel McCubbin downstairs in the lobby with several other men, so I dashed back up."

That wasn't good. McCubbin was the chief of the Confederate military police. This was beginning to look like a trap.

Lewis tossed Scully his coat. "You might need this in prison," he said.

*****

John had remained quiet throughout the entire odd visit from the two men—Pryce Lewis and John Scully. It was obvious that something was wrong between them and the visitor, Chase Morton. Only moments after Lewis made his farewells, Morton gave a nod of his head, and his partner, Mister Clackner, departed in a rush. John could not help but notice that Clackner had a revolver tucked into his belt, and he wondered if he might be a policeman. A few minutes later, Mister Morton made his farewells.

"I don't like this," Miss Hattie whispered to Webster when Morton had gone. "Do you think he recognized Lewis and Scully?"

"It appears so," said Webster. "I thought it was foolish for Pinkerton to send men to check on me."

"Should we leave town? Tonight?" asked Miss Hattie.

"We wouldn't get far," said Webster. "Besides, even if Morton suspects Lewis and Scully of being spies, that does not implicate us. I still have my good reputation as a Confederate courier."

"If you need a place to hide, you could go to the Van Lew residence," John said quietly.

Webster smiled at him. "Thank you, John, but let's hope it doesn't come to that. I suggest you head on home now. No sense in you getting caught up in this."

I'm already caught up in this, John thought.

"Maybe you should leave town for a spell," Webster suggested, looking at Miss Hattie.

"Even if I wanted to leave you, it wouldn't look normal for a man's wife to leave him unattended in your condition," she said. "I'm staying by your side."

"If you left me in charge of tendin' to Mister Webster, then people might not wonder why you are leavin' a sick husband, Miss Hattie," said John.

"He has a point," said Webster.

"No." Miss Hattie was adamant. "I will not desert you."

"Then, John, you should consider slipping out of town for a time. Until this blows over."

But John was as adamant as Miss Hattie. "Wouldn't think of it, sir." His father hadn't raised him to run from a fight, especially when a friend was in trouble. Even a white friend.

"If I had the energy to argue, I'd try to convince you *both* to leave town," said Webster. "But I suddenly feel terribly tired, so here we are."

Webster asked John to track Lewis and Scully and find out if they made it back to their hotel without being arrested. It was seven o'clock, so John still had a couple of hours before the curfew forbidding blacks from being on the streets of Richmond.

John went off in search of Lewis and Scully, reaching the lobby just in time to see Clackner, Morton, and McCubbin escorting the two men out of the hotel. They were joined by four rough-looking characters, who probably worked for McCubbin and General Winder. Winder's thugs were known as Plug-Uglies, and they were as brutal as they sounded. They had roots in the mobs of Baltimore and would beat a man senseless for even making a joke about the Confederate government.

A small crowd began to gather in front of the Monumental to gawk at the arrests. Lewis appeared to be taking their capture stoically, but Scully had the look of a trapped rat. John followed the parade of curiosity seekers as the Plug-Uglies, armed with clubs, hurried Lewis and Scully through the streets. The growing crowd gave off the kind of excitement you see at lynchings or tar and featherings, and it made him feel conspicuous being one of a few black faces in the mob. Once Lewis and Scully disappeared into the bowels of General Winder's office on 9th and Broad Streets, there wasn't much more for him to do than report the bad news back to Webster and Miss Hattie. With that done, he scurried on back to the Atwater house before the nine o'clock bell rang signaling the curfew—the time when night patrolmen could turn his head into a smashed pumpkin.

"You're back later than normal," said Peg, as John climbed under the quilt, and she put her head on his chest.

"Mister Webster was feelin' more poorly than normal."

"Mmmm." She draped an arm around him.

"Go on back to sleep," he said, but she had already done just that.

35

P EG SPOTTED THE HEADLINE FROM ACROSS THE TABLE AS SHE
served breakfast to Captain Atwater and Missus Hicks. YAN-
KEE SPIES shouted the front page of the Sunday *Richmond
Enquirer*. She tried to read the stack of headlines below the main
header, but could make out only a few choice words as the captain
rustled the paper, holding the *Enquirer* in one hand as he cut into his
fried eggs with the other. The paper said something about two spies
being captured Thursday night and something about Henrico Jail.

When the captain set down his fork and opened the paper wide,
Missus Hicks started reading the front page from her seat across the
table; when he tried to turn the pages, Missus Hicks ordered him
to stop so she could finish reading without being distracted by the
rustling of pages. The captain peered over the top of the newspaper,
patiently waiting for her to permit him to continue flipping through
the news.

"Two spies caught red-handed," she said.

"I read the article—most of it, at least."

"I hope they give them swift justice. Set them up against a wall
and fire away."

"Swift justice is often no justice at all, Henrietta."

"Tell that to all of our dead lying in fields in northern Virginia."

Peg nearly dropped a cup and saucer. Could Timothy Webster
and Hattie Lawton be the two nabbed spies? She felt light-headed,
and her entire body was charged by panic, like she was plummeting
from a high roof. John had been with Webster and Miss Hattie at the

Monumental Hotel just three nights ago—the night these spies were captured.

John was out back, cutting firewood for the Atwaters, and he would be in shortly to get dressed up for Sunday worship. She fought the urge to dash outside right then and there and ask him about what had happened, and she continued to work through breakfast in a fog of worry.

Missus Hicks noticed. "You look a million miles away, Peg."

Peg wished she really were a million miles away.

"Sorry, ma'am."

The old lady finished off her coffee and studied Peg's face. "That's the way I like it."

Peg stared back, confused, and Missus Hicks clarified. "Your head wrap. You have the tie in the back, the way it's always done. Very nice."

"Thank you, ma'am."

When breakfast had been cleared and the dishes taken care of, Peg nearly sprinted up the servant's staircase, and she found John stretched out on their bed, hands laced behind his head.

"Why didn't you tell me?" she said, closing the door too firmly; it banged shut.

John sat bolt upright. "Tell you what?"

Peg put her face within inches of him. "Why didn't you tell me about what happened Thursday night?"

John put a hand on Peg's right arm. "Was there somethin' in the papers?"

Peg shook loose and walked over to the dresser, then turned. "It's all over the paper. Was it Mister Webster and Miss Hattie who got nabbed?"

"That's not what the paper said, was it?"

"I only saw headlines. Somethin' about two spies bein' captured. Was it them?"

John put his feet on the floor, but he didn't rise from the bed. He scratched his chin with his forefinger. "It wasn't Webster or Lawton. It was two other spies—Pryce Lewis and John Scully."

That brought some relief. "So you ain't got a connection to them?"

John paused before answering. "I wouldn't quite say that. Lewis and Scully were in Webster's hotel room Thursday night. They're Pinkerton men."

"Oh, Lordy. *They were with you?*"

"With me and Webster and Miss Hattie."

"John, you gotta run."

"I ain't desertin' Mister Webster and Miss Hattie. And I certainly ain't desertin' you."

"You wouldn't be desertin' me. I *want* you to go."

"My papa didn't raise me to be no coward."

"Your papa ain't here no longer. And it ain't cowardly to run to safety for a spell."

"And leave you here unsafe?"

"Then we could run together," Peg said.

"Don't be foolish. No one suspects either of us of anything. If we run, we wouldn't get far. A black couple goin' North is somethin' people notice."

"But you had no problem leavin' town to go North back in June."

"No problem? I got caught by Confederates."

"Miss Hattie can take us with her. We can pose as her servants."

"Miss Hattie ain't leavin' Webster's side neither. She's not a deserter."

"Then she's a fool too."

"You think I'm a fool?"

"I don't think it. I know it."

Peg had enough of him playing the "obedient boy" to Webster. She had enough of Miss Lawton and her white-woman charms. And she had enough of his infernal sense of honor. When she wanted him to stay in Richmond back in June, he left. And now that she wants him to go, he stays.

"A man doesn't just run out on his friends."

"No, he just runs out on his wife."

"That ain't fair."

"Besides, you really think they're your friends? They're just usin' you for their purposes."

"No one's usin' me. I'm free to choose."

"Then choose me. Run away. Run for my sake."

"I *am* choosin' you. I'm choosin' to stay here to protect you."

"You can't protect me if you're dead. *Run.*"

John walked over and kissed her on the forehead. "I'll be waitin' for y'all outside. Church is startin' soon, so you best get dressed."

Peg felt like screaming.

*****

It had to be on a Sunday. That was the only day on which Ichabod could be sure that the Atwater house would be empty all morning. Captain Atwater and Missus Hicks would be attending St. John's Church, while the Negro help would all be at First African Baptist for a long day of preaching and worshipping.

Ichabod brought along Ahab because he would bark an alarm if anyone came by unexpectedly, but all appeared quiet and desolate as Ichabod approached the servant's entrance from the alley. The door was unlocked, as the butler, Gilbert Mann, ensured him it would be. Ichabod had talked to Gilbert and discovered that the man detested John Scobell. So Ichabod had worked that fact to his advantage, telling Gilbert he knew things about Scobell that could get him tossed in jail, but that he needed to collect evidence from his room. Gilbert was more than cooperative after that, telling him exactly which room John and Peg Scobell occupied on the third floor and ensuring him that the door to the servant's entrance would be left open.

Ichabod eased open the door and slid inside, with Ahab right behind. He had to be careful. After all, if he dropped the doll in his hands, he would be engulfed in flame, and his body parts would wind up as decorations in several different rooms. His bomb-making friend, Bat, had fitted the doll with a modified Schenkl shell with a percussion fuse. The cylindrical shell was sewn into the doll's belly, making the doll unusually heavy, but it would still do the trick. The percussion fuse, a brass cylinder filled with primer, would ignite the shell when struck. Drop the doll, it explodes. Set it on its back with any amount of force, it explodes. Jam a knife in its back, looking for hidden documents, it explodes.

One way or another, this doll was going to blow John and Peg Scobell off the map—as long as Ichabod didn't drop the thing going up the stairs. He carried the doll as gently as a newborn baby—careful to keep it face down in his hands since the percussion fuse faced toward the doll's back. There was always the risk that any explosion would kill Captain Atwater along with the Scobells, but he could accept that. After the captain's foolishness with the Union spy living under his roof—the Baker woman—he doubted that the man was all that innocent.

The Scobells' room on the third floor of the house was tiny, but much too comfortable for the likes of these spies. If he were wealthy enough to have black help, or own a slave or two, he would have them sleep in the barn or a shanty. Anything but under the same roof. He entered the room and looked for the most obvious place to set the doll. *The bed.* They couldn't miss it there.

But he had to keep reminding himself: *Remember to place the doll face down.*

Ichabod laid the doll on the Scobells' bed. With sudden inspiration, he decided to place the doll *beneath* the covers, providing yet another way for them to accidentally set off the device. They probably would not notice the lump in the bed, and if they plopped down on the mattress, they would land on the doll and be blown to atoms. He smiled at the idea of John and Peg, wrapped in a loving embrace, tumbling together onto the bed—and going up in flames. Even if they somehow discovered the doll under the covers, chances are they would set it off while investigating it.

There were many ways for them to die.

*****

Peg was glad to be taken away from her worries—at least for part of the day, swept up in the Spirit at church. She was never one of the shouters at church, worked into a frenzy by the music, but today she let herself go. It was the only way she could cope with John's stubborn determination to stay in Richmond, as well as confront her worries about her brother and the war. They all pressed on her mind with a combined weight that was hard to bear.

On the way home, as John tried to console her, they bumped into Mary Bowser, who was heading to the Van Lew house.

"You hear the news?" Mary asked.

"About the two spies?" John said. "Yes. It will blow over."

"I think you're right."

Peg stood by scowling. Blow over? She thought that both Mary and John were fooling themselves.

"What about Shadrack?" Mary continued. "Any word?"

"I think he's long gone," John reported.

Peg had told Mary everything about her brother, in the hopes that her connections would know something about the whereabouts of Shadrack. They didn't.

"I don't suppose he will ever dare return to Richmond," Mary said. "But I guess the consolation is that at least he is out of your life for good."

"I would much rather he be here facin' justice," John growled.

Peg could see that John was still irritated with Mary for involving her in spy business. Mary probably noticed it too. She gave Peg a hurried hug and made her farewells, and then Peg and John continued on to the Atwater home.

They could hear Matilda banging away in the kitchen and singing to herself as they approached the back door. When they entered, Matilda broke into a smile and patted herself on the head, which displayed another head wrap variation. This one had a large knot on the front of her head, with a little bit of hair showing in front.

"You like, Peggy?"

"Very nice," Peg answered, but without her usual enthusiasm.

Matilda stared at Peg carefully. "Y'all feelin' all right? You look like you're havin' to drag your body along like it's a sack of corn." Then a knowing look crossed her face, and the cook grinned even bigger. "Y'all feelin' sick in the morningtimes? Is there somethin' you ain't tellin' us, sister?"

"No, no, absolutely not." Peg wished she could say she was with child, but her barrenness was just another disappointment in her life.

"Well I wouldn't be so sure, dear. You just ain't been yourself, and I often found that if you ain't yourself it's because there's a himself or herself growing inside."

"I pray you're right," said Peg, offering Matilda a weary smile.

"If you ain't feelin' right 'bout bein' around food preparations and all, I can talk to the mistress and see if she'll excuse you."

"That won't be necessary. I'll be down shortly."

"You rest that weariness away," Matilda called, and Peg and John trudged up the servant's staircase and into their room on the third floor.

"Matilda's right," John said, hanging his straw hat on a hook. "You need to rest some."

Peg didn't answer. She was still too angry at John for refusing to run to safety. They sat together, side by side on the edge of the bed, and John put an arm around her shoulder. She felt weary and a little sick, and she doubted that Matilda could possibly be right about her being with child. She assumed that this feeling of heaviness, which had been dragging at her steps like an anchor for days now, was just her reaction to Shadrack and the arrest of those two spies.

"Tell you what," John said. "I'll go on downstairs and help Matilda in the kitchen. You rest."

Rest would be nice. Her eyelids felt heavy, and she would like nothing better than to just fall back onto this straw-filled mattress and dream away the next year of her life.

"But Missus Hicks will want me down there servin.'"

"When it comes servin' time, I'll fetch you. For now, you rest." John kissed her on the side of the head.

"Perhaps y'all are right."

"I'm always right," John said, rising and heading for the door. "Go on now. *Sleep.*"

Peg forced a smile, a small consolation to her husband, and after he departed she just sat on the edge of bed, staring into space. Eventually, her eyes landed on Lucy Ann, the doll that John had brought back from the forest outside Manassas. She had sewn the doll back together after they had extracted the hidden stash of quinine. Lucy Ann had come to represent the child she wanted so badly and maybe could never have because of what had been done to her by Cager Johnson—and others. She tried to ignore the fact that the doll had a white face.

Rising, Peg walked over to the chair where Lucy Ann sat with her unchanging expression. She picked up the doll and brushed it against her cheek, feeling the softness of the clothing. Then she set it back down and turned toward the bed. Sleep. She needed sleep. She should just cast herself onto the bed and vanish from reality.

She would have done it too if she hadn't noticed the slight bulge in the very center of the bed. She groaned, because John was always leaving his brogans in the oddest places in the room. She nearly tripped on his shoes just two days ago because he left them right inside the door. But putting a shoe beneath the covers? That was just plain odd.

Then it occurred to her: John was *wearing* his shoes, so what was this?

Curious, she pulled aside the covers and gasped. Lying on the bed, face down, was another doll. She smiled. Even with the doll lying face down, she could tell that its face and hands were the same color as her own skin. It was a black doll.

But where in the world had John found this gift? It was just the thing to raise her spirits, so she reached out for the doll, ready to embrace it.

36

ATILDA INSISTED ON INSPECTING JOHN'S HANDS BEFORE HE helped her in the kitchen. So he held out his fingers, and she looked them over, one digit at a time.

"Can't trust men not to come into the kitchen with dirt all over them hands," she said, pulling back his right thumb to check in the creases of his finger. "But y'all are lookin' fine. You musta scrubbed up for church good."

She started John off with something simple—cutting the white ends off of the asparagus, about six inches from the top. Matilda continued to sing as they worked—but not too loudly because the last thing she wanted to do was disturb Missus Hicks.

Missus Hicks and Captain Atwater came by the kitchen anyway, about ten minutes later, both of them curious about why Peg wasn't working.

"She wasn't feelin' so good, so I'm pitchin' in until dinnertime," said John. Missus Hicks sniffed in response, but she didn't demand that he retrieve Peg. Still, she was in an ornery mood, and she targeted Matilda's head wrap.

"You have the knot on the wrong side," she observed icily. "You normally wear the wrap tied in back."

Matilda smiled. "I'm mixin' things up, Missus Hicks. Just like I wouldn't want to cook y'all the same meal every single day, I'm lookin' for variety and hope you approve."

Captain Atwater chuckled. "She has a good point. I wouldn't want to eat liver every single day of my life. Come to think of it, I have a hard time stomaching it for even one day of my life."

"Don't you worry then, Captain Atwater. Tonight is lamb and asparagus. No liver in sight!"

"I am eternally grateful, Matilda."

Missus Hicks didn't crack a smile, but she didn't push the matter of the head wrap any further. She must be tiring some lately, John thought. She had been sleeping later and holding her fire in minor skirmishes such as these. So she just let Matilda's head wrap be, and shuffled in the direction of the staircase, probably heading upstairs to take a nap. John hoped Peg had found some sleep as well.

*****

Peg lifted the black doll from the bed—gently. It felt unusually heavy for a doll, but that just made it seem more real. She wondered what this doll might be carrying inside, but she hated the idea of John tearing into its small back to find out. The other doll, Lucy Ann, looked more like a young woman, dressed in a bonnet and fancy gown, but this black doll was made to look more like a baby with its oversized head and chubby cheeks. She cradled it in her arms like a real child.

Peg's mother never seemed to lack for the ability to pop out babies. Shadrack had been Peg's only sibling in their home, but Mama said her first three children had been sold away before Peg was born. Papa had also forced Mama to give away two illegitimate children, so there were plenty of brothers and sisters out there somewhere, wandering the world or already dead. It puzzled her why Mama, so unfit for motherhood, would be blessed with an abundant brood, while she had trouble conceiving. It didn't help having John gone for half of the year.

She sat on the bed and rocked the child in her arms and sang a Scottish lullaby, taught to her by their old master, Dugall McQueen.

Ho-ro-ro, hi-ri-ri
Sleep until dawn,
Oh, hush thee, my baby,
Thy sire was a knight,
Thy mother a lady,
Both lovely and bright;
The woods and the glens,
From the towers which we see,
They all are belonging,
Dear baby, to thee.

Oh, fear not the bugle,
Tho' loudly it blows,
It calls out the warders
That guard thy repose;
Their bows would be bended,
Their blades would be red,
Ere the step of a foeman
Draws near to thy bed.

Oh, hush thee, my baby,
Thy sire was a knight,
Oh, hush thee, my baby,
So bonnie, so bright.
Ho-ro-ro, hi-ri-ri
Sleep until dawn;
Ho-ro-ro, hi-ri-ri
Sleep until dawn.

Ever so gently, as she finished the last verse, Peg laid the baby down on a pillow on the window seat. Then she kissed the child's face and crawled into bed where she would give anything to be able to sleep until dawn.

*****

Ichabod stared up at the Atwater house. Ahab stood at his side, tongue lolling out. The house was dark, except for a lone candle on the first floor. The third floor window, where Peg and John Scobell's room was found, was completely dark. Even more shocking, the room was still there. He had fully expected to see a gaping hole in the home, where his explosive had taken a big bite out of the third floor.

Was his bomb a dud? Bat had a good reputation, so duds were unlikely. But perhaps he had not made the percussion fuse sensitive enough. Ichabod didn't want it to be too sensitive for fear of it going off in his own hands, but maybe he had had Bat overdo it.

Crouching down, Ichabod scratched behind Ahab's ear.

"No fireworks tonight, boy. But tomorrow . . . If this bomb is workin', there is no way they could survive a second day without settin' it off."

Ahab licked his face, the big, sloppy tongue running up and down his cheek. Patting the dog on the back a few times, Ichabod stood up, took one last look at the house, and shook his head.

37

John opened his eyes. It was Monday morning, but still dark, and he was wide awake. No chance of going back to sleep now. He heard Peg's steady breathing inches from his face. Her leg was draped over his foot because Peg preferred some contact as they slept. An arm draped over his waist. Legs tangled together. Any type of physical connection.

He sat up in bed and rubbed his eyes before getting up and fumbling around in the dark for the horsehair brush for his teeth. Peg had trained him well, and now he used it first thing every morning. She would not kiss him until he had used the tooth powder concoction, so he had a strong incentive. He used the bucket of clean water tucked beneath a small end table.

"Mornin', laddie."

John turned around and found Peg sitting up in bed, hugging her legs to her chest. "Mornin', lassie," he said. "Feelin' better this mornin'?"

She shrugged.

John went to the window and opened the curtains. Faint light on the horizon filtered into the dark, early morning sky, and he could sense a steady, stealthy increase in brightness. As he moved away from the window, his eyes grazed across the window seat, and he stopped.

"What's this?"

Lying on the window seat was a new doll—a baby doll with a black face. He grabbed it by one arm and lifted it; the doll was hefty.

"Don't y'all know how to carry a baby?" said Peg, appearing at his side and reaching for the doll.

"You do know it's not real, don't you?"

"But it's good practice. Here, let me show you." Peg took the doll out of his hands and then cradled it in her arms, staring into its lifeless eyes, as if the thing were flesh and blood. "This is the way it's done, John."

"But where'd you get this thing?"

Peg looked up at him, obviously puzzled. "You got it for me, didn't you?"

"No. You thought I got this?"

"When I came up to take my nap yesterday, it was just there beneath the covers."

"That's strange. I didn't put it there. Could it be Matilda's?"

"Maybe she was hidin' it from Missus Hicks, afraid the old lady would get rid of it, seein' as it's a black doll and all."

John reached to his waist and produced his hunting knife. "It might contain more quinine. It's awfully heavy, don't y'all think?"

Peg put her hand on his and gently steered the knife away. "Don't cut into it, John. Not just yet."

"Peg, we need to inspect this thing, find out what it contains. We can sew it back up."

"Just let me enjoy it for a day."

This was all so peculiar. John knew how badly she wanted a child, but treating a doll like it was flesh and blood worried him. He should just grab it out of her hands and cut into the back, and pull her out of this fantasy.

"Please, John. You can check it tonight. Besides, if it is Matilda's doll, she won't be too happy if you cut into it. So let me ask Matilda about it. You wouldn't want to cross her."

John sighed and ran the handle of his knife across his morning stubble. "I suppose you're right. Find out if Matilda hid it in our room. If it's not hers, we gotta check its contents tonight."

"I will, laddie. I promise."

"Gotta head down to the hotel then."

Peg clutched his right arm, squeezing his bicep. "You don't have to go. You *shouldn't* go, not with all the mess about those spies."

"You know I gotta."

"You don't gotta do anything."

Peg let go of John's arm, and he made for the door, pausing to look back. "We're gonna be all right," he said.

Peg didn't answer. She was just staring at the doll when he slipped through the door and headed downstairs.

38

PEG WAS ON THE SECOND FLOOR ON HER HANDS AND KNEES, scrubbing the guestroom floor, when she heard a commotion from downstairs. It began with Missus Hicks' raised voice. Not much new there. But then she heard a strong response by Matilda. Matilda usually knew how to tiptoe around the explosive Missus Hicks without setting her off, but it didn't appear that way today.

Squeezing out the dirty water and draping the rag over the edge of her bucket, Peg stepped into the second-floor hallway and went to the top of the staircase.

"It's just a knot!" she heard Matilda say. "It don't matter which side it's on!"

"If it doesn't matter, then change it!"

They were arguing about the head wrap.

"I like it this way, and I'm *keepin'* it this way!"

Matilda's strong words were terrifying, for you never knew what Missus Hicks was capable of doing; but the words were also strangely exhilarating. Matilda was storming the fort.

Peg couldn't make out the next exchange because the two women were talking over each other, so she moved down four stairs and leaned over the railing. The next words from Matilda rang out sharp.

"I'm a free woman!"

"Not under my roof, you aren't! When you step through that front door, you do what I tell you to do!"

"It's just a knot! Why do you care whether it's in front or back?"

"It's always in back! If you plan to work in our house, you change it right now!"

Captain Atwater had gone for his morning constitutional. She wished he were around, for he would know how to defuse things. Peg was afraid Missus Hicks would fire Matilda on the spot, before he was back from his stroll.

The weight of the week was so wearying, and Peg could not take any more from Missus Hicks. She felt a sudden shudder of frustration and anger.

"If you like the knot in back so much, then pretend my face is the back of my head!" Matilda exclaimed.

The sound of the battle raged, as Peg walked back up the stairs slowly, wondering if she had the courage to do what needed to be done. She entered her room, and the voices below became more muffled, but there was no sign of a ceasefire. Peg went to the lone dresser, jammed against the wall.

Opening the dresser, she looked down on the four head wraps she owned, neatly folded like small battle flags. Then she reached for the yellow one.

*****

When John arrived at Timothy Webster's room in the Monumental Hotel, he found Webster asleep and Miss Hattie by his bedside, reading the *Richmond Enquirer*. He couldn't miss the gargantuan headline: SPIES IN CUSTODY.

"I heard it's all in the news," he told Miss Hattie.

She peeked around the edge of the paper. No smiles from her this morning.

"The paper says Lewis is in Henrico Jail, and Scully is in Castle Godwin. Take a seat, John."

John grabbed one of the chairs and dragged it squeaking across the floor. Then he sat at the foot of Webster's bed. Timothy's breathing was raspy, like a pipe leaking steam.

"How is Mister Webster farin'?" John asked.

"Not good. The stress of the past days must have been too much. His fever is up, and he sleeps most of the day. When he's awake, he's delirious. I am seriously worried."

"You think he's well enough for y'all to move him out of the city? For your safety and his?"

Miss Hattie shook her head slowly. "I'm afraid he wouldn't survive a trip. He can't even stand."

Miss Hattie folded up her paper and fanned herself with it. "You are probably wondering if there is any mention of us in the article."

The thought had crossed his mind so many times that it had worn a path in his brain. He assumed they hadn't been mentioned, or the authorities would have already been at their door. But he still wondered.

"Rest assured, the paper made no mention of us. I suppose we can thank the Lord for lazy journalists. The writer had all manner of things wrong. It said that Lewis and Price were identified by a lady from Washington, who passed them on the street and recognized them as spies."

Although the facts of the case were jumbled now, John wondered how long it would take for reporters to untangle all of the facts and put Lewis and Scully in this very hotel room on the Thursday night of their arrest. And how long would it take for people to discover that he too had been in the room?

Miss Hattie handed him the newspaper. "Take a look for yourself. I know you're a reading man."

"Thank you, ma'am."

While John dove into the front-page article, Miss Hattie dipped a towel in a pail of cold water, squeezed it, and then draped it over Webster's forehead. Webster's face was beaded with sweat, and at times it almost sounded as if his breathing had stopped completely.

John was relieved that the writer said Lewis and Scully had been discovered in a private house, not the hotel. "It is clearly shown, by evidence not prudent to detail at this place, that they are paid hirelings of the enemy," the article declared.

"I'm not sure there's much you can do here today," said Miss Hattie, using another rag to dab the sweat from Webster's face. John wondered again how strange it was for a married woman to be tending to another man like she was his true wife. All of this playacting bothered him, and it made him question the entire enterprise of spying. Too much skulking and lying, even for a good cause. He was so weary.

"Go on back to Peg," Miss Hattie said, and John was surprised she knew his wife by name. "I think y'all should stay away from the hotel until we are in the clear. Understand?"

"I understand." John rose back to his feet and returned the chair to its spot, pushing it up against the wall. "I'll pray for y'all and for Mister Webster's recovery."

"You do that, John. But don't dawdle. You need to be with your wife."

John agreed, and he didn't dawdle. As he exited the room, he had a spooked sense that someone was coming at him from behind. Several times, he cast a glance over his shoulder and saw no one behind him, but the sense was still there, tickling his back, so he rushed down the stairs, taking them two at a time, as if the building was on fire.

39

EG DARED TO USE THE MIRROR IN THE GUESTROOM ON THE second floor once again—only this time with Missus Hicks in the house. She didn't care any longer what the old lady would say or think about anything she chose to do under this roof. She was a free woman, and if she was caught using the mirror, so be it. Letting her fury and frustration take her places she had not gone before, she also decided to tie her wrap in a completely novel way. She wrapped it around her head like a headband, leaving much of the hair on the top of her head exposed. Then she tied the loose end into a thick knot on the right side of her head, and the excess material dangled down to her shoulder.

The argument downstairs had subsided for a spell, and Peg wondered if Matilda had caved in to Missus Hicks' wishes, or whether the old lady had simply tired and given up trying to bend the cook to her will. She couldn't imagine either one of them waving a white flag (or white head wrap) in surrender.

Peg didn't feel any fear—nothing conscious at least—as she made her way down the stairs. She walked slowly, head high and back straight like royalty, as she passed through the hallway leading into the kitchen. Missus Hicks was still in the kitchen, saying, "That's much, much better. Now you do that every day, and we won't have any trouble."

It sounded like Matilda had given up and readjusted her head wrap. Time for the reinforcements.

Peg entered the kitchen as if this was just another ordinary day and nothing amiss had happened. "What would you have me do, Matilda?" she asked nonchalantly, not even batting an eye in Missus Hicks' direction. However, she could see, in her peripheral vision, the old lady staring at her in utter disbelief. Even Matilda's jaw dropped. Not only was Peg wearing the *yellow* head wrap, but she had left much of her head exposed. She was in open rebellion. She had done more than burn her bridges with Missus Hicks. She had *blown up* her bridges.

"Do you think you are being funny?" Missus Hicks said.

Peg, much taller than Missus Hicks, swung around, looked down on her, and smiled. "How am I bein' funny, Missus Hicks?"

"Take that rag off and go on up and put on a white one."

Peg smiled. "You talkin' about my head wrap?"

Matilda continued to stare in wonderment. She had a large spoon in her right hand, and it dripped flapjack batter on the wood floor. The cook didn't seem to notice.

"You know good and well I'm talking about your head wrap. And you know that I want you wearing *white* wraps, tied neatly in the back. Like the way Matilda has it."

But when Missus Hicks motioned toward the cook, Matilda was already in the process of unwrapping her head covering and retying it in the same style as Peg's. She tidied it up with a few pats to her head. "Do you like it, Peg?"

Missus Hicks had gone rigid, and she spit out her next words like they were poison. "You are both dismissed from my services at this very hour."

Peg felt a stab of panic; she had known that losing her position in the house was a real possibility, but now that it had happened, she wondered if she had gone too far. She also felt a twinge of guilt for dragging Matilda into this. The woman had cooked for the Atwaters going on twelve years.

Turning on her heels, Missus Hicks charged out of the kitchen. "I want you out of my employ and out of our house, and I will help you clear out right this moment."

Missus Hicks stormed the staircase, and Peg guessed that she was heading for her room. Peg followed close behind, trying not to run, trying to maintain her composure. "That's all right, Missus Hicks. I'll clear out myself."

"No you aren't. I'm *tossing* you out, and I am going to do it myself."

Peg was tempted to grab the old lady by the shoulder, spin her around, and give her a slap, but such a thing would be guaranteed prison time—or worse. She restrained herself and followed Missus Hicks up the two flights of stairs and into their room. Peg and John didn't have much in the way of possessions, beyond a modest number of clothes. So Missus Hicks went for the dresser. She yanked open the bottom drawer harshly, didn't see what she was looking for, and then went for the middle drawer. She reached in and began tossing Peg's head wraps over her shoulder, one after another, like a magician pulling handkerchiefs from his sleeve. Peg began scooping them up from the floor.

"I will do my own packin', ma'am."

But Missus Hicks paid no attention. Her face had gone as red as a ripe tomato, and she pulled open the top drawer of the dresser so roughly that it came out entirely and crashed to the floor. She began yanking out Peg's few dresses and John's britches, wadding them up in a ball, and hurling them across the room.

"Missus Hicks, no! Please, stop!"

But Missus Hicks had become a force of nature, a human cyclone. Peg scooped up the clothing as it landed on the floor, continuing to plead for her to stop. Meanwhile, Matilda had entered the room and helped Peg gather up the clothes. The old lady was so out of control that Peg wondered if she might bust an artery right in front of her. She could only hope.

Every article of clothing that they owned was soon strewn around the room, and Missus Hicks paused, breathing heavily, her upper lip sweating. She scanned the room for something else to throw. There wasn't much left that the woman could harm; the furniture belonged to Captain Atwater, except for the rocking chair where Lucy Ann sat.

Missus Hicks' eyes landed on the doll, Lucy Ann. Then her gaze shifted to the window seat, where the Negro doll lay on its back with its arms slightly raised, like a real baby eager for its mother to pick it up. Missus Hicks' eyes lit up at this new opportunity to express her rage.

"No!" Peg shouted.

But Missus Hicks had already gone for the dolls.

*****

It was the morning of the second day since Ichabod had put the explosive in place, and still nothing. The Atwater house had not been rattled. Ichabod and his dog, Ahab, had already made a pass by the home two times on this Monday morning, and the house just stood there, unscathed, mocking him. No explosion. No sign of life at all, except for Captain Atwater, who had left for his morning constitutional about a half hour earlier. The day was a mixed bag of weather, with a storm brewing in the west, where the horizon was lined with bluish-black clouds, filled with wind and rain. Directly overhead, the sky was still clear.

"C'mon, boy, no fireworks today."

Ichabod booted a stone and sent it bounding across the dirt road as they made their way back down Franklin Street, away from the Atwater house. He was scheduled to put the new torpedo boat into use in Hampton Roads in less than a week, and he wanted the matter of Peg and John Scobell settled by then. He wanted them gone, and he had almost run out of patience waiting for the explosive to trigger.

He was a full block from the house when he heard the wondrous sound. An explosion rumbled behind his back. At first, he wondered if it was a crash of thunder, but the storm wasn't close enough for the sound to be so loud. It had to be a man-made rumble. Ahab turned and barked before Ichabod could even fully absorb the sound. Then Ichabod spun on his heels and stared down the road. Smoke was coming from the Atwater house.

*****

John rushed through the lobby of the Monumental Hotel, ignoring the white man who ordered him to carry his suitcases.

"I thought I'd find you here," said Cleon. John's friend must have been waiting in the lobby for him to show up, and Cleon fell into step beside him. "Y'all are in an awful hurry."

John slowed his pace as they exited the Monumental Hotel onto Grace Street. "Sorry, Cleon. Just been on edge."

"I can believe it, brother. I heard the news." Cleon looked around to make sure no one was within earshot. "Did y'all know the two spies who was apprehended?"

John nodded. "I met 'em Thursday night."

Cleon whistled. "That's the night they were arrested. Then you need to leave town, John."

"I ain't leavin' Mister Webster and Miss Hattie in the lurch. And especially not Peg."

Cleon tried to argue with him, but John made it obvious he was not budging on this point. His father hadn't raised him to run out in times of trouble.

"Sometimes runnin' is your only option. Y'all don't always gotta stand and fight," said Cleon. "Joshua and Caleb from the Bible didn't stand and fight when they were spyin' out the city of Jericho. They went runnin' out of the city fast as they could so they could fight another day. And look what they made happen to that city—the walls came tumblin' down."

John made no comment and didn't even bat an eye at Cleon. He kept looking straight ahead and increased the length of his stride. Cleon had to jog to keep up. In the silence between them, they suddenly heard what sounded like distant artillery; it reminded John of the faraway cannon blasts he had heard at Manassas during the first major battle of the war. Was it thunder?

"What in the world . . .? Sounds like someone just fired up some gunpowder," said Cleon.

They turned onto Franklin Street and spotted smoke, a small cloud drifting across the street. Black smoke was coming from Captain Atwater's house. Other people had heard the blast, and they began to flock to the scene.

John took off sprinting with Cleon just behind.

40

CHABOD WAS ONE OF THE FIRST TO ARRIVE ON THE SCENE, AS people up and down the block emerged from their homes to find out what had happened. Richmond had been bracing itself for a Yankee attack for almost a year. Had it finally come to pass? Only Ichabod knew the true source of the blast, but he pretended to be just as perplexed as everyone else. He looked the Atwater house up and down, from base to roof, and his feigned confusion slowly became real bafflement because he didn't understand why the structure was still in one piece. He stared up at the third-floor window and saw that the explosion hadn't even so much as broken out a windowpane.

As he stared up, a black woman's face appeared in the open window and looked down on him. It was Peg Scobell, and she was in one piece. Or was he staring at an apparition? Their eyes locked, and then Peg drew away from the window and disappeared from sight.

"Somebody tell me what just happened!" a lady shouted.

Missus Hicks, an occupant of the house, rushed out of the front door, waving arms and demanding answers.

"Did you see it? Did you see it? Speak, man!"

"Did I see what?" Ichabod asked, still reeling from the sight of Peg Scobell unharmed. Something had exploded, that much was certain. So how had she survived?

"Did you see the explosion, you fool?" Missus Hicks pointed toward a patch of grass next to the edge of the front porch—a scorched circle of ground, where something had burst. His bomb?

Ignoring the sputtering Missus Hicks, he strode over to the patch of burnt grass, crouched down, and noticed bits and pieces of the doll scattered about, like the severed limbs of a battlefield casualty, torn apart by cannon fire. He scanned the area while Ahab sniffed around, nose to the ground. Then he stood back up and discovered, about fifteen feet from the blast site, the Negro doll's head, blown cleanly from its shoulders. He realized that somehow the explosion had taken place on the ground, which explained why the house wasn't harmed. But how did it all happen? How had the doll wound up down here?

Picking up the severed doll's head, he went back to Missus Hicks, who was demanding that other people in the street tell her what they had seen. She was uncontrollable in her rage, using language that would turn a sailor beet red, and it took Ichabod a good two minutes to get her to settle down.

"I found this near the blast," he said, displaying the doll's head, which looked about the size of a shrunken skull. She went abruptly quiet.

"That's the doll I tossed out the window! One of them at least."

Groaning inside, Ichabod tried to coax her into telling him what had happened in the house.

"That is not any of your business, young man!"

"But what happened inside might have a bearin' on what happened out here."

"I don't see what on earth one has to do with the other! I hurled a couple of dolls out the window, that's all."

"I suspect the two actions are connected," he said.

She stared at him and puzzled over those words. "Are you trying to say there was a bomb inside one of those dolls? Would Yankee devils stoop so low as to plant infernal torpedoes within the walls of our very homes?"

"I wouldn't put it past them, ma'am."

"*Peg Scobell.* Where is that devil?"

"Who, ma'am?" Ichabod asked innocently.

"My maid. They were her dolls. I'll have her strung up for this."

At that moment, Captain Atwater appeared, back from his morning walk and clearly confused by the curious crowd in front of his house. It took some doing for Missus Hicks to explain to him what had happened, so Ichabod saw his chance to wander around to the back of the house and enter through the servant's door. Time was slipping away, and he didn't want Peg Scobell to slip away either. He found the Atwater's cook sitting at the kitchen table and staring into space, stunned into silence. She was no help whatsoever, claiming she had no idea where Peg Scobell had gone.

Cursing, Ichabod checked every floor of the house and found no one else around. So he turned to Ahab, the best tracking dog in all of Richmond. They had to act quickly before the scent was blown away by the wind or burned away by the sun. Scents were a fragile thing, hanging on to the tracks left by a person's shoes or created by tiny flakes of skin dropped to the ground like a trail of invisible breadcrumbs. His dog could track day-old scents, but the fresher the better. Not all Cuban bloodhounds are natural born trackers like Ahab. Ichabod had never seen a better one in all of his days. For most dogs, it would take them close to 100 yards of keeping their nose to the ground to finally lock onto a scent trail, but not Ahab. He could do it in 10 to 20 yards.

Missus Hicks gave Ichabod one of the head wraps worn by Peg Scobell, and he used it to give Ahab a good long whiff of Peg's scent. She couldn't have gone far, so he was confident that Ahab would bring her down in no time. His dog began with a tight circling motion, trying to sort through the thousands of scents bombarding his nose from all sides, sifting and sniffing and finally locking onto the target. Ahab had found the scent of Peg Scobell.

As they moved down Franklin Street and then into the alleys along 20th Street, Ahab weaved from side to side, following the scent in a meandering path, but in a consistent direction. One block down, he began circling again, which meant he had lost the scent and was searching. It didn't take long for him to lock back on to the smell and break out of the circle. Ahab was good at not being distracted by the hundreds of competing scents, particularly any whiff of food, and in a city the size of Richmond, there were thousands of competing smells coming at him from every angle. Ichabod had worked his dog hard to get him to focus his nose.

Ahab moved out of the alley and onto Grace Street, cutting back from side to side as he eliminated alternative directions, working the smell, creating an odor map through the city. Occasionally, the bloodhound would raise his head and check out a passing person, but then he would quickly dismiss the passerby and put his nose back to the ground and return to the invisible trail. Ichabod had him on a long leash, feeding out the line to give his dog room to work. Pedestrians on the street also gave Ahab plenty of room, especially colored folks. Ichabod loved to see the fear in their eyes as they caught sight of his working bloodhound.

"Who y'all trackin', mister?" asked a white boy, no more than eight years old. The barefoot boy in overalls ran alongside, skipping here and there.

"Ain't none of your business."

"Can I pet your dog?"

"If you wanna keep two hands and ten fingers for the rest of your life, I wouldn't recommend it. Now scat!"

At the mention of missing body parts, the boy gave Ahab a healthy distance, but he continued to follow, along with three other white boys who joined the hunt. They moved down Grace Street, and when they passed 22nd Street, Ahab's tail began to wag—a good sign they were closing in. Ichabod stared ahead down Grace Street as they passed 23rd, and he saw the stately mansion of the Van Lew family looming on the south side of the street.

Elizabeth Van Lew's house. Ichabod should have known that this was where Peg Scobell had fled.

41

WHEN JOHN AND CLEON REACHED THE ATWATER HOUSE, they found a crowd of gawkers and gossipers clogging Franklin Street. Cleon said he would remain in front and see what he could learn, while John went around back and entered by the servant's entrance. John found Matilda in a tizzy, and she blubbered something about an explosion; but before he could even absorb the possibility that Peg might have been killed, his wife passed by the kitchen, moving at full tilt. She looked shocked to see John, but also quite relieved, and she threw herself into his arms. She told him, in the midst of her sobs, that she thought the new doll contained an explosive, and it had gone off when Missus Hicks tossed it out the window.

That's all he needed to hear. He took her by the hand, told Matilda to forget what she had just heard, and they ran for their lives, weaving down the back alley to Grace Street. He could smell approaching rain, and he prayed for a downpour because that would add to the chaos and reduce the chances of an immediate pursuit. He also hoped the rain would wash away any scent trail they left on the ground.

Peg said they should go to the Van Lew house, and he agreed. Despite his misgivings about Peg's involvement with Mary Bowser and Elizabeth Van Lew, he knew that their house was the only sanctuary in Richmond. So they pounded on the servant's entrance to the Van Lew residence, and John was relieved to see it opened by Mary Bowser. He had never been happier to see her face.

Mary could see immediately that they were in trouble.

"Come in and tell me what happened."

Peg did most of the talking, and the words came pouring out in an almost unintelligible, unstoppable flow. She told about the dolls, the fight with Missus Hicks, the explosion, the fear.

"Miss Van Lew has gotta hear this, but she's at Libby Prison, bringing more food to prisoners. But I know she'll want y'all here in the house, where you'll be safe. So follow me."

Even though it was daylight, Mary handed unlit candles to both Peg and John, and she motioned for them to follow her up the staircase, past the second floor, past the third floor, to a narrow door in the hallway—a door opening up on a dark, cramped flight of stairs to the attic. The floor of the attic slanted like a ship in heavy seas, the ceiling was low, and John's head nearly brushed it. Against the far wall was an old chest of drawers, and Mary stood behind it and pushed. Behind the dresser, built into the wall, was a small, square panel—a door. Mary pulled away the panel, revealing a secret room behind.

"Don't breathe it to a soul that you saw this," Mary said, as if John and Peg needed to be told.

"You go in first," Peg said to John. "Never know what might be in there."

"True," said Mary. "Found a family of bats in there once—got in through the ceiling cracks somehow."

John saw Peg biting her lips and staring at the hole nervously, for his wife hated enclosed spaces, and Mary didn't need to add that information about bats. After lighting his candle, John crawled through the opening and found himself in a small, stuffy space, barely ten feet long. Inside the room were a musty-smelling mattress and two small end tables, and he placed his candle on one of the tables. It was obvious they weren't the first occupants. John had heard rumors about Miss Van Lew hiding Union prisoners in this house after escapes, and now he wondered if there was truth to the stories. This was the ideal hiding place.

"Is it safe in there?" Peg called. She crouched at the doorway, framed by the square.

John inspected the ceiling and noticed cracks where bats could enter, but he saw no sign of the flying rats.

"Looks like we got the room to ourselves, lassie."

Peg climbed in, snagging her dress on the lip of the doorway, and it tore slightly as she extricated herself. Once she was in, Mary handed her the second candle.

"It's small but cozy," said Mary. "If you need to get out, don't worry about the dresser in front of the door. It's on wheels, so it will push out of the way."

"Thanks," said John.

Mary reached in and gave Peg's hand a squeeze. "I'm going to fetch Miss Van Lew down at the prison, so you stay put until I can get her here. She'll know what to do next."

With that, Mary put the door in place, and they heard her shove the chest of drawers back in front—like heaving a stone to seal a tomb. The room was not much bigger than a dead-man's vault and equally claustrophobic. John stretched out on the mattress with his back against the damp wall, and Peg lay next to him, her head on his chest and one arm draped over him. They didn't dare make a sound.

42

F ROM ACROSS THE STREET, ICHABOD SPOTTED A BLACK WOMAN come around from the back of the Van Lew property and march down Grace Street at a quick clip, as if on a determined mission. It was the one they called Mary Bowser. He waited for her to disappear around the corner of 20th Street before approaching the front of the Van Lew mansion. With Ahab alongside, he passed through the black wrought-iron front gate and slipped around the side of the house, where evergreens provided cover.

Behind the house, he found the door to the servant's entrance locked. He tied Ahab to a nearby tree so he could investigate on his own before daring to enter the house with a dog in tow. Then he went to a window at ground level, cupped his hands against the glass, and peered inside. No sign of life inside the house, so he used his elbow to punch it open. After plucking out the jagged pieces still caught in the sash like shark's teeth, he stepped through the window. Once inside, he stood perfectly still and listened, but he didn't hear any sound throughout the home except for the ticking of a grandfather clock coming from the front of the house.

He moved from room to room and found the first floor desolate and dim, for the advancing cloud cover had darkened the day, letting little light into the house. He decided to put Ahab to work before Elizabeth Van Lew arrived on the scene. So he unlocked the back door, retrieved his dog, and placed Peg Scobell's head wrap back beneath Ahab's nose.

"Track," he said, giving the command word that triggered Ahab's senses and put him to work. It didn't take long for Ahab to catch Scobell's scent once again, and he pulled Ichabod in the direction of the staircase. There was no doubt now. Peg Scobell was definitely in the house, definitely somewhere upstairs. He pulled out his pistol as the dog, straining on his leash, drew him up the stairs.

*****

John put a finger to Peg's lips and motioned for her to stay back against the wall. Then, in a crouch, he moved to the door of the secret room and put his ear to the wood. Someone had entered the attic, but how could Mary Bowser have returned so quickly from fetching Elizabeth Van Lew? She hadn't been gone long enough, but maybe he hadn't judged the passage of time properly.

Then he heard what sounded like the clicking of claws on the wooden floor of the attic and the panting of an animal. A dog? It was possible—and then it was confirmed. He heard a bark and a man's muffled command that silenced the animal. John drew out his hunting knife and cast a glance toward Peg and saw that she had pushed herself into a corner, and was continuing to push with her feet, even though there was nowhere else to go. When he heard the chest of drawers being shoved, sliding across the floor, he realized he had little time before the door would spring open and the dog would attack.

"Off the mattress," he hissed to Peg, and she rolled off. He grabbed the mattress and wrestled it across the small room, jamming it against the opening a split second before the door to the secret room opened, and he heard the single-word command: "Kill."

*****

Ichabod gave the command, not even taking the time to confirm that the person inside this hidden room really was Peg Scobell. He knew it had to be her, and he wanted Ahab to spring immediately, without warning and without mercy.

When he pulled away the door, Ahab leaped—and crashed face-first into something soft. His dog backed up, shook his head, and sneezed; the woman had jammed a mattress in the opening. Smart little devil. Ichabod holstered his gun, crouched down, and threw his shoulder into the mattress, expecting it to give way easily, but a power from the other side pushed back. A woman wouldn't be capable of such stonewall force. Someone was inside this hole with her. A man. Probably John Scobell.

Grunting, he threw his shoulder against the mattress again and the bedding gave way slightly; Ahab began to go wild, snorting and clawing at the mattress, trying to squeeze through the small opening that appeared where the mattress had been slightly dislodged from the doorway. A woman screamed from inside the hole.

"Back!" Ichabod shouted, and Ahab obeyed. He didn't want his dog to jam his neck through the small opening and get stuck; if the man behind this mattress had a knife, his dog's neck would be exposed and vulnerable.

Ichabod crashed against the opening a third time, and he heard a man groan from the other side. Only twelve inches of bedding separated him from this rascal, so he decided to use gunfire to penetrate the barrier. He drew his Colt revolver, stood back, and guessed where the man's body might be positioned. Then he fired, and the bedding shuddered under the force, a puff of feathers erupting from the hole. The man gave out a startled shout.

*****

John felt like his hand had been bitten or stung, and he pulled it back from the mattress instinctively. A bullet, as big as a bumblebee, had gone through the mattress and through his hand, leaving a bleeding, puckering hole in his palm. A mattress wasn't going to work against a man armed with a gun, and he realized he had no choice but to take the offensive—although how he was going to fight off a large dog and an armed man simultaneously was beyond him, especially with a battered hand. When he heard the man's gun cock again, he tore away the mattress and gave out an inhuman growl as he threw himself toward the opening, armed only with his modest-sized hunting knife.

It was like hurling himself into a moving brick wall. As he went for the opening, the dog came crashing through from the other side, knocking him onto his back. His knife went flying out of his right hand, and the door to the secret room slammed shut; the man had sealed John and Peg inside with a killer animal in a space not much bigger than a closet. Peg screamed. The struggle became a chaos of disjointed images: Fur, teeth, claws, muscle. The dog latched onto his arm, but hadn't gone for his neck yet. With his free hand—his bleeding left hand—he tried to jam a thumb in the animal's eye sockets, but the bloodhound was moving too wildly, shaking his arm from side to side. Finding the animal's eyes would be next to impossible. His strength was draining away with his blood, and the mauling became inevitable.

*****

The nightmare animal was on top of John, tearing into his arm. Only one candle lit up the confined space, for the other one had tipped over and extinguished. So all that Peg could see was a roiling mass of fur, flashes of teeth, and glimpses of berserk canine eyes, moving in and out of light and darkness. The dog's body and John's body became a confused tangle of legs and arms and shadows. John struggled underneath, legs kicking, his left fist landing on the animal's body with useless thuds. Peg had seen the knife fly out of his hand, and she searched the space for any sign of it. How could it have disappeared in such a small room? It had to be here! She screamed in frustration.

Then she spotted it. The knife was pinned beneath John, the handle visible under his right shoulder blade. She moved in closer and slid the knife out from underneath him, with the dog's teeth and mouth only inches from her face as it continued its frenzied attack on her husband. The image of gutting pigs flashed through her mind as she drew back the knife and plunged it into the dog's side. Peg became wilder with every stab as she drew out the knife and plunged it in. The dog yelped and let go of John's arm and came after her. The bloodhound lunged straight for her face, and she could smell its fetid breath as it came for her—then stopped short. John had wrapped his arms around the dog's body and brought down the weakened, bleeding animal. Peg found a vulnerable spot in the dog's side, and she plunged the knife in again and again and again and again and again and again, and it wasn't until John wrapped his arms around her that she finally stopped her stabbing frenzy.

John was covered in blood, both his and the dog's. Peg's face was splattered with blood, and she looked down on the dog's motionless body. More blood puddled the floor, black like oil in the dim candlelight.

*****

Ichabod enjoyed the show. In fact, he had pulled up a chair and sat in front of the sealed door to the secret room while he listened to Ahab maul the man and woman. Ahab had killed before, and he knew that the smell of blood drove his animal wild. He heard the man scream, then the woman scream, and he wished he could be seeing this. But he knew it was better to keep the door closed, cutting off all retreat for the man and woman inside. Still, he wished the door were made of glass, so he could witness the demolition of the human body. He understood perfectly why ancient Romans loved to watch lions maul Christians. There was nothing better than death on display.

When he heard Ahab suddenly yelp, he had a momentary twinge of fear, but the man had probably landed a lucky strike to a sensitive area of the animal's body. He was confident in Ahab's killing instinct—and in his dog's invulnerability. He and Ahab had come through so much together. They were linked in a mystical bond, and he liked to think that his imperviousness to death had bled over into his dog.

Then all went silent.

He leaned in closer to the door. He heard the faint sound of someone moving inside, but he couldn't tell whether it was the sound of a human moving about or a dog.

"Speak!" he shouted through the door.

No answer. No bark.

This could not be possible.

"Speak!"

Still no answer. No bark.

Ichabod drew out his gun once again and pointed it at the door. The hairs on the back of his neck stood up.

43

"SPEAK!"

John heard the man's command from the other side of the door, and he glanced down at the motionless dog, just in case the animal showed any sign of life. But the dog didn't even flicker with involuntary muscle movements.

John knew they were still in deep danger, and he had to think of something quickly. He put his arms beneath the massive dog, guessing that it must weigh up to 130 or 140 pounds. He had lifted that much before, but not dead weight—not a dog with a dangling heavy head and a torso slick with blood. He tried to make as little noise as possible because he didn't want the attacker to know who was alive and who was dead inside the room. So he stifled his groan as he crouched down and brought the dog up and onto his knees. His face was slick with sweat. Or was it blood? His left hand, where the bullet penetrated, had begun to swell and ache, as if on fire, and his right arm throbbed where the dog had bit down. Now that he had time to assess the situation, he realized this was the very dog that had attacked him in the cabin.

He crouched only a couple of feet in front of the doorway, with the dog weighing heavy on his knees, sprawled across his lap like a bulky rug. He waited. He knew the door could spring open at any second, and the man's gun would be aimed at his forehead.

*****

Ichabod heard scuffling and groans inside the secret room, and the sounds seemed human-like. His dog should be barking by now, unless he was too busy tearing flesh off of bones. He feared the worst.

If anything had happened to Ahab, he would make Peg Scobell pay. He would delight in killing her man in front of her eyes before turning his gun on her. He wanted a good clean shot, preferably in the head, so he crouched down and aimed his gun at the door to the secret room.

He cocked his gun and used his left hand to get a finger-hold on the edge of the door. He took a deep breath.

Then he yanked out the door panel.

Ichabod caught himself, holding back on his trigger-finger. He was confused, for the first thing he saw was not a black man or black woman. It was his dog's body filling the frame of the doorway. Was Ahab alive? The shock of seeing his dog in the doorway slowed his reaction time, and it took a couple of seconds to realize that he was looking at the dead body of his dog, being held up by human hands. Black hands.

The man holding Ahab surged out of the hole, and he used the dog as a shield and a weapon, shoving the animal in his face. It was like being attacked by the bloody puppet of a dog. Ichabod stood up straight and backpedaled, hoping to find a clear shot at the black man who was charging forward, shoving dead dog in his face. But all he could see was Ahab's lifeless eyes coming at him. He could smell the blood and the animal stink, and he fired wildly. But the man kept coming, pushing the dog in his face. The man was strong, much stronger than him, and it didn't appear that his shot had come close to hitting anything. He was being shoved backward, and it was all he could do to simply keep his balance. Then he felt his back come up against something firm. A wall? He heard the crashing of glass, and he realized that the man had shoved him clear across the attic and through one of the windows.

*****

It worked. As John used the dog as both a shield and a battering ram, the man fired a shot, but it went wide. His attacker went crashing through glass and wood and landed on his back on the roof outside, and then John shoved the massive dog through the window after him. The animal carcass landed on top of the man, who groaned beneath the weight. The man's gun was knocked out of his hands, and the weapon went flying over the side of the house; just like that, the attacker was disarmed and pinned beneath the dog.

It had begun to rain—a light rain—so there was no one in the street to see the outlandish scene that had just unfolded on the Van Lew roof. He considered going out onto the roof and overpowering the man and tossing him from the three-story house, but he couldn't take the chance of being spotted. A black man being seen throwing a white man off a roof would not be the kind of attention Elizabeth Van Lew would want to bring to this house. So he crouched by the shattered window with his bloodied blade in hand, in case the man reentered.

*****

Ichabod considered going back into the house to kill off the man, but his gun had slid off the edge of the roof, and Scobell's strength scared the life out of him. His back ached from crashing through the dormer window, and he felt a spasm clench his muscles as he heaved Ahab's dead body off of his chest. Glass had also sliced a thin red line across his forearm, and he was bleeding badly. His shredded shirtsleeve was moist and red.

He decided he would retreat for now, bind his wounds, and then he would return and carry out his revenge. Peg and John Scobell would pay for killing his dog.

The Van Lew's roof was slanted, but not too steeply, and a white railing ran all along the roofline, so he felt safe as he made his way across the surface, slick with rain. Three dormers stuck up from the roof like bulging eyes, and directly below the middle dormer was the roof of the front porch. He gauged that he could lower himself down onto the porch roof and then climb to the ground from there. He didn't dare return through the heart of the house; he did not want to face that black devil again—not without a gun.

The cold rain increased in intensity, and he blinked drops from his eyes as he began to work his way down the roof to the white railing. He looked back and saw the body of Ahab, lying in a bloody, unrecognizable heap in the rain—his side torn in many places.

Ahab had been a part of Ichabod's life for ten years, his only remaining companion. He realized he couldn't just leave the dog on the roof, where large birds would pick him apart. The Van Lews would probably bury the dog, but he didn't like the idea of them handling the body. He had buried a mother, father, friend, wife, and child. Now he would bury his dog, his only living relation.

So Ichabod worked his way back up the tiles toward Ahab. He didn't think he could lift the dog and carry it on his back, certainly not while balancing on a tilted roof. His dog's eyes were lifeless, looking as blank as one of those infernal dolls, and he fought back the tears. Taking hold of Ahab's rear legs, he dragged him down to the railing overlooking the top of the front porch. The body left a streak of red, like spilled paint on the roof, and the rain carried the blood over the edge of the house in red rivulets. He would try to lift the dog over the railing and then drop it a short distance onto the roof of the front porch. He looked down, gauging the distance, and noticed a man standing across the street, holding an umbrella and staring up at him.

"What are you doing, mister?" the man shouted.

Ichabod just cursed at the man, but the stranger didn't move.

Bracing his leg against the railing for support, he put his arms beneath Ahab's body, and he groaned and growled as he lifted up the dog's body and slung it on top of the two-foot-high railing. He intended to take a breather before lowering it down from the railing and onto the porch roof, but the weight of the dog was too much. The wooden railing snapped beneath the dog, and Ahab's body began to fall. Ichabod instinctively tried to grab his dog to keep him from falling, and the weight of Ahab yanked him forward. Ichabod's feet slipped on the slick roof, and he too plunged over the edge.

In disbelief, he went down, face first, still holding on to Ahab's body, but he wasn't perfectly centered over the porch, so he didn't hit the porch roof squarely. His forehead struck the sharp corner of the porch and he bounced off and fell all three stories. But there was a calm within, for he knew he would survive. He was the Master, and Death was his slave. In the few seconds he had left, he had a sense that Fate would step in and his dog's body would brace his impact on the ground and he would survive once again. But he was no longer holding on to Ahab. He had lost his grip on his dog and they were falling, side by side. Directly below them was the wrought-iron railing that curved in a half-circle along a staircase leading from the front porch to the ground. The railing was lined with a long row of black wrought-iron tips, sticking up like sharpened teeth. This could not be happening, for he was the Master, he had the power, he had the control, and Death bowed and scraped before him.

The wrought-iron tips, as sharp as Nat Turner's pikes, were the last things he saw before he touched Death one last time.

44

"YOU SURE KNOW HOW TO LEAVE A PLACE A MESS," MARY BOWSER told John as she finished wrapping his right arm with a bandage.

"I woulda cleaned up after myself if I wasn't bleedin' half to death," John said with a grimace.

Mary had been an angel since she and Miss Van Lew returned home to find the dead bodies of both a man and a dog in front of the house. John had seen Ichabod plunge from the roof, but being afraid to step out onto the roof into the full view of the street, he had no idea the man had died until Mary and Miss Van Lew told them what had happened. The only one who had witnessed the skewering of Ichabod was the man holding the umbrella and standing across the street, and he had immediately pounded on the front door of the house, shouting for someone to answer. John and Peg heard the pounding and the shouting, but they were not about to answer any doors while covered in blood. So the man had finally concluded that the house was deserted, and he left to retrieve the authorities. But he hadn't gone more than a block before he ran across Elizabeth Van Lew and Mary Bowser, hurrying back to the house. The man knew Miss Lizzie, and he told her that an intruder had been inside her house, exiting from the roof, and he had seen the man fall—impaled on the railing.

Miss Lizzie dealt with the authorities and the dead body on her front railing, handling it with calm efficiency. She too had been an angel of mercy, and John gained a belated appreciation for the two women with whom Peg had been working for the past eight months.

This was the first time he had been introduced to Miss Lizzie, the small, bird-like woman with endless energy.

The men from the Richmond Day Watch put down the death as a burglary gone awry, and Miss Lizzie led them to believe that the dead dog belonged to her and had been savagely killed by the intruder. The broken window in the back of the house, the broken window in the dormer, the dead dog, and Ichabod's accidental fall from the roof all pointed at an unlucky intruder who had encountered a guard dog and died while trying to flee the house through the attic.

Mary had some nursing training, so she tended to John's wounds on both his arm and palm of his hand, and she scrubbed away the blood from the attic floor. Then she used a fresh bucket of water to wash down the secret room.

"Good thing the bullet went clean through," Mary said.

She was right. If the bullet hadn't exited his hand, all of that contained energy would have wreaked even more havoc inside his palm. The wound hurt like nothing he had ever felt, but it would have been much worse if the bullet had hit a thicker part of his body, such as a thigh, and become lodged inside. In the weeks leading up to the Battle of Manassas, he had seen doctors root around for buried bullets, and it was horrifying.

"If you'd a been carryin' your Bible, the Scriptures woulda stopped the bullet," Cleon announced half-seriously when he showed up at the house later in the evening, along with Abram and Gallus. While Abram and Gallus helped Mary with food preparation, Cleon talked quietly with John and Peg in the secret room—with their only light coming from two fresh candles. "I know a fella who got shot once, and the Bible in his breast pocket stopped it cold."

"If a twelve-inch-thick mattress didn't stop the bullet from such close range, I don't think the Bible woulda done much," John said.

"The Word of God is a rock, and a rock is a lot more solid than a mattress."

John smiled. "I'll remember that the next time a crazed Confederate hunts me down with a Cuban bloodhound and shoots me point-blank through a mattress."

"You do that. But right now we need to be gettin' y'all out of town, quick as can be," Cleon continued. "Tonight, in fact. With what happened at the Atwater house, with the explosion and all, people might come here lookin' for y'all."

"Maybe we should stay hidden in this room to give John some time to recover," Peg suggested.

"Too dangerous."

"Cleon is right," said John. "Don't worry, lassie, the bleedin' is under control."

"But you said it earlier: A black man and a black woman leavin' in the dead of night is bound to raise suspicions," Peg said.

"That's why I'm gonna get in touch with Ethan Hancock," said Cleon.

"He's in town?" John said.

Cleon nodded. "He's stayin' over at the Lumpkin place, posin' as a slave trader. That man is a wonder. They take him to be an authentic slave trader and Rebel sympathizer. I'm sure Hancock will be happy to take y'all out of town, with you two pretendin' to be a couple of his new purchases."

John put his arm around Peg's shoulder and drew her close. "If Hancock can get us to Washington, I can seek medical help from a Yankee doctor."

John gave Peg a quick kiss on the lips, and she responded with a more lingering kiss.

Cleon cleared his throat. "Don't mean to be interruptin', but I been wonderin', John. You ever seen that white man with the dog before? Why'd he come after y'all?"

"That's the same dog that attacked me in the cabin. And I think the man mighta been one of the fellas that tried to run Miss Hattie and me down."

"He did what?" Peg asked, and John realized he had never told his wife about the incident with Miss Hattie—or the first dog attack.

Cleon let out a soft whistle. "Makes me wonder if he's also the fella who's been trackin' down Lincoln Leaguers and killin' us one after another."

"Could be," said John. "But I thought you had your suspicions planted on Timothy Webster."

"I ain't ruled out Webster. But the dog man is a strong suspect."

"And a dead suspect."

"I'll go on and fetch Hancock while it's still light and find out if he can take y'all out of Richmond. I ain't wantin' to go near that Lumpkin place after dark because it's probably swarmin' with demons." Cleon took hold of the cross around his neck, drew it to his lips, and kissed it.

Then he crawled out of the secret room, while John leaned back against the wall and tried to ignore the throbbing of his bandaged hand. He stretched out on the bare floor with Peg beside him, her head on his chest. The mattress, soaked with blood, had been removed to be burned.

45

IT WAS STILL DARK IN THE EARLY MORNING HOURS WHEN PEG AND John were loaded into the back of a wagon and Hancock took them north out of town. On the outskirts of Richmond, they were met on the road by Rebel pickets, and Hancock flashed his pass; it was just a formality because one the soldiers recognized him as a loyal Confederate and had no reason to question his claim that John and Peg were recent purchases at the Lumpkin trading post. John and Peg had agreed to be chained at the legs for effect, although it was the first time in years that either of them had worn chains. Master McQueen never abided chains or whips, but Peg's former master, Cager Johnson, had been fond of both.

"I heard about the explosion at the Atwater house," Hancock said to John and Peg after they had put the pickets far behind them. He sat up front, steering, while John and Peg huddled together in the back next to Hancock's luggage and boxes of tobacco. Hancock had told the pickets that he was delivering tobacco to the boys up in Manassas. "I heard folks saying that you and the missus tried to blow up the captain's house with a string of bombs."

"That kind of talk is why we need to get North," John said. "There was only one explosive, and it was targeting me. It was hidden inside a doll given to Peg."

"A doll? Given by who?"

"I don't know," said Peg. "It was placed in our room, but we wonder if maybe the man with the Cuban bloodhound done it."

"If the bomb was put in a doll, it sounds like someone was targeting *you*, Peg."

"I don't think so," John insisted. "What reason would anyone have to kill Peg? But me . . . I mighta been a target for the fella who's pickin' off members of the Lincoln League."

John didn't want Hancock—or anyone for that matter—to know that Peg had been spying in Richmond, making her a possible target as well.

"So you think the man with the dog's the one pickin' off Lincoln Leaguers?"

"I *hope* he's our culprit 'cause that would mean we don't gotta worry about him no more."

Hancock glanced over his shoulder. "I, too, pray you're right, John."

They rode on in silence. John and Peg hadn't slept a wink, and a heavy drowsiness came over them as the wagon rocked back and forth. The morning was still dark, but they could hear the sound of birds active in the branches all around them. The wagon rolled through a thick, dark woods, with trees on all sides crowding the narrow road, and it felt like they were moving through a black tunnel filled with bird sounds. Off to their right, they heard a series of short bursts of "kee-ah, kee-ah, kee-ah!"

"Red-shouldered hawk," John said.

"Red-*tailed* hawk," Peg corrected.

"No. Red-shouldered hawks have the shorter call. The red-tailed has a longer scream."

In the dark, they had no idea who was right, but they kissed anyway.

*****

Mary Lumpkin was happy to see Ethan Hancock clear out from their slave trading post. He wasn't as greasy and depraved as some of the slave traders who stayed on their property, but she didn't like the way he stared at slave women. Seeing men like Hancock made her feel especially guilty about the business her husband Robert had built in Richmond. She felt the vileness soaking into her like a bloodstain.

As the sun rose on a new day, she strolled across the yard, past the dogs to the lodging place for guest slave traders like Hancock. She unlocked the door and entered with her mop and bucket because it was her job to clean up after one slave trader left, to prepare for the next. She opened a window to air the room and heard the sound of a woman weeping, a ghost-like sob that carried across the yard from one of the slave pens. Mary Lumpkin saw herself in the faces of the women slaves—like staring into a mirror. She knew that the destiny of these women could have been her own fate back when Robert Lumpkin first laid eyes on her. She had been much thinner in those days, long before she had five children with Robert, and he had stared at her with unusual intensity when she first showed up as a slave at his trading post so long ago. He took her on as his supposed wife, and she was relieved at not being sold deeper South, but she tried not to think about the fact that she was "married" to the man who ran the Devil's Half Acre. Did that make her the devil's wife? Sometimes it felt that way. Her job was to tidy up his kingdom.

When she first became his woman, her conscience began eating at her right away, and the more she settled into this life, the more the guilt grew. About the only time she had felt relief from the guilt was when Robert sent her and their two daughters to the free state of Pennsylvania for their own safety—and for an education for her girls. When the war began in the past year, she was crushed when he brought her back down to Richmond. Living away from the trading post for a spell had made this hell seem even more evil than she remembered. She secretly rooted for the Yankees to come into Richmond and burn the place down. She sometimes thought about doing it herself, but instead she did little things to revolt, like sneak food to the slaves.

Before mopping, she tidied up the room where Hancock had stayed. Lumpkin treated his slave traders well, for the room had a comfortable feather bed, almost as nice as the one she shared with him. The walls were even decorated with framed photographs of families—daguerreotypes that Robert had purchased down in New Orleans. She had no idea who these families in the photographs were; Robert just wanted to give the slave traders a cozy sense of family while they traveled.

Mister Hancock was normally a fussy man, but he had left in a rush, not long after Mary Bowser and a black man named Cleon Fisk had come to him with urgent news. That was the only explanation for why he had left his dinner plate and cup in a tumble on the floor—uncharacteristic of him. He also left two days' worth of newspapers in the bottom drawer of the dresser. She reached in and gathered up the newspapers and noticed that they covered up something beneath. It was a folded American flag. Strange. She had no idea why a Rebel would be carrying around a Federal flag. Setting aside the newspapers, she pulled out the folded flag and noticed that there was writing on the cloth—something scrawled in red. She unfolded the flag and snapped it like a rug before taking a good hard look at it.

The flag carried a baffling message. It said, THIS IS THE FOURTH.

46

HEN JOHN OPENED HIS EYES, IT WAS LIGHT OUT AND THE wagon was parked along the side of the road. His mouth felt dusty, so he looked around until his eyes fell on the canteen in the back of the wagon. He popped the cork and drank down a couple of mouthfuls, taking time to swish the water from cheek to cheek. He also had to make water, but he was still chained to Peg, and he didn't want to wake her up. So he looked around for Hancock to get him to unlock the chains that connected his right ankle to her left ankle.

He spotted Hancock about twenty feet from the wagon, sitting with his back against a ramrod-straight tree—his rifle across his lap. His hat was tipped over his eyes, and John wondered if he was asleep.

"Good morning, John," said Hancock from under the hat.

"Mornin', Mister Hancock." John spoke just above a whisper so he wouldn't rouse Peg, but loud enough for Hancock to hear. "Would y'all mind unlocking me for a spell? Gotta make water."

Hancock just sat there, his hat still covering his eyes and most of his face.

"Nah. Don't think so."

John's heart froze. It was the way he said those words that did it. The words were spoken casually, with an edge of menace.

"I really don't want to wake Peg, so if you can just disconnect us," John insisted.

Hancock didn't answer. He tipped his hat back, and John saw his eyes. The man stared at him with reptilian intensity. The last time he had seen that look in Hancock's eyes was back almost eight months ago, the night before the Battle of Bull Run. Hancock had wanted to kill him then, and John had the feeling he wanted to kill him now. John looked around for any sign of a weapon.

"Don't waste your time, John. Why would I leave a gun in the back of the wagon?"

John stared at Hancock, who smirked back at him. He could not believe he had been so blind, so gullible. "So y'all are workin' for the South after all?"

"You're just working that out now, John?" Hancock suddenly switched from his Southern accent to a Northern one.

"You're really a copperhead, ain't you?"

Hancock raised the copper one-cent piece that hung around his neck, put it to his lips, and kissed the image of lady liberty. "I prefer to think of myself as a Peace Democrat, standing up to a tyrant like Abraham Lincoln. This war is such a bloody waste of people."

"So is slavery."

"If you think Uncle Abe wants to rid the country of slavery, then you're a bigger fool than I took you for, John Scobell."

John had to keep him talking. The moment Hancock's words stopped, he might decide to start shooting. John had heard plenty about copperheads in the North who opposed Lincoln and the war. Some were political, while others were downright dangerous—like the difference between nonpoisonous and poisonous snakes. Hancock was obviously the poisonous sort.

"Are you a Knight of the Golden Circle?" John asked.

"A Knight of the Golden Circle? You do realize that the idea behind a secret society is for it to remain secret. But to answer your question: no."

"I suppose that would be your answer, whether you were a member or not."

"Then why bother asking?"

To keep you talking, of course.

John just shrugged. "Did you kill those men in the Lincoln League?"

"Save your breath. I'm not answering—although that reminds me . . ."

Hancock stood up tall, unfolding his lanky body, and he strode across the narrow muddy road to the wagon, which was positioned off the side of the road opposite from where Hancock had been sitting. John instinctively leaned away from Hancock, wondering if the man was going to shoot him here and now. Peg stirred, but did not wake. John preferred it that way. No need for her to wake up to terror.

Hancock leaned over the edge of the wagon and peered into the back. "Toss me that haversack there, will ya, John?"

John grabbed the gray haversack and peered inside before hurling it at Hancock's face. Hancock snatched it out of mid-air and smiled. "Control that temper, John. You don't want to irritate the man with the gun."

Stepping away from the wagon, Hancock pinned the butt of his rifle beneath his right arm while he rooted around among the clothes in the haversack. He cursed and tossed the haversack to the ground.

"It appears I forgot my flag! Musta left it back at the Lumpkin place."

That pretty much answered John's question. Hancock was the man who had been draping his victims in the Federal flag.

"So am I the fourth?" John asked.

"You soon will be—or your wife will. I'm thinking that I might let you see your wife die before you follow her into the void. That would make her the fourth, and you'd be the fifth."

"I can count."

"And read. I have always been impressed. But we could use one less darky in this world who reads and writes."

John's hand nonchalantly drifted down to his belt, where his hunting knife was sheathed.

"Don't bother, John." Hancock reached around his back and produced John's blade—the same one used to kill the dog.

"Did you plant the bomb in our room?" John asked.

"Explosives make me nervous. I'd a been too worried I'd blow myself apart."

Peg stirred once again, only this time her eyes opened slowly. She stared at John, oblivious to Hancock's presence. "Good mornin', laddie," she said, smiling. John tried to reassure her with a smile, but it was difficult to conceal the tension in his face. "What's wrong, John?"

John stared at Hancock, and Peg followed his gaze. When she saw Hancock standing there, aiming his gun at them, she sat bolt upright in the wagon.

"John, what's happenin'?"

"Mister Hancock ain't who he said he was."

"None of us are who we say we are," Hancock said. "Timothy Webster says he's a Rebel courier. Hattie Lawton says she's his wife. You say you're their servant. There's too many actors in this world, John. Who are you pretending to be, Peggy?"

She didn't answer. She clutched tightly to John's shirt, twisting it in her fist.

"As soon as I deal with the two of you, I'll head on back to Richmond and finish off Webster and Miss Hattie."

"Why'd you let him live this long? You knew he was a Northern spy."

"I wasn't completely certain which side he was working for, but now I am. Simple as that."

"How do you know he isn't workin' for the South?"

"I don't have time for arguing, John. I still haven't had my breakfast, and I am famished. Climb outta the back of the wagon."

John and Peg didn't budge.

"Oh come on, John, I don't want your blood all over my boxes of tobacco. The boys serving the Confederacy wouldn't much like that."

If John weren't chained at the ankles to Peg, he would at least have tried to charge at Hancock in the hopes that his gun would jam and he would overpower him. But if the gun didn't jam, John would simply be hurrying up his death—and he wanted to squeeze every last minute into what remained of his life—and Peg's life.

"At least let Peg go," John said. "She ain't done nothin'."

"Sorry, John. She's connected to you in so many ways, not just with those there chains. Besides, she knows me now, who I really am."

"Did my brother help you track down those men you killed?" Peg asked. John could tell that she too was stalling for time.

"He's quite the tracker, that Shadrack. I learned about his talents several years ago before he earned enough money to buy his freedom."

Slowly, chains clanking, John and Peg climbed out of the back of the wagon, and Hancock motioned with his rifle. "Over there by a tree."

With his right arm around Peg, John and his wife hobbled off the road. The ground was covered in decayed leaf matter, still moist from the previous day's rain. "If he raises his gun to shoot, we should try runnin'," John whispered into Peg's ear. "Lead with our chained legs first."

"No secrets now," Hancock said, and John was startled to realize that the man had slipped to within a few feet of them. He wondered if he had overheard what he said to Peg.

"And I wouldn't suggest running. You aren't going to outrun me in those chains. And if you do attempt to run, I'll make Peg's passing much more unpleasant than if you cooperate. I'll do things to her you won't like seeing."

John and Peg exchanged looks. John slowly shook his head, as if to tell her not to run. It wouldn't be worth it. At least this way, they would die standing up, like soldiers on a battlefield. They would die with honor, not like dogs.

They turned to face Hancock, and John thought about Cleon's constant refrain that he was not afraid of dying. He wished he could welcome the other world as eagerly as Cleon. John believed in heaven, but he still clung to living as desperately as he and Peg clung to each other. A bullet had passed through his hand just one day earlier, and he hoped a bullet to the head or the heart would not hurt any worse. He wondered if it would be just like waking up from a deep sleep, as Cleon said. He and Peg would open their eyes and touch the glory.

John told himself that everyone has to die someday, and this was as good a day as any. He would have preferred old age, so he came up with a helpful fiction; he tried to pretend that he was eighty-some years old, and his time had finally come. He put on one final act by pretending in his mind to be an old man, ready to face his Maker after a long life. He was a good actor. He could live one last lie.

"Tell you what, John, since you're taking this like a man, I will shoot you first. You don't have to watch your wife die in front of your eyes." Hancock stepped back to load his rifle and ram the charge into the barrel.

Peg wrapped her arms around John's waist tightly and squeezed. John closed his eyes and buried his face in her hair.

"Northern cardinal," she said softly.

John pulled back. "What?"

"I hear a Northern cardinal."

John listened. Sure enough, he heard the whistle of a bird in the trees, a song that sounded like "birdie, birdie, birdie, birdie . . ."

"You're right," John said. "Northern cardinal."

They kissed.

"Oh that's sweet," said Hancock, "but I don't have all day here." He took a few steps closer so he was only about six feet from John and Peg. The man obviously wanted to be sure he didn't miss.

As John and Peg broke apart, John's gaze drifted down to the ground, where he spotted a rat snake coiling its way through the thick grass. Snakes were just becoming active this time of year, preparing for the mating season, and the harmless rat snake had a striking similarity to the poisonous copperhead. Its gray blotches were often mistaken for the larger hourglass shapes emblazoned on the bodies of a copperhead.

Hancock began to raise his gun, and John realized he had only a few seconds to spare. So he lunged down, grabbed the snake around the neck, and hurled it at Hancock's face—all in one smooth flow of movement.

The gun went off.

47

OHN WASN'T SURE IF HE HAD BEEN HIT WITH A BULLET, BUT IF he had, it hadn't killed him instantly. Very much alive, he charged Hancock, who was hopping around, peeling the rat snake off of his shoulder and making the sound of a scared schoolboy. John plowed into the man before he could rip away the snake, and they tumbled into a heap; Peg fell into the tangle as well because she was still attached to John by ankle chains. In their struggle, John grabbed the snake by the neck again and jammed its head into Hancock's open mouth. The snake writhed and hissed, and it was obvious from Hancock's bug-eyed stare that he did not realize the snake was harmless. The man tried to scream, but the sound was muffled by the snake stuffed in his mouth.

The terror boiling in Hancock must have given him a charge of energy, because he grabbed the snake and tossed it aside, pushed his way out from under John, scrambled to his feet, snatched his rifle back up, and clubbed John across the face with the butt of the gun. The forest began to spin, and John felt an instant sickness seize his stomach. He was still conscious, and he could see Hancock quickly reloading his rifle. He took two steps toward the man, but the spinning images in his head staggered him, and Hancock backpedaled out of reach.

Then a gunshot went off.

John was confused. He didn't think Hancock had finished reloading, and yet he had heard gunfire. He noticed Hancock staring down the road from where they had come, and John turned to look. Three horsemen thundered down on them, riding side by side and kicking up spouts of dirt. All of them appeared to be armed, and all of them were most definitely black. When one of them took aim, Hancock took off running into the woods; he probably figured he couldn't be run down by a horse if he disappeared into the thicket.

John's spinning head had begun to settle, and he could clearly see that it was Cleon, Abram, and Gallus who had arrived. Swinging down from his horse, Cleon aimed at the fleeing Hancock and fired, but missed. Cleon was not the finest of shots.

"Your gun! Now!" John said to them.

Gallus tossed him his rifle, and John swung around to draw a bead on Hancock, who was rapidly vanishing into the forest. The gun was a smoothbore musket, not a rifle and not capable of shooting nearly as far. So Hancock was almost out of range. The tree cover made the shot doubly difficult. John took aim and was thankful that Hancock didn't have the good sense to run in a zigzag pattern. There was still a clear pathway through the trees—barely. John squeezed off a shot.

Hancock kept running.

"Missed him," John muttered.

Abram cursed.

But he cursed too soon. Even from such a distance, John could see Hancock suddenly stagger and buckle at the waist, then straighten up, then buckle again and fall. He disappeared from sight behind a thicket. John couldn't pursue with the chains still connecting him to Peg, but Cleon and Abram took off through the forest, while Gallus stayed back.

In silence, John, Gallus, and Peg watched as the two Lincoln League men reached the spot where Hancock had fallen; then Cleon crouched down and disappeared from sight, probably checking whether Hancock was alive or not. A moment later, Cleon was back on his feet and Abram was pointing his revolver toward the ground. His shot echoed through the forest.

48

ASEBALL SERVED AS A TONIC FOR JOHN ON THIS STUNNING mid-April day in Washington. The wound in the palm of his left hand was still tender, so he had to catch with only one hand, but he could swing a bat without too much pain. Cleon, Gallus, and Abram were also playing ball on this day. John and Peg were indebted to the three men, who had come to their rescue after Missus Lumpkin marched to the Van Lew house with the flag she had uncovered in Hancock's dresser.

John and Peg had made Washington their new home ever since the incident with Hancock. But when John learned that Webster and Miss Hattie were both arrested just before sunset on Thursday, April 3, he very nearly ran back to Richmond to be at their sides. He would have gone if Peg hadn't raised such a fuss.

According to reports, Scully had broken down in prison and given up Webster and Miss Hattie as spies. Now, John's two friends were imprisoned in Castle Godwin, awaiting trial—and he felt guilty roaming free in Washington. But Peg made him promise that he wouldn't dare go back South until everything with Webster and Miss Hattie settled down.

Cleon clapped him on the back as John picked up his wooden bat. The two of them, along with Abram and Gallus, made up part of a team of nine free blacks, which they called the Lincoln Leaguers, and they squared off against another team of black men in a cow pasture on the edge of Washington. John stepped up as striker and faced the hurler, who gripped a ball that they had constructed by winding socks around a bullet.

John waited for the perfect underhand pitch and smacked the ball solidly, sending it on a line into the outfield where it became lost in deep grass, and he took off running. They had set up four makeshift bases—two rocks, a shrub, and a piece of lumber. The piles of cow dung that dotted the field were not bases and were best avoided.

Legs burning, arms pumping, he rounded third and was heading for home base when the other team finally found the ball in the weeds. John sensed the missile coming straight for his head. Ducking, he saw the ball pass right in front of his nose, and the sight brought his mind back to the Battle of Bull Run, where bullets crisscrossed the air all around him, whistling past.

But this particular bullet had missed him, and John made it home, scoring the first ace of the Lincoln Leaguers' eventual 15 tallies. The match turned out to be a close one, with a final tally of 15 to 12.

"We have fought the good fight, and laid up for us is a crown of righteousness," said Cleon, bringing in Scripture wherever he could, even in a game of baseball. John strode off the field, flanked by Abram, Gallus, and Cleon. The smell of grass and flowers was springtime sweet. Peg met him at the edge of the field and hooked an arm in his. But they hadn't gone more than a few steps when she looked down and noticed the blood seeping through the bandage on his left hand.

She took his hand and studied it. "Laddie, please take it easy or this'll never heal over. Maybe y'all should skip the second match."

John shrugged and gave no defense. He knew he wouldn't win this argument with Peg, so he hoped his smile would satisfy her.

"John ain't one to sit things out," said Cleon, following one step behind. "Ain't you learned that by now?"

Peg had packed a between-game meal, but as they headed for the picnic basket, they spotted a white man moving swiftly across the field. A stocky man, puffing on a cigar. As he came into focus, John realized it was Mister Pinkerton, probably come to press him for an answer.

"Good afternoon, all," said Pinkerton, arriving breathless.

"Afternoon, Mister Pinkerton," said John.

Peg didn't say a thing. She stared at Pinkerton with fire in her eyes.

"Mind if I take John aside to talk?" Pinkerton asked, turning his gaze on her.

"Yes, we can talk," John said before Peg had time to answer. He didn't need permission, so they strolled out of earshot.

"How's the hand?" Pinkerton asked as they drifted away from the others.

John held up his palm and displayed his red badge of courage.

"Maybe you should give it a rest," the secret service man said.

"If you think I should rest, then why are you here askin' about another mission?"

Pinkerton laughed and blew out a puff of smoke. "I mean you should rest *your hand* by sitting out the second match. The mission I have in mind for you would not put a strain on your wound—not like this game of baseball is doing. So have you thought about it? The war is a long way from being over, and the Peninsula Campaign is in the early stages. We need all of the eyes and ears we can get scouting the enemy."

"But wouldn't they know who and what I am if I go back to Richmond or northern Virginia?"

"You are a Negro, John."

"But I'm also a spy, and I worked for two people sitting in prison for espionage."

"People still don't see you as a threat. You're a Negro, and they don't fear the black man as a spy."

"They see us as too ignorant?"

Pinkerton tossed the stub of the cigar to the ground and drove it underground with the heel of his boot. "That's what some people think, yes."

"But I'm linked to Mister Webster and Miss Hattie."

"That don't matter. They still don't think a black man is capable of spying. Don't complain. It's a blessing in disguise!"

Don't complain? These people thought he was no more capable of spying than a dog off the street. John had a hard time thinking of that kind of attitude as a blessing.

"How is Miss Hattie faring?" John asked.

"She was sentenced to one year, but she has been given permission to petition Jefferson Davis for clemency. We can only hope and pray."

"What about Mister Webster?"

"It's not looking good."

"But he's British born. Won't that mean something?"

"He renounced his British citizenship a long time ago. He's a Yankee through and through, so the Confederates won't be merciful. He did a lot of damage to the Rebels over the past year."

Pinkerton pulled out a pair of cigars from his coat pocket and offered one to John. John accepted, but neither of them lit up immediately. Pinkerton used his cigar like a conductor's wand, emphasizing his words as he spoke

"John, you did wonderful work for Mister Webster and Miss Hattie. We need you again. Uncle Abe needs you."

"Then why can't I put on a blue uniform and fight with honor in the field?"

"I believe it will come to that someday."

"When President Lincoln becomes desperate enough?"

"Maybe sooner."

John spoke harshly, but he knew he was being too hard on Pinkerton. The man seemed genuine in his belief that black men should be allowed to fight in this war.

"Until you are permitted to wear the uniform of a soldier, this is your way to fight. Will you accept this mission?"

Pinkerton wiped some flakes of tobacco from his fingers onto his pants leg and then extended his hand.

"Will you shake on it, John?"

*****

Peg served up chicken to Abram, Cleon, Gallus, and several others, and the men dug in eagerly once Cleon had finally finished blessing the food with his short sermon. She had plenty good reason to be thankful to God for this meal. Food and other supplies were becoming scarce in the South. Flour, sugar, vinegar, salt, coffee . . . all were becoming as precious as California gold. But she was in the North now, and she was able to put her hands on a chicken—a fresh one at that, not a long-gone bird.

Peg didn't partake of the meal. She was too riled, and she spent the time pacing back and forth, the hem of her dress brushing against the tall grass.

"Settle down and have a bite," Abram said. "You're making me edgy just watchin' you."

"Then don't watch."

"Just mind your food, Abram, and let her stew if she wants to," said Gallus.

Peg stomped off, put her hands on her hips, and stared across the field at John and Pinkerton. After everything they had gone through in the past year, she could not believe that John was thinking of doing it all again. She reminded him twenty more times that this was a white man's war, and he should stay out of it. But John was stubborn, and he had an overblown sense of honor. Peg considered storming over to them and giving Mister Pinkerton a piece of her mind. But if she did such a thing, John would only spite her by agreeing to *two* more missions. She folded her arms across her chest and stared, hoping he would glance over and see in her stare exactly what she was thinking.

Finally, she saw John shake hands with the man, and she felt like kicking the plate of food out of Cleon's hands. As if reading her mind, Cleon shielded his plate. John and Pinkerton separated, and John came trudging back in her direction, head hanging low. He wouldn't look her in the eyes.

Cleon, Abram, and Gallus stopped eating and stared; they looked like gawkers at a fisticuffs fight.

Head still down, still bobbing, John came to a stop, only about four feet in front of Peg. He didn't look up.

"Well?" she said.

John raised his head slowly, looked her in the eyes. "I'm goin' again."

Peg's heart nearly stopped. She felt like hitting him hard, but he still showed a bruise from where the butt of Hancock's rifle cracked him hard. She couldn't do that to him, even as angry as she was.

"John, you can't go runnin' back to Richmond. You can't leave me here. And you certainly can't—"

"Easy, easy," said John, and he finally let crack a smile. He reached out and played with the knot on her sky-blue head wrap. "I meant that I'm gonna play a second match here today. That's all. But I ain't goin' on any more spy missions."

"You're stayin' with me?"

"I'm choosin' you, Peg."

"You ain't goin' on a job for Pinkerton?"

"I ain't goin'—for now."

Peg didn't like the "for now" that he added, but she wasn't complaining. She wrapped her arms around him and squeezed. And when he put his hands on her waist, she pulled back abruptly.

"John, you're gonna get blood on my nice new dress. Now go on and get some chicken."

As John fetched a plate, Peg watched Pinkerton stroll away across the pasture, stopping twice to check the bottom of his shoes. John played the second baseball match, and she had to re-bandage his hand because the strain of striking the ball had irritated the wound. Peg found a seat on the grass and ate a chicken leg and drank down a glass of tea and wondered if it might be possible to find a stretch of peace in their lives during a war like this. Probably not, but at least she had this afternoon to savor, as eighteen free black men—nine on each side—played baseball until darkness set in.

Epilogue

John Scobell was never mentioned again in the historical records after the arrests of Timothy Webster and Hattie Lawton.

Timothy Webster was hanged as a spy on the morning of Tuesday, April 29, 1862. When the trapdoor released beneath Webster's feet, he slipped out of the noose and crashed to the ground. "I die a double death," he said as they brought him back up on the scaffold, fixed the noose tighter, and released the trapdoor a second time. He was the first spy executed by either side during the Civil War.

Hattie Lawton was released not long after she wrote to Jefferson Davis, president of the Confederate States of America, on October 13, 1862. People still referred to her as "Missus Timothy Webster."

Allan Pinkerton resigned as chief of the Union Intelligence Service in November of 1862 to protest Lincoln's removal of General George McClellan from command. Pinkerton was replaced by Lafayette Baker.

Elizabeth Van Lew and Mary Bowser continued their spying activities in Richmond. In fact, some believe that Mary Bowser worked as a maid in the home of Jefferson Davis, spying in the very heart of the Confederate White House. When General Ulysses S. Grant and his forces finally arrived in Richmond, he met with Miss Van Lew and declared her to be one of his best sources of information during the war.

Mary Lumpkin remained true to her word that the infamous slave trading post, Lumpkin's Jail, would not remain "The Devil's Half Acre" forever. When her "husband," Robert, died soon after the Civil War, Mary Lumpkin leased the property to Reverend Nathaniel Colver in 1867. The property was used as a school to teach blacks and eventually became the Richmond Theological Seminary and then the Virginia Union University—now in a different location. The site of Lumpkin's Jail was excavated in 2006.

That piece of land became known as God's Half Acre.

Author's Notes

John Scobell is a real spy from history, and all that we know about him can be found in the 1883 book *The Spy of the Rebellion*, written by Allan Pinkerton, head of the Union Intelligence Agency during the first year of the Civil War.

Pinkerton's book recounts a string of disconnected episodes about Scobell, which I decided to tie together with a common thread. In most accounts about Civil War spies, there is no mention of the information being collected other than troop numbers and movements. So I tied John Scobell's activity to the work the Confederates were actually doing on submarines and torpedoes. (At that time, a "torpedo" referred to what we now call mines—both water and land mines.)

The Spy of the Rebellion recounts Pinkerton's first meeting with Scobell (a scene I depict), as well as how John waylaid Doctor Gurley to retrieve papers, how he followed the red-headed spy to the cabin, and how he and Miss Hattie were chased on horse by the red-headed spy and three other men. All of that is true. It's also true that John was a master at taking on the guise of different characters, and he really did startle people with his ability to sing Scottish songs with a convincing brogue.

We also know that John and his wife were freed by their Scottish master just before the war, and that John left to serve the Union as a spy while his wife remained in Richmond. But unfortunately we know nothing more about his wife, not even her real name. However, I was intrigued by the fact that John ran off to spy while she remained in Richmond, so I decided to create a separate storyline for Peg, tying her story into several real-life spy operations taking place in Richmond.

The first true-life spy operation was that of Elizabeth Baker, the Northern woman from Chicago who really did visit Captain Atwater and collect information on submarines right under his nose. With today's level of security, it seems hard to believe that Captain Atwater had no qualms about taking Missus Baker with him on a tour of the

Tredegar Iron Works and a demonstration of the new Confederate submarine along the James River. But it is true.

I also linked Peg with Elizabeth Van Lew and Mary Bowser, two of the most famous spies in Richmond. Van Lew, a Southern belle loyal to the Union, coordinated the most extensive network of spies in Richmond. Miss Van Lew, or Miss Lizzie as she was known, sent ciphered messages to a farm on the outskirts of Richmond, hiding them in hollow eggs and shoes. She also slipped messages to Union prisoners by hiding them in a dish with a false bottom.

Miss Lizzie had freed her family's slaves, including Mary Bowser, whom some believe became a maid (and a spy) in Confederate President Jefferson Davis' household. There is a lot of mystery surrounding the real Mary Bowser and many stories about her are disputed, including the claim that she went by the code name Ellen Bond. (If this were true, I would have loved it if she identified herself as "Bond. Ellen Bond.")

Timothy Webster and Hattie Lawton were real spies as well, although some sources list Miss Lawton as "Carrie" Lawton. More sources referred to her as Hattie, so I went with that name.

Webster was Pinkerton's top double agent working in the South, and John Scobell did pretend to be the servant for Webster and Miss Hattie. Webster became ill in the Monumental Hotel, much as I depicted, and his cover was blown when John Scully and Pryce Lewis were sent to Richmond to find out what had happened to him. Scully and Lewis were both blamed for his blown cover and eventual execution, although some historians believe it was Scully, not Lewis, who broke down and gave up Webster. Lewis later killed himself, throwing himself from a tall building in New York.

One other prominent spy, who is only briefly touched upon in *The Lincoln League*, is Rose Greenhow, the Southern socialite who lived in Washington and spied for the South. In fact, some maintain that she sent critical information to the Confederate leaders near Manassas just prior to the first major battle of the war. She sent information about the North's point of attack, which led the South to send needed reinforcements and ultimately win the battle.

The submarine operations I depict actually took place during the first year of the war, and this early submarine was detected and sunk by draglines and nets in the waters of Hampton Roads, much as I depicted. However, Ichabod is a purely fictional character. Also, it is not known with certainty which ship sank the submarine. Some have speculated that it was the USS *Minnesota*, which was attacked by a submarine in October of 1861, but that incident doesn't fit the timeline described by Pinkerton. So I went with the USS *Congress*, which took the precautions against submarines that I describe in the story. But whether the USS *Congress* really sank the submarine, I do not know.

Dolls really were used for smuggling, with the most famous being two dolls that can be found at Richmond's Museum of the Confederacy. The dolls are named Lucy Ann and Nina, and it is believed that Confederates used them to smuggle medical supplies, such as quinine and morphine, through the Union blockade.

The scenes of the First Battle of Manassas (known as the Battle of Bull Run in the North) are fictional, but I based my account of the Eighth Georgia on information from David Detzer's excellent book *Donnybrook*. I also paid a visit to the battlefield near Manassas, where the park ranger on duty gave a fabulous description of how the battle unfolded, first on Matthew's Hill and then on Henry Hill.

Hackey Pickens, Abram Fox, and Gallus Turner are fictional characters, although the name "Gallus Turner" is a combination of the names of "Uncle Gallus" and "Uncle Turner"—the only other Lincoln League members mentioned by name in *The Spy and the Rebellion* besides John Scobell. Also, I based Cleon Fink's vision on several spiritual visions recounted by slaves in the book, *God Struck Me Dead*, and Shadrack's attempt at conjuring by using a mixture of cow manure and red pepper was based on a story straight from a slave narrative.

Finally, I should note that my one scene with Lincoln and Pinkerton is *not* based on an actual conversation. However, the story about the bull that I have Lincoln recount is one he actually told, and the details about submarines that Pinkerton relates is information that the North gleaned from Missus Baker's espionage.

The Spy of the Rebellion was my primary source, but I turned to many other key books (in addition to *Donnybrook*). Here are some of them:

Ashes of Glory: Richmond at War, Ernest B. Furgurson, Vintage Books: A Division of Random House, 1996.

Double Death: The True Story of Pryce Lewis, the Civil War's Most Daring Spy, Gavin Mortimer, Walker and Company, 2010.

From the Ballroom to Hell: Grace and Folly in Nineteenth-Century Dance, Elizabeth Aldrich, Northwestern University Press, 1991.

A History of the Negro Troops in the War of the Rebellion: 1861–1865, George Washington Williams, Fordham University Press, 2012, originally published in 1887.

Infernal Machines: The Story of Confederate Submarine and Mine Warfare, Milton F. Perry, Louisiana State University Press, 1965.

The Negro in the Civil War, Benjamin Quarles, Da Capo Press, 1953.

The Negro's Civil War, James M. McPherson, Vintage Books, 1965.

Southern Lady, Yankee Spy: The True Story of Elizabeth Van Lew, Elizabeth R. Varon, Oxford University Press, 2003.

Spies for the Blue and Gray, Harnett T. Kane, Doubleday and Company, Inc., 1954.

Spies and Spymasters of the Civil War, Donald E. Markle, Hippocrene Books, 2004.

The Spy With Two Hats: A Life of Timothy Webster, Rosamond McPherson Young, David McKay Company, Inc., 1966.

Submarine Warfare in the Civil War, Mark K. Ragan, Da Capo Press, 1999.

A Yankee Spy in Richmond: The Civil War Diary of "Crazy Bet" Van Lew, edited by David D. Ryan, Stackpole Books, 1996.

Discussion Questions

1. Do you think John should have stayed in Richmond with Peg rather than leave to work for the Union cause? Explain your reasons.
2. Honor was important to John Scobell. What does honor mean to you? Is honor valued today? Why or why not?
3. How did new technology, such as submarines, challenge notions of honor during the Civil War?
4. The name Cleon means "glory" and the name Ichabod means "glory has departed." How did those characters reflect the meaning of their names? How did Cleon and Ichabod each view death?
5. Birds and animals show up in many different ways throughout the story. How were animals used in the story and what was their significance?
6. What was the meaning of the head wrap in the story? Why was it so important to Peg and Matilda?
7. Who did you suspect was picking off members of the Lincoln League? Did your suspicions change throughout the story? How?
8. Why did so many African Americans and women become effective spies during the war?
9. Which character did you relate to the most? Why? How did John and Peg change over the course of the novel?
10. How did this story alter your view of the War Between the States? What did you learn that was new?

Praise for Doug Peterson's History by the Slice Novels

The Disappearing Man

Based on the amazing true story of a slave who mailed himself to freedom.

Doug Peterson takes us into the story of Henry "Box" Brown, a slave in Richmond, Virginia, who makes a daring escape attempt by allowing himself to be shipped north in a wooden box. I got hooked on the storyline in the past—the abuses, the romance, the friendships—only to find myself hooked again on the harrowing portions dealing with Henry's imprisonment in the box. . . . It is more than just fast-paced entertainment; it is an eye-opening and educational reminder of the importance of grace, acceptance, and equality. Even as the lives of many slaves blew away like windswept leaves, those leaves spread seeds and life that continue on into today.

—Eric Wilson, *New York Times*
Best-Selling Author

What a wonderfully inspiring story! The way the novel is written, I could see the scenes playing as if I was watching a film. It would make a terrific movie. This book is full of great historical details, and has moments that will choke you up, and others that will make you laugh out loud. One of the most unique and fascinating novels I've read in a long time!

—Deborah Raney, Award-Winning Novelist

The Vanishing Woman

Based on the true-life escape of a slave woman who posed as a white man, while her husband pretended to be her slave.

The Vanishing Woman is a well-researched and wonderfully written account of the amazing journey of Ellen and William Craft from slavery to freedom. Doug Peterson captures the ingenuity and the danger of this bold escape in a novel that will appeal to both adult and young readers.

—Andy Ambrose, PhD, Executive Director,
Tubman African American Museum, Macon, Georgia

Do not doubt the work of Doug Peterson. I know, because I've now read three incredible works by this man, and *The Vanishing Woman* is merely the latest. Check out Doug Peterson! He's as good as anybody out there.

—Wolfe Moffat, Amazon Reviewer

Doug Peterson is an amazing author. He does his research very well, writes in such a way that you are really pulled into the people's lives and makes you not want to put the book down.

—Nita Cichy Hanson, Amazon Reviewer

The Puzzle People

How do you complete a 600-million piece puzzle and solve two murders? Based on events surrounding the rise and fall of the Berlin Wall.

Peterson is a master at combining intriguing fiction with historical events. I highly recommend *The Puzzle People*.

—Dave Trouten, Division Chair, Kingswood University

This is one of the most well-researched, superbly written books I've read in a while! Doug writes with such dynamic imagery, depth of overlapping plot lines, historical accuracy, and intrigue that it is hard to put his books down.

—Jenny L. Cote, Author of *The Amazing Tales of Max and Liz* and the *Epic Order of the Seven* series

The Berlin Wall forms an almost literal backdrop to *The Puzzle People*. The story follows the lives of a handful of people whose lives have been ripped apart, sometimes brutally, by the totalitarian East German government, and the lure of freedom only yards away on the other side of the Wall. The story has many elements of a Cold War thriller. There are spies, soldiers, government agents, and more than one shoot-out. But ultimately this book is about finding peace with an often very painful past. . . . Overall, an excellent read. I can't wait for Peterson's next book!

—Chuck Payne, Amazon Reviewer